Critical

DANIEL O'

"Daniel O'Thunder is a triumph—a frightening,
funny, moving, page-turning romp.
Deserves to be shelved where they keep Charles Dickens
and Robertson Davies and Sarah Waters.
Ian Weir is a storyteller of extraordinary ability."

STEVEN GALLOWAY, author, *The Cellist of Sarajevo*

"Marvellous from the first paragraph."

THE GLOBE AND MAIL

"A pugilist-turned-preacher returns to the
boxing ring with the ultimate goal of going toe-to-toe
with the devil—what more could you want?
Weir's unique retelling of the Gospels,
set in mid-19th-century London, is Charles Dickens
meets *Tom Jones*... A knockout debut."

NATIONAL POST

"A deliciously dark, funny and surprisingly
moving romp through the misty, grimy streets
of Victorian London. *Daniel O'Thunder* is completely
compelling, driving the reader on to learn what
comes of the battle between a prize-fighting evangelist and
the devil himself. Rich in character, plot and setting,
Daniel O'Thunder has it all. A terrific story vividly
imagined and consistently well told."

CANADIAN AUTHORS ASSOCIATION

"A terrific, fast-moving narrative.
The scenes of rat-infested brothels, drizzle
and mud are convincing, with overtones
of menace and a certain wistfulness."

GUARDIAN

"Weir's plot steps smartly, and the language
crackles with the immediacy of shifting
first-person voices. There are murders, rapes,
hangings, prizefights, a city-wide riot, and lots of thrilling
escapes. He also has more than a few plot twists
up his sleeve. By the time the novel reaches its dramatic
conclusion, set in the Klondike during the
gold rush, the story has landed in a place somewhere
between dementia and the supernatural."

QUILL & QUIRE

"A romp *Daniel O'Thunder* most certainly is.
The chief attractions here are that
braided plot, and the giddy pleasure its author
takes in the ornate linguistic tropes
of the Victorian era. This is wonderful stuff."

THE GEORGIA STRAIGHT

DANIEL O'THUNDER

'He nobbed Daniel with a muzzler, and followed with a half-arm dig, and then landed a grave-digger that shocked us all...'

IAN WEIR

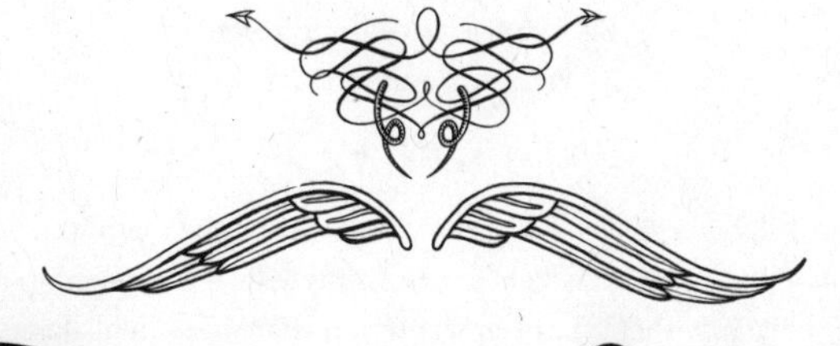

Daniel O'THUNDER

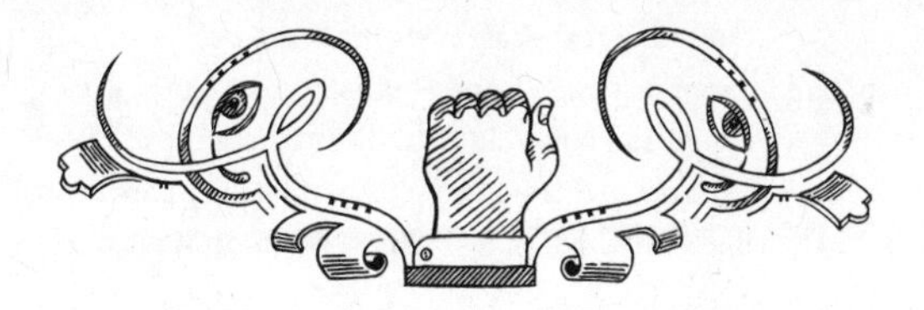

DOUGLAS & MCINTYRE
D&M PUBLISHERS INC.
Vancouver/Toronto/Berkeley

First paperback edition 2010
First U.S. edition 2011

11 12 13 14 15 6 5 4 3 2

Douglas & McIntyre
An imprint of D&M Publishers Inc.
2323 Quebec Street, Suite 201
Vancouver BC Canada V5T 4S7
www.douglas-mcintyre.com

Cataloguing data available from Library and Archives Canada
ISBN 978-1-55365-435-3 (cloth)
ISBN 978-1-55365-564-0 (pbk.)
ISBN 978-1-92670-682-5 (ebook)

Editing by Ramsay Derry
Cover and text design by Peter Cocking
Cover and interior ornaments and frontispiece by Laura Kinder
Printed and bound in Canada by Friesens
Text printed on acid-free, 100% post-consumer paper
Distributed in the U.S. by Publishers Group West

We gratefully acknowledge the financial support of the Canada Council for the Arts, the British Columbia Arts Council, the Province of British Columbia through the Book Publishing Tax Credit, and the Government of Canada through the Canada Book Fund for our publishing activities.

To Jude and Amy

for more than they realize

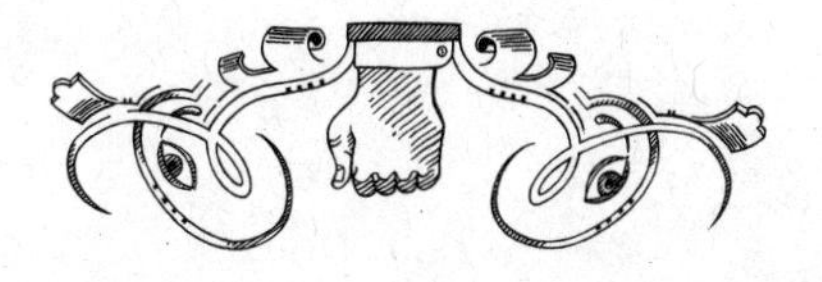

DANIEL O'THUNDER

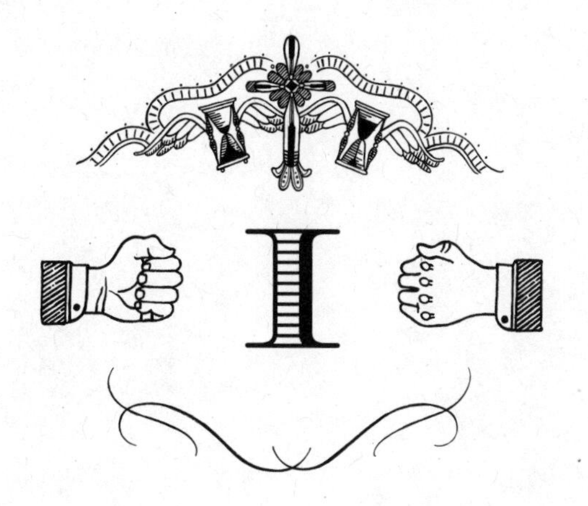
I

*N*IGHT HAS FALLEN *as the Devil emerges from his lodgings in Mayfair, lingers for a moment in the baleful sputter of a gas-lamp, and then limps away through the London fog towards Regent Street. He has been awake since late afternoon; or rather, he has been awake all along, for the Devil does not sleep. Instead he reclines for periods of malevolent immobility, in which he broods upon ancient hatreds and marshals his energies for reprisal. At such times his eyes glow crimson with the fires within, and wisps of smoke issue from the neck of his shirt, causing whosoever might be lying alongside him—such as an actress, or a half-guinea whore from Mother Clatterballock, or just the crumpled ruination of a flower-girl—to utter exclamations agonizing to our Saviour and leap to her feet, clutching her smock in consternation. Afterwards he sits before the mirror with his pencils and his paints, preparing himself. This may take an hour and more, for the Devil is ancient, and lined, and vain as a fading tragedian.*

Regent Street is a clatter of carriages; a young whore in exotic plumage loiters on the corner. She steps forward with a brazen greeting as the Devil approaches, but it dies in a start of recognition. The Devil had her once before and the horror is with her still, for he was in one of his moods that night and *he rode her as if she were a jade, until she thought her bones must bow and her sinews burst. The whore shrinks back with a hissing intake of breath and hurries away, followed by the desiccated gentlewoman who attends her. The Devil continues on his way, his footfalls echoing iambs on the cobblestones, clip-*clop. *He wears a low slouching hat with a curved brim, and tall riding boots in the Regency fashion, and a black coat that has been* démodé *these thirty years, for the Devil stalks through the world at a measured pace. Of late, indeed, he has been nagged by the sense that his pace remains unchanged whilst all around the world is accelerating, harnessing dark inchoate energies as it tends towards some point of culmination, as yet unglimpsed beyond the horizon. It is a vertiginous sensation; he hates it. It leaves him with a vague and creeping dread.*

The Devil pauses as he turns towards the Haymarket, trying to decide what he will do with the evening. Suddenly fingers are plucking his sleeve.

"Is it the doctor, then?"

A ragged woman has emerged from an alleyway behind him. Apparently she has mistaken the old-fashioned black coat for a medical man's, or perhaps she is simply trying to impose her last frail hope upon a hopeless situation.

"God save you, sir, are you the doctor?"

Here at least is something to engage his interest, so the Devil suffers himself to be led. The alley is foul with refuse, human and otherwise. The ragged woman takes him through a door and up a narrow stinking stairwell to a tiny stinking room. There are tens of thousands of such dwellings in London, scarcely bigger than coffins, where sons of Adam and daughters of Eve live six and ten and four-and-twenty to a room, all curled together like maggots in a wound. In the guttering light of a candle stub there is a weak-eyed man who rises to one elbow, and a filthy pock-marked boy, and an even filthier girl. A bundle of rags in the corner mutters to itself and weeps, thus identifying itself as a living entity of the grandmaternal species. In another corner an infant lies on a bed of straw. A little boy, wrapped in a shawl. He is pale as death; the breath rattles in his tiny chest, and he shivers uncontrollably. "Oh, sir, can you help him?" the woman asks, beseeching.

Mingled with the human stench of the room is the sickly sweet odour of cholera. The Devil smiles. By morning the boy will be stiff and still, and the others will follow soon after: the eternal marionette-march to the grave. Assuming a look of professional assessment, the Devil takes the shawl from the infected infant, and leaves him naked in the straw.

"Expose him to the air," he recommends. "Don't give him water, no matter how he cries. And place your sure and certain hope in Providence."

Departing, the Devil takes the shawl with him. The Haymarket throbs with activity: carriages and gentlemen and louts and nymphs of the pave, all jostling together. Shouts from a gin palace, and an altercation spilling from a chophouse doorway. Perhaps the Devil will go to the theatre tonight, or perhaps not; the theatre bores him past endurance, as does all of London. A handbill informs him of a pugilistic exhibition above a dance hall near Lincoln's Inn Fields; possibly he will go to that, although pugilism is no longer what it was in the blood-red days of Broughton and Figg. He sees a boy and a little girl, huddled in a doorway, and slants towards them.

He comes upon them from the left, of course, for such is his ancient tradition. The Devil always approaches from the sinister side.

"Would you like a penny?" asks the Devil. He produces one out of the air, a playful conjuring trick he employs for the entertainment of the weak-minded. "Take it, then. A penny for your soul."

The Devil smiles, but the boy just looks at him. He is ten or twelve years old, the boy, sullen and filthy. The little girl is younger, with hollow cheeks and hair that might be golden underneath the grime. A little sister, apparently: clumsily cared for, dearly loved. She shrinks against her brother as the Devil's gaze falls upon her, and the urchin hugs her protectively. There is of course no hope for such as these, nor should there be.

"Is she cold?" asks the Devil.

The boy shakes his head, but the night wind is keen, and the little girl shivers. The Devil extends the shawl. "This will keep her warm."

The boy hesitates, but finally he takes it, and wraps it around his sister's thin shoulders.

"There," says the Devil. "Snug as a bug."

*When the boy looks up, the Devil is stalking away, trailing a faint odour of sulphur and eau de toilette. Clip-*clop. *Clip-*clop.

Perhaps he will go out into the country. The Devil despises the countryside even more than he despises London, but at least it is different there.

JACK

I AM NOT the devil. I need this to be understood, from the outset. If you won't accept it, then please stop reading. Set these pages aside, and go away. Go and judge someone else.

God knows I am not an angel, either. I don't even profess to be a very good man, for we are none of us good, not in the way that Heaven yearns for us to be. I am just a man. I have needs and desires, some of them lamentable, for like yours my nature is Fallen. I have from time to time indulged these desires, for like you I am weak. At moments indeed I have walked at the Devil's side, and heard his sweet seductive whispers, and perhaps even for the span of a heartbeat been his man—as you have—body and soul. But at all times I swear that I have wished to be better. I have prayed to be *good,* and fixed my eyes upon the image of Goodness Itself that winked and glimmered on the far horizon—so remote from us, and separated by such torturous terrain. I have staggered towards it all my life, and stumbled and fallen, and grovelled for a time and then stood up and staggered some more, though my feet were lacerated and my poor heart ready to burst. Just like you, my friend. Just exactly like you.

Are you still there? Still reading? Wherever it is you like to read—in the comfortable chair in your parlour, perhaps. Or stretched out beneath your favourite tree, with Trusty the spaniel dozing close to hand. Fine: if you're still reading, then I'll trust we have a bargain. You will not judge—and I will tell the truth. Or at least you will withhold your judgement as far as seems humanly possible—which is seldom very far—and I will tell as much truth as can reasonably be expected from a man—which is seldom as much as one might hope—and between us we'll do the best we can.

Yes? Then we begin.

It is 1888 as I write these words. I am an old man now, scratching syllables by candlelight at an old desk in a dingy room in Whitechapel. The wallpaper peels in the ever-present damp, and a filthy window overlooks Dorset Street. Sometimes I write of the Devil, and of his activities amongst us in London some decades ago, my connection to which may grow more clear as we proceed. But mainly I write of a man named Daniel O'Thunder. I write of Daniel as I knew him, and since no man may know the entire truth about anyone or anything, I have collected as well the accounts of others. In some cases these have been set down in writing by the teller. In other cases I have had to go beyond an editor's role and conjure the tale as the teller would surely have told it, had he or she the opportunity. In these instances I have relied scrupulously upon such details as have been made available to me, supplemented where necessary with judicious suppositions and my own insights into human nature. In short I may here and there have invented certain facts, but always in the service of a greater Truth. As indeed did Matthew and Mark and Luke and John—and every single word they wrote was Gospel.

Daniel O'Thunder was—and remains—the most remarkable man I have ever met. He was a complicated man of deep and abiding contradictions, and yet he was at one and the same time a simple man with a very simple goal. He wanted to call the Devil forth, and face him and fight him, and—finally and forever—defeat him.

This, then, is my Book of Daniel.

In writing it—in telling you the tale of Daniel O'Thunder, and his deadly Enemy—I am of course telling the tale of myself as well. And to tell my story we must begin where it all began to go so wrong.

A SUNDAY MORNING in 1849. We are in Cornwall. More specifically we are in the little church of St Kea's-by-the-sea. It is a church in the stark Gothic Perpendicular style, dating originally to Norman times, set upon a hillside above the village of Porthmullion. The churchyard is a riot of colour, for it is spring and the daffodils have begun to bloom amidst the headstones. There is a towering grey Cornish Cross outside the front door, carved atop a granite column. Nearby is the Holy Well where miracles were wont to occur in bygone days, and might—we are Christians, and live in hope—occur again. Here inside the church it is cool; it smells of damp and piety and distant sea-brine. Sun slants in through stained glass, and dust-motes dance like angels. Mounted upon the walls are slate tablets with inscriptions commemorating bygone parishioners, such as young William Barnstable:

Short blaze of life, meteor of human Pride,
Essayed to live, but liked it not and died.

In the windows are Bible scenes, and images of the Four Evangelists. Set into the west wall is a portrait of St Kea. His golden head is haloed, and his eyes glow with an unsettling admixture of humility and fervid derangement. This conceivably reflects the limitations of the artisan, but possibly it doesn't, St Kea being one of those Dark Age divines who paddled to Cornwall from Ireland on a boulder. There is in Kea's expression a certain agitation as well, an incipient alarm, as if he glimpses Someone Else amongst us, and would call out a warning if only he weren't trapped forever in stained glass.

The saint is quite correct, of course. The Devil is here, and he is watching. He's watching dear old Petherick, the verger, nodding off in the choir. He's watching young Bob Odgers—pay attention, Bob, and stop pinching your sister. He's even daring to watch Sir Richard Scantlebury, *Bart.*, slumbering in his family pew. Oh yes he is—open your eyes, Sir Richard. Beware! He's watching right this second.

And on that fine spring Sunday, looking out from the pulpit in my cassock and my jampot collar, I told them so. Behold the young Revd Mr Jack Beresford, in earnest oratorical flight.

"For the Devil does not sleep," I said, "and he does not blink. The Devil's eye is a basilisk's eye, and it is fixed upon you, and you, and you, and upon each and every one of us, from the moment we draw breath until the moment we are Judged. And if in this Judgement we are found wanting, then that eye will remain fixed forever."

In a different parish such ruminations might well have been seen as alarmingly Low Church, or indeed slightly mad. But here in St Kea's there was a little frisson of dark satisfaction. Mine was a congregation composed primarily of labourers and fisherfolk. Cornish labourers and fisherfolk to boot, dour and stolid men and women who quite liked the idea of their neighbours being Judged, especially if they should also be Found Wanting.

"Now, I have met with those," I continued, "who maintain that the Devil does not exist. They say to me, 'surely the Devil is just a story, made up to frighten children.' And what do I say to this? I say: 'my friend, if you don't believe in the Devil, then I'm not sure I believe in you. For if you looked at yourself closely—if you looked down deep in your heart—I suspect you'd see a devil soon enough.'"

I happened to be looking straight at Sir Richard, *Bart.*, as I said this, which was unfortunate. Sir Richard, *Bart.*, had awakened with a snort and a fart a moment or two earlier, and he was a man who felt perceived insults keenly. The Scantlebury pew was curtained and carved and raised above the rest to balcony level, for the Scantleburys were the local aristocracy—which is to say that they were a clan of inbred horrors descended from smugglers and pirates. Sir Richard's great-grandfather was the notorious Reeking Scantlebury, a freebooter equally noted for his rapacity and his contempt for personal hygiene. He married Black Bess Timberfoot, a twenty-stone one-legged pirate queen who was known for flaying her captives alive and feeding their vital organs to her parrot, Beaky Norman. From them are descended the present generation of appalling pig-farming gentry.

Granted, I'm supplying one or two details of my own here. Such as the parrot, and the pirate queen, and Reeking himself. As you come to know me better, you will learn that I have a vivid imagination, and an instinct for the dramatic. Still, many Cornish fortunes did indeed begin in smuggling, and these guessed-at details would go a long way towards explaining the present occupants of Scantlebury Hall. Sir Richard was a man of porcine bulk and ponderous self-regard, sitting like a champion boar amidst his brood. On his right scowled the son and heir, Little Dick, half a head taller and even broader athwart. Beside Little Dick was young Geoffrey: a pouting thing of twelve or so with a head of yellow curls, proof that the breeding of sons is not as exact a science as the breeding of Dorsetshire Saddlebacks, and that even the saltiest sea-captain may sire the occasional cabin-boy. On Sir Richard's sinister side sat Bathsheba, the most unsettling Scantlebury of all.

Bathsheba Scantlebury was one-and-twenty. She was her father's daughter, and clearly destined for the Scantlebury bulk, complete with the squinting Scantlebury eye and perhaps even a wen upon the snorting Scantlebury snout. But not yet. Bathsheba was still beautiful—or if not precisely beautiful, then nonetheless keenly desirable, in an ill-tempered sluttish up-against-the-cowshed sort of way. She had a gaze that pinned you wriggling to the wall, and a curl to her lip that said: "I know what the world is like, and what it wants in its filthy black heart—and more than that, *I know you.*"

I gripped the sides of the pulpit and continued, like a mariner in his cockpit gazing down upon a troubled sea.

"You say to me, 'Mr Beresford, I have looked high and low—I have looked within and without—and I have never seen the Devil, no not once.' Well, I'm afraid I must reply that this is very bad indeed. For if you don't see the Devil, what it almost certainly means is, he's already got you.

"For the Devil is a busy man, my friends. The wide world is his hunting-ground, and all of humankind his quarry. So when he passes a hardened sinner, he exults: 'This one is already mine—pass on to the next!' A grasping man of business, extracting the last mite from a widow? 'Pass on.' The man and the woman eyeing one another, aglow with the secret fires of lust? 'Well done, my good and faithful servants—you'll join me soon enough, and *my* flames are everlasting. Pass on!' So take no solace when you cannot see the Devil, and never suppose that he has forgotten you. For the gates of Hell are gaping wide, and the Devil is forever rising up."

I shot a swift guilty glance upwards to Bathsheba Scantlebury. Her own eyes had widened slightly—for damn it all, these infernal musings had provoked a certain agitation down below, and the Devil was rising up indeed. The pulpit hid this from most of the congregation, but Bathsheba in the elevated Scantlebury pew stared down from above. And she had seen.

Oh, Lord. I could hear my voice growing constricted, and sought refuge in shrivelling images.

"Once the Devil has risen up, he will not rest until he has dragged you down. And what does it mean, to be dragged down by the Devil? Well, let me tell you. You are sealed in your coffin, and plunged head downwards into the Pit. And this Pit is like a mine shaft, except far narrower, just wide enough to accommodate your coffin, which in turn is so close that your face presses up against the wood, so tightly that you cannot draw a single breath, even if there were air to breathe in Hell, which there is not. There you are, pinioned upside-down, suffocating in the stench of the unquenchable sulphur flames—and yet ice-cold, a cold that gnaws into your very pith and marrow, for the flames of Hell generate no heat, but a cold so intense it cannot be conceived.

"And there's worse to come. After an age of agony, there comes an instant of hope. You hear a scraping sound above, and a voice crying, and your poor heart leaps with the thought: 'They've come to fetch me out of this!' Your coffin gives a lurch and a shudder and a grind, but the cry you heard was not the angels winging to deliver you. It was the sinner next in line, who has just been loaded in on top. An endless line of sinners, each one atop the last, each one forcing you six feet deeper down that suffocating shaft.

"And now comes the worst of all. You realize: you are utterly alone. God has turned His face from you—now, and for all eternity. God has forgotten you ever existed. He has let you go."

I had shaken them. I could see it in the faces staring back at me: some of them slack-jawed, a few of them frankly appalled. Even Sir Richard blinked, and shifted his bulk uncomfortably. I could have continued. I could have told them: trust me—it's true—*I know.* I've read my Calvin and my Dante, and a hundred hellfire evangelists beside. What's more, I've looked into my own heart, and understood what I deserve. I felt the prick of tears, and there was a moment—there really was—when I might have fallen to my knees, and wept, and confessed my sins to God and the people of Porthmullion, and vowed to walk the paths of righteousness all the days of my life.

But Bathsheba Scantlebury was staring down at me. Her head was cocked appraisingly, and her lip said: "Oh, you dog—I *know* you."

The Devil stared straight back at her, and twitched.

I SHOULD NEVER have been a clergyman in the first place. That should have been my brother. Tobias was two years younger, a boy who could pray for hours at a stretch, and who would utter things like, "God sees the little sparrow fall, but He trusts in you and me to mend its wing." He nursed wounded birds in his bedchamber, did Toby, keeping them in a little box beneath a picture of Our Lord holding a lamb in his arms. Our Lord had a tiny sad smile on his face—you know the smile I mean. He smiles because he loves us, but he is sad because so many of us are damned and just don't know it yet. Late at night, passing by, I would hear the sweet earnest murmur of brother Toby entreating Our Lord to forgive me. Toby was in short a sanctimonious little horror. But just as you were on the verge of ducking him in the pond, he'd finish all your chores and disappear before you could thank him, or else ask you why you were crying and impulsively give you his new compass, or perform some other such act that would send you slinking away with a withering sense of your own selfishness, and the deeply discomfiting realization: my God, he actually is *good,* isn't he?

In this he took after our maternal grandfather, an ineffectual but beloved provincial vicar who occupied pride of place in my mother's personal canon of saints. So when Toby announced—at the age of three—his vocation for the priesthood, it was a day of rejoicing for my mother, not to mention a vast relief to me. Now that Toby's chubby hand had taken up the torch, I was free to follow my own true nature, which much more closely favoured our father. He was a provincial solicitor—we lived on the outskirts of a bleak Midlands industrial town, whose belching smokestacks fed my child's intuition that Hell's Gate was just beyond the next hill. More to the point, my father was the second son of a second son, a man of feckless charm and determined demons who frittered away a modest patrimony in a sequence of ill-conceived initiatives. After each catastrophe he would plunge into drink, proceeding through fury to despair and tearful encomiums to self-slaughter, before staggering back to his feet in the renewed conviction that something grand might turn up next week.

But my brother never took up holy orders. A chill gripped Toby on the evening of his fifteenth birthday, and he withdrew to his chamber under the sad watchful gaze of Our Lord. By morning the chill had become a racking cough, and by nightfall a fever that made the doctor shake his head in gloomy resignation. Toby departed at dawn, brave and devout, actually whispering with his last breath: "Don't cry, Jack. Look—my angel's come—he's reaching out to take my hand."

Well, this is quite the legacy to leave your older brother. I was seventeen at the time, and had almost settled upon the Law as a suitable career for a young man with decent intelligence and keen material expectations, but no particular gift for application—my father's son, in other words. But now the weight of maternal hope had nowhere else to fall. My poor mother was sufficiently distraught to clutch at any straw, even the belief that I might make a clergyman after all—so how could I say no, with the flowers still fresh on Toby's grave? Besides, I was genuinely haunted—and have remained so, all my life—by the look on my brother's face as he struggled to lift his hand towards his angel. It was a look so radiant that it could make even a wretched Doubter half-believe that it was true—that Toby's angel *was* there—and more, that there was a second angel in the room, reaching out to Toby's brother and telling him: "This is your destiny. Put down your nets and follow me."

So. You conjure consolatory dreams of deanships and bishoprics, which soon wither in the reality of a third-class degree from Oxford and a family with no money and less influence. Finally the Future presents itself in the form of a seventy-pound-per-annum curacy in the outer reaches of Cornwall. And what do you do then? Why, you do your best.

MY BEST IS WHAT I was doing on the afternoon of that fateful Sunday.

I had spent an hour or so alone after service, despairing over failures and inadequacies, and dreaming of escape. Today's dream had to do with California, whence news of a Gold Rush had reached the newspapers even in Cornwall. This conjured an agreeable image of myself, ministering selflessly to spade-bearded miners in a verdant wilderness, before succumbing to a fever even more spectacular than the one that had taken my brother. I had just come to the point where news of my death reached Bathsheba Scantlebury—she was secretly shattered—when I saw that the hour was nearly two o'clock. God's Work awaited just down the road, and so I gave myself a shake and roused myself to it.

Old Ned Moyle had been failing badly these past few months. He was past ninety and no longer able to walk to church, so I'd fallen into the habit of taking the Communion bread and wine out to him. This meant a five-mile trudge along the cliffs to the fisherman's cottage where Old Ned lived with his son, Young Ned, and then of course a five-mile trudge back, which was no bargain—let me tell you—when the weather was up. But on a fine spring afternoon, I confess I enjoyed it—a walk that was all sharp salt air and plunging ocean vistas, with prowling waves and secret coves where you could picture low-slung sloops at anchor under the black flag, and Reeking Scantlebury plotting his depredations, and Black Bess in the fo'cs'le feeding your kidneys to Beaky Norman.

The Moyles lived in the sort of rough dwelling you'll find all along the Cornish coast, clinging to the rock like barnacles. Their low stone cottage was set into the hillside, with a steep path winding past a desultory vegetable garden and down to the sea. The sun was sloping westward when I arrived. Young Ned was at work out front, mending his nets. "Why, it's the young Reverend, coom to zee us," he exclaimed, as surprised as he had been last Sunday afternoon, and each Sunday afternoon before that. Young Ned was well on the shady side of seventy himself—still as strong as a bull, but his memory was no longer what it once had been. The result was that life was full of surprises for Young Ned, and some of them were pleasant, which I suppose must count as a blessing.

"Coom in, young Reverend," he beamed, wringing my hand and leading me inside. It was cramped and damp but surprisingly clean, though full of clutter and fisherman's paraphernalia. The stick that was Old Ned reclined in a cot by the window, covered with a tatty old shawl. I performed the Eucharist with my customary sense that someone else would be more convincing in the role, pausing as usual while Old Ned gummed the wafer and worked it down. Afterwards I stayed for a chat, which was identical to the chat we had enjoyed the previous Sunday, and all the Sundays preceding, the gist being as follows:

YOUNG NED: "Well, Da. Here's the young reverend."
OLD NED: "It's the legs, you know. They've give out."
REVD BERESFORD: "I'm afraid God sends these things to try us."
OLD NED: "*WHAT?*"
YOUNG NED: "*E ZAYS, GOD ZENDS THESE THINGS!*"
OLD NED: "Aye, God zave the Queen."
(*Brief interlude, in which are vague patriotic noddings.*)
YOUNG NED: "Well, Da. Here's the young reverend."

Et cetera. The chat lingered, as it often did, owing to the excellent quality of Young Ned's ale. We toasted the Queen, and the Prince Consort, and various heirs to the throne, and it was well past five o'clock by the time I rose and blessed Old Ned—something that always made me feel utterly fraudulent, but also oddly happy. Young Ned walked me out to the head of the path. It was clear there was something on his mind, and I waited while he hummed and hawed.

"'E's not entirely well, is 'e?" he said at length, with a sidelong look, as if half hoping that I might contradict him.

"He's an old man, Ned," I said. Sometimes it's best to stick with the blindingly obvious.

"'Is legs've give out."

"His poor old legs."

"Aye. Them legs."

Young Ned stood pondering his father's legs for a few moments, rocking from toes to heels, sucking ruminatively upon his teeth.

"But it's more than that, isn't it?" he resumed. "I'm ztarting to think . . . 'e might be gone, one of these days. One of these days quite zoon."

There was such wistful look in his eyes—a man of more than seventy, about to be orphaned—that my heart went out.

"We'll all be gone one of these days, Ned. But here's what I think. I'm pretty certain—I think I can say for a fact—that he'll be here when I come back next Sunday afternoon. So we'll raise a glass of your excellent ale, and we'll toast Her Majesty and all her loyal subjects, and we'll spend a splendid afternoon."

Sometimes when we open our mouths, the right words come spilling out. Young Ned began to nod, a happy look creeping across his weathered old face. "Well, young Reverend," he said. "We'll all look forward to that."

I LEFT WITH a feeling of warmth inside that wasn't entirely due to Ned's ale. For a few lovely moments I was buoyed by the sense that God's business had just been carried out—and carried out by me—and that against all odds I might actually have a vocation for this after all. I imagined Toby and his angel smiling down in dewy-eyed approval, and all at once I felt a powerful urge to go searching for fallen sparrows. But this passed, for the weather was turning.

It was later than I'd intended. Twilight was creeping across the hills, and with it came a rising wind and dark clouds massing overhead. I pulled my coat more tightly round myself and hurried; you didn't want to be caught on the cliffs after dark, especially with a storm rising. I had reached the crest of the headland, just where the trail grew narrowest and the rocks plunged most precipitously into the sea below, when I heard the sound of hoofbeats behind me, emerging out of the roar of wind and waves. I looked back, and shouted in alarm, for the rider was already upon me.

"Look out, you fool!"

This being the rider's shout, not mine. A moment later I was raising myself to hands and knees, winded and indignant, having sprawled for safety half a heartbeat before the hooves thundered past. Ahead, the horse was brought skittering to a stop.

"I say, look where you're going—you could have killed me!"

"Then stay out of the damned road!"

A great grey gelding shied and pranced, and I recognized the rider. It was Bathsheba Scantlebury, in tall black boots and a black riding cloak. She gave a little start as she recognized me in return.

"Is that the curate?" she exclaimed.

She brought the horse skittering closer, to be sure.

"The Revd Mr Beresford—it *is* you. What the Devil are you doing up here on the cliffs, with a storm coming on?" Her hair was loose, and her colour was high with the wind and the gallop. Cocking her head, she eyed me with jaundiced appraisal. "I'd best not discover you've been poaching."

"P-poaching?"

You try getting the word out without a splutter—an accusation like that, when you're already fair dancing with the indignation of it.

"This is all Scantlebury land. Lay a hand on a single pheasant, and I don't care who you are—I'll have you horsewhipped."

"You sulky supercilious bitch," I cried—or at least, imagined myself crying. Indeed, I imagined stalking forward in seething masculine dudgeon, and saying other things besides, such as: "You're the one who should be horsewhipped, Miss Scantlebury. I've half a mind to turn you over a knee myself—and I see by the wanton gleam in those eyes that you might jolly well like it!"

But of course I said no such thing, being a man of the cloth.

"In point of fact I've been to see a parishioner," I said, clutching what tatters of dignity I could lay hands upon. "Not that it's any particular business of yours. I just walked five miles to comfort the afflicted, and now I'm walking fives miles home again. That's what a priest does, Miss Scantlebury, because that's what the Lord expects of him. I am also called to feed the hungry," I added, "and clothe the naked."

Damn. The instant it was out of my mouth.

One eyebrow arched. "Yes, I can well believe that the naked concern you, Mr Beresford. I suspected as much this morning."

I could feel the morning's humiliation rushing scarlet to my face. And she just looked at me, brazen as Babylon.

"Come on, then—I won't leave you out here in a storm. Climb up, and you can ride behind."

But a man has his pride. I straightened my back, and met that gaze with actual—yes—*froideur.*

"Not if yours, Miss Scantlebury, was the last behind in Cornwall."

I admit, an unclerical thing to say. But by the God who made me, it was splendid to say it. Bathsheba's jaw actually dropped, as she searched for a suitable retort. But whatever it might have been, it was lost in a startled exclamation. Lightning had flickered a few moments before, and now thunder cracked, directly overhead. Her horse, already skittish in the rising wind, reared back; taken unawares, she tumbled.

"Miss Scantlebury!"

She was on her back and rolling, and in another instant she must have gone straight over the cliff-edge. But I had already leapt forward, and caught her by the arm to steady her. Bathsheba lay breathless for a moment, stunned by the fall and by the narrow escape—for this had been a near-run thing. We stared down at the jagged rocks and the heaving sea far below.

"Are you all right?"

"Take your hands off me!"

I released her and stepped back, expecting her to stand. Instead she lay where she was, gasping for breath and glaring furiously up at me.

"I've hurt my leg, damn you."

"That's hardly my fault."

"I damned you on general principle. I say it again: damn you, and damn that look you're giving me right now. That's supposed to be manly concern, is it? And I suppose you think you're fetching—the young curate, with his soulful eyes. Well, don't bother, because I *know* you."

I hesitated. "May I . . . ?"

"No, you may not!"

But I did. I knelt and asked which leg was hurt, and she lifted the right one an inch or two. It seemed to be her ankle—a surprisingly delicate ankle, at the end of a beautifully formed calf, above which there was of course a knee and—oh dear God.

"I don't think it's broken," I hazarded. But clearly it was badly sprained, for the gentlest touch made her gasp, and when I glanced up her eyes had actually filled with tears. For a heart-stopping moment she was a child again, hurt and vulnerable and secretly frightened.

"What do we do now?" she asked, for clearly we faced a dilemma. Her horse was already gone and galloping homeward, and here we were—a good two miles from the Moyles' cottage, and at least another three from Porthmullion, with night falling and the storm beginning to rage in earnest.

"Lean against me," I urged, helping her up. "Here, we can manage it!"

But we couldn't. This was clear enough after the first few hobbling steps, which left just two possibilities. The first was to leg it for home myself, leaving Bathsheba to rot—which I confess I considered. The alternative was an old abandoned shepherd's hut. It was above us, in a cleft between two hills.

I pointed. Rain lashed down, and I had to raise my voice against the wind. "It isn't much, but at least there's a roof. It'll keep us dry while we wait out the storm. Look, I'm going to have to carry you, all right?"

"I swear, I really will have you horsewhipped!"

Which under the circumstances I interpreted as agreement.

The uphill path was arduous, and several times I nearly fell. But as I struggled onward—her arms round my neck—I began to see myself as I still do, frequently, to this day: as an actor thrust into a role upon the stage, wholly unprepared and fearing himself unequal to the task, but plucky and determined and finding his light, and discovering resources that he had never dared hope he possessed. I believe I had an image of myself as the hero of one of Mr Boucicault's melodramas—the one in which he rescues the foul-mouthed slut. But after an eternity of slips and strangled oaths and "Christ, watch where you're going, you imbecile!", the old stone hut was there before us, and we staggered in.

It was small and dank, and it smelled of piss, but it had a roof, and a door that pulled shut with a tattered leather strap and kept out the howling wind. There were even a few sticks of furniture. I kicked apart a rickety chair for kindling, and after a few attempts I managed to start a little fire, which crackled and generated actual warmth. We stripped off our sodden cloaks and huddled in front of it. I discovered I still had half a jug of ale, and this improved things even further.

"Young Ned gave it to me, before I left. Young Ned and his father—that's who I went to see."

"You mean you really were seeing a parishioner?"

I wasn't offering it as proof that I'd been telling the truth, but apparently she took it as such.

"Do you want to search my pockets for pheasants?"

"Oh, don't sulk. You think it makes you look dark and brooding, but it doesn't."

Her expression was sour, but there was also a certain—well, if not warmth, then at least neutrality. She was sitting on an old blanket that I'd found on a shelf and spread out in front of the fire. Her dress clung to her, and as I uncorked the jug I caught her sneaking another sidelong look in my direction.

The fact is, I was a good-looking fellow in those departed days of 1849. It wasn't the face I show to the world these four long decades later, ruined by the years and much else besides—a face that would cause you to start if you saw it, and flinch. For that's what you would do—oh yes you would—if I looked up abruptly from my glass in some low tavern, or perhaps came upon you suddenly in the London fog. But back then I was quite the lad, in a crookedly smiling boyish sort of way. The brown eyes were large, and there was a wing of brown hair that would fall down over them, which I had a way of flipping back with a movement of my hand. The overall effect might indeed have been too boyish, except for the scar: a horseshoe-shaped scar by my left eye, courtesy of a childhood set-to with a butcher's apprentice who had been bullying my brother. I'd been carried home in a cart, to be sewn up on the kitchen table, but apparently I'd inflicted some damage in return, for my adversary never troubled poor Toby again. And I afterwards discovered that the girls were quite affected by my scar—it gave me a rugged cast—so all in all I decided I'd come rather well out of the bargain.

Miss Scantlebury and I shared the ale, and divided the loaf of bread and the lump of cheese that I'd brought with me too. Soon enough we were feeling warmer, and beginning to talk. Then we were talking some more, and laughing, and agreeing that this was a very odd place for a picnic. I found myself telling her about the old Welsh pony I rode as a boy, and never saw the Devil until it was too late.

"The last behind in Cornwall?" She eyed me aslant.

"Yes, well. I apologize," I said. "That was rude, and ungentlemanly."

"I shouldn't forgive you," said she, with a little pout. "But under the circumstances, I suppose I shall."

"You're very good."

"No I'm not. I'm not very good at all. That's what you like best about me."

"Miss Scantlebury, what are you doing?"

For a hand was upon my leg.

You'll have guessed the sequel, of course. Someone like yourself, who knows the way of the world and the frailties of the human heart. And of course I knew it was wicked, and wrong, and hateful in the eyes of God. But the Devil had slipped in from the storm without our noticing, and now there was the dark sweet murmur of Infernal blandishments—*go on, my friends, for you want to so much; it's lovely, it's harmless, and who's ever to know, on a night so dark and God's eyes surely elsewhere?*—and then the lash of his riding crop. Before I quite realized what was happening, Bathsheba was a wondrous writhing rubbery thing. Breasts burst from linen; she cried out. The first hot cascading plunge, and finding the stride, and then the great gallop—ears pinned back and the Devil's whip-hand flailing—thundering around the turn and down the stretch to the last gate, the storm raging both within us and without. We were up and over and tumbling down the other side, utterly spent and lying limp as rags. And then, just as triumph began to give way to the first cold stabbings of remorse—that familiar sick lurch into self-loathing—just at that very point, I felt an icy gust of wind. The door was open, and someone was standing in the doorway, holding up a torch.

"Bathsheba?!"

It was her younger brother, the Cabin Boy. Behind him loomed Little Dick. I exclaimed, grabbing at the blanket to cover myself. Despite my confusion, I expected to hear Bathsheba's voice, uttering furious oaths and ordering them out.

"Help," whispered Bathsheba.

"I beg your pardon?" I said, bewildered.

"I tried to fight him, but he forced me."

"I did not!"

"Oh God, oh God, oh God, my Virtue."

I sprang to my feet. But a sledge-hammer fist came whistling, and the world exploded into blackness.

THIS IS WHERE my account grows unreliable. The memory of what happened next has the swooning unreality of nightmare; I have been forced to conclude that some of it—much of it?—was pure hallucination, brought on by that first concussive blow. But I have pledged to tell my tale to the best of my ability, and so here is what I seem to recollect.

I am swimming back to consciousness. A vast echoing room, with great rough wooden beams, lit by torchlight. A cavernous fireplace, and tapestries on the walls, and animals stuffed and mounted: the heads of stags and boars, and the entire forms of smaller predators—ferrets and badgers and stoats—frozen forever in attitudes of coiled malevolence. Among these are human portraits: bloated grandsires with bulging eyes, and cold-eyed viragos as coiled and malignant as the stoats.

Even in my disorientation, I can guess whose ancestors these were. This shrine to slaughter and misanthropy is Scantlebury Hall, and here assembled are the current denizens. Sir Richard on a vast oaken chair, with Little Dick louring beside him. Bathsheba recumbent nearby on a low divan, wrapped in a blanket and managing to look shattered, attended by the curly-haired Cabin Boy.

I struggle to my knees.

"Look here," a voice says woozily, as if from a good distance. Apparently it is mine. "I don't—you can't just—dear God in Heaven."

The voice that replies is like metal grinding upon stone. "The charge against you is as follows. That you did lie feloniously in wait for a virgin of unimpeachable character, viz. my daughter, upon whom you did perpetrate an act of savage assault and rapine, in such a manner as to place you beyond any appeal to common humanity, and all hope of mercy in this life or the life to come."

Sir Richard Scantlebury, *Bart.*

"A charge? What are you talking about?"

"How do you plead?"

"I didn't touch her!"

This is not of course strictly true. A stammered emendation: "I mean, yes, of course I—well, you know. And it was wrong—a priest—obviously. A shitten shepherd—a disgrace to the cloth—I condemn myself utterly. But we walked down that path together, and I swear I am not the sort of man who would ever—just ask her!"

"You ask me to believe," grates Sir Richard, "that my daughter—what—*seduced* you? That she participated in the act? Of her own volition, and without protest?"

"Yes!"

They stare: a convocation of stoats contemplating a rabbit.

Bathsheba's bottom lip quivers.

What happens next is assuredly an hallucination. I seem to see young Geoffrey stepping forward. Inexplicably, he seems to be wearing a peasant smock and carrying a basket of baguettes. He points a finger in righteous venom, as if standing in the shadow of the guillotine.

"*J'accuse,*" says the Cabin Boy.

"What?" I exclaim, bewildered. "What's he saying?"

The room gives a lurch, and steadies. Geoffrey is himself again, and he is lying through his teeth.

"...and I was hurrying home with my brother, Sir, when I heard my sister screaming. We ran to help her, thinking she was being murdered by ruffians, or tortured by Red Indians, so terrible was the cries. Instead we found her in the embrace of the curate, him standing right there, rutting in his lust with his bottom bare and horrible, and shouting, 'Scream all you please, my Pretty, for I only like it better when you do!'"

All eyes are upon me. Sir Richard and his brood, and their ancestors upon the walls, and the ferrets and the stoats. Such eyes as I have glimpsed in my darkest dreams of perdition.

"Do you have anything to say," says Sir Richard, "before sentence is passed?"

"Sentence? This is no court!"

"This is the manor court, convened by ancient baronial privilege, and I am the baron."

"You're all mad!"

Or else I am. But things are happening very swiftly now.

"Kill him!" cries Bathsheba, bursting into tears. "Kill him—but geld him, first!"

Little Dick reaches out. But in moments of crisis we discover what we are made of, and this moment confirms what had been intimated in the Battle of Butcher's Apprentice—to wit, the Revd Mr Beresford is descended from warriors. If not actual warriors, then at least the sort of men who could survive a skirmish on the fringes of the main conflagration—men who could raise their heads a few breathless moments after the last cannon had echoed into silence, and look around, and blink, and exclaim: "Are we done, then? By the Lord Harry, that was almost too close for comfort."

I duck my head and charge, butting Little Dick in the solar plexus. He staggers back, trout-faced. The window—quick! The Cabin Boy skitters to block my way, too late. A bound and a leap and a shattering of glass, and I am through the window headlong and landing with bone-jarring impact.

All air is driven from my lungs. Howling wind and lashing rain. Somehow I am back upon my feet. But there are shouts behind me, and a gunshot. Christ! I am running now, running blind. Then the ground is gone beneath my feet. I pitch forward. A sickening sensation of falling—and falling.

Even in my wild confusion, I know what this means. There is a sheer cliff on the windward side of Scantlebury Hall, and I have blundered over. Now there is nothing but the icy black sea and the jagged rocks below.

But now comes the most incredible moment of all. I swear this to be true. In that moment of horrid realization—plunging helpless, like a minor rebel from the fields of Heaven—there is a light in the darkness. I seem to see a shining face, and a hand reaching towards me. In my confusion it seems to me at first that this is the visage of blessed stained-glass St Kea, paddling to my deliverance on a boulder. But it is another face entirely. A man's great laughing face, lumpen and scarred from old battles but somehow beautiful nonetheless, with a lopsided jaw and a tumult of yellow hair. The face of a warrior archangel, and a voice like the flight of eagles, saying: "Fear not, brother, no never fear at all, for I am with you always."

"Who are you?" I cry.

He says: "O'Thunder."

· LONDON, 1851 ·

NELL

IT WAS EARLIER that night when I seen the Devil, outside the theatre. The Kemp Theatre, north of Holborn, near King's Cross. He was on the corner, passing out handbills. Or not the Devil himself, but one of his demons, spindly and wretched and black with sulphur smoke. Leastways that's what I assumed, cos what else would he be, outside a theatre? An actor, got up as one of Satan's henchmen, passing out handbills for the play.

But he wasn't. I realized when I got closer and looked again—the sulphur smoke was ink. So he was a printer's devil, an apprentice in a print shop. Apparently he wasn't much good at it either, cos he'd got inkstains all over. He was skinny and shabby, with hands that stuck out the ends of his sleeves and trousers that come halfway up his shins, and it wasn't handbills for the play he was giving out. It was tracts—you know, the Christian ones, all about living a better life and what happens to you if you don't. Well, I don't live the one, so I can hardly afford to care about the other, can I? So I ignored him and elbowed my way in with the crowd, and I'd never have give him another thought the rest of my life, if it hadn't been for what happened later.

I always loved the theatre. I loved it more than practically anything. Back then, all those years ago when I lived in London, I'd go nearly every night of the week. I'd go see any kind of play, even Shakespeare. I seen Charlie Kean play Hamlet once, and Macready, and afterwards I went with one of them. Not Kean or Macready, but one of the others. We went to a night house nearby, and had a drain or two of pale, and then took one of the little rooms. Nothing happened much, even though I gave it a good try. It just dangled there like a wrinkled stocking, between his skinny old shanks. But he paid up like a gentleman, and we drank some more, and he blubbered a bit and called me his own dear child who reminded him of his salad days when he was young and the world was full of hope—yes, he talked like that—so perhaps he got his half crown's worth. If he didn't, ah well. Fuck 'im.

But the ones I really liked were the melodramas. Mrs Dalrymple used to take me when she was alive, and now that she was dead I'd go to the theatre with one of the other girls, or lots of times just by myself. A highwayman and a lass, and a toff who was really the villain, and a first-rate murder and a duel, and everything going horribly wrong before turning out right in the end—those were the plays for me. Or the ones that made you shriek out loud, with blue demons dancing, and red demons rising up, and the Devil disappearing with a *BANG* through a hole in the floor. This particular night—the night I'm telling you about—it was a play about two Corsican brothers. The one gets foully murdered by a villainous French toff, and of course the other has to take re-venge. It was the first time I'd seen it, so naturally I had to watch it close.

"This is wrong."

A voice in my ear.

"What?"

"These are bad places."

It was him—the Printer's Devil. He was right behind me in the crowd.

"I shouldn't be here, I shouldn't have come, and neither should you, such places lead us into wickedness."

He spoke like that, a low worried voice and the words all spilling out on top of each other. He was staring at the stage like it offended him so much he just couldn't look away from it for a second. I was familiar with that look, from all the times it was directed at me, by gentlemen with high moral principles and low filthy longings. This one was no gentleman, and of course he was just a boy, sixteen maybe, although he was tall for his age. A lot taller than me.

"You're gay, ent you?" he asked.

"Never you mind what I am."

"You're gay, you're a whore, you're here to flaunt yourself and have carnal connection."

"I'm here to watch the play. So fuck off."

He was right, though—the part about me being a whore. Why deny it? There was lots of us gay girls here—dozens of us, just like every night—and most of 'em had come for the business. At the big music halls, the ones where four thousand punters could crowd in, there might be two hundred girls at work, and private rooms behind the boxes, where a gentleman could retire for half an hour with a girl and a bottle of wine. There were no little rooms at theatres like the Kemp—it wasn't grand enough for that. But there was the night houses across the way, and alleyways behind, where the world could go round as the world has gone round since Adam met Eve, and will continue doing till Judgement Day comes. But me personally, I was here to watch the play. Besides, there was something just a little bit wrong with this one, the Printer's Devil with his gabbling worried voice. You get so you can sense it straight off, the ones you'd better steer clear of. So I edged forward, through the crowd.

We were way up top, of course, cos that's where you'd go for a sixpence. The theatre was packed, like usual, and I'd come in too late to get a seat on the benches, which left me standing at the back. The pit was a shilling, and them who could afford three shillings were in the boxes—merchants and such and the real titled gents and ladies—though they steered pretty much clear of theatres like this. Up here it was tradesmen and shop-girls and apprentices and dollymops, and all manner of riff-raff like myself, crammed in cheek-to-giblets and craning to see round someone's hat. The smell was what you'd imagine, all mixed in with gunpowder from the explosions and oranges being eaten by the crowd, and the heat was terrible, from all the bodies and the gaslights. But the play was prime.

It had just got to the part where the ghost of the one brother appears to the other, all quavery and beyond-the-grave with his hair standing straight up on end, and blood and gore on his breast from the sword that foully struck him down. There were gasps at the sight of him, and shouts to his brother of, "hear him, hear him!" and "it was the Frenchman done this!"—you know, in case he wasn't clear on who he should be killing for revenge. For they were enjoying this, and not jeering as they do when the play's no good, although they weren't impressed with the actor who was playing the Frenchman's friend, and there'd been a few orange peels flung at him already.

"They incite the passions, that's what they do, they stir up our animal spirits, such low and lewd entertainments."

Fucksake. He'd come up behind me again, talking low and faster than ever.

"The door is open, just a crack but that's all he needs, the door is open and the Devil slips in. That's why it's wrong, I shouldn't be here, I should leave."

"Then go."

"I want you to come with me. I want you to come right now."

"What for?"

But of course I knew what for. He was pushed up against me in the press of bodies and I could feel it, sticking into my back.

"Christ, would you take that bloody thing—?"

"No, not for that!"

The look on his phiz was pure distress—enough to make you laugh out loud. Cos of course I had him pegged from the first second he started gabbling. One of them bible-thumpers so horrified by the goings-on in his breeches that he torments himself barmy. Suddenly—Gawd help us—he was Bearing Witness. Something about being a norrible sinner and in the Devil's clutches till he was Saved by the Light and it was someone called the Captain who rescued him.

"The Cap'n loves me, he said 'I love you Young Joe like a son.' He said so this very morning and I could of wept with happiness. And I dreamt one time of how the Devil come for me, but the Cap'n was there to stop him. He seized the Devil by the nose, the Cap'n did, and thrashed him with a stick, Cap'n Daniel O'Thunder!"

The name meant fuck all to me, and besides I'd had enough of this. Now he was clutching my arm to keep me from getting away.

"I swear, he thrashed the Devil till he howled, and—*argh!*"

What you do is, you stamp down hard with the sharp heel of your boot on his instep. It works a treat if you do it right, and I'd had plenty of practice, trust me. With a shriek he lurched back into the punters behind him, who didn't like this one bit, and let him know it. I slipped through the bodies, quick and nimble, for I can flit like a swallow when needs be. When I looked back I seen his face for just an instant, twisted and clenched, and then he was swallowed up in the crowd.

So I forgot about him, and watched the rest of the play. It was very satisfactory. The French villain who killed the first Corsican brother tried to flee in his carriage, but crashed in a forest. He was with his friend—the friend being another Frenchman, tricked out in a great black wig and the worst stage whiskers I ever seen. He couldn't act a lick to save his soul, this friend, but it was a small part so it didn't matter so much. Anyroad, the second Corsican brother stepped through the trees and challenged the villain to a duel. There was a great swordfight and the villain fell dying in agony and at the very end the ghost appeared again to talk to his brother. Both brothers were played by the same actor, a wonderful trick that must have been done with mirrors, and you should have heard the shouts and applause. After the play there was an acrobat, and then the burlesque, and it was nearly midnight when it was finished. You tell me where else you'd find yourself an evening like that for a sixpence, because you wouldn't. You wouldn't find it for a pound.

And if I'd seen my mother on that stage, it would have been perfect. I was watching for her, of course, like I always did. But, just like always, it turned out she was somewhere else.

THE NIGHT AIR was cold, coming out of the theatre, and Christ the noise and jostle. The street out front was clattering with coaches, looming at you out of the fog—cos what else would there be except fog, on a London night? Yellow fog in the gas-lamps, waiting to swallow us, and rivers of Londoners flowing in all directions. That was London, all hours. Just slip into the current and let it carry you away, like a tiny lump of something—don't ask what—bobbing along on the Thames.

Just before it carried me round the corner, I seen the Printer's Devil again. He was standing under a gas-lamp clutching his tracts. Someone had stopped to take one—a tall old gentleman in a queer old-fashioned black coat and boots and a slouchy low-brimmed hat. The gentleman was standing very close, looming over him like a hawk on a tree branch. I only seen them for a second, and it was hard to be sure with the fog, but it seemed to me like the gentleman was saying something. The Printer's Devil was shrinking back with his eyes wide and white, like a horse's when a fist is raised to strike.

That's when the gentleman looked across and seen me. Just an instant. His face beneath the low-brimmed hat, staring at me from out of the fog, like something coiled up in a cave.

I WAS ANGLING SOUTH and west towards the Haymarket, so the route took me along the edges of the old rookery of St Giles. The Holy Land itself—the biggest and worst of all the London slums.

It wasn't like it was in the old days, or so I'd been told. In the old days the Holy Land was one great maze of tiny stinking streets and blind alleyways, stretching from Drury Lane west to Charing Cross Road, and from Great Russell Street in the north all the way to Long Acre. You could stumble in and not come out again, not ever—just wander lost till someone took pity and slit your throat. A lot of it had been torn down, but parts of it remained. Houses so rickety you'd think the next big wind would blow them over, all jumbled together so close that one couldn't fall without taking a hundred more with it. Broken windows patched up with rags and paper, with poles sticking out for hanging clothes, and slops being emptied look-out-below. In the old days there was paths through the Holy Land that never saw the light of day—you could go from one end to the other through windows and cellars. This was wonderful handy for thieves and footpads, for how was the Watch to follow? Nip in and just disappear, like a rabbit in a field of brambles. There were still routes like this, if you knew where to look—and I did, since the Holy Land is where I'd lived with Mrs Dalrymple.

But I wasn't deep into the rookery that night, just on the very fringes. The roads beyond were still crowded and busy, but here it was just filthy and quiet. Dark too, and choked with fog, for who'd waste good gaslight on a shit-hole like St Giles?

That's when I knew someone was following me.

I looked quickly round, but of course there was no one there.

"Hello?"

Nothing.

I started forward again, and tried to tell myself I was just being a fool, and frightening myself with imaginings. But I was moving fast, now. This was London, and you knew the risk you took. There were gangs who roamed these streets at night, looking for a girl on her own, to rob and do things to and leave half dead. There was eyes watching from alleyways, belonging to God knows who. And if you were *really* unlucky, there was the London Burkers. Luna Queerendo laughed at this, but Luna was a twat. God forgive me for saying that, but she was, no matter what happened to her afterwards.

The London Burkers were a gang of murderers. They crept about in the London fog slitting throats and selling the corpses to medical students, who wanted them for cutting up and studying. When Luna heard me mention this, she gave that laugh of hers—hooting like an owl, all smug—and said the last of the London Burkers was hung at Newgate twenty years ago, which everybody knew except for poor Nell apparently. And anyway the law'd been changed so medical students could get their corpses other ways, poor Nell she's such a daisy isn't she, hoot-hoot-hoot.

Twat.

Besides, there was worse than the London Burkers. There was Spring-Heeled Jack. I knew for a fact he was out there, cos everyone knew about Spring-Heeled Jack. I knew someone once who actually seen him. She nearly died. He jumped up from behind a wall—jumped twenty feet into the air—with his eyes burning and two horns on his head. Except you couldn't think that way. You couldn't slink about scared all the time, cos then you couldn't live a life at all.

I'd been listening to my own footsteps echoing on the cobblestones: one-two-one-two. And then I heard the others: muffled and uneven. They stopped, half a second after I did. But I'd heard them, behind me.

Clip-*clop*.

I stood very still.

"Who the fuck is there?"

Silence and fog, growing thicker by the second. A deadly chill creeping over the cobbles.

"You better know, I got a knife. I know how to use it. You don't believe me? Then try."

Fog like a living thing, moving.

There. Something moving that wasn't fog.

I ran for my life, with him behind me—whoever it was. I slipped, and almost fell, and every second I expected to feel hot breath on the back of my neck, and hands laying hold. But I was fast, and he wouldn't catch me. I knew these streets—I knew where I was going. Except I'd turned the wrong way, or this was the wrong street, cos it was a dead end. In front of me was a wall of brick.

The yellow glare of a bull's-eye lantern came lurching at me out of the fog. There was a face. I screamed.

"Good God!" he exclaimed.

A chalk-white face with the eyes black and horrible. "Christ, you startled me! No, it's all right. Look, I'm sorry. I think I got turned around—bit lost—the fog and these damned winding... Look, I really wish you wouldn't wave that thing in my face."

Cos I had the knife in both hands, never mind how both of them was shaking. "You bastard—keep away!"

"Yes—fine. Look, I'm not going to hurt you..."

The two of us, in the yellow pool of light from the bull's-eye. I'd seen him before—I was suddenly sure of that. But where?

"Stop following me!"

"Following you? How could I be following you? I was coming the other way. I was back there—whichever way it was. I was coming from the theatre, and now I'm completely turned around."

The Kemp Theatre. The black around his eyes was make-up. *That* was where I'd seen him. He stood uncertainly, the lantern rocking in his hand.

"Look, I'm sorry if I frightened you, but look here, could you please stop—*Christ!*"

He broke off with a shout of pain. He'd put his other hand out, and this startled me, which was too bad for him, cos I was still very twitchy—even though I recognized him now.

"You're him. You're that French turd."

"Look what you've done! What did you do that for? You've sliced my hand to the bone!

"Not the first turd—the other one. You're the French turd's friend. From the bloody play."

I was so relieved I started to laugh. He was shorter without his high-heeled shoes, and of course his face was different, without the black wig and glued-on whiskers. But it was him, all right. Now he was clutching his hand and tottering back, staring at me all shock and disbelief. You'd think I'd just run him through the heart.

"Fucksake, it's a nick. Look at you, a grown man, carrying on. Besides, it's your own fault, cos you startled me—so don't go blaming me, I fucking hate that. And mister? Maybe this ent the time, but someone's got to tell you the truth. You just can't act for dogshit."

PEOPLE CLAIMED Mother Clatterballock had been a famous beauty in her day, with men from all over London queuing up with guineas in their hand. Hard to believe, but looking back I suppose it makes sense. It would explain how she'd managed to earn the money in the first place, to set herself up in business—that and a great grasping fist, and a nose that could sniff out an advantage like a bloodhound, and an ear that could hear a farthing drop onto a feather bolster half a parish away. Now she was twenty stone poured into a purple velvet dress, with a great braying laugh and a nose like a potato and her bosoms billowing up from her bodice like two great wobbling blancmanges. But she had her charm, when she wanted to use it—give the old girl her due—and she was decent enough to me, more or less, much of the time. So you take the bad with the good, and get on with your business, don't you?

Mother C kept a house in Panton Street, across from a dance hall and wedged between a hot baths and Dalley's Oyster Rooms. Two floors up rickety stairs there was rooms for the girls, and down below was the night house. It was like any such house, with wooden benches and trestle tables all crammed in, and piss-smelling sawdust, where you could get a drink and a meal at all hours, providing you weren't too particular. There was always a few sporting gentlemen, meaning gamblers and swells and layabouts, mixed in with a regular working man or two and maybe a table of law students out on a spree. And of course them as come creeping out of their holes after dark. Thieves of all manner, for thieves came in every category you could imagine, and they all had names. Burglars and sneaks and dog-thieves. Cracksmen who specialized in breaking locks, rampsmen who specialized in breaking heads, and bug-hunters who preyed on them as was staggering drunk. Swindlers and card-cheats and sharpers, and hard men talking flash, and girls from the Haymarket. There was a painting of Tom Cribb on the wall, who was once champion prize-fighter of all England, and a story that the great man once raised a glass here years ago, long before Mother C ever came. People said he danced a sailor's hornpipe on top of a table, though whether there's truth in that I couldn't say. Another time a man come in and emptied an entire sack of rats out onto the floor. I can tell you that was true, cos I was here the night it happened, and Lord you should have seen it. A hundred people in a room thirty foot by twenty, shrieking and yelling and brown sewer rats running everywhere and biting. I'm not sure why the man done it. He was a sporting gentleman.

I was hardly through the door before old Lushing Mary spotted me. She came screeching like a seagull.

"Where did you get to? Where? I was frantic!"

I rolled my eyes a bit, and reassured her. "I'm fine, Mary. I went out, but now I'm back again, ent I? Back again safe and sound."

"And what if you weren't? What if you were floating in the river right now? Or face down with your windpipe slit like a chicken's, you selfish little slut! For then just think what would happen to me!"

It was a fair enough point. I wasn't supposed to go out at all, except when I had Mary with me. This was the arrangement for all the girls who lived at Mother Clatterballock's, and such places. Mother C couldn't have a girl sneaking off to do her business and pocketing all the coin for herself, or perhaps sneaking off and never coming back at all, wearing clothes on her back that belonged to Mother C, since she provided the dresses we wore. So when a girl went out, she had an old lady with her, and mine was Lushing Mary.

I slipped off fairly regular, of course, whenever Mary was in her cups or turned the other way. Mother C knew about it, too, but she didn't make too much of a fuss, cos she trusted me, as far as she ever trusted anybody. Or at least she was willing to take a chance where I was concerned, after first explaining what would happen to me if I ever tried to sneak away from her. Explaining very carefully, and in specific detail. Besides, Mother C done well out of me—selling me for a virgin every night for three weeks running, when I first turned twelve and was old enough. It's an easy enough trick, with a bit of acting and a few drops of sheep's blood. She'd done well enough from me ever since, seeing as I had a bright eye and a fine set of teeth—every one of them still in my head.

"I'd be in the park—that's where I'd be, if something happened to you!" cried Mary. "You want me to end my days in the park? God save us, the girl's a monster—she's got no feelings at all. An old woman in the park, reduced to all manner of depravity!"

When gay girls got too old and lost their charms, they had to find another way to scrape their living together. Some of them, like Mary, managed to get themselves kept on at houses like this, cleaning up in the daytime, and at night minding one of the girls. In return, they'd get a roof to sleep under, and food to eat, and enough gin to keep them limping through another day. If Mary lost her position, then where else would she go? Except down to the river to drown herself, or else to the park, like she said? And the river was the cleaner of the two, for all the stench and the shit floating down, pumped in from every sewer in London.

You could see the women in Hyde Park every night, as soon as it was dark. The old ones who couldn't show their faces in the gaslight, no matter how heavy they painted. They'd creep about like crows, and in the end they'd be just a bundle of rags a-laying on the ground, to be discovered when the sun come up and carted off like all the bundles of rags before them. But till then they'd sell themselves for pennies to men who wanted things they couldn't get from anyone else. Things you couldn't even think of without your stomach turning. Things you'd die before you'd ever do, except here you were in the park, doing them.

"Come on, now, don't cry," I said. My arm around her shoulder, giving her a squeeze, cos she was working herself into a state. "We'll get you something to drink. For Christ's sake, buy her a glass of daffy—it's the least you can do."

"The least *I* can do? Jesus wept!"

This being my actor gentleman.

"Who's the injured party, here?" he demanded. "*I'm* the injured party!"

"And I gave you my handkerchief to wrap it with, didn't I? A brand-new handkerchief, practically new, and now it's ruint—got blood all over. So stop moaning and buy a lady a fucking drink."

He was cradling the hand in his lap, like it was a kitten that got run over in the street. Milking this for every last drop, and being most wonderfully wounded and aggrieved. A bit dramatic, was my actor gentleman. He would surely have been even worse if he hadn't also been hunkering himself down in the darkest corner of the room, and hoping that Mother C's fine customers would fail to notice him. But they did, of course, and were currently eyeing him pretty much exactly the way you'd expect: which is to say, like a pack of wolves noticing a piglet.

"I shouldn't be here," he muttered, out the side of his mouth. "I just wanted to see you home safely. And now I'm liable to end up floating in the Thames. Christ, no good deed goes unpunished."

He tried a rough little laugh as he said it, like a man accustomed to risking his life as if 'twere nothing at all. Like I said: dramatic. Give him a cloak and a French accent, and he'd be the Count of Monte Cristo.

"He's an actor," I said to Mary.

He essayed another rough laugh. "But not, apparently, a particularly good one."

"Dogshit," I agreed, with a shrug. "Sorry."

"An actor. D'you act in Shakespeare?"

This was Old Mary. She'd stopped her blubbering once the glass of daffy was in her hand, for being alive is never so bad if there's gin to take the edges off. Now she actually perked up.

"I approve of Shakespeare." She was sitting up a little straighter on the bench—as straight as she could manage, with a back bowed like a question-mark—and God save us if there wasn't a spark in her eye. "My father was a schoolmaster, you know."

I'd heard her say that before. I'd also heard her say her father was a Member of Parliament, or else a vicar. This last was something you'd hear an astonishing amount, with gay girls. On any given night, the dens and night houses of London was apparently chock full of vicars' daughters, all painted and flat on their backs. How much of this was true I couldn't say, though I certainly had my suspicions. If I had to guess about Mary, I'd guess she wasn't sure herself, any more. But I'd actually seen her reading books. I'd even given her a book once, and told her it was for her birthday, though God only knew when her birthday was. It was a book of poems, with a cover of dark green pebbled leather. I wrote her name inside—*to my friend Mary Bartram, on her birthday*—and she grew all grave and said it was a treasure. She didn't speak like she come from the streets, either, or from the servants' quarters of some dirty provincial town. She spoke like someone who'd had an education, even after all these years, and falling all this long way down—all the way down to Mother Clatterballock's, gulping her gin and holding on by her fingertips, with nothing but Hyde Park beneath her. There was a thought to cheer you up, wasn't it? To comfort you about the ways of the world, and give you hope.

Often I heard Old Mary, when dawn finally came and the house was quiet, sobbing herself to sleep. I did that sometimes too, of course. But I was quiet as a mouse, and you'd never have known.

"That's him!"

A woman's screech, and my actor gentleman went rigid.

"That's the one! Him right there!"

It was Luna Queerendo. She'd come in a minute ago, and now there she was with Mother Clatterballock, rearing up like an angry stick-bug. She was long and skinny, was Luna, with a little head wobbling on a long stick-bug neck, and a great long nose for looking down at you, and long bony fingers like Death himself in an old painting, and one of them was pointing straight at my actor.

Mother C peered through the haze of smoke, and saw. "Tim!" she called, in a voice like doom.

There was a stirring across the room, and Tim Diggory raised his awful head.

Tim was the bully here, which is to say he made sure gentlemen took no liberties but the ones they paid for. He was six and a half foot tall, with a chimney-pot hat on top of it, and a lantern jaw that worked from side to side when he was trying to get his thoughts round an idea, for Tim weren't swift. Not even to begin with, and that was before a hand with a cosh in it had reached out from a drunken brawl one night. It laid Tim out twitching, and he never rose again for three days. He finally got up, but the cosh had broken something crucial, some kind of spring deep inside the brainpan, and Tim was never quite right again—even by Tim's standards.

Now he came looming up behind Luna, who had that finger in my actor gentleman's face. He was shrunk back against the wall like the last rat left alive in the rat-killing ring.

"He never pays for his drink last time, the shitsack! He never pays for me neither! He pulls it out, I reaches for the basin, and he's gone—out the door and down the stairs, still hoisting his breeches up over his spindly erse!"

Tim Diggory fixed his left eye upon my actor gentleman. His right eye drifted across the room. Tim's eyes always looked in different directions, and the left eye—the one he used for fixing upon you—was changeable. Sometimes it was sleepy, like a child's. On those occasions there might even be a little smile on Tim's lips, like he'd just remembered something that used to make him happy. But then without warning his eye would go all narrow, and flash like a telescope on a hill. When that happened, God help somebody—which God never did of course, either because he didn't care to look round in places such as Tim Diggory was to be found, or else because God was no fool, and lay low like everyone else when Tim's left eye went flash.

It was flashing right now.

"No, look, I'm sorry," my actor gentleman was stammering. "I'm terribly sorry, but there's been a misunderstanding. I've never been here in my life."

"Fuck you ent been here!" cried Luna.

"All right, then I was—you're quite right about that, ha ha—but I paid—I did—I left the money on my way out—at least I thought I did. Ha ha ha. There's clearly been some mistake, and—"

"There's been a mistake indeed," Mother Clatterballock wheezed, for she'd put herself out of breath hauling her bulk across the room, "and you're the one who's made it." She held out a great grubby hand. "Two pound."

"Two pounds?"

"A pound for Loo, five shillings for the drink, five shillings for putting me out of temper, and ten shillings for the hinsult to the hestablishment. Plus the collection fee and something for Tim—better round it out to two guineas. Payable instanter."

I laughed out loud.

"Oh, come on. Luna was never worth a pound on the best day in her life—and God knows *that* day came and went."

"You shut your pie-hole, Nell Rooney!" cried Luna. "I'm worth more than you'll ever be, with your pinched little phiz like a weasel. And my name isn't Luna, you little scrawny slut, it's Louise!"

Matter of fact, this was true. Her real name was Louise Maggs. I started calling her Luna Queerendo after finding out she'd been married once. The marriage happened years earlier, when some poor wealthy gentleman actually fell in love with her, and him with three thousand pounds a year. Well, this was the magical pot of gold she'd been dreaming of all her stick-bug life. But when the gentleman's family found out they got themselves a writ—*de lunatico inquirendo,* which meant some magistrate had to judge whether he was soft in the head. Sure enough, guess what? That was the marriage annulled, and the pot of gold snatched back again, which would have been very sad I suppose if I hadn't hated her. And of course I felt bad as anything about what happened to her in the end. I wouldn't have wished that on any living creature in this world.

"I don't have two guineas!" my actor gentleman was stammering. "Dear God, where would I get hold of two guineas? Look, here's what I've got. I've got a shilling—that's all the money I have, I swear. But you can have it. It's yours, with my very best wishes. And I won't come back. At least, I *will* come back—yes—I'll come back directly, with the rest of the money. All right? You just wait here."

He looked from Luna to Mother C to Tim, all charming and desperate, like a piglet hoping these wolves might like vegetables instead. There was silence.

"It's the cheek of it," said Mother Clatterballock. "That's what stuns you. The sheer gall." She looked to Tim Diggory, like a magistrate about to reach for the black cap. "Tim? I don't believe I want to see this one again."

"No, listen to me. Wait—please—!"

My actor gentleman's voice was sounding strangled, but nowhere near as strangled as it was about to be, cos Tim Diggory was already reaching out to take him by the throat.

"Oh, leave him be, for Christ's sake. I'll pay what he owes."

"You?" Mother C shifted to stare at me. "Cos why?"

"Cos he's my brother."

Even Tim stopped.

I'm still not sure why I said it. It's not as if I liked him, even. Probably it was just me being contrary.

"And it's not two guineas, it's ten shillings. Three for the drink, two for the trouble, and five for Luna—which is at least three shillings on the generous side, where's she's concerned."

That was the other reason I spoke up. I couldn't stomach the smarmy sneer on Luna's face, with her supposing anyone could value her at a pound.

"Don't you have a doll to go play with?" Luna flung back after sputtering for a bit, this being her best go at deadly sarcastic wit.

Mother C wasn't listening. Her eyes were fixed on the guinea I had fetched out of my pocket.

"You can take it out of this," I said, very casual. "I was give it by a gentleman I met this afternoon—a *real* gentleman, with a carriage, who liked what he saw, and knows you have to pay top price for quality."

This was God's own truth, or some of it at least. I was never a beauty, but I was small, and there are gentlemen who like that. This one wanted a naughty child that required correction, so that's what I gave him. I was a naughty child that stole things too.

"Oh, you peach," wheezed Mother C, and had the guinea before I could think twice. "Is this my clever girl? Oh, my."

I'd never see that guinea again, nor any part of it. But the expression on Luna's gob almost made me forgive myself. Besides, I still had the gentleman's gold watch, which was in his weskit when the gentleman wasn't. It was worth a good sight more than a guinea, and Mother C was never going to know about that. Anyroad it was always a good investment to stay Mother Clatterballock's peach. Then there weren't so many questions about coming and going as I pleased.

"Your brother, eh?" Mother C was eyeing my actor gentleman. "And 'as 'e come to rescue his little Nell from out o' this life?" She said it with her old whore's squint, the one that said both *I'm just having a joke with you, ducks,* and *think very careful what you say next.*

"No," I said, "he's here to ask money of me. For there has to be one in each family that'll do a day's work, and he ent it."

I don't suppose I fooled her one bit. But after a moment, Mother C's squint relaxed into a leer. "Well, then, enjoy your family time," she said, "for this hestablishment is built on family walues. At least, enjoy yourselves for a minute or two. But after three minutes, I'd best see you back at work, Nell, for the sake of all concerned. And you, sir," she added, with another look at my actor, "won't be showing your phiz 'ere again without you got coin of the realm clinking in your pocket, family or no family, brother or no brother, for Tim Diggory is here seven days o' the week, every week o' the year, and that hincludes Christmas. Ent that right, Tim? Yes it is. So nod your 'ead, Tim, and let go the gemmun's windpipe, and we'll take our leave—and so will the gemmun. 'E'll be on his way directly, and won't be 'anging about like a fartleberry from an arsehole. Come on then, Loo. Loo! I'm talking to you, you surly slut. Pinch your cheeks all rosy-nice, and smile for the lads, for no one wants to fuck a lemon."

So they left, with Luna shooting unspeakable looks every second step. That left me and my actor gentleman, staring at each other.

"Yer welcome," I said.

"Yes. God, yes. Thank you."

He sat with a whump on the bench, like his legs had clean give way beneath him. I matched the saving of his hide against that guinea of mine in Mother C's fat grubby palm. *Good exchange, Nell,* I said to myself, *you twat.*

"I'll pay you back, of course."

"Yes you bloody well will. You'll pay me back with fucking interest. By the time you've finished paying back, you'll wish you'd gone to the moneylenders instead."

He started to laugh, with the sheer relief of it. He was actually nice looking, when he laughed. In fact, he was almost handsome—or at least he would've been if he'd had a bit more in the way of a chin. All that Count of Monte Cristo business—the brooding stranger, rough and bitter—that was nothing but an act he tried to put on. But just when you were fed to the teeth with him, he'd cock his head a quarter of an inch, and sneak a peek at you out from under the wing of soft brown hair that had fallen over his eyes, as if to ask: *how am I doing so far?* Then he'd flip it back with a movement of his hand, and give a crooked boyish smile. A rake's younger brother, maybe—wishing he could be dangerous and wicked, but not getting much past coy.

Maybe I didn't dislike him as much as I'd thought.

"My name is Hartright," he said. "Jack Hartright. At least, this is the name I go by, in these days of my exile from a former life."

"Then go buy me another drink, Jack Hartright, just before you fuck off. Cos your three minutes are about up."

He laughed again, and shook his head. He had a scar at the side of one eye—a strange thing to see on such a smooth face. It was shaped like a horseshoe.

"My God, but you're a curious little creature, aren't you?"

There was several things I could have said to this, and probably would have, in another half a second. Starting with: "Tim Diggory? Come back here please, cos I've decided I'd like you to kill him after all." But I didn't get the chance.

"I'll be glad to buy you a drink," he said.

Except it wasn't Jack Hartright who said it.

Tall and thin and dressed in black, with a limp and high boots and a low slouching hat. The old gentleman from outside the theatre. He'd come in behind me, without my knowing he was there. He'd brought the night in with him; suddenly the air was cold.

"What would you like to drink, my dear?"

"Nothing," I said. "Thank you very kindly, but I ent available."

"No? But I think you are."

He had a coin in his hand. He'd plucked it out of the air, some fucking conjurer's trick.

"I'll pay you a crown."

It was good money—except you always knew, when it was wrong. In the first second, you just knew, before they said a word. But this was different. This was all wrong, but wrong in a way I'd never come up against before. I opened my mouth to call for Tim Diggory.

"A guinea," I heard myself saying instead.

His lip crept up over his teeth. I suppose you'd call it a smile.

I STOOD BY the window. My room was at the top of the stairs, on the third floor, at the back. There was a bed, and a little low table with a pitcher and a basin and a candle fluttering, and a trunk against the wall by the door. He looked round the room. He looked at the trunk. Then he sat down on the lid of it, slow and creaking, and looked at me.

The room was icy with him.

"Let's have the guinea, then," I said.

All my things were in that trunk he was sitting on. Everything I owned. Bits of clothes, and other things too—most of them useless, but they were mine. An old clock with some of the insides missing, except maybe I'd meet someone who could mend it. A wooden soldier with arms and legs that moved when you pulled a string. My hat with a feather and some lace and a real silk handkerchief. I had some books, too. One of them was lying on top of the trunk. He picked it up.

"You can read?"

"Of course I can bloody read."

"Well done."

It was a little book about Dick Turpin's famous ride. I had some other books too, inside the trunk. One about Tom Thumb, and also Bewick's *Birds* with beautiful drawings.

"My guinea," I said. "You said a guinea, so let's have it."

He plucked it out of the air—that fucking conjuring trick of his—and smiled. "Here," he said. He held it out, but only partway, so's I'd have to step closer to take it. When I did, his other hand moved faster than I could see. I gave a cry and pulled back, thinking he was grabbing at my throat. But it was my locket he wanted—the one I had on a chain around my neck.

"Give that back!"

He turned it with his fingers, examining it in the candlelight.

"I mean it. Give it here. Look, it's only brass, all right? It isn't gold—it ent worth anything to you, so just give it here. Mister? Fucksake . . . !"

"What do I get," he asked, "for my guinea?"

His eyes, pinning me. Narrow dark eyes, with flecks of colour in them. They didn't blink. There was a smell about him, a strange smell of lavender water and something else, something dark and sharp. Sulphur?

"I expect you'd do almost anything I asked," he said, musing. "A girl like you. For a guinea."

"Then you'd be wrong, mister."

"Would I?"

"Yes. You'd be expecting wrong."

"But you'd do anything for five guineas, wouldn't you?"

"Five?"

With five guineas in my hand I could leave this hole. With five guineas every week, I could be someone different completely. I could have my own rooms, and a servant. I could have a carriage. There were girls all over Mayfair, set up like ladies, cos they had a gentleman who would give them five guineas a week.

He smiled a little, as if he'd seen the thought cross my mind.

Oh, Christ—but not five guineas from this one. Not five hundred guineas, if it had to come from this one.

"What would you want," I heard myself asking, "for five guineas?"

He mused for another minute. He was trying to pass for a younger man, maybe five-and-forty, but that was done with paints and dye. He was much older, but there was a ropey strength about him too.

"I think what I want most of all," he said finally, "is for someone to die. Yes, I believe I'd like someone to die, for sheer love of me. For five guineas, would you do that?"

The window behind me was tiny. Even small as I am, I'd never squeeze through. To reach the door, I'd have to get past him, and he knew it.

"I think you'd best leave, now."

"It's only dying. Everyone does it, sooner or later. One way or another."

"I'm warning you. If you don't leave, I'll shout for Tim Diggory."

"You'd certainly die for ten guineas—because I'd give them to Mother Clatterballock. For ten guineas, she'd hand you over with her blessings. She'd applaud while the deed was done, and for an extra shilling she'd lay on refreshments."

"Were you the one that followed me, tonight?"

It came in a cold flash. I remembered his footsteps on the stairs as he followed me up to the room. With a limp: clip-*clop.*

"Tim!"

But Tim was three long rickety flights below. *Oh Christ,* I thought, *you've done it now. You've really done it, haven't you, Nell? You've finally done it this time.*

"God's blood, you're so much like her."

He'd opened the locket, and was looking at the little picture inside. Something had shifted in his face.

"You truly are. You're so much like your mother."

This came so unexpected that I just stared at him.

"Her picture, in the locket. That's your mother, isn't it? Yes, I saw it in you straight away, outside the theatre. It's not the features, exactly, but the expression. The eyes, and the set of the mouth. For a moment, I actually thought it was her, come back to me."

I made a grab, and snatched my locket back. He was looking at me with the strangest expression.

"You never knew my mother."

"I knew your mother well. I had her many times."

"You're a liar!"

"But not about this."

I was trembling. From the cold of him, and more than that.

"Where is she, then? Tell me about her." My voice was shaking now. "If you can tell me where she is, I'll do what you want."

But whatever he was going to say was lost in the ruckus that bust out suddenly from the next room. It had been brewing for a bit—a man's voice, muttering, and a woman's, rising. I'd hardly noticed, for obvious reasons. But suddenly it was shouts and crashes, and the man hollering that he'd been bit, and someone's head being pounded against the wall, and the woman—it was Luna Queerendo; I'd know that voice anywhere—shrieking for Tim Diggory. Except she wasn't shrieking for Tim, but shrieking *at* him.

"Take yer filthy—stop it! Oh please, for Christ's sake—no!—you filthy—help! Murder! *Murder!*"

How it happened I don't exactly know, but in the next second I was out the door and onto the landing. There was a great splintering as Luna crashed clear through the door of the next room, with Tim on top. More people were coming up the stairs, shouting for Tim to let her go. But none of it was going to help, for Tim was going to kill her.

He'd always been sweet on Luna, and followed her about—being just her type, since no one was softer in the head than Tim Diggory. He never quite worked up his nerve to touch, cos I think he actually had a notion that she might yet fall in love with him, even though she treated him like a dog. Besides he was terrified of Mother C, who warned him if he pestered the girls she'd have him gelded like a Clydesdale, and his onions stewed for oysters. But tonight, something had happened. I suppose he'd turned that eye on Luna—the one that flashed—and now all Hell had risen up inside. He had her by the hair with one hand, pinned down on the landing, and in half a second Luna was dead. Cos Tim was rearing over her and in his other hand he had a cudgel.

But the killing blow never fell. Tim went staggering forward and headfirst into the wall, so hard I swear the whole house shook. Someone had come thundering up the stairs behind, and slammed straight into him. It was a man with a shaggy head of yellow hair, and a great wide face, crying in a voice with an Irish lilt: "This won't do, brother! No, brother—this won't do at all!"

He had a spider's legs, long and spindly—except they weren't really, which I didn't realize till afterwards. It was just that the body on top of them legs was so wide, a great barrel body and the arms of a blacksmith.

But Tim Diggory was even bigger. Tim had his cudgel too, and now both Tim's eyes were wild. When the Irishman seen them eyes, he groaned.

"It's the Devil!" cried the Irishman. "Aw, look at this poor man—it's the Devil himself has risen up within. But we don't despair—no, never that, no matter what. For when the Devil rises up, we cut him down to size again."

Tim Diggory swung his cudgel in a blow that would dash the Irishman's brains out. But the Irishman's mauleys were raised, and he stepped inside the sweep of it. One, two—them mauleys landed on Tim's ribs with a sound like pumpkins dropped from the roof to the cobbles.

"Forgive me, brother—and I hope you and I may yet be friends—but I will not abide the Devil."

The next blow was flush on Tim's jaw like chopping wood. Tim's legs gave a wobble, and then down he went like an ox in a slaughteryard.

"And look how strong the Devil is still."

Tim was struggling to rise to his knees again, grovelling for his cudgel. So the Irishman dropped onto his haunches, which put a stop to whatever the Devil had in mind, since the haunches were on Tim's head.

The stairs were packed with gawkers now, peering and exclaiming, and trying to get a glimpse of what was going on through the bodies wedged in front. In the midst was two nice-dressed older women in grey cloaks and bonnets, fluttering wide-eyed with distress and making little strangled cooing sounds like doves. It crossed my mind to wonder what on earth they was doing in a place like this, but like all the rest I couldn't take my eyes off the Irishman. His face was broad and ugly and red with breathing hard, with side-whiskers like hedges and a nose like a knob of gristle. But there was something about him that made you hold your breath and pray he'd look your way.

"That's it!" shrieked Luna. "Now kill the bastard!" She was standing in the doorway, clutching bits of her dress to cover herself.

But the Irishman shook his head in sorrow, as Tim give off little muffled protests from underneath his hindquarters.

"Kill him? No, we'd never do such a thing as that, for he's our own poor brother. We love him and we forgive him—not because he deserves it, but just because it's in our power to do—exactly the same as our Lord forgives us, even though we none of us deserve it, not for a second. We don't deserve from him anything at all, but he loves us still, the Lord Jesus, no matter what we do in return. And one day he'll come back, and on that blessed day he'll beat the Devil like a yellow dog."

That voice of his—I'd never heard anything like it. The words soared out of him like birds. I thought: *I could listen to this voice forever.*

"Yes, Our Lord will beat the Devil till all the welkins are ringing with his howls. Then he'll fling him down into the Pit and bar the doors, and that'll be the Devil done for once and all. But until that great day dawns, brothers, the battle's in our hands—brothers and sisters too, for we're all battlers together, battling for the Lord. So when you see the Devil, you stand up to him, and twist his nose, and fetch him a clout to rattle his teeth, and let him know what he's up against! For the Devil's a great coward, brothers and sisters—he won't stand against a healthy Christian. And now I'd like us to sing. We'll raise our voices in a hymn together, and we'll make this house resound with a gladsome noise—all of us singing lustily, including our brother here I'm sitting on, for he has gone quiet now and still, and I believe this to indicate that the peace of our Lord has come upon him at last."

There was uneasy exclamations at this point. One of the Dove Ladies caught the Irishman's eye and fluttered enough to indicate that Tim wasn't still from the peace of God upon him. It was more that the Irishman's hindquarters was upon him, and he was suffocating. So the Irishman got up instanter, with a sound of dismay. Mother Clatterballock arrived at last just in time to see this—Mother C having wheezed her way up three flights of stairs. She exclaimed, "Christ Jesus, 'e's squashed Tim like a bug!" But a bit of brandy got Tim restored, and sitting up again, with all the wildness squashed right out of his eye. The Irishman looked relieved.

"Are you a madman, then? Or just a fool?"

It was the tall icy gentleman in black. He was standing behind me in the doorway to my room, staring at the Irishman. His smile was wintry and mocking, but there was something else too—like he'd seen the Irishman before, and was trying to place him. The Irishman seemed like he might be thinking the same thing in return, cos they neither of them moved for a moment or so, the way two fighting dogs will do when they meet by accident. Stiff-legged and bristling. Waiting to see if the other will lunge, or pass by.

"I am a man who goes here and there," said the Irishman, "in the name of the Lord. If that makes me his fool, then it is my honour to be so."

"And what does the Lord's fool call himself?"

"My name is Captain Daniel O'Thunder. And who, brother, are you?"

The tall icy gentleman looked him slowly up and down again, the way an actor does on the stage, to show contempt.

"I am one who is beyond you," he said. "Utterly."

He put on his hat, and raised his lip, and shouldered through the press of gawkers. They all flinched back to let him pass.

"May the Lord bless you and keep you," the Irishman called after him, "and mark you for his own forever."

The tall icy gentleman looked back, and raised his lip again. Then he passed down the stairs—clip-*clop*—and was gone.

JAUNTY

DANIEL'S ESTABLISHMENT was in a dilapidated stretch of the Gray's Inn Road, where Holborn slouches into the East End with patches on its elbows. There was a low public house on the corner, and a worse one three doors down, with eyes in low doorways watching slantways as you passed. There were costermongers hawking this and that from barrows, such as you'd find in any street, and flower-girls, and of course the customary assortment of beggars, most of them missing limbs or wits. Outside a butcher's shop was one poor wretch whose arms and face and neck were covered in hideous festering sores—which is to say an expert practitioner of the Scaldrum Dodge, by which hideous sores were simulated with soap and vinegar. A few hours from now, you'd be liable to meet this same fellow in a tavern half a mile away, miraculously cured and enjoying a plate of sausages. I tipped my hat to such artists, and if I were flush I might even toss 'em a coin, for I have always respected a professional.

Finding the place had required a deal of asking, and a deal of tramping about the streets, followed by a deal more asking and another few miles' expenditure of boot-leather. But I was accustomed to such expenditure, being an old infantryman. I'd expended boot-leather across half the world, in the service of Empire, God, and Dooty. Or so at least they'd told us at the time, and Tom Lobster in his red coat doesn't ask, does he? No sir, he does not. Being told what to do—and what to think—and who to shoot—is plenty good enough for the likes of Tom Lobster. So he just marches where they send him, and shoots where they point him, and then ducks.

I was with the old Forty-Fourth, if you're asking. That's where I'd encountered Daniel in the first place. He was just a lad when first we met, a great laughing boy of fifteen, while I was an old campaigner twice that age, with a store of splendid tales—some of them even true—and the finest side-whiskers in the regiment. And yes indeed, it was *that* Forty-Fourth—cut to ribbons in Afghanistan in January of 1842. The Khoord Caboul and the infamous retreat to Jellalabad.

But I'm getting ahead of myself. Just now, I'm telling you about a Saturday afternoon in the late spring of 1851, on the Gray's Inn Road.

Next to it, above a second-hand clothing shop, was a doctor's surgery. So on your approach to Daniel's establishment you might hear the shrieks of some poor soul having his boils lanced or his leg sawed off. A few more steps and there it was, a little yellowing cardboard notice propped in the window: O'Thunder's Academy of the Manly Arts. Beside it was another card, advertising instruction in Swordplay, Pistolry, and Pugilism, and stuck below this a scrap of paper with carefully printed letters—you could practically see the man who printed them, tongue clamped between his jaws in concentration—assuring the reader: "Persons of quality will be given the utmost tenderness, for which reason mufflers are provided, that will effectually secure them from the inconweniency of black eyes and broken jaws." The building was an ancient creaking thing with a list to starboard, as if it had itself suffered the inconweniency of one too many whacks to the coconut, and was about to topple sideways. Like the sawbones next door, O'Thunder's Academy was above. So up I went, a flight of narrow creaking stairs, and stepped through the door.

IN MY SALAD days when I was green, I met an old-timer or two who could still remember Jack Broughton's Boarded House in Oxford Circus. This had been a great theatre of battle, where instruction was offered by day. By night displays of skill with sword and fist attracted vast hordes of punters. One night the great James Figg fought a three-stage duel with Ned Sutton, the Gravesend pipe-maker, who once shaved it overly fine while demonstrating his technique with the short-sword, on account of which his opponent suffered the inconweniency of having his nose sliced off. First there was a battle with backswords, and after a gentlemanly break for port they boxed, and finally they brought the cudgels out. Figg was bloody and reeling when he delivered a sudden blow that broke Sutton's knee and secured a famous victory, to the great delight of all, excepting of course poor Sutton himself, and the punters who bet on him. But then no situation can be perfect, for then you wouldn't be in London at all, but in Heaven. And if you were in Heaven, then you'd have been no friend of mine, and I fear we'd have very little in common—but here I go, I'm prattling. I freely confess it—I'm a talker. I like people, you see—I just like 'em, I like to be around 'em. I'm told I'm fond of my own voice too, and I fear there may be some justice in that. I put it down to being Welsh on my mother's side—I have a Welsh singing voice too, if I may say so, a fine Welsh baritone—so put the two of them together and you'll just have to bear with me.

O'Thunder's was not such a place as old Jack Broughton's. It was just a rectangular room, sagging in the middle, with a few small cracked filthy windows and a retiring room in back, all of it smelling of sweat and liniment and piss. The piss-smell was a bit off-putting but entirely understandable, especially when you paused to consider what they were doubtless doing to themselves this very moment next door at the surgeon's. There were benches and chairs along one wall, and swords and mufflers piled up in a corner, and a table with pistols laid out. Just inside the door a very large party in a chimney-pot hat sat hunched on a stool, looking for all the world like something you'd encounter underneath a bridge, girding its loins for billy goats. He had a battered metal cashbox on his knee, to collect money from the clients as they came in, or possibly as they staggered out, having suffered some degree of inconweniency, despite the best intentions to the contrary. But the battered cashbox was nothing compared to his face.

"Yeh?" said he, through a pair of split lips.

He looked me over. Or rather one eye did—the other was drifting up towards the rafters. Both eyes were blackened, though, and half-closed, which gave them something in common. In fact his whole face was a mass of spectacular lumps and welts.

"Good God," I exclaimed, for I couldn't help it. "What does the other man look like?"

"'E looks," said the large party, "like salvytion. Is that what yer 'ere for? Or t'other?"

I may have looked perplexed, as I took a moment to try and disentangle this.

"I've been syved, myself," said the large party. He cleared his throat, and proceeded to bear witness. "I was a norrible sinner, right up until last week. I drank and I fornikyted and I laid wiolent hands upon uvvers. I was a-going to Hell, and the Devil had prepared my plyce. But then the Light of God bust through the clouds, bruvver—it bust clear through and sat upon my head, in the person of Captain Daniel O'Thunder. So now I'm syved, just like you can be syved, and I printed that note."

"Note?"

"In the winder. Down the stairs. That was me. I wrote that note with this wery 'and."

"Ah, yes."

"D'ye like it?"

I assured him I did—I liked it of all things—for despite the rosy glow of salvation there was the stirring of something down deep in that eye that you didn't want to prod.

"And is by any chance the Man Himself here present?"

His eye veered away before he answered, his attention being caught by a disturbance on the other side of the room. A thing of rags and tatters was trying to impress upon two harried ladies in grey cloaks and bonnets that it was owed a bed to sleep on, and was here to claim it. The thing of rags and tatters was more specifically a female person of the Cockney Irish sort, which is to say the loudest and most argumentative sort, especially when they're reeling drunk, which this one was. She'd gotten it into her head that O'Thunder's Academy of the Manly Arts was in fact a mission, run by Christians who'd welcome in the dregs from the streets, and feed 'em and clean 'em up, and send 'em back to the world sober and hopeful of a fresh start in life, and welcome 'em back a week later roaring drunk and worse off than ever. And the remarkable thing was, she was absolutely correct.

I'd heard it from the landlord at the Horse and Dolphin. My old friend Daniel O'Thunder had found the Lord, he said. Or the Lord had found Daniel O'Thunder, which worked out to the same thing. This much I knew from my last meeting with Daniel nine years earlier—what I didn't know was that the close relationship between Daniel and Heaven continued to thrive. For who would have suspected that Daniel would show such fortitude? And this planted a certain Idea in my head. Did the landlord (I asked casually) happen to know where Daniel might be found? And indeed he did. It seemed that Daniel was operating a ramshackle little academy of pugilism that had the distinction of being the only one in all of John Bull's England—as far as was known—that also served as a ramshackle little mission society, ministering to the creatures of the streets. This meant there was a mingling of two very different purposes, as when a respectable patron of the academy going out would encounter a park woman or a badly fallen dollymop coming in. This could lead to awkwardness, and occasionally to sharp words, and not infrequently—so the landlord gave me to understand—to the patron and the dolly-mop striking up an understanding and disappearing together into the retiring room, where they'd be subsequently discovered in lively interchange by another patron, or else by one of the evangelical helpers, such as the two grey-cloaked ladies. These, I later learned, were a pair of middle-aged spinsters named the Miss Sherwoods, Peggy and Esther. They were committed to their charitable work, God bless 'em—and completely committed to their belief in Daniel O'Thunder. They actually saw him as a latter-day apostle, which goes to show you yet again that human beings have amazingly constituted eyesight and will see the most remarkable things.

Just at the moment, they had their hands full with the Cockney Irish party, who was holding forth at full volume—the gist being that she wanted the bed she was owed, and wanted it now. Then she sat abruptly down on the floor, flopped back, rolled over, and commenced to snore. Miss Esther (the older and rounder of the two) exclaimed "Lord bless us," while Miss Peggy muttered something that may have been less Christian. But after a moment's indecision they concluded that there was only one man for the problem at hand.

"Captain O'Thunder!" they called.

And Daniel O'Thunder came in from the back room. It was the first time I'd laid eyes on him in nearly a decade. He nodded a general greeting in my direction—the way you'd acknowledge the arrival of a stranger—before abruptly realizing who it was.

"By the Lord Harry," said Daniel.

"It's grand to see you too," said I. "You're looking well, Dan. Fit as a fiddle."

He was in fact looking jowly and florid, the way a big man does as he's going to seed, and older than I'd been prepared for. It's odd how you can leave a friend for nine years, then feel surprised when he turns up looking a decade older. In fact, you feel betrayed, as if he's aged you along with him, and personally dragged you a decade closer to the grave. But I didn't say any of this, of course. You don't say such things to an old friend, even one who didn't look quite as joyful to see me as he might have done—and especially considering the nature of my errand.

Tell the truth, Daniel looked as if he'd seen a ghost, and promptly excused himself to attend to the Cockney Irish party. She was snoring loudly now, and lying in a small but spreading puddle, which commenced its contribution to the overall aroma of the place. But Daniel paid no mind at all, and picked her up, as easy as you'd pick up a kitten. It pleased me to see that he still had his strength—although this was to be expected, since old prize-fighters always hold their strength to the end. It's the speed that goes first, and then the wind, and then the coordination, till finally they just stand stiff and splay-legged like slaughteryard cattle while a young man chops 'em down.

"I'll do that, Captain!" the newly saved troll was exclaiming. "That's dirty work—let me!" He had risen to his feet as Daniel had entered the room, and was now bounding towards him like a great galumphing Newfoundland dog. The look on his face was absolute devotion.

"No, Tim Diggory," said Daniel, "it's not dirty work at all. There's no dirt where the Lord's work is to be done, and nothing to flinch at in a fellow human soul. But here you are, so we'll do it together."

While they went off into the back, I made myself pleasant to the Miss Sherwoods, offering amiable observations about this and that and the other—the weather and the price of ribbons—for I'm the sort of man who's at ease wherever he finds himself. When this petered out I amused myself by looking round at the pictures on the walls. O'Thunder's Academy was decorated with pictures both religious and pugilistic in nature. It was a remarkably eclectic mix, such that St Peter shouldered up against Molyneaux, and gentle Jesus with his lamb appeared to be gazing straight across at a portrait of Mendoza, stripped to the waist and set to settle someone's hash.

"Daniel Mendoza," I said, to the Miss Sherwoods. "Before my time, but the old-timers say he was one of the greatest of them all. He was champion of England until soft living caught up with him, alas, along with Gentleman Jackson, who seized him by the long dark hair with one hand, and battered him senseless with t'other. The other gentleman," I added, indicating the picture of Jesus, "I believe you know already. But do you know what the two of them had in common?"

"They were both warriors," said Daniel, who had returned in time to hear this question. "They both fought fearlessly, asking no quarter, regardless of the consequences."

"Ah, there you go," said I. "There you go—Daniel puts it in a nutshell. Lacking his sure grasp of the essence of things, I was simply going to say: they were both Jewish, and a credit to their people."

Daniel had recovered from his first shock at seeing me. Now he found a smile and extended his hand. It was like taking hold of a bag of nuts. As with all old prize-fighters, every bone in those hands had been broken, at one time or another. For Daniel had been a pugilist, of course, after the two of us had left the Army. I had been a trainer of pugilists—and still was.

"My old friend John Thomas Rennert," said Daniel, almost as if he meant it. "After all these years. Welcome, brother—and doubly welcome if you've come to confess your Christian faith and join us in our work. No? Ah, well—for I can tell by your merry laugh that this is not the case. Or at least not yet, for who can say when the Lord may come to each of us, and rap upon our door, and call upon us to open? But welcome nonetheless. I'll pour you a glass for old times' sake, and we'll sit and chat awhile in fellowship. After that you'll be on your way, for I'm sure you're a busy man as you always were. And these days I have myself so very much to be getting on with."

That voice again, after all these years. I'd half-forgotten what an instrument it was. Daniel could always talk. So could I, of course, as I've confessed already—but that was talking in a different way. I could talk the sparrows down from the trees. Daniel could halfways convince them they were eagles.

He opened a cabinet and took out a bottle of the pale and a single mug. "For I no longer have truck nor trade with spirituous drink," he said. "If you cast your mind back, perhaps you'll recall the reason why." A shadow crossed his face, and of course I remembered vividly. "Nine years sober," he said, quietly. "Since that morning in Bristol—you were there, John Thomas—when God reached out and lifted me from the mire."

"Then I compliment you on your resolve. Your very good health," I said, raising my brandy, and added with a wink: "Captain O'Thunder. For I understand it's 'Captain' these days."

He gave me a look. "I am many things these days, John Thomas, and Captain is one of them. But I'm not at all the man you used to know."

He had taken me to a little sitting area off in a corner, with a bench and a rickety wooden chair. It happened to be out of the immediate earshot of the Miss Sherwoods, who had gone back to mending hand-me-down clothes, and also the Diggory party, who had returned to sit with the cashbox by the door. For no man is comfortable when his past comes strolling up the stairs to introduce itself to his new friends, especially a man with a past like Daniel's.

"I can see that you've changed indeed, old friend," said I, privately doubting this very much. For none of us ever changes, not really. "And yet in one important particular, you're exactly the same man as ever. You're fit, as I said already, as a fiddle. You look as fit as the man who licked Long John Jurrock in fifty-two rounds—remember that? You look as if you could step into the ring this afternoon, against the Tipton Slasher himself."

Daniel laughed out loud. "The Tipton Slasher? My friends would carry me out in a horse blanket, John Thomas, half a minute after I stepped in. I haven't fought in nearly a decade. I'm fat and thirty-three years old. I feel it, brother—and more than that, I look it. So why don't you tell me what this is about, and what you're angling towards, so I can shake your hand one last time and wish you well and be done with it?"

A smile remained on his face. But there was a resoluteness too, that hadn't been there in the old days. I wasn't sure I liked that resoluteness.

"What you're saying is true enough, Daniel—or part of it, at any rate. You're not as young as you were—who is?—and perhaps you wouldn't stand for long against the Slasher. But the fact remains, you retired from the prize-ring too soon. You departed from the green faerie circle before you'd had a chance to reach your prime. I've mused upon this many times, these past nine years—I've thought upon it with a lingering sadness, Dan—I've wondered often and again, 'What might Daniel O'Thunder have achieved, had he stayed with the game just a little while longer?' And I wager you've done so too."

I leaned forward, for now I was in my stride, and closing in on the quarry. "You're a fighter, Daniel—that's what you are, and always will be. And I have a Proposition."

"You always did, John Thomas. The answer is no."

"Hear me out. It concerns a young man I've taken an interest in, called Spragg the Ruffian. You've heard of him? I see you have, for he's been mentioned in the sporting papers. Well, we've fought him a few times up North, and he's done well. A strong, strapping lad—not much in the way of technique just yet, but he's learning, and he can deliver a blow. He bested the Croyden Drover—remember him?—and stretched out the Onion Boy, flat as a mackerel, after twenty-seven minutes. So now it's time to bring him South, closer to London, for that's where the potential for glory lies, and reputations are to be made."

"You mean, that's where the money is."

"I don't deny it. 'Give us this day our daily bread'—except it don't get given, does it, Daniel? It must be purchased, with coin of the realm. So. It's time for the Ruffian to be introduced to the wider sporting public. More than that, it's time to find out what he has for bottom, for he hasn't been tested yet. I need a man who'll test his chin. I also need a man who'll draw the Fancy. And you still have a name—no, don't be modest, you do. You had a certain little popularity in your day, and there are those who remember. Most of all, I need a story that I can tell. For that's what it is—beyond the fine old English art of self-defence, and the hearts of oak, it's the story that draws 'em in. I admit this freely, because we're old friends, Daniel. It's always been honest-as-the-livelong-day between us, and I intend to be honest now."

The shaggy head was cocked to one side, and there was a little smile on that great ugly mug. If fighters weren't ugly when they started, they were ugly when they'd finished—or more to the point when the game had finished with them. The cauliflower ears, and the flattened nose, and the knots and lumps like boles on a tree trunk. But you could see a kind of nobility in a face like that, if you chose to. Give him credit, Daniel O'Thunder had a kind of nobility.

And now it was time to bring this home.

"Daniel, I'm afraid I must shock you. For whatever you've been told about the character of Spragg the Ruffian—whatever rumours you've heard about riotous living and addiction to all manner of vice and abandonment—it's worse. I don't say that his heart is bad, for few men's hearts are truly so, not rotten clear through. But he's fallen into a bad way of living, Daniel. He's a braggart and a bully and a man of violent outbursts. When you tax him with his duty to his fellow man, he sneers. And when you speak of the Judgement that awaits us all, he laughs in your face—for Daniel, he don't believe in God. And that," said I, building towards the very nub of it, "*that* is the match I want to make, and the story I want to tell. Spragg the atheistic Ruffian, against O'Thunder the evangelist."

Daniel was silent for a moment, musing. "Preacher O'Thunder, God's Warrior, that sort of thing?"

"I was thinking," said I, "of Battling O'Thunder, and his right hand the Hammer of Heaven."

He moved his jaw a bit, from side to side, as if trying out the feel of it in his mouth. "That's good," he admitted. "I have to say, brother, it has a ring."

"It rings like the bells of St Paul's."

And now I played my trump. "Daniel, I've spoken to the Ruffian. He says if you can beat him, then he'll admit that he's been wrong. He'll amend his ways, and accept the Lord who is Saviour of us all. So how's that—eh? How's that for a story? And more than that, it's a young man saved from a life of depravity, and snatched clear out of the Devil's grasp. So let me hear you say no to an opportunity like that."

"Let me see," said he, "if I've got this straight."

"Of course you have, Daniel. Dead-straight, for there's naught that's crooked in it."

"You've got a young fighter with a rising reputation, but no character to speak of," Daniel said. "So you'll cook up this story of yours, and match him against an old warhorse—a decade out of the ring—who'll go off at odds of ten to one, or higher. The Ruffian gets paid to lose the match, and meantime you've wagered everything you've got on the old warhorse. But you're not finished yet. For lo and behold the warhorse has become a celebrated old nag, and more than that he believes he won the fight fair and square—he actually believes he's rediscovered his youthful powers. So you persuade him to make another match. You match him against the real article, a genuine contender, and spin the story that he's on his way to the Championship of All England. Then you wager all you've got—and more—on the contender. For of course this next fight isn't a cross—it's on the up-and-up—and the warhorse is naught but a wind-broke jade on his way to the knacker's yard. So John Thomas wins a pot of gold, and no one loses at all—excepting for all those who were duped, and wagered the wrong way. And of course the warhorse himself, who had his few remaining wits a-beaten out of him—and his integrity too, which he gave away, just gave it away, for he hadn't even the sense to put a price on it."

Well. I made no return for some while, for what can you reply to such cynicism?

"Old friend," said I at length, "you wound me."

"John Thomas," said he, "I know you. Brother, you'd have matched your grandmother against Cribb, if you could have thought of a way to get the old girl up to the line of scratch."

I began to feel a certain desperation. I needed money badly, for reasons we don't need to enter into just at present. And this was a solid scheme—the best I'd been able to come up with.

"Look: one fight, against the Ruffian. A purse of twenty guineas to the winner—half to you, half to me. I plan to wager my share on your good self, and I'd urge you to do the same. Ten guineas at ten to one—a hundred guineas—and you use it all for God's own work. A hundred guineas to feed the poor, or clothe the naked, or whatever holy purpose you prefer. Think of the lives you could save—think of the *souls* you could save—and then tell me no, that your conscience is too nice, and the Lord don't want money that was wagered at a prize-fight."

He looked at me with sadness, and shook his shaggy head. "Just listen to yourself, John Thomas—like Satan himself in the wilderness, tempting Our Lord. Not that I'd ever mistake myself for the One—I hasten to say it—and not that you're the other. No, you're not the Devil, brother—just a crafty old sharper with an eye for the main chance and an angle to work, same as you always were." The smile had faded completely. "And now it's time for you to leave. Go with my blessing and the assurance that we're still friends, John Thomas, and always will be, for I bear no malice at all against any man in the world, and certainly none against you. But go at once, brother, before I kick you down the stairs."

I suspect he'd have done it, too. But suddenly there was a sound of shouting on the street below. A moment later there were footsteps, and then a ragged apparition burst through the door. It was a lad, sixteen perhaps, in scarecrow clothes. He was a printer's devil, apparently, filthy and stained with ink.

"And here's Young Joe," said Daniel warmly, his face lighting up. "Have you finished with our printing, then?"

"I need somewhere to hide oh Cap'n please oh Lord they're right on my heels!"

He was in a state of pure panic, and Daniel grew dismayed.

"Who's after you, young Joe?"

There was a rusty brown blossom on the scarecrow's breast. Daniel's face began to grey, as if with awful premonition.

"Is that blood, Young Joe?" he said. "It is—that's blood that's dried upon your shirt. What's happened? Are you hurt?"

"I never did what they're saying! It isn't true it wasn't me I'm a good boy Cap'n help me!"

Too late, for more voices were shouting, and more feet thundering up the stairs. A man burst through the door, followed by two Peelers. He pointed and cried out, in triumph and revulsion.

"There he is—the one who done the deed. He butchered that girl like a calf!"

"I didn't!" the printer's devil cried, and burst into tears.

MURDER NEAR CURZON STREET

Citizens Pursue Nightwalker Slayer

By William Piper

The Morning Register

27 May, 1851

. . .

The talk of St Giles Street, Holborn, is of a murder discovered yesterday morning, and a subsequent chase through the streets. It began when the body of a young woman, later identified as Louise Maggs, a prostitute, was found in an alley by an early rising tradesman. Our information, gleaned from witnesses who came upon the scene shortly thereafter, is that the woman had been assaulted and then most horribly slashed by a knife or similar cutting instrument, as if her assailant had begun with one intention but then worked himself into a frenzy. Members of the Watch being summoned, a search of the area was commenced, leading to the discovery that the perpetrator had gone to ground in a nearby cellar—either for fear of discovery in his gore-soaked habiliments, or (which is thought more likely) because like a wild beast's his instincts compelled him to watch over his kill. Flushed from his hole, he took to his heels. But the hue and cry was taken up, and chase was given by constables and members of the citizenry, who sprang instantly to their duty. For a time, the killer appeared to give his pursuers the slip, before the scent was found again and pursuit resumed. At last he was traced to a well-known house of vice and sedition in the Gray's Inn Road, and apprehended, following a violent struggle with his friends, including a great Scottish brute who put witnesses horribly in mind of Sawney Bean, and two ancient slatterns who fought on the murderer's behalf like shrieking harpies. The killer has been identified as Joseph Gummery, who is notorious in the district, being known as the Devil's Printer.

ERRATA

The Morning Register

28 May, 1851

. . .

Upon further investigation, certain details contained in yesterday's account have been found to be in error. The notorious house of vice and sedition in which the murderer was apprehended has been more properly identified as an academy of self-defence which serves also as the office of a laudable Christian charitable organization. The great Scottish brute referred to by our correspondent is in fact a godly Irish evangelist, bearing no similarity whatsoever to Sawney Bean, the Hibernian highwayman and cannibal. Contrary to our report, there were no ancient slatterns on the premises. The *Register* apologizes unreservedly to the Misses Sherwood, two mature philanthropists of unimpeachable character, who mildly urged members of the police to observe due process and decorum while carrying out the arrest. The suspect Joseph Gummery is not in fact notorious throughout the district as the Devil's Printer. Rather he is an apprentice in a printing house, or a "printer's devil." The *Morning Register* stands by the remaining elements of the account, particularly those details reflecting upon the industry of the police and the courage of local citizens.

JACK

SPECTACLE, DEAR BOY. Never mind the mirror held to nature. If they want nature they'll look at a tree. Bangs and whizzes—startling effects—characters who shriek and stab and get on with it. That's what they want, and so naturally that's what we give them. And why? Because we are not muffs."

Edmund Cubitt peered down at the boards beneath his feet, and raised his voice. "Are we ready down there?" Silence below. Sounds of carpentry from the wings. He gave an impatient stamp. "Can you hear me? One knock for yes."

Two muffled raps were given in reply on the underside of the stage, like goblin-knocks in a mineshaft. Cubitt rolled his eyes. "No, of course we're not ready. We go up in two hours, and it hasn't worked yet, so why would we be ready now?"

"About my play—"

"Could we be ready *soon?*" Cubitt's voice rose into his tragedian's register. This was the register he used for climactic moments of doomed heroism, and the hailing of cabs down the full length of crowded thoroughfares. "Could we aspire to readiness at some point in the identifiable future, or shall I just chuck it all over and go back to Punch and Judy in the provinces? I merely ask."

Silence below.

Edmund Cubitt ground his teeth.

He was First Tragedian and Manager of the Kemp Theatre: a man of five-and-forty, brisk and brusque, with strands of boot-blacked hair painstakingly arranged upon a startlingly large head. He was already half costumed for his performance as the vampire lord in this evening's melodrama, which meant he was kitted out in kilt and tam-o'shanter. No, don't ask.

"My play?"

"Right. Short answer?"

"Well, yes, if—"

"No."

I admit, this came as a blow. This time, I'd been so sure.

"You've read it?"

"Most of it. Enough of it. Can't use it, dear boy."

"Could I—could I ask why?"

I heard the damnable note of bleating in my voice, and for an instant had an image of myself as a cartoon drawing of the wretched fawning Poet: knock-kneed in supplication, clutching my scribblings in both hands, prevented from tugging my forelock only by the absence of a third hand to tug with. Christ, what is it about literary endeavour that strips a man of all dignity?

"A Scottish vampire," Cubitt was muttering to himself. "Jimmy MacRevenant. Ah, well—why not, eh? Why not."

He had fallen to contemplating his costume, having apparently forgotten completely about my play, which was one of the problems with him. His attention span was a hummingbird, darting incessantly from one topic to the next, and invariably returning to the one topic above all that riveted his attention: Edmund Cubitt.

"Romania—Hibernia—it's all much the same to the gallery. Yes, they'll like it well enough. They'll like it a damn sight better than Shakespeare."

The decision to mount a Scottish vampire play was not in fact an artistic one, incisive or otherwise. It came in consequence of an earlier decision to remove a production of *Macbeth* from the repertory, after audiences dwindled to the point at which there were scarcely enough lungs to give it a proper booing-off. This left the Kemp with both a yawning hole in its schedule and a wardrobe full of Highland costumes, which coincidence brought Cubitt darting to the honeysuckle-bush of inspiration: he would remount *The Vampire,* a melodrama written by Mr Planché some decades past and inexplicably set in Scotland. Cubitt had seen a pirated version as a boy, and later played it himself to some minor acclaim in the provinces. The story made relatively little sense, but it had fangs and imperilled virgins, both enduringly popular in the three-penny seats. Cubitt had added some innovations of his own, including Scottish ballads and dances, some caber-tossing, and a heroic charge by the Black Watch Regiment, complete with pipers. These had now begun rehearsing in the wings, setting up a plaintive Highland wheezing. In short it was a complete dog's breakfast, bereft of any artistic merit whatsoever, and likely to be a great success. Cubitt was an indifferent tragedian, but a shrewd manager, occasional lapses into Shakespeare notwithstanding.

"I forget, dear boy—there's the problem. I sit down with my text of the Scottish Tragedy, and I exclaim to myself, 'This is good—this is in fact sublime—it is a mirror held to the Human Condition. But I forget about the audience. Anyone who can spell Condition—or Human—or The—is at the opera. The ones we've got are mutinous before we're fifteen minutes in. 'I liked them witches—they was all right—and it was prime that bit where they stabbed the feller. But why do they have to *talk* about it, rest of the bloody night?' It's the same with *Hamlet.* Give them the Ghost, and the Gravedigger and the five minutes of slaughter at the end, and they'd go off happy as clams. It's the other four hours that bores 'em rigid."

Cubitt's limitations as Chief Tragedian had something to do with this failure as well. The last time he had essayed Hamlet, vocal elements had begun urging him on to self-slaughter by the middle of Act II. But there was a straw here, and I reached for it, albeit morosely.

"Are you saying that my play is beyond the grasp of the Kemp Theatre audience as presently constituted?"

"No, I'm saying your play's no damned good. Same as your other ones. Sorry to say it, dear boy, but spade a spade. I'd put the quill away, if I were you, and look about for something I had a talent for. Ah, *finally?*"

An apparition had uncannily manifested down below, poking its head out through a little door in the stage apron and waving one bony hand to Cubitt. It looked for all the world like something the faeries had left behind, on one of their nighttime depredations into some ill-starred nursery. Remarkably this was not a performer in the evening's extravaganza, but the boy who operated the trap. He was not above twelve or thirteen, with lank white hair and great unblinking eyes in a pale and sharp-chinned goblin's face. We called him Tommy—short for Tommyknocker.

"We're ready? My stars, can it be true?" Cubitt demanded, in the register he reserved for moments of tragic irony.

Tommyknocker disappeared beneath the stage without a word. He never did say a word—never a syllable, for apparently he was mute. He had been discovered at the stage door one morning, huddled and shivering, one of those waifs that the metropolis vomits up upon the cobbles. But one of the actresses took him in, and one of the carpenters found him a corner to sleep in, and eventually someone else discovered that he was no fool, and in fact ingenious with pulleys and mechanisms—amazingly so, in a child so clearly defective.

"Then let us screw our courage to the sticking point." Stepping forward, Cubitt assumed the attitude of Lord Ruthven, Highland fiend, and declaimed: "Demon as I am to walk the earth to slaughter and something-or-other! Something else about a black heart sustained by human blood—oh, deuce take it, they're not coming for the bloody dialogue." With that,

Cubitt precipitated himself headlong and disappeared, with a suddenness that would elicit great gasps and cries from the three-penny seats, for in tonight's performance it would be accompanied by a hiss of smoke and a belch of hellfire. I gave a little jump myself, despite knowing how the illusion was produced. It was a simple stage trap, consisting of two India-rubber flaps underlain by a wooden slide fitting close beneath. This was slid back at the appropriate instant, letting the actor plunge through to be caught by a blanket affixed below.

As Cubitt disappeared I had a glimpse of Tommyknocker, staring up at me through the opening with those great uncanny eyes. For a disconcerting instant he might have been an imp squatting upon the infernal coals, contemplating the inevitability of my eventual arrival. Then the flaps snapped back into place and I stood alone, clutching my poor rejected manuscript while the muffled voice of Cubitt wafted up through the boards.

"Give it up, dear boy. I'm sorry, but give it up. Off you go then—I'll want my supper at six o'clock—and don't flounce."

I HAD BEEN in London for nearly two years by this point, having fled there from Cornwall when my old life collapsed in ruin. For of course you have already made the requisite connection. The Revd Mr Beresford, pursued by Furies—this actor Jack Hartright, with his murky past and distinctive horseshoe-shaped scar—by God (you've exclaimed) they're one and the same man! And so they are—or rather, so they were, for as I set this down four decades later I find I have transformed once again, and call myself by a third name. It is a dark one, this third name, but that need not concern us at present, for just now I am telling you of the bygone events of 1851, by which so much was set in motion—some that was great, and some alas that was terrible.

I won't describe in detail my flight from Cornwall. Suffice it to say that there was a chance outcropping of rock along the cliffs below Scantlebury Hall. It broke my fall, although it broke my ankle as well, so badly that it never really healed. There was a friend who found me and took me in—Young Ned Moyle, bless his true heart—keeping me hidden and nursing my injuries until I could walk again, and then arranging secret midnight passage over the waves. Picture in your mind a cutter setting out from Sawle, and a young man shrouded in a cowl. Imagine an unseasonable storm arising, with such ferocity that the sailors began to mutter with white rolling eyes that there was surely a Jonah on board, carrying God's curse. But picture safe harbour at last, and a post-carriage rattling through the night, and then finally there I am: stepping out into London under cover of darkness, with neither friends nor resources beyond a last few shillings and my own frail certainty that a new day must eventually dawn.

Going home to my family in the north was clearly no option. My father had intimated prior to my departure to Cornwall that arranging for my curacy was pretty much the last effort he could be expected to make on my behalf, although I should certainly write if I ever became a bishop. Besides, that was the first place the Scantleburys would look for me. No, it had to be London, where a man could dwell unnoticed amongst the teeming masses, and create himself anew. And on that first morning, as I gnawed a sticky bun from a coffee stall in the Strand, I felt that there was hope. London was vast and surging and bellowing—half the world, it seemed, was upon this thoroughfare alone. Carriages jostling, and pedestrians streaming, and costermongers with their barrows and their bullhorn Cockney voices, rising above the cacophony: *Ni-ew mackerel, six a shilling... Wi-ild Hampshire rabbits... Fine ripe plums!* No one pausing, and no one caring, and most of all no one noticing—not noticing the marks of deformity upon the poor, or the mute despair upon the faces of many, or indeed the fugitive priest who was sidling away from the coffee stall without having paid his penny.

"Oi!"

This from the stall-keeper, a burly oaf in an apron, who turned with a gentleman's change just in time to see our hero disappearing into the throng like a river otter into bulrushes. The rushes closed behind me, and I was gone.

I confess to my shame that there were various such episodes in those first days and weeks in the metropolis, for after all a man must survive. But a chance meeting with some players in a public house led to a few pennies for passing out handbills advertising the Kemp Theatre's new season, which led in turn to the discovery that the theatre manager, Mr Edmund Cubitt, required a secretary. This invaluable person would handle the great man's correspondence and keep the books in order, and might in addition be required to appear on stage from time to time when an actor was indisposed—"indisposed" being a theatre term meaning "even drunker than the rest of them." Naturally I clutched at the opportunity, although soon enough I discovered that the position involved other duties as well, such as washing the great man's linen and mending his hose, not to mention putting up with his moods and indulging his maunderings, for it turned out the great man was in fact a mediocre man at best—indeed in many ways an utterly paltry and inadequate man—not least when it came to appreciating dramatic literature.

I had written several plays. I had done so in a joyful creative fever, having discovered that dramatic poetry was my true and genuine gift. I had scribbled them by guttering candlelight, often working clear through the night until dawn. My writing made the rest of it bearable—the moods and the linen, and the orange peels flung at my forays onto the stage—and as I completed each play I would convey it with buoyant hopes to Mr Edmund Cubitt, who wanted his supper at six o'clock.

But on this particular evening, he was not eating supper at six—or at seven o'clock either. By the time eight o'clock chimed, I'd been sitting for three hours in the corner of an unfamiliar public house. Having bolted from the theatre in high dudgeon,

I had chosen the pub at random. It was dingy and dim, even by the standards of such houses, with a fire in a great stone fireplace that flickered upon the denizens and gave them rather the appearance of robbers in a cave. This impression was not completely fanciful either, for it turned out that this was a notable haunt of the sporting crowd. It was called the Horse and Dolphin, or more commonly the Nag and Fish. The walls and the mantel were festooned with sporting memorabilia, and pictures of horses and dogs.

I paid no attention to any of this. I sat in my corner, drinking my claret and brooding.

Perhaps my first few plays had indeed been lacking. One had for instance been a melodrama after the manner of Boucicault, about a virtuous young vicar who is falsely accused of a crime. I could accept that this was an apprentice piece, glittering here and there with flecks of gold, but admittedly the work of a Poet still finding his stride. But my new play—the play I sat clutching tonight—was different. *John, Baptist; or, The Devil Distraught:* a five-act drama that broke new ground in its treatment of the early life of the prophet—portraying him as a compelling but undisciplined youth, chafing in the shadow of a saintly brother, who was nearly undone by the erotic fascination he exerted upon women in general, and on one of them in particular, the duplicitous daughter of a Galilean pirate. But he redeemed himself, abjured the Devil, single-handedly cleared a path through the spiritual wilderness for the coming of the Lord, and finally triumphed in a last desperate battle against his Old Enemy, who came to him at the eleventh hour in the form of the beauteous Salome and sought to seduce him to his ruin. It was a work of truth and terrible beauty, despite the inability of Mr Edmund Cubitt to see this: Edmund Cubitt, purveyor of tartan ghouls to the illiterate, a man who tooth-picked his soul each morning in case stray bits of poetry had lodged there.

Except Edmund Cubitt was right, and as I reread the play I knew it. *John, Baptist* was a turgid sham, filled with wooden characters and leaden discourse, stinking of spilt poetry. And nothing I would ever write would be one whit better, because I had no talent. This was nothing but an illusion I had conjured, in my desperation to reinvent myself after that Cornish debacle. But it was time to face the truth about myself. Or at least to face a few selected glimmers of the truth, since this is really what we mean when we commit ourselves to self-knowledge, with all the tearful fervour that accompanies such moments. We won't face the whole truth until we are dragged out shrieking upon Judgement Day itself, when each one of us will find himself loathsome—oh yes we will, my friend—beyond all hope of enduring.

LOOKING BACK ACROSS the years—scribbling these lines in my crabbed old hand here in Whitechapel, four decades later—I have to shake my head. What a preposterous youth I was! Hunkered in that public house, wallowing in self-pity, and scourging myself with self-hatred. *Ecce homo,* behold the man: the disgraced priest, fled to the metropolis and hiding under an alias like a rat in a bolt-hole—not that a rat has an alias, nor indeed a bolt-hole, but we'll let that pass by—and now shaken to his very foundations by the discovery that his plays were drivel. Dear absurd self-aggrandizing idiot boy.

But at the time it seemed shattering. I was drunk enough—on claret and despair—to make a Gesture. Thus I bolted to my feet and shouldered to the stone fireplace, where a gingery man stood warming his hands. Ignoring him, I consigned *John, Baptist* to the flames, watching with savage satisfaction as my fondest hopes writhed and blackened and expired. With a bleak little snarl I turned away, but in doing so I lost my balance, and reached out to brace myself against the low table behind. That's when I saw Him upon the wall. He was reaching out to me.

Prominent amongst the sporting pictures were images of pugilism: portraits of bare-knuckle fighters in sparring poses, and dramatic drawings of desperate battles. It was one of these that riveted me now.

It was a pen-and-ink engraving of two pugilists at close quarters, hemmed by a bellowing fight mob, surprisingly detailed and lifelike. The warriors wore breeches and clogs, and their bare torsos were improbably well-muscled, for the sketchers of prize-fights are notorious for seeing past the actual to the Ideal. The one on the left was hunched down, coiled to launch a blow at his opponent's midriff. He was the shorter and stockier of the two, swarthy and black-haired and snarling with bad intent. His opponent arched over him in an elegant parabola. He was fair and perfectly formed and beautiful, this second pugilist, in the way that rugged men can have beauty. His left fist was held low, and with his right he was reaching over and past his hunched opponent, as if reaching out towards someone he had just seen in the crowd. His lips were slightly parted, and his eyes had just begun to widen, as if in surprise and welcome at whoever it was he had glimpsed.

But there was distress in his eyes as well. The artist had caught a moment late in the fight, for the ravages of terrible bare-fisted blows were evident on both men. When you looked more closely you saw that a ragged cut had been torn open on the fair man's brow. Evidently the cut had been inflicted just an instant before, because it was clean and white; the blood had not yet begun to flow. Thus the distress—and yet it wasn't distress, not quite. I gazed for fully half a minute before realizing what those eyes in fact contained. It was an enormous empathy—a great sorrowful complicity in the suffering of the world. This fighter recognized that his pain was commingled with your own—and he was looking straight at you. In his pain and sorrow, he was reaching out to you.

He was reaching out to me.

Evidently I'd exclaimed this out loud, because there was a chuckle at my elbow. "Reaching out to you? Naw, mate—he's missing with his right, is what he's doing."

It was the gingery man who had been warming his hands. He regarded me with wry amusement.

"Missing him with the right, and dropping his left into the bargain, daft Irish bog-trotter, which was a terrible habit he had. And that's what ended the fight, about an eye-blink later. The Gardener landed him a doubler to his liver—that being the Gardener on the left, there—Tom Oliver, the Battersea Gardener, famous for his sweet peas and nectarines. He followed that with a leveler to the conk, and that was that. Down goes our man like a toppling tree, and nothing I can do will bring him back again."

"You?"

"I was his second, that afternoon. There I am, right there."

He pointed to the picture—guiding me to a closer look with a hand on my side—and there he was indeed, just outside the rope by one of the ring posts. The man who stood beside me tonight was older—fifty years old, perhaps; his hair was thinning, and his whiskers were patchier than they once had been. But he was unmistakably the man in the sketch: frozen forever in an attitude of dawning horror, arching back and raising his hands as if to ward off the blows that were about to rain upon his champion, with all the wide-eyed woefulness of St John at the foot of the Cross.

"We did what we could, of course. Carried him to the corner, and blew brandy up his nose, and at the end of thirty seconds we carried him back to the line of scratch and prayed he'd stay upright when we let go. But down he went—flat down on his phiz in the mud—and that was that. Well, the Gardener's friends hurried over, and I held up our man's hand so the Gardener could shake it, for that's what you do. You shake the man's hand—partly for sportsmanship, but mainly in case you've killed him. The handshake can be cited in court to prove there was no hard feelings, y'see, and with luck the judge will reduce your sentence accordingly. All goes well, it's six months for manslaughter—but if you're not careful it can be worse. It's a terrible thing when a man gets killed in the prize-ring—tragic beyond measure, for they'll throw the seconds in jail as well. But nobody died that day, thank the Dear, though Daniel never fought again, and doubtless just as well. Do I presume that you're a sporting man yourself?"

I was not in fact a sporting man. And yet I knew the man in the engraving—I'd seen that face. But where?

"My name's Rennert, though my friends call me Jaunty. And if you'd care to stand us a drop of the daffy, I'd be honoured to count you among that number, and tell you tales all night."

I was no longer listening. I was in fact on my way out of the door, for the room had all at once grown hot, and the claret was curdling in my stomach. But as I lurched out I had the most extraordinary conviction that the eyes in that engraving were following me. And moments later, as I disgorged the curdled claret onto the cobbles and straightened with a feeling of clammy relief, it came to me in an overwhelming flash of certainty.

I lurched back into the Nag and Fish, to discover that my new acquaintance Mr Jaunty Rennert had inexplicably disappeared. It wasn't until some while later that I discovered that a small but rather valuable item—a silver snuff-box, with the masks of comedy and tragedy etched on the top and bottom—had disappeared as well, from my vest pocket. This discovery brought with it the memory of a hand being placed on my side and guiding me to a better look at the picture, and suggested a plausible reason for Mr Jaunty Rennert's abrupt departure.

But in this moment I was hardly thinking of snuff-boxes. I was staring thunderstruck at the face, in the engraving. That face and the hand reaching out. And now I knew.

It was the face I had seemed to glimpse that dreadful night outside Scantlebury Hall, as the rocks had given way beneath my feet. The laughing face of the warrior archangel.

O'Thunder.

I WAS STILL unsettled when I arrived back at the theatre, but marginally more steady on my feet. Bagpipes were wailing as I slipped through the backstage door, and cabers were thudding. This meant *The Vampire* was well into its second act, and Edmund Cubitt had been left to struggle unaided through three costume-changes. Doubtless I would pay tomorrow, but tonight the spirit of bitter rebellion seethed.

"Well, look what the cat dragged in. Where've you been?"

It was Mrs Beale, emerging from the dressing area underneath the stage.

"Himself is going to have your little onions."

"Himself can go to the Devil."

Mrs Beale was a flirtatious young thing of forty, as fresh and blooming as paint could counterfeit. She normally played the second ingenue, and had been doing so since anyone could remember. These days, the strategy was to keep her upstage as far as possible, in a bad light. She wasn't precisely Mrs Beale, either, in the sense that there had never been a Mr Beale, although a considerable number of men had over the years presumed upon his conjugal privileges. But appearances must be maintained, and the great British public is jaundiced concerning unmarried women upon the stage. The public entertains doubts about their virtue.

"He says to send you straightway, the second you're spotted. He says you didn't even lay his costumes out, before you left. And he wants to know, have you seen his snuff-box?"

"What?"

"His silver snuff-box, with the masks etched on it. He says it was on his dressing table, and now it's missing."

"Why would I have seen his bloody snuff-box?"

"Because you're his bloody dresser?" she said, starting away. "Oh, and someone came here, looking for you. A young *lay-dee.*" She said it with a look of exaggerated innocence, as if to counter any imputation of sneering sarcasm. "And there she is right now."

I froze. Ever since arriving in London, I had been haunted by the dreadful foreboding that I would one day turn a corner, or open a door, and find Bathsheba Scantlebury waiting for me, with vengeance in her gaze and Little Dick looming behind her.

With my heart in my throat, I turned.

It was Nell Rooney.

She was standing in the corridor behind me, wearing an improbable hat, and round her slender shoulders a fox-fur tippet with dangling head and paws. The fox glared with glassy accusation, and Nell's own expression was quintessentially hers—the exact expression I continue to see to this very day when I close my eyes and conjure the memory of her. A look of secret shame overlain with jaw-jutting defiance, as if she half-admitted she had no right to be here in the first place—to be anywhere at all—but was damned if she'd step back without a fight.

"Oh, God bless you!" I exclaimed.

In that moment I could have fallen at her feet, and adored her for the sheer goodness of not being Bathsheba Scantlebury. But vast relief gave way to a stab of guilt, as I guessed what brought her here. "I don't have the guinea I owe you, just yet. But next week, without fail. Or—or the week after."

I could hear the shiftiness—knew my smile had gone false—and inwardly I cringed.

"I ent here for the money," she muttered. Then quickly she added: "When I come for the money, you'll know it. Cos I'll have Mother C's new bully with me, and he's twice as mean as Tim Diggory ever was. He'll twist your leg off and beat you with it."

She punctuated this with a scowl, and a further little jut of her chin. I didn't stop to ask what had become of Mr Diggory. I'd heard rumours of a ruckus at Mother Clatterballock's the other night, not long after I'd slunk away into the fog, but I had not as yet learned the details.

"You saved my life," I told her—which was an exaggeration, but probably not by much—"and I won't forget that. You'll have the money, just as soon as I have it myself. I promise, as—as your brother. But let's find a place to sit down, and you can tell me what brings you here."

"I'm looking for my mother."

HER MOTHER'S NAME was Joanna, and she was lovely. She had brown ringlets, and bright lively eyes, and cupid's bow lips that were on the very verge of sparkling with a smile. At least, thus she looked in the tiny oval portrait in Nell's locket, and Nell swore it was a good likeness.

"I mean, I hardly remember—I was so young, when she had to leave. But Mrs Dalrymple always said this was my mother in the flesh—Mrs Dalrymple who looked after me. Mrs D said that's exactly the way she looked the day she walked out the door, except she was weeping that day, cos of feeling so bad at leaving me behind. They hung her for thieving, the bastards."

"They hung your mother?" I exclaimed.

"Of course not!" she said indignantly. "If they'd hung my mother, I wouldn't be looking for her, would I? I'd know where she was, if they'd hung her—she'd be in a coffin, all covered in quicklime, like poor Mrs Dalrymple."

"Ah. So Mrs Dalrymple was the unfortunate soul who—?"

"No one hung my mother, Jack. No one *ever* hung my mother. And they never put her in any fucking coffin."

She glared with such pugnacity that the suspicion occurred: this very thought was a spectre that haunted her, and must be barked back into the shadows before it could take shape.

"My mistake. I should have known." I returned my eyes to the picture in the locket, and scrutinized it closely. "Your mother. Yes, I can see you in her."

Nell's eyes had gone wistful, and she reached to angle the locket for a better look. Her fingers brushed against mine as she did. "My mother was beautiful."

"So are you."

"Fuck off."

"It's true. I wouldn't lie to a sister."

She was wearing too much paint—it didn't suit her, not at all—and she could have used a wash. In fact, when you sat close—as we were sitting, in the snug of a public house across the alley from the theatre—she was a shabby little thing altogether. The fox fur was patchy and coming out in clumps—it put me in mind of the whiskers of Jaunty Rennert—and that preposterous little hat with a feather sticking up. Her arms were bony and her face was too thin, but her green eyes flashed with life, and somehow she was beautiful. At least, so she seemed to me.

"Have you seen her, though?"

"What's that?"

"My mother, for Chrissake! Who else are we talking about? Or maybe you've heard the name. Joanna Rooney—leastways, that's the name she used to go by."

I shook my head.

"Not that this means anything," I added quickly, for a tiny bloom of hope on her cheek had faded. "I've only been in the theatre for a matter of months—I've met hardly anyone. If you like, I could show the locket round to the others. There's a chance one of the old-timers has seen her."

She hesitated. "Mind I get it back," she muttered, her jaw jutting out again. "Cos it's all I've got of my mother, and it means more than your life will be worth, if it turns up missing."

"Mother Clatterballock's new bully," I agreed.

"That's right."

"Twist my leg off."

"And it's nothing to smirk about! Same goes for you," she added, with a scowl towards an ancient hulk who had paused to leer.

The public house was the Three Old Cocks: small, and blue with smoke, and reeking of malt and humanity. We had never set foot outside at all, Nell and I, the Cocks being accessible by a tunnel running under the alleyway from the theatre. There were many such tunnels in London, including one—or so I'd been told—that connected a certain West End brothel to the north bank of the Thames, into whose dark waters unlucky patrons could be slipped after they'd been robbed and beaten senseless. My eyes were smarting and my head was beginning to swim with the brandy I'd just poured down in place of the regurgitated claret from the Nag and Fish. But it had seemed a good idea to clear out of the theatre, to avoid prying eyes and impertinent questions, not to mention Edmund Cubitt, who would—just about now—be plunging down through the vampire-trap to the pit beneath the stage, there to curse his way through another single-handed costume change.

"Tell me about Mrs Dalrymple," I said, on an impulse.

A shadow crossed Nell's face, and she was silent for a moment. "She was all right, Mrs Dalrymple," she said at length. "She was good to me, I suppose, in her way. She liked to smoke a pipe."

"There must be more to tell than that."

"She had a house in the Holy Land. She let me stay there, and other girls too sometimes, girls with nimble fingers. She got took up with stolen goods. They accused her of other things, too, most of which she done."

"And?"

"And that was that. Fucksake, what more do you want? She went quick, thank God, at the end. She didn't struggle more than a minute, even though she was skinny as a rail, and those are the ones that can take forever to strangle. Afterwards she hung there like a bundle of old rags."

Nell's voice had grown husky, and I could almost swear her eyes were moist. She sat there small and frail and achingly young, and all at once I felt a yearning to look after her. Without doubt I was far from the first to feel that way, and would be far from the last—and neither the first nor the last to feel like an utter fool afterwards, for Nell was after all a whore. But the heart has a mind of its own, let the head say what it will. And looking back, I suspect this was the moment I began—fond young daisy that I was—to fall head over heels in love.

"So you'll show the locket round to them at the theatre?"

"I said I would."

"Men say lots of things." She had snatched that glimpse of vulnerability back from the window in which it had inadvertently been displayed, and replaced it with a look of disdain. "And don't think this changes nothing, neither. You still owe me the fucking guinea."

"I know."

"But I don't ask nobody for favours, cos I don't do favours in return. So let's settle up. There's a room upstairs we can use, or just the alley, if a suck will do."

"No, I'm afraid it won't do at all."

"What, then?" A guarded look had come into her eyes, as she waited to hear what might be asked of her. I expect she'd had requests that would turn your stomach, and leave you sickened about humankind. I expect she'd said yes to them, too.

"I want you to walk with me, on Monday afternoon."

"Walk where? The fuck are you talking about?"

"I want to take you walking in the park."

IF YOU ENTERED Hyde Park from the southeast, you'd pass first under the great triumphal arch, erected in 1828 from designs by Mr Decimus Burton. There was a screen of Ionic columns, and three arches for carriages, and two for those on foot. Just to the right was Apsley House, the town residence of the Duke of Wellington. If you were especially lucky, you might see the grand old Iron Duke himself—he turned eighty-two the year of the Exhibition—setting out in his carriage, perhaps accompanied by a lobster-red column of the Life Guards, whose barracks were on the south side of the Serpentine River. And of course you'd smell the Serpentine—that's the very first thing you'd smell, and probably the last thing, and (depending on the wind) quite frequently the only thing. The Serpentine was an open sewer, stinking of fish and worse, for it was also the last resting place for the mortal remains of delinquent dogs and superfluous cats. But of course this never kept anyone away from Hyde Park and its four hundred Arcadian acres of hill and dale and wood.

If you came on a Sunday afternoon, you'd see half of fashionable London out for its weekend promenade along Rotten

Row, with splendid carriages passing up and down, ogled by throngs of the unwashed who stood or sat in chairs that had been placed all along the way. Amidst the carriages trotted beautiful young creatures on horseback. Though they rode alongside the wealthy and high-born, these women—for all their brazen airs and splendid dress—were neither. They were the "Pretty Horsebreakers," kept mistresses flaunting their ravishing riding habits and their delightful little hats—much to the disgust of the middle classes, who nonetheless must keep close watch, for from time to time the wind would flutter a skirt and expose an ankle. There had been an amusing letter in *The Times* that very day, concerning a notorious horsebreaker named Skittles—identified by the letter-writer only as Anonyma—whose manifestations along Rotten Row were causing serious traffic congestion. I read it aloud to Nell.

> About six PM a rumour arises that Anonyma is coming. Expectation rises to its highest pitch; a handsome woman drives rapidly by in a carriage drawn by thoroughbred ponies... but alas! she causes no effect at all, for she is not Anonyma; she is only the Duchess of A——, the Marchioness of B——, the Countess of C——, or some other of Anonyma's eager imitators. The crowd, disappointed, reseat themselves and wait. Another pony carriage succeeds—and another—with the same depressing result. At last their patience is rewarded. Anonyma and her ponies appear, and they are satisfied. She threads her way decorously, with an unconscious air, through the throng, commented on by hundreds who envy her. She pulls up her ponies to speak to an acquaintance, and his carriage is instantly surrounded by a multitude; she turns and drives back towards Apsley House, and then—away into the unknown world, nobody knows whither. Meanwhile thousands returning from the Exhibition are intolerably delayed by the crowds collected to gaze

> on this pretty creature and her pretty ponies, and the efforts of Sir Richard Mayne and his police to keep the thoroughfare open are utterly frustrated.

I laughed. "What do you think of that?"

Nell had finished the ice I had bought her as we arrived, and tossed the paper wrapper to the ground. "I think Skittles is prob'ly worth every penny Lord Whoosit gives her, for tending that shrivelled scrawny cock of his—and twice as much besides, for pretending it's big. 'Oooh, Sir, take care wi' that—and me such a little slip of a thing!' Don't tell me about actors on the stage—it's every day of my fucking life. And I can read, you know. I know my letters. So you don't have to read out loud to me, like an eedjit."

She took the paper, scowling, and scanned it herself.

I sighed. Nell had been in a strange mood ever since we had arrived—indeed, ever since I had first proposed walking in the park.

"The park?" she had demanded, with a kind of dark incredulity. "Why would you want to take me to the park?"

"Well—because it's a place people like to go walking," I had said, a little baffled by her reaction. "It's a nice thing for two people to do together. It's... ordinary. Wouldn't you like," I added wistfully, "to feel ordinary?"

She just stared. "Ordinary? The fuck kind of way to feel is that?"

"Well—"

"Would 'common' do just as well for you? I could feel common as dirt for you, if that's what you'd like."

"I just meant—"

"I could feel common as dogshit, if that would make you happy. Common as dogshit on your boot."

Now, as we arrived at the park, she walked the way a cat picks its way through foreign territory: hackles at the bristle, set to spook at any second. And of course she had been subdued by the news I had brought with me, that nobody at the theatre had recognized the face in the locket, or the name. This included Edmund Cubitt, who had after a day or two descended from the alpine heights of silent wrath to deliver a jeremiad upon the sin of pique, and the sacred demands of duty, and the sure and certain consequences if such dereliction were to recur—and by the way, did I have a pinch of snuff that I might offer him? For his snuff-box had gone missing, though he refused to presume it stolen, preferring to believe better of human nature, despite the bitter lessons of experience.

But here we were, the two of us, walking in Hyde Park together. Nell remained for the moment buried in the newspaper—either to prove her claim to be literate, or more probably to avoid having to talk to me. But the sun was shining and the Serpentine was stinking and despite myself I felt—for just a moment, a tiny slice of time carved out of the world—absurdly happy.

Nell took a sharp breath. "They fixed the day for hanging him."

"What's that?"

"Him they arrested for killing poor Luna. Not Luna, Louise." She was riveted upon a paragraph on an inside page of the newspaper. Her face had paled.

"You mean the whore who was found murdered a few weeks ago?"

I remembered reading something about it at the time, although I didn't recall the specifics. Just that she'd been attacked in an alley not far from Mother Clatterballock's dreadful house, and that the one they'd convicted was just a boy.

"I mean Louise Elizabeth Maggs—cos she was a person, and that was her name!"

"You knew her?"

She turned on me, accusing and incredulous. "Of course I knew her—and so did you. Luna—Louise—you fucked her!"

Respectable passers by veered away and glared, but I scarcely registered this. "What, that skinny girl at Mother

Clatterballock's? She was the same poor creature who was found—? Oh dear Lord!"

I snatched the newspaper back, and there it was. The murder of Louise Maggs. Joseph Gummery of St Giles Parish, aged sixteen, was to hang on Monday. He was still protesting his innocence.

"Sixteen years old." I sat down slowly on a bench, as one shaken yet again by the depravity of humankind. "Dear God, why do you suppose he did it?"

"He killed her cos she was low," said Nell. She spoke so quietly that I could scarcely hear. "She was low as dirt—just like me. That's why he done it. But she was a person."

Now the words came welling out, as if she were entering them into some universal ledger. As if saying them could somehow make a difference.

"Her friends called her Loo—and she had friends, even if I was never one of them. She could be kind. She had a bird she kept in her room. She'd let it out of its cage and it would sit on her finger. She was twenty-seven years old, and she'd been a shop-girl till she met a sodger and one thing led to the next. But everything would have been different if they'd just left her and her soft-headed gentleman alone, him with three thousand a year. She'd have had her own house. She'd have had children. That's who she could have been. And God damn them all for taking it away from her."

I sat clutching the newspaper. The look on Nell's face—that forlorn jaw-jutting bulldog defiance—was enough to break a man's heart.

"You're not low," I said. "I don't want to hear you say such a thing again."

"What am I, then?" She glared at me, suddenly savage. "Go ahead, then—you tell me what I am."

It was on my tongue to tell her: "You're my friend." But in the next moment, she gave a bitter laugh.

That was Nell—from the day we met, until the day it all came to an end. She was a child. I don't mean in her years, or her capacity for understanding. But a child in her temperament. She was changeable as a day in early spring, veering from one extreme to another. And just as you'd catch up she'd be gone again, darting like a swallow.

"You know what I am?" she snapped. "I'm here to see the fucking Exhibition. So let's go see it."

THE GREAT EXHIBITION of the Industry of All Nations: that was the whole world's reason for coming to Hyde Park in the summer of 1851. It had been opened by Queen Victoria in May, as a symbol of Great Britain's unquestioned industrial, military, and economic superiority. At least, this superiority was unquestioned by Great Britain herself—and really, what other opinion mattered? It was housed in the Crystal Palace, a vast structure of steel and glass that shone in the sun like a gigantic faerie fortress. In the planning stages, engineers had raised fears that a large crowd, moving regularly inside such a structure, could create "resonance"—vibrations that would escalate in speed and pitch until, like some Siren-shrill discord of the Spheres, a terrible crescendo was reached and the whole thing came crashing down. So first they built a test structure, on which three hundred workmen walked back and forth, first one way and then the other, then jumping simultaneously into the air. Finally columns of army sappers and miners were summoned, and marched repeatedly in step. But the structure stood, and so the Crystal Palace was raised. Once completed, it spanned nineteen acres, making it six times the size of St Paul's, with over a million feet of glass. It was seventy feet high at the apex, at which two sparrow hawks could often be seen circling. These had been introduced at the suggestion of the wily old Iron Duke of Wellington himself, to deal with the flocks of sparrows that must otherwise infest the building. From time to time one would stray in unawares, and there would be a shadow, and a plunge, and a tiny tumult, and a handful of feathers wafting down upon the multitudes.

Sundays were five-shilling days for the great folks. Mondays, at a shilling, were for the rest of us. Today was a Monday—a day of honest families wearing their humble best, gnawing on hunks of bread and cheese, and sucking at small beer from small bottles. Most of all it was a day of wide-eyed examination and cries of frank amazement—for this was a palace of wonders, everywhere you looked, and the unwashed were unafraid to show it.

"My God, just look at the fountain."

Nell flitted forward. A bright, brittle amazement was upon her.

And of course the fountain was wonderful. It was gigantic, the centrepiece of the entire Exhibition—which in its entirety was entirely wonderful. Come: let us marvel.

At the northern end were tropical plants and forest trees. Arranged on every side were sculptures, many of them colossal and beautiful. In the midst was a series of courts depicting the history of art and architecture from ancient Egypt to the Renaissance, and courts displaying industrial wares from all corners of the world. There were marine engines, locomotives, hydraulic presses and anatomical models—silks and shawls, laces and embroideries, locks and clocks and watches—the great British furniture court—the cotton fabric and carriage courts, and wooden power-looms in motion. There were chemicals, and philosophical instruments, and toys: whirligigs and rocking horses and porcelain dolls from France in billowing silk dresses; wooden toy soldiers, kites and croquet sets and ingenious clockwork animals that moved.

"Look there," Nell exclaimed. "It's an elephant!"

And of course it was: a great stuffed elephant, with a spectacularly bejeweled howdah, as part of the Indian court. The Koh-I-Noor diamond was here on display, and over there a mighty steam-driven threshing machine, and there—God bless us—a pair of "terrible lizards," on an island in an artificial lake. Cement and tile models of Iguanodon and

Megalosaurus—*dinosauria*—as they are said to have looked before they perished in the Flood.

"Do you believe in that?" Nell asked suddenly.

"What, you mean believe in the *dinosauria?*"

"No, not them," she said impatiently. "Of course I believe in *them*—I can see them, can't I? They're right there, big as elephants. I'm asking, do you believe in the Flood, and Noah and that? And Adam and Eve and the Snake—God making the sun and moon on the fourth day—all them stories."

She was eyeing me in that sidelong way she had—dogged and challenging—and I hesitated. "Well, they're not just stories," I said. "They're written in the Bible."

"Of course they're written in the Bible, you eedjit. I know where they're written. What I'm asking is, do you believe 'em?"

And I hesitated again. I told myself this was to choose my words, for you had to be careful how you answered such questions, especially to someone who thought as a child. But that wasn't really what troubled me at all.

Nell's brittle bright energy had scarcely flagged in all the time we'd been here. But as she had flitted from one exhibit to the next, I had been gripped by the strangest feeling. I had read all about the Great Exhibition—I had listened avidly as others described the marvels. Now that I was actually here, I felt . . . uneasy. But why? Surely it wasn't the crowd, for I had never minded crowds, not even such a Monday mob as was jammed in here today. In the midst of such a crowd you can be as solitary as you like—you can be invisible—and that was something I always liked.

No, the problem was all these wondrous devices—these engines of the future. A carriage that created its own railway, laying down tracks as it proceeded and picking them up as it passed. Here was a model of an aerial machine, and there a navigable balloon. Surrounded by such devices, it grew more difficult to believe in things we *must* believe in. And here came that cold and vertiginous sensation I had been fighting to hold back all my life. The sense that a wrong answer—a single unguarded admission—might produce a tiny crack, like an unseen fissure in a gigantic structure of steel and glass. But it would spread, spiderwebbing through the foundations without my even noticing, until all at once in a terrible cascading thunder the entire edifice collapsed around me.

"Of course I believe in the Bible," I said doggedly.

"Do you think she's in Hell?"

"What?"

"Luna. Louise. Louise Elizabeth Maggs, who got her belly slit from her cunny to the breastbone, and her innards all over the cobbles. Do you think she's burning in Hell?"

Her mood had veered again. She was trying to show that sardonic look, but now her voice was unsteady. "If she is—if she's burning in torment, right now, right this minute while we're standing here—then it's all my fault. Cos it was supposed to be me. D'you understand? I was the one he was after—not the same night he killed Luna, but a week earlier. I was the one he meant to kill."

And it all came pouring out.

"He come up behind me in the theatre, pressing himself up and talking about how it was filth, and afterwards he followed me. I know it was him—it had to be. I got away—I was running away from him when I run into *you*. And it was him they arrested—it was the same one—no, don't try to tell me I don't know that for certain, cos I *do*. I went to the court when they put him on trial—I went to the Old Bailey—and it was him! Gabbling and blubbering about how he never, and it was someone else, and he was nothing but a good boy and had been all his life. I knew it was a lie—I knew he done it—and I said so. I stood up and shouted it, and that judge threatened to put *me* in jail, and they dragged me out, them bailiffs. But I was right, wasn't I? That judge knew that himself, knew it just as much as I did, cos he put on his black cap afterwards and passed the sentence. And now they'll hang him—they're going to hang him next Monday—and it'll all be over. Except it won't be over at all, cos she's in Hell and I should be there instead."

Tears of desolation streamed down her face. Oh, my poor Nell.

"I deserve it, too," she said. "I deserve to be in Hell—and that's where I'll be, soon enough—for being such a horrible bitch when Luna was alive, and thinking such thoughts about her. I'll be in Hell, and won't the Devil be rubbing his hands."

"Don't talk rubbish," I said firmly. "Hell does not exist for the likes of you."

"How would you know?"

I almost blurted: "Because Hell exists for the likes of me." But instead I told her: "I'd know because I'm a priest."

This stopped her dead.

"Look here, it's time I told you the truth about who I really am. If we're to be friends, then you should know. I used to be a curate in the Church of England, until—well, let's just say that life did not unfold as I had expected. Something quite terrible happened to me, and I had to run away. I turned my back on my past, and I suppose I turned my back on God as well. But perhaps he hasn't turned his back on me, not quite yet. And I know for a fact he hasn't turned his back on you, or your poor friend either. I mean that."

Nell's eyes were still brimming with tears. She gave a cynical little snort of laughter.

"I meet a lot of gemmen who once was vicars and curates," she said, "in my particular line of work. Most of them was curates and vicars right up till yesterday afternoon, and never laid hands upon a girl before, so how would I feel about half price? I once had a gemmun who'd practically been Pope."

"You think I'm lying? Why would I lie?"

"Why would you tell the truth?"

But her face was softening. She brushed at her eyes with the back of her wrists.

"Mister, I don't care who you are, or who you've been, or what you'll be when you wake up tomorrow morning. But good for you—you made me laugh—and I suppose I should thank you for that."

She stepped suddenly forward, put a hand on my arm, and stood on tiptoe. A tiny brush of lips against my cheek, and she stepped back again. As she did, for just a moment she was smiling.

Oh, my sweet soiled lily. And oh my poor wayward heart.

"It's absurd, of course. Nothing but puffed-up human pride and folly. How would he know what they looked like, even if they existed in the first place?"

Nell gasped.

He had come up behind me, and was looking past my shoulder at the *dinosauria* on their lake. The tall old man in black, from that night at Mother Clatterballock's. His queer old-fashioned riding boots and low slouching hat. Eau-de-cologne, and something else.

"Mr Richard Owen," he said dismissively, waving a hand at a plaque identifying the scientist upon whose designs the terrible lizards had been constructed. Long fingers with thick black hair on the back of them. "Was he there to see them, pray? Has he spoken to anyone who was? Was Mr Richard Owen walking the earth when it was created—what has Bishop Ussher determined—nearly 6,000 years ago?"

He spoke with disdain, but the look on his face was darker than that. He regarded the display with something closer to hatred.

"He didn't need to see them," I found myself replying. "He reconstructed them from ancient bones—from fossils."

"Yes, Mr Richard Owen found some very old bones, by digging holes in the ground. He claims they were left there by the *dinosauria*."

"How else would they get there?"

"I would suppose someone put them there."

"Someone like who?"

"I don't know. The Devil?"

"And why would the Devil put bones in a hole?"

"Why, to delude Mr Richard Owen. To puff him up in his pride, and encourage him to delude others. It all seems clear enough to me." The tall man continued to gaze fixedly at the *dinosauria,* but his lip twisted slightly in a sardonic smile as he added: "But of course, the Devil does not exist."

"That is where you make your mistake," said I, "Lord Sculthorpe."

For I knew his name. I'd asked after it, that night at Mother Clatterballock's, when he'd plucked a guinea from the air and taken Nell away from me. *Why, that's His Lordship,* I'd been told. *You see 'im about, in the strangest places. And don't he half give you the heebie-jeebies?*

His eyes flicked towards me. Ice-cold eyes. They looked me over—up and down—as if taking the whole measure of me in less than a moment. And yes, it more than half gave me the heebie-jeebies.

"You think the Devil exists, then?" asked Lord Sculthorpe.

"I know he does," I said.

"And what makes you so certain?"

"I live in the world. I see his handiwork, everywhere I turn. But perhaps I'm not such a forward-looking man as you yourself, my Lord."

It was an impertinent thing to say to a peer of the realm in a Regency hat. Somehow I was gripped by a compulsion to goad the man—an idiot schoolboy impulse to prod befanged things with sticks. But Sculthorpe had already dismissed me from his consideration. His eye sought out Nell, and he smiled thinly down upon her.

"What a pleasure to see you," he said.

Nell made no reply. All this while she had stood very still, shrinking into herself, like a small bird sheltering in tall grass.

"I'd like to see you again. I'd like you to come to my house."

He held out a card. When Nell didn't take it, he pressed it into her hand. Nell's other hand had slipped itself into mine. It was small and hot. A child's hand, burrowing for reassurance.

"I'd like you to come tomorrow afternoon. Three o'clock."

"Thank you," said Nell, in a very quiet voice. "But I think I won't."

Lord Sculthorpe's thin smile widened by half an incisor. "Oh, I think you will."

With a last seething look at Mr Richard Owen's terrible lizards, he turned and walked away. In the back of my brainpan, something began to nag—a small thought creeping on silent rat's paws. There was something I had noticed, if I could just lay my hands on what it was.

It came to me much later. That night, as I walked alone in the dark London streets, reliving the afternoon in my mind. Thinking of Nell, and poor Luna Queerendo, and the Devil. That's when it hit me—Lord Sculthorpe had come up on my left. He'd come up on the sinister side.

*T*HE DEVIL *does not like the future. He does not like the look of it at all. The future hurtles towards him at forty miles per hour, drawn by steam locomotives. Forty miles in a single hour—forty miles in each and every hour—and the Devil's own pace remains so measured. It is the exact same pace he has maintained since he first stepped out upon the Fields of Light—a pace that has served his purpose in all the aeons since. But the world is accelerating, all around him. Rushing at him. Unbalancing him. Now they're about to dig tunnels for trains beneath the earth itself, probing like great one-eyed worms through all his dark and secret haunts, leaving no place under the sun to hide.*

One evening in May, walking in Hyde Park, he had looked up from a smouldering reverie to discover the Duke of Wellington standing beside him. The old man had tottered from Apsley House to take a turn, now that the flood-tide of humanity had ebbed with the coming of twilight. Stillness had descended upon the stately trees. Beyond, the Crystal Palace blazed in the dying rays of the sun. A willow tree bowed its sleepy head over the Serpentine; a little boy gambolled on the bridge while his father knelt at the water's edge, drowning a sackful of kittens.

"Good evening," the Devil had said, "Your Grace."

The old man snarled something unintelligible in reply, having just discovered something on his waistcoat. He squinted, then picked at it disgustedly with a yellowed thumbnail. But it was unmistakably the Duke. That famous falcon profile.

"It's a fine evening," said the Devil, by way of making conversation. "Have you been to the Exhibition?"

"Shat upon by sparrows," the Duke exclaimed in bitter grievance. He searched arthritically in his pockets for a handkerchief.

"Here," said the Devil, "take mine."

He produced a handkerchief from thin air in one of those conjuring gestures that he could never quite resist. The Duke blinked, and for the first time he looked the Devil in the face. There was an instant of uncertainty, and then an ancient memory stirred.

"I've seen you before, haven't I?"

"I don't know," said the Devil, who always enjoyed such moments. "Have you?"

The old man's eyes sharpened with recognition. "I saw you upon the field at Waterloo."

The Devil felt a thin cold trickle of gratification—the closest to pleasure he ever experienced. He began to formulate a response, one that would combine droll understatement with the glitter of dark triumph, and the insinuation that upon such unholy fields—amidst the roar of the great guns and the shriek of destruction—were many of his masterpieces made.

"I saw you on the field that night," exclaimed the Duke. "After the battle was done. You were out there amongst the corpses."

The Devil remembered the scene vividly, as he remembered so much of Waterloo. He had spent the night before the battle in a little pension *in Quatre-Bras, locked in the embrace of the innkeeper's fourteen-year-old daughter. She had been such a sweet, shy thing when he had arrived, and so haggard afterwards. He had enjoyed the battle from a nearby hillside, peering with a spyglass through the smoke and combustion. When at last the dreadful day was done, he had come down to walk in the darkness, in the moaning of the wind and of the dying. There were thousands of them dying there, amidst the thousands—men and horses—already dead. A thin horrid gibbering rose and fell; an endless aria of desolation. The Devil saw a horse, still quite alive but with both its back legs blown away, looking round in vague accusation. There were hundreds of women upon the field, flitting like wraiths, calling out names. These were camp-followers, the wives and sweethearts of soldiers who had not returned from the battle, now searching desperately through the vast swath of carnage. And of course the scavengers were out—peasants and rogues and deserters—robbing the bodies of the dead and the not-quite-dead, and slitting the throats of more than a few who had not been dead at all. The Devil had been gratified to see his little innkeeper's daughter amongst these ghouls, her sweet ruined face as savage as any.*

It had been getting towards midnight when he saw Wellington. The Devil had been kneeling beside a sobbing boy, consoling him with promises of imps with red-hot tongs and the weight of a vast millstone crushing eternally down upon his lungs. As he rose, he was startled to see the Duke on a hillock nearby, attended by an adjutant. Their eyes met, and the Devil had it half in mind to stroll over—or perhaps to gain the hillock with a single unnatural bound, like Spring-Heeled Jack—and there to say with a smirk and a nudge, "Why, look what we've accomplished, the two of us!" But instead he found himself ducking his head, and moving away, for there was something about Wellington that put the Devil on edge. It had something to do with the man's icy resolution. Despite himself, the Devil felt unsettled by so much resolve, in human form.

By contrast, he had always enjoyed his encounters with the little fat Corsican. The little fat Corsican had considerable resolve of his own, but mainly he liked to talk about the purifying flame of human aspiration, and of course the Devil always encouraged such talk. Several years before, the two of them had spent an entire night drinking together. The Corsican's eyes had grown shiny and moist as he spoke of the road that stretched before him, proposing that his own triumphs should stand as an emblem of the triumph of the human spirit. The Devil had warmly agreed, and poured out another glass of the Corsican's splendid claret, and hazarded the suggestion: "Russia."

"Yes, that was *you, wasn't it?" the old Duke was exclaiming now. There was an expression on his face that the Devil didn't quite like. "Robbing the bodies, you sneaking prick—I should have had you shot."*

The Duke drew back his walking stick to cut the Devil a blow, but in that very moment his thoughts gave a lurch and fixed upon another topic entirely, as an old man's thoughts will do. Staring sharp-eyed into the Devil's face, he said with a sudden gleam of inspiration: "Of course—sparrow hawks."

NOW, SOME MONTHS later, the Devil stands alone amidst the humanity that teems in the Crystal Palace, drawn back yet again to those horrid dinosauria. He hates them, even more than he hates the gigantic steam threshing-machines of the future, because the Devil does not remember dinosauria. He cannot remember them at all—does not recall their being created, or living, or perishing. This brings with it a nameless, gnawing dread—a sense that the ground itself could at any instant drop beneath him, like a hangman's trap. For if he has forgotten dinosauria, then what else may he have forgotten? Worse yet, what memories may not be memories at all, but instead just the fragments of dreams and the echoes of distant voices imperfectly heard, mere phantoms that he imagines to be real? If this is possible, then nothing can be known at all, and where does this leave the Devil? In a Hell far beyond his own conception.

The Devil can stand this no more. With a crack of pinions he rises up seventy feet, and circles as a hawk. Down below, amidst the throng, an honest mechanic walks with his good wife and their four children—all good Christians in their shabby best clothing—plump white souls for the plucking. "Oh, look!" they cry in happy surprise, for they have just seen that wonderful elephant. In their excitement, the parents fail to notice that the youngest and plumpest of their little birds, the dearest little apple-cheeked girl, has toddled a few steps away.

With a silent shriek the Devil plummets.

PIPER

Hangings were always at eight AM. Sharp upon the hour, as the bell of St Sepulchre tolled. But the crowd would begin gathering outside Newgate Prison by four, with dawn still a rumour of red on the horizon. Gradually, as the sky grew light, the prison would take form, great and grim and grey.

The event had actually begun the previous afternoon, which was a Sunday. Hangings were done on a Monday, always on Monday—even in the old days, when there might well be a hundred hanged in a calendar year, so you might see three or four done at once. By early Sunday afternoon the drinking would begin in the nearby taverns, and the bartering for choice vantage-points. Five pounds to hire the attic storey of Lamb's Coffee House, directly opposite—up to five times that amount for a private balcony. Such a price to pay! But then, it was such an event. The revelry would be in full swing by Sunday evening, when the mood would start to shift. Workers would have begun erecting the barriers and platforms outside the prison. Then—a shock of excitement—the gallows itself would emerge. A black stage with a trap door, and three parallel beams above. Drawn by horses from its storage place within the walls. Trundled into place like some old-world siege engine being wheeled out yet again to do its duty in the ancient war against evil.

Revelry would continue through the night. This was heard of course by the wretch in whose honour this celebration was being held. Heard faintly but distinctly through the walls, like an echo from a time before all hope had been lost. By six AM, the crowds would be streaming past St Sepulchre's, and up Snow Hill. At seven, just about the time when one or two of the earliest arrivals had fainted with exhaustion, the wretch within the walls would be escorted down to the cold stone holding cell. There he would be pinioned by the Yeoman of the Halter and offered spiritual sustenance by the Prison Ordinary, on this his last morning in the world.

Or so I had been told. I had never been to a hanging before. There's an admission for a Londoner to make, and a London newspaperman to boot.

That's me. William Piper—perhaps you've come across the name? It appears from time to time in the pages of the *Morning Register,* usually above short entries that had been much longer before a sub-editor laid waste to them. Purveyor of sturdy English facts, set down in good plain English words, all laid out in a row, penny apiece. What else do you need to know? A man in his thirties, at the time this narrative begins, without matrimonial connection but earnestly committed to his filial responsibilities.

And I can see a sub-editor's eyebrow arching already, so fine. In good plain English words: thirty-seven, unwed, lives with his Ma. Hair: thinning. Eyes: bulging. Physical contours: toad-like. Disposition: vaguely optimistic, though God knows why.

There we go. Introductions completed. On we go.

I arrived outside Newgate at seven-thirty that morning, alongside Daniel O'Thunder. To be honest, he was the last companion I'd have expected, on this or any other morning. But here he was, shouldering forward through the crowd. Ashen, but determined to keep his promise. I began to wonder if I had misjudged him.

O'Thunder was a brute, of course—I kept reminding myself of that. He was first and foremost a brute, as all prize-fighters are brutes—never mind the chirping of the Fancy that this murderous bruiser or that appalling thug is in fact a rough unlettered aristocrat of the spirit. Granted, brutes can be fascinating, even compelling, as this one undeniably was. He had a kind of surging animal spirit, and upon this capital had founded his second career as a street preacher. But let us be honest (I reminded myself). When we find a brute charming, what we're in fact feeling is relief. He grins a crooked grin, and calls us brother, and in gratitude we inwardly exclaim: "Why, the brute is not at this particular moment twisting my head off like a chicken's—how immensely I like him!" And indeed this one had come within a whisker of twisting my head off before we'd even been properly introduced.

Things had begun on the wrong foot with that paragraph about Joe Gummery's arrest—perhaps you read it, in the *Morning Register?* The one that mentioned ancient harpies and notorious Scotch cannibals? This was an unfortunate lapse into literary flourish (*reminder to self: sturdy English words, you fool, the plainer the better*). And unfortunately I had one or two facts wrong—well, most of them, actually—which never helps. I hadn't been present at the arrest, and trusted in reports from sources who—as it turned out—hadn't been there either. They'd heard it from a man who knew a man who'd heard it straight from a girl whose cousin was a constable. But what can you do? You admit your mistake, grovel a bit, and then clutch at the possibility of redemption.

It was this that had taken me to the Dog and Duck on the Friday prior to the hanging. The clutching at redemption part, that is—I'd already been grovelling for two weeks. The Dog and Duck was a public house at the foot of Fleet Street, much frequented by gentlemen of the daily press. I found my Editor in a snug at the back with his usual coterie of cynical lickspittle underlings. There was the expected volley of drolleries and witticisms, which consisted largely of juvenile plays upon my name.

"Why, here's the man himself. What do you have to offer us, then? I'll wager it's another retraction—served up Piping hot."

Merriment, etc.

"As a matter of fact," I told them coolly, "I'm offering an exclusive gaolhouse confession from the Printer's Devil."

This stopped them in their tracks. The Editor looked up sharply. He was a brisk little Scottish thug named McKay, with eyes like bright black buttons and drooping black whiskers that put one inevitably in mind of an Aberdeen terrier.

"A confession?"

"A full and wretched confession. Brimming with sensational disclosure and tears of woe. A thousand words, at tuppence apiece."

McKay stared at me. I was reminded that the Aberdeen terrier was originally bred to fight badgers. "You've spoken with him?" he demanded.

"I have."

I uttered the syllables with measured dignity. McKay and the others stared back at me with—could it be? Oh yes it was—the first glimmerings of actual respect.

"At least, not precisely," I conceded. "Not yet. But I *will* be speaking to him directly—this very night."

At times one is conscious of a leaking sensation, like a punctured hot-air balloon. I did my best to rally.

"No, look. I have a connection to one of the turnkeys. We've made arrangements—he's going to let me in to see the Printer's Devil—exclusive interview. This is a coup."

And it was. No one had been allowed in to see the wretch at all—not since he'd been dragged from the Old Bailey after hearing the doom pronounced upon him, shrieking and raving and carrying on. He'd been in such a state—swearing his innocence and flinging himself against walls—that they clapped him into solitary lock-up and kept him there, in shackles. But I had arranged to see him. Thus I would be the man who heard his exclusive confession.

"And what makes you think he'll confess, Piper?"

"Well—well, because they all do."

Brief stony silence. Further leakage.

"I mean, it's human nature. The shadow of the gallows—remorse welling up—the awful certainty of... et cetera. Just wait, you'll see. But fair enough, all right, we'll call it a penny a word..."

There was a barking sound.

They were laughing at me.

IT WAS LATE Friday night when I saw Joe Gummery, the Printer's Devil. On Saturday morning I sought out Daniel O'Thunder.

He was of course the last man on earth I wanted to see.

Ever since the arrest, O'Thunder had been frantic with activity. I hadn't seen it myself—I'd been careful to steer clear, for obvious reasons—but I'd heard. He had rushed to Bow Street Police Station, protesting that a terrible mistake had been made. When they threw him out, he launched an investigation of his own, pounding upon every door within a mile's radius of the murder. Searching for a witness—any witness—who would contradict the official account. He had led a delegation into the courthouse during the trial, and in a terrible voice had cried "No!" when the verdict was returned. He had thundered the killer's innocence on street-corners, and his followers pleaded the case in ill-spelt letters to Members of Parliament, and every newspaper in London.

This campaign was continuing as I arrived at the Academy on that Saturday, two days before the hanging. The room was full of O'Thunder's ragtag little band.

The man had his followers, give him his due. They were beggars and whores and drunken costermongers for the most part. But there were also a few honest mechanics, and mixed in with them ladies from good families. Doggedly doing the Lord's Work down here amongst the dregs of London. The women were the keenest followers—O'Thunder had an effect upon women, despite that ugly mug of his. Half of them dreaming of taming the beast, I expect. Half of them dreamed of I shan't say what. A handful looked as if they expected he might at any minute mount a white mule and lead them into Jerusalem. Just now, the lettered were scribbling last desperate missives to Her Majesty. A cadaverous printer was passing out pamphlets for distribution. A florid bakewife had just arrived with a basket-load of Save Joe buns. There was din and flurry and desperation, and the distinctive odour of O'Thunder's rabble—a curious and pungent combination of sweat, stale piss, and piety.

I was standing just inside the door, looking for a sticking point to which to screw my courage, when the older Miss Sherwood spotted me. She gasped and exclaimed something to her sister, who had been earnestly scribbling. The younger Miss Sherwood turned her head, and her gaze glittered.

More heads turned. A hush began to descend. An immense party in a chimney-pot hat arose in the midst of the others, like Moloch from the Underworld.

Finally O'Thunder saw me. He had been striding back and forth through the room—exhorting here, encouraging there, covering his own desperation with activity. Seeing me, he went still.

I am not a courageous man at the best of times. Just now, I felt utterly unscrewed from anything resembling a sticking point. I cleared my throat.

"Good morning," I said. "My name is William Piper. I am—that is to say—you may be possibly familiar..."

"Oh, indeed," said the younger Miss Sherwood, in a remarkably cold voice. "We know who you are. You're the man who writes such extraordinary things in the newspaper. The question is, what are you doing here?"

O'Thunder spoke. That tenor voice of his—such a curious high voice to come fluting from such a brute. "Why, Brother Piper has come to help us. He's come to help us save poor Joe. That must be the case, for why else would Brother Piper be here? So come in, Brother Piper—come in friendship."

His eyes were red-rimmed. His face was unshaven, and his linen had clearly gone unchanged for several days. I wondered briefly if he'd slept at all since Gummery had been taken. But he smiled as he took me by the arm—a grip that would choke a Clydesdale—and led me forward. Rumbles from round the room, and glares of Christian murder from the Miss Sherwoods. "Clear some room for Brother Piper—here, this table will serve—and someone fetch him a quill and paper."

It wasn't sarcasm, either. He was actually determined to believe the best of me.

"I saw him," I said.

"What's that?" said O'Thunder. He still wore that smile, and now it twisted into a rueful chuckle. "I'm afraid you've spoken into my right ear, Brother Piper, which is my wrong one, being the ear the Barrel Boy clouted those many years ago on Finchley Common. I've never heard a human voice since, not in my right ear—although I've heard another Voice. The Still Small Voice that whispers to us all, if only we'll open our hearts to listen—it's always the right ear that hears. I mention this purely for information's sake, Brother Piper, and by way of asking you to speak into my left."

"I saw Joe Gummery."

It stopped him, for of course he hadn't seen Joe Gummery since the sentencing. They'd refused to let him in, even when he and his followers stood outside Newgate for two days and a night.

"You saw Young Joe?"

"Last night."

"How is he? Tell me!"

"Not well."

A flurry of exclamations. They clustered round.

"And why did you go to see him, Mr Piper?" demanded the younger Miss Sherwood, who had angled to stand beside O'Thunder. "To comfort him in his affliction, as the Lord commissions us to do?"

I told the truth. "I wanted to extract a confession."

Miss Sherwood's jaw clenched. O'Thunder himself looked confused, as if he could not at first connect such an answer to the question. "A *confession?*"

"But he wouldn't confess. He just—well, he carried on. Weeping, and whatnot."

More exclamations. O'Thunder had begun to understand.

"In other words, you set out to trick him—is that what you're saying, Brother Piper?"

"No, of course not! I mean, not precisely..."

"To bait him and badger him, and torment the words from his poor lips. Corkscrew them out, and then print them in your newspaper, for pieces of silver."

"All right, I—well, perhaps—but I wouldn't put it *that* way."

"And how would you put it, precisely? Because I want to be certain I'm understanding you, Brother Piper. I want to be very clear in my mind, for I don't want to do you an injustice."

"Look, what matters is, I think there may have been a terrible mistake. I think—"

Events grew momentarily chaotic. I saw the dark flush of fury on O'Thunder's face. There was a sensation of rising, and choking, and a dreadful impact. I discovered that my feet were kicking and dangling. This was owing to the fact that I had been hoisted by the windpipe and slammed back against the wall with a force that made the timbers shake and my teeth rattle.

Subsequent interviews with eyewitnesses confirmed my initial impression: Mr William Piper was pinioned two feet above the ground, his tongue protruding and his eyes bulging like eggs. His short legs pedalled furiously, while Captain O'Thunder held him in place with one hand. Several witnesses remarked upon this feat of strength, Mr Piper being, in the words of one, "no small slab of beef." But in the moment itself, my preoccupation was the wild look in O'Thunder's eyes. Not to mention the alarming size of O'Thunder's right fist, which was balled to smash my skull. I swear he'd have done it, too, if the younger Miss Sherwood hadn't wrapped herself round his bicep like a lemur clinging to a bough, crying: "No, Captain O'Thunder! No, for they'll hang you too!"

"Stop!" I croaked desperately. "I think he's innocent!"

At least, this is what I attempted to croak. What actually came out, I couldn't say. But after a moment the grip on my windpipe mercifully slackened. I discovered I was once more standing with my back to the wall, down which I now slid to sit weakly upon the seat of my trousers. I looked up, wheezing the breath back into my lungs.

O'Thunder gazed blackly down at me, still trembling with his anger. "What did you say?"

I managed to get the words out. "I think you're right—they're about to hang an innocent boy. He's begging to see you. I think I can arrange it. That's what I came to tell you."

For a moment, he seemed not to comprehend. He shook his great head from side to side, like a baited bear half maddened by his wounds. His eyes, still wild, found mine once more. I recognized them for what they were: the eyes of the most dangerous man I would ever meet.

They began to fill with tears.

"I must go to him, poor soul," he said. "For God's sake, brother, take me there."

IT WAS MIDNIGHT by St Sepulchre's clock as O'Thunder and I stood outside Newgate Prison. The turnkey peered out through the slitted opening in a thick oaken door, like the porter at Hell's Gate. Two shillings elicited nothing but a stony stare. But a third jarred loose the recollection that he had admitted me last night, and might conceivably do so again.

"But not that one," he muttered. The eyes peered past me to O'Thunder, who stood behind in the darkness.

"He's asked for me, brother," O'Thunder told him. "I must see him."

"Can't be done. Such an hour? Impossible."

"Dorcas sends her best regards," I said.

Dorcas was my mother's servant. She was also—following a recent chance encounter at a fishmonger's stall—the apple of the turnkey's eye. This was the talisman I had exploited to gain access the night before, and with luck it might prove sufficient again.

There was a moment's silence. "Tell Miss Dorcas, Waldron sends 'is regards in return."

I assured him I would certainly do so, immediately upon returning home.

"Tell Miss Dorcas, Waldron hinquired hafter Miss Dorcas's 'ealth."

"I'm glad to say her health is excellent."

"And tonight is four shillings."

I fetched out my last coin. There was the hollow rasp of a bolt being drawn back, and the door creaked open.

In the old days, by all accounts, Newgate Prison had been a fine old circle of Hell. Jammed to the gunwales with criminals of every stripe—the strong oppressing the weak, the vile contending for advantage with the merely venal. A teeming pit of treachery, misery, and vermin. It was less chaotic these days, but no less terrible. For Newgate was the last earthly home to London's condemned, awaiting their Monday morning appointment with Mr Calcraft.

We followed Waldron through the entry lodge. He was a man of five-and-thirty, a shambling party with a palsied eye. Or at least he seemed to have one, until you realized that those intermittent twitches were in fact mordant winks.

We passed a wall festooned with irons, including the set that had been used—or so tradition had it—upon Jack Sheppard himself, the highwayman and escape artist. "Oh, Mr Sheppard were quite the lad, were Mr Sheppard," Waldron was telling us. "Yes, escaped full 'alf a dozen times, did Mr Sheppard, cheating the 'angman on each and every hoccasion. On each and every hoccasion, gentlemen"—mordant wink—"except the last. This wye."

He led us down a winding stone corridor, eerily lit by sconces. Every few steps, it seemed, was another great wooden door, iron-bound and studded, to be closed with a hollow boom and locked behind us. With each door closing, I felt as if another breath of air had been stifled from me.

The corridor led past the Chapel, with the Condemned Pew in which the soon-to-die would receive his final Communion. In the old days, his freshly carpentered coffin would be placed beside him for the occasion—this to help him gather his thoughts, which might otherwise flutter in frivolous directions. Then through the Press Yard, and down a narrow staircase into another corridor, lined with cells. Waldron stopped before the last of these, and clanked through his various keys to find the one he wanted.

"This 'ere is where the Patient resides. Let's 'ope"—mordant wink—"we find 'im 'ome."

The door swung open onto a small stone dungeon, eight foot long by six foot wide. There was a small high window with a double-row of crossed iron bars. Below it the Printer's Devil huddled on the bench that was his only bit of furniture. Joe Gummery had been hysterical and wailing when I had left the night before—those terrible wails had pursued me down the corridor. But now he sat silent and drained and shackled. Thin and wretched to begin with, tonight he seemed less substantial still. In the fluttering light of his single stub of candle, he was so pale as to be almost opaque, as if he had already begun his awful journey from this world to the next.

O'Thunder stepped forward into the cell. The turnkey and I hung back, looking on from the shadows of the corridor. Joe Gummery raised his head, and a look of wonderment crept onto his face.

"Is it you, Cap'n? Is it you come to see me at last?"

He struggled to rise, but the shackles held him down.

"Hello, Young Joe," O'Thunder said. His high voice was husky, but somehow he dredged up a smile. "I've come indeed, to see you. I tried to come before now—I tried and tried, but they wouldn't let me in."

"But now you've come."

"I've come."

"And then you'll leave again?"

"I'll stay as long as I can, Young Joe."

"But you mustn't Cap'n, you mustn't stay, you must go quite soon. And when you leave you must take me with you. Please?"

Joe Gummery summoned a beseeching smile. He spoke with a forlorn earnest reasonableness, as if O'Thunder must surely see what a sensible idea this was.

"I'd love to do that, Young Joe. I'd love nothing better than to take you home with me—and I pray that I'll be able to do that, before very much longer. For we're fighting to free you, Young Joe—all of us, all your friends. We've been fighting all along, and we're fighting still."

Joe Gummery's forlorn smile faltered. "Perhaps you don't understand, Cap'n. Perhaps they haven't made it clear to you. If I stay here very much longer, they're going to hang me. They want to hang your poor Joe."

He cocked his head, desperately searching O'Thunder's expression for any sign that this had been understood. Like a dog trying forlornly to communicate mute distress. His face crumpled slowly, and he began to weep.

"It's all right, Young Joe." O'Thunder's voice was not quite steady. "There, there..."

"It's dark where I'm going, Cap'n. I'm afraid of the dark. Nothing but darkness when my candle dies, and look at it Cap'n, look at my candle, the last one I have and now it's burned down to nothing at all."

Such despair on a human face I hope I never see again. O'Thunder reached out a great paw, and put it on the boy's shoulder.

"Now, don't you worry, Young Joe. And don't cry, neither." For the boy had dissolved into desolate tears, moaning and rocking from side to side. "I'll see to those candles, Joe. I'll make sure you have all the candles you need—I'll pay for the candles, and this good fellow will bring them to you."

As he spoke, O'Thunder fished out a few coins. He turned and handed them to Waldron, standing by me in the corridor. The turnkey took on a shifty expression and opened his mouth. I suspect it had crossed his mind to imply that these particular coins were not quite up to the task at hand. But a savage look from O'Thunder persuaded him that he had been mistaken and they were entirely sufficient after all. So he clapped his mouth shut and inclined his head.

"There we are, Young Joe. That's your candles, taken care of. I'll be back tomorrow"—another dark glance to Waldron—"so I'll see those candles myself. I'll see that a candle is burning just as long as you remain in this place. So dry your eyes, Young Joe—that's the way—no more tears tonight. Dry your eyes, and we'll have a picnic, you and I, for look—we've brought a hamper."

I handed it to him. O'Thunder smiled still, but his hand shook as he opened the hamper and took out the treasures within.

"Here we are, Young Joe. Here's bread and cheese and wine—and something more." He fished out two of the big sticky buns that the bakewife had brought to the Academy. "These were baked specially for you, Young Joe. See? 'Save Joe,' they say—the one word written on top of the bun, and your name right there on the bottom. I don't have the letters like you do, Joe—I was never a clever lad, like yourself. But I know what these letters say, and I know they tell the truth, because Joe is going to be Saved—yes he is—you mark my words. If not in this world, then most certainly in the next."

Joe Gummery just wept.

"I didn't do it Cap'n, what they said. I didn't kill that girl, I never hurt her, I never hurt anyone."

"I know that, Young Joe. So do all your friends, and we're trying to convince the others. We've written a letter to the Queen herself—imagine that."

"He wanted me to do it. He told me to kill her but I wouldn't."

"Who told you, Young Joe? Who said such a thing?"

"The Devil." Joe Gummery looked up in anguish. The words came tumbling one after another. "He showed me a girl at the theatre, a whore, he told me she was low he wanted me to kill her but I wouldn't. I didn't touch her and I didn't touch that other girl, that poor girl lying in the alley. I was the one who found her Cap'n, that was me, I was hurrying to work and I found her. I knelt beside her and I tried to lift her head, that's how the blood was on my shirt. But I wasn't the one who killed her. They wouldn't believe me, they cried 'Stop murderer' and I ran but it wasn't me. It was someone else who did that—the Devil made someone else kill that poor girl—but now they're going to hang me Cap'n, they're going to hang your poor Young Joe. The Devil knows it too, and he's laughing Cap'n, the Devil laughs at me. I hear him laughing and it drives me mad, a horrible laugh rising up from beneath the stones because he knows he's got me now. He'll be waiting underneath the scaffold and he'll catch me by the ankles and drag me down!"

O'Thunder's face in the flickering candlelight had clenched at the mention of the Devil. It grew darker with every word Joe Gummery uttered. Now he knelt before the wretched boy.

"You don't need to fear the Devil, Joe—no, listen to me. The Devil can't touch you, because you're innocent."

Joe Gummery shook his head and moaned.

"I'm innocent of killing, but I've done other things. I've told lies, Cap'n, and stole things. I stole money from my master once, a Christian man who was always kind to me. I stole other things too, I stole pies from shops, and a handkerchief, and many times I had wicked thoughts in my heart, wicked horrible lustful thoughts."

"These aren't such dreadful sins, Young Joe. And besides, all you need to do is to repent."

"But I can't!" Joe Gummery burst out in abject despair. "I can't repent, because he won't let me pray. I try to lift my hands and pray but the Devil holds them down!"

Beside me in the corridor, Waldron rolled his eyes and twirled a sausage-fat finger by one ear. I had a strong urge to punch him. But instead I leaned forward into the circle of candlelight. Clearing my throat—somehow or other there seemed to be a lump—I hazarded a suggestion.

"Actually, I believe—look, it's not really the Devil, I don't think, holding down your hands. It's actually just the shackles..."

I don't think anyone heard me. I don't suppose this mattered much.

O'Thunder had taken Joe Gummery by both shoulders. His voice was hoarse, but it rang.

"Look at me, Joe. The Devil won't touch you—no, look at me—for I won't let him. Do you understand? If the worst comes to pass, then I'll be with you on Monday morning. I'll be right there with you, at the end. And another fellow will be with me, too. He's a far greater Fellow than I, Young Joe, and you're in His good hands. You're in His hands forever, for He never lets a single one of us go, so long as we truly repent with all our hearts. So that's what we'll do. We'll lift our hands and pray, the two of us. We'll pray together, and drive the Devil howling back down to the Pit. And there'll be such rejoicing in Heaven, Joe, for the angels themselves will cry out: 'Look, it's Young Joe Gummery, and he's on his way to join us!'"

THE HANGING WAS quicker than I'd expected, when the time finally came.

The whole world was outside Newgate, or so it seemed. We later estimated it at forty thousand. "We" being the gentlemen of the press, for of course I attended in my professional capacity. Why else would I have been there? Indeed, why else would I be anywhere? Eyes clear, heart uninvolved. Just the facts in good plain sturdy English words, penny apiece. So: forty thousand Londoners assembled on a fine morning in early autumn to watch a boy hang. The high and the low, the great and the small, parents and children. Look—an eager lad on his father's shoulders. Altogether an impressive turnout, though not as large as the crowd that had gathered to watch Mrs Manning hang in '49. Mrs Manning who'd poisoned her lover. She'd appeared on the platform in a black satin dress—and black satin dresses had promptly gone straight out of fashion, and never come back since. There you go: public hanging is highly influential.

I'd been outside O'Thunder's Academy since five-thirty AM, waiting. The streets were strangely clean at this time of morning, as if they had been washed down in the night. The air was scented with promise. At seven o'clock O'Thunder came out, with a dozen of his followers in grave procession. The Miss Sherwoods, dressed in black, with black bonnets. Moloch, whose name I had discovered was Tim Diggory, in his chimney-pot hat. They exclaimed in startled indignation when they saw me, but O'Thunder held up his hand. "No, let him come. Brother Piper is one of us."

I wasn't, of course—I was no such thing. I was accompanying them for professional reasons, and began to say so. But the others were already on the move, following O'Thunder south along the Gray's Inn Road. That spider-legged stride of his, torso slightly angled as if he was shouldering his way through a mighty wind. I huffed alongside.

Hangings were at eight o'clock. Upon the instant of the hour, St Sepulchre's bell began to toll. The vast crowd had been relaxed until this very moment—bizarrely so, chatting about this and the other. A man with a honking voice had been holding forth about the idiocy of Such-a-bill that Lord So-and-so had introduced. Festive jokes and ginger beer, and an old woman selling pies. But with the first sound of the bell there was an instant's hush, and then a dark rising murmur. The bodies, already closely packed, gave a surge. I had the suffocating sense that I could lift my feet and never fall, but be swept forward in the awful press. Forty thousand souls becoming one vast Being—a creature of no thought at all, but merely instinct.

And of course I wasn't sticking to O'Thunder's side for journalistic purposes. I just was terrified to be alone.

"Make way!"

O'Thunder's tenor cry rose above the clamour. And astoundingly they did—the mob fell back. I cannot swear to how it was, because the cobbles were somehow unstable beneath my feet. I hadn't gone home the previous night, having decided—or so I told myself—that the dawn came early, and the clarity of sleeplessness was better than the fog of an hour or two's slumber. So a lengthy session at the Dog had led to a night house or two or three. A dram too many, perhaps, because the morning had begun to swim about me. I seemed to see a pathway parting, as through the Red Sea. O'Thunder surged forward, and I stumbled after.

The tolling bell echoed away into silence—and nothing. A moment in which it seemed possible that nothing would happen at all, and no one would come. Joe Gummery had been reprieved, or else had hanged himself already in his cell. Then dark figures, ascending the platform. The sheriffs first, and the Prison Ordinary, then a small figure—a lad. Limbs like sticks, hands pinioned in front, white as marble.

"It's him—the Printer's Devil!"

"Hats off!"

"Down in front!"

He wore a pitiful smile, and a wild imploring look. He was facing the clock, but a sheriff took him by the shoulders and turned him towards Ludgate Hill.

The noise from the crowd—I had never heard such a sound. I hope I never hear it again. A shriek and a rising roar, with a horrible metallic jangling noise mixed in. I have no idea whence it issued—human throats? And there was old Calcraft: hoary-headed, ancient, rheumy eyes blinking in the morning sun. He'd begun his long career by flogging boys and now here he was, Her Majesty's Hangman, in all his doddering incompetence. A man at the Dog last night had said: watch below. The old fool won't drop him far enough to break the neck. But he'll go down below to the pit, Calcraft, and if the strangling goes on too long you'll see his hands reaching up through the trap, and tugging on the ankles.

"I'm here, Young Joe! Here I am!"

Calcraft had the white nightcap in his hand, but in that last moment Joe had seen O'Thunder. We were in the suffocating press of humanity directly beneath the scaffold, gazing up.

"I'll be with you, Young Joe," he had promised that night in the cell. "I want you to look at me, just as long as you can, and know that I'm still there even when the darkness comes. I'll help you pray, and I want you to lift your hands, as a sign. They'll be bound, Young Joe, your hands—they'll bind your poor hands, but if you lift them even half an inch then I'll know, that you've reached out to Him and He's forgiven your sins and it's all right."

O'Thunder shouted the words now, his eyes locked onto Joe's: "Our Father, who art in—pray with me, Joe!—our Father, who art in Heaven..."

Joe's lips twitched—drained of blood, they moved. Or perhaps they didn't. Perhaps it was a trick of the shadow as the nightcap came down over his face. The halter round the neck, and then attached to the black chain dangling from the centre crossbeam.

Forty thousand faces in the mob. Faces cramming every window opposite, faces on the rooftops. A man had clambered up a gas pipe and looked down from a shelf. In the window below, an odd tableau: a tall dark man in an old-fashioned Regency coat, and beside him a slip of a girl with a blaze of red hair, in a preposterous gay little hat with a feather. The girl distressed, raising a hand to cover her eyes. The tall man smiling thinly, catching her wrist.

The flag went up. The crash of the bolt, the clatter of the trap, and a vast cry of rage and horror and joy, wrenched from forty thousand throats. A lad choking his life out, with his feet kicking at old London Town. But in the instant before the trap had fallen, Joe Gummery had raised his pinioned hands an inch.

I didn't watch anymore—but I knew what I'd already seen. Seen in that creature of forty thousand faces, and heard in that vast inhuman cry. I said so to O'Thunder, after it was all over—after the crowd had dispersed, and the body been taken down, and Wm. Piper had finished spewing upon the cobbles. We sat on a low stone wall across the square, with the ragged crew about us.

"I saw the Devil," I said. I was still shaking like a leaf, and deciding that a second spew might be required.

"So did I," said Daniel O'Thunder.

He sat with his shoulders slumped. Head hanging, drained by the ordeal. He looked somehow very old, and haunted.

"I saw the Devil this morning," I repeated. "Metaphorically speaking."

"The Devil was here—but he didn't catch Young Joe. Did you see? Joe raised his hands at the last—he prayed with me. The Devil snatched at Young Joe's ankles, but he couldn't drag him down."

His followers exchanged uncertain looks.

"That were the 'angman, Captain," said Tim Diggory. "Them were Calcraft's 'ands you saw, reaching up from hunderneath."

"I'm not talking about the hangman, Tim," said O'Thunder. "I'm talking about the Devil. He was bested this morning, but he'll be back—and it's up to me to put a stop to this."

A look of desperate resolve had settled upon O'Thunder's face. His right hand clenched in a fist.

"Someone find John Thomas for me. Go and find John Thomas Rennert."

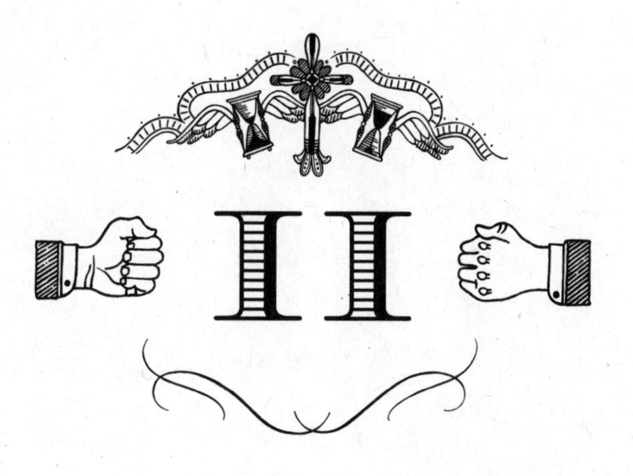

· OCTOBER, 1851 ·

JAUNTY

I'D MET DANIEL for the first time in the summer of 1833. We began by getting him roaring drunk.

That's how the thing is done, when you're recruiting soldiers. You march into some little town, a Recruiting Sergeant and a few select companions. There's a drummer with you, for nothing stirs the blood like the flams and the paradiddles, and oh you're a fine sight. You're wearing red coats and you all have the most wonderful whiskers. Straight you march to the nearest tavern, where you stand a few drinks and tell a few tales of adventure and derring-do. When the time is right—when some clodpoll is reeling with gin and excitement—then it's out with the King's shilling. Slap it down on the table, and who's-for-the-life-of-a-hero.

Well, Daniel snatched the shilling up. Fifteen years old, straight out of the potato field and up to his shins in mud, a great gangling beautiful lad. And having snatched the shilling up, he slapped it right back down again and stood us drinks, for such was the spirit he had. A bog-ignorant gulpin who couldn't even write his name—he made an X on the recruiting contract, and I stood witness—with no more sense of tomorrow than a starling has. But such a spirit that you couldn't help but love him, a joyful laughing spirit such as I'd never encountered before, and don't suppose I'll ever meet again. In the morning he woke up with his head like a pumpkin and realized what he'd done. He looked sick for all of half a second, and then he laughed out loud. He said there was nothing for it, and besides he had no family to speak of, excepting an uncle who would probably forgive him if his head were blown off, and some cousins who wouldn't mind at all. In fact, they'd probably decide this was the best use a head such as his could be put to.

"So it appears," said young Daniel to me, "that we'll be having adventures."

"It appears," I replied, "that you're correct."

Both of us grinning like schoolboys. When we marched off an hour later, he was wearing a red coat three sizes too small, and carrying a Brown Bess musket, and whistling "Garryowen," as British soldiers have done for generations. Five years after that, we were in Afghanistan together, and not long afterwards... but let that be for now. We won't discuss that yet.

Let me just say that I always liked him. I probably loved him, even, in the way a man loves a comrade. I can't claim I ever really understood him, though. Just when you thought you had the hang of Daniel O'Thunder, he'd slip away on you again, like water through your fingers.

And now here it was, October of 1851. We were setting off on our strangest adventure of all.

"I SPEAK AS your friend. I speak as one who wishes you nothing but well. And the fact of it is, you are blubber-headed."

"I am no such thing."

"Daniel," said I, "don't contradict."

With a pleasing *pock,* another well-aimed rock rebounded from his cheekbone.

"John Thomas, I give you fair warning. If you continue throwing whoreson rocks at my head, I will not be answerable for the consequences."

"Then pick up those feet. Look at you—you're waddling like a washer-woman."

"That's because I'm tired, you villain."

"It's because you're fat. You are corpulent, big-bellied, and full of gross humours. You are short-breathed and your skin is all wrong. And to top it off, you're blubber-headed."

Pock.

Daniel turned a brighter shade of scarlet, and questioned my ancestry.

"For shame, Daniel. Is that spoken like a Christian? Remember your religion, and your dignity."

Though all things considered, the dignity would have to wait for another day. He was toiling on foot through the trees up a bleak Essex hillside, while I stayed just ahead of him on horseback. Lobster-faced and puffing like a steam engine, was Daniel. He belched great clouds into the frigid air. He wore two coats and a vest and three shirts underneath, which gave him the bloated appearance of a four-days-old corpse dredged up from the Thames, and he had a towel tied round his head like a Hindoo.

"For we must sweat the head, Daniel," I told him. "When extra weight lies about the chops, the man is seen to be blubber-headed. And when the man is blubber-headed, that blubbery head must sweat."

Pock.

This was in fact a time-honoured training technique. It had been invented by the great Captain Barclay, while training Cribb for his first legendary battle against Molyneaux. Captain Barclay had taken the old champion up into the Scottish Highlands for three months, running him over hills and heather, and encouraging him to greater efforts with a leather pouch full of smooth Scottish stones.

"For Cribb was very much like you are yourself, Daniel. He was a fine fellow, but a fat blubber-headed oaf, and needed to pick his bloody feet up."

Pock.

With a great bull's roar of rage, Daniel broke into a lumbering gallop. I gave my nag a nudge and we trotted on ahead.

THE BOWELS, the lungs, and the skin: that is where the science of training begins, and where it ends. Some day, when I have time, I may write a monograph. You'd be shocked at the degree of ignorance that abounds, to the ruination of many a good fighting man. I repeat: bowels, lungs, and skin. If your man is superior in each of these, then he has his chance to win.

You build from the bottom up, meaning start with the bowels. Three weeks of salts and emetics, the dosage calculated just so, for our goal is to evacuate the man completely without actually killing him. In those first weeks of training I had to remind Daniel of this principle on numerous occasions, as piteous groans and dark oaths came issuing through the door of the privy. Daniel was always a great complainer during training.

"You've poisoned me! You villain, I've no insides left at all."

"You must take your medicine like a man," I would tell him. "Otherwise you'll be taking your medicine from Spragg the Ruffian, and I'm afraid you'll find he dispenses bitter physick indeed."

"I'm dying, John Thomas. You've killed me. You'll hang for this."

"We must prime those bowels, Daniel. That's how Tom Cribb triumphed over Molyneaux. I was there at the match. I was just a lad, but I was there and I'm here to tell you now—the American overmatched our Tom. It's the truth. Molyneaux was the better man in wind, and activity, and strength of sinew, and even pure science—for Molyneaux was a scientific miller, Daniel, despite he was a great black heathen, though I never say a word against the colour of a man's outside, for it's what's inside that counts. And inside Molyneaux that day was unprimed bowels."

"You horrible whoreson ginger-headed—ooohhhhhhhhh! Both ends at once!"

"And you'll thank me for it soon enough."

Next, of course, you must feed your man, and build him up again. You do this with meat, always meat, never vegetables, which are watery and bad for digestion. Beef and mutton chops are best, taken from full-grown animals, and boiled. Bread is acceptable in small quantities, but only bread that is day-old, and *never* bread that is London-baked. It's the alum in London bread, and the yeast. They shrink the alimentary canal, and may close it completely, with consequences too dismal to be described. Beer of course is the recommended beverage for a pugilist in training, with a glass or two of wine at meals.

On this point Daniel was implacable.

"John Thomas, take the tankard away. Bring me good cold water, drawn from the well."

I attempted reason. "No good has ever come from the drinking of water. This is scientifically proven."

He regarded me with quiet reproach. "You knew me, John Thomas, in the days when I did not drink water."

True. A pause, and a flicker of memory. A strapping young Irish infantryman with a head of golden curls, reeling and roaring on the ran-tan, dismantling the premises of a landlord who had declined further service. Other memories as well, some of them considerably more unsettling.

"Water it is," I conceded.

Next you must exercise your man. Captain Barclay would begin by sending Cribb off each morning with a fowling-piece, and the woods would ring with gunfire for the first two weeks of training. Once your man can walk twenty miles without being blown, then he must run: four miles in the morning, and another four miles in the afternoon, to build his wind. Other manly forms of exercise are also excellent, such as chopping wood and brushing down a horse and playing leapfrog—but never dancing, for dancing involves women, bless their hearts, which leads a man in training to a.) Notions, and consequently b.) Ruin. While building your man's wind, you must simultaneously attend to his skin. It must be smooth, elastic, and transparent—that's when you'll know he is trained up properly. Wash him daily, with soap. Rub him down with coarse linen. This will properly open the pores, through which the fat will chiefly be evacuated during sweating, particularly the fat that hangs about the kidneys, intestines, ribs, and heart.

Finally, sparring. We erected a makeshift ring in a grassy hollow half a mile or so from the village, fringed on three sides by trees, where we might undertake our preparations in private. At first I served as Daniel's partner myself, for although undersized I had been a miller of nimble feet and some small scientific capability in bygone regimental days. We wore mufflers, of course, for you never sparred bare-knuckled. Bare knuckles were strictly for the mill itself. I took great care to remain just out of range, nipping in to plant a facer and then dodging back to safety while Daniel flailed like a baited bear, for the timing of his blows was all in a ruin. All the while I exhorted him with encouragements, such as, "look at you, wallowing about like a great fat blubber-headed pig—oh, won't the Ruffian enjoy his bacon." This continued for some days, until a ball from a sixteen-pounder came whistling from I-have-no-idea-where. Following the explosion there was a period of incoherence, emerging woozily from which I found myself lying sprawled against a tree-stump with the songbirds singing and Daniel's mug peering down at me.

"Are you alive, John Thomas?" He sounded concerned, though perhaps not quite so keenly as I might have preferred.

"I believe my jawbone may be broken, Daniel, in three or four places."

"Then perhaps, John Thomas, you should give your jawbone a rest."

I did so, after first calling for Tim Diggory.

Tim had come up from London for the purpose of sparring with Daniel once this crucial juncture in his training had been reached—this being the juncture at which Daniel's timing had improved, leaving Jaunty's head in danger of coming clear off Jaunty's shoulders. For say what you like about Daniel O'Thunder: despite his flaws, as a miller and as a man—and God knows he had his share on both counts—Daniel O'Thunder could strike a blow. Even with the mufflers on, he could bring down the walls of a city.

With a week remaining before the match, he could run a mile at his top speed—not that Daniel's top speed was anything much. Daniel did not, shall we say, slash forward as a corvette upon a wind-swept sea. Daniel was rather a ship-of-the-line: heaving ponderously into view on the horizon, and then more or less remaining there, while onlookers tapped their toes and consulted their tickers and peered through their spyglasses and wondered, "Is it actually moving at all?" But once in motion a ship-of-the-line is relentless—and oh, those great guns firing and recoiling and then firing again. Each time I approached the sparring ring, I half expected to find a cloud of smoke overhanging, which would gradually clear to reveal Tim Diggory's arm draped over the rope, and his leg lying beside the pond, and his head rolled up against the corner-post. But if so, there'd have been a great glassy smile frozen onto Tim's dead phizog, for he worshipped the very ground on which Daniel walked. He received the blows like St Sebastian welcoming his arrows, until a final volley of punches killed Tim dead.

At least I was afraid it had, for he dropped like a felled ox, and did nothing for quite some time but twitch. But after some slapping and exclaiming and a bit of brandy up the nose, he came round—to our very great relief—and abjectly apologized.

"Orful sorry, Daniel. Just give us a minute. Orrible sorry. Right as rain."

We were carrying him back to the inn, at this point. Tim's head was swollen up like mumps. Both of his glims were battered shut, and his knob of a nose was an inch or two west of where it had begun the morning.

“’Alf a minute,” said Tim, and spit out a tooth. “Back up on me trotters. Finish the session.”

That’s what pugilism does: it brings out the best in a man. I said so to Daniel afterwards. First we got poor Tim settled on the couch and wrapped up his ribs, for it turned out a few of them had been a bit broken. Then we went out again.

“Pugilism brings out the best in a man’s character, Daniel. It brings out courage, and humanity, and greatness of spirit. And it slays me, the way they’ve outlawed the sport.”

We were walking along a country lane, the two of us, in the quiet of an Essex evening. The day had been unexpectedly warm, and the sun was just descending behind the hills. I had a small bottle of brandy in my hand, as a precaution against chills. I had taken several pre-emptive swallows already, and was waxing philosophical.

“Pugilism is what makes this nation great. They don’t have pugilism on the Continent, Daniel—or at least, they don’t embrace it, as we do—and you can see what results. For what does your Frenchman or your Spaniard do when he has a grievance? Why, it’s the dirk in the hand, and skulking down the alleyway, and cowardly backstabbing murder. Every last one of them has a knife, tucked inside his shirt or hidden in his boot. They’re steeped in treachery, Daniel, and it’s all because they’ve been raised without pugilism. But when two Englishmen have a grievance, then it’s all the difference in the world. It’s face to face and fist against fist. It’s manly blows and stout courage, Daniel, and none of this Continental rib-sticking. And when it’s over and done, then more often than not it’s the shaking of hands and the purchasing of drinks on either side, and two fast friends forever after. It makes me proud to be an Englishman, Daniel—and I include the Irish in this too, and the Welsh of course, and even the Scots. It makes my heart swell up with pride—just as you shall make hearts swell on Saturday.”

I discovered that my sparklers had gone misty. Apparently I’d worked myself up to a bit of a pitch. “You’re going to make us proud, Daniel. For you're going to thrash the Ruffian, and bring him to right-thinking, and inspire him to mend his wicked ways."

BUT THERE WAS the question, wasn't it? The question upon which so very much depended, including Jaunty's future prospects and quite possibly Jaunty's neck: *could* Daniel O'Thunder lick Spragg the Ruffian, at thirty-three years old and a decade removed from the prize-ring? For there was nothing else for it—this fight was on the up and up, and the man left standing would be the best man. Daniel had set those terms at the outset.

"There's no one sold and nothing purchased, John Thomas," he had cried, thumping his fist upon a table. "I want you to make a match for me, but I want it on the square. This is not to be a cross."

This had been a month or so earlier. Tim Diggory had tracked me down, and dragged me back to that ridiculous Academy, where Daniel was pacing.

It was night. We were alone in the room, save for two or three ragged hulks snoring in a corner. Daniel was distracted and dishevelled, and my first stomach-sinking thought was: back on the blue ruin. But it wasn't gin at all. He was just fearfully upset about that boy they'd hung, though how a hanging required the resumption of Daniel's prize-fighting career was something I was not quite clear on. Only later did I understand that it all connected somehow with standing up to the Devil and calling souls to Jesus, which is the sort of realization as will make a trainer swallow hard, and call up a brave smile, and think quietly to himself: ah well, no matter if he's mad as Bedlam, so long as he keeps punching.

"I mean it, John Thomas." He veered back to the table and thump went the fist again, even harder. "If the mill turns out to be a cross, I'll have nothing more to do with you."

"Daniel sets the terms," said I, "and Jaunty accepts them."

My hand was upon my heart, but the cranial gears were turning. So the task was to choose the proper opponent—"proper" meaning one who would put on an acceptable show before falling down like a good lad, and neglecting to mention that he'd been bought, for it takes two to make a mill but only one to make a cross.

"And if you've bought the other man," said Daniel grimly, "then I'll know it."

He'd brought his face in close, six inches from mine.

"Even if I don't know it for a certainty, I'll suspect. And if a suspicion crosses my mind, John Thomas—if it so much as flutters like a moth at the window—then I'll denounce you right there in the ring. I'll wash my hands just like Pilate washing his hands of Our Lord, John Thomas, only you won't be the Lamb of God. You'll be an old sharper a-standing there on his lonely in the green faerie circle, with the crowd he's duped staring back at him. And we know what happens next, don't we?"

Yes, we did.

"You've made your point," I said, with a plucky smile and a sinking heart. "Fair and square. May the best man win, and Devil take the hindmost."

THE HORRID POSSIBILITY existed that the hindmost would turn out to be Jaunty himself, whose financial difficulties—already mentioned—were bad and getting worse. For of course my whole dodge depended on Daniel winning the first few mills. But for the past eight weeks, he had actually trained.

If you'd predicted this, I'd have scoffed. If you'd said, "Jaunty, your old friend will accompany you to Darkest Essex, where he will rise at cock-crow every morning for eight weeks, and lumber over hill and dale, and chop wood and spar and sweat the blubber right off his head," I'd have laughed out loud. I'd have said: "Friend, you mistake me for a fool. I have known Daniel O'Thunder man and boy for nearly twenty years. I have trained him on numerous occasions, each one more dismal than the last. For Daniel's idea of training is to eat and drink and sing and be joyful, and then to be drunk and obstropolous and assault someone, frequently a constable, and upon his release from the spike hotel to moan and spew and then drink a great deal more, with time out for taking the barmaid down the back alley for a knee-trembler, and her sister at the same time, if she has one."

But damn me, this time the man had actually trained. I told them so the night before the mill. We were jammed into the taproom of the Plough, the country inn where Daniel and I had been staying these past weeks. It was rough diggings, but commensurate shall we say with current financial realities, and besides there are worse things than fleas in the bed. The taproom itself was as salubrious as a stable, with straw and sawdust on the floor and hams hanging from low rafters overhead. If they hadn't been smoked to begin with, they certainly were now, for a pall of blue smoke hung over us, thick as a London Particular fog. Like country taprooms everywhere, it was the natural habitat of unwashed men with curious humps and lumps and squints, and far fewer teeth than they'd started with. I ignored these, and addressed myself to the Quality wedged in amongst 'em.

"Gentlemen, he's in prime twig. I've never seen him in such fighting trim—and I wouldn't say that unless I meant it."

"Of course you would, haw-haw." The Honourable Alfred Duckworth brayed like an amiable well-bred donkey, and looked round for approval. "You'd say any deyvlish thing at all, if it suited you."

Duckworth was the sprig of minor gentry somewhere in Norfolk. But he was worth five thousand a year, God bless him, and loved to wager. Best of all, he was an imbecile, as eager to be liked as a Labrador puppy. He'd arrived an hour earlier with his usual flock of chinless cronies and tuft-hunting hangers-on. Late this afternoon, the sporting crowd began arriving from London—the Fancy, as we called ourselves—by the dozens at first and then the hundreds. For I had been right—O'Thunder was remembered, and the story was a good one, and there was interest in this battle.

I'd been cultivating Alfred Duckworth lately, and had actually tried—without success—to convince him to put up the fifty guineas as O'Thunder's half of the prize. The Ruffian's backers had in turn put up fifty guineas for their share—winner to take all—for such was the way these things worked. It actually mattered little to the backers which man won. The prize was small beer compared to the betting that would go on, and they could just as easily bet against their man as for him. I had pointed all of this out to Duckworth, but he had turned me down all the same, the scrub, thus forcing me with grave misgivings to seek the money elsewhere.

"Seriously now, Jaunty. Tell me the truth, ye deyvil, and enough of your eyebrow-waggling. D'ye think he has any chance at all?"

"Yes," I said. "I do."

I may almost have meant it.

"Then let's have a flutter upon it," drawled another voice.

It was a crony of Duckworth's, a party with a permanent sneer and a shock of premature silver in his hair. I recollected his name was Soames—one of those superior young nobs who goes up to Oxford a twat and comes down worse three years later. He had just arrived on the fringes of the group, with his usual air of boredom, and two or three companions. One of these had turned away to say something over his shoulder, but it seemed to me there was something familiar about him. A young man of five- or six-and-twenty, flushed with drink and unsteady on his feet. He might almost have been dashing if he'd had a bit more chin. There was a wing of brown hair falling over one eye and a horseshoe-shaped scar by the other.

But Soames was talking, and the subject was coin of the realm. I gave him my full attention.

"What do you say?" he asked, eyeing me down his nose. "Put a pynde or two upon your man?" Like many of his species he strangled his vowels at birth.

I hesitated. Faith is one thing, but finance is another. Soames smirked.

"Haw," he said. "There's a trainer who trusts his man."

"A pound it is, then," I said stoutly. "A pound on Daniel O'Thunder."

"Haw to you, Soames!" exclaimed Duckworth, and looked round for approval of this witticism. "Haw right back to Soamesie, eh? Haw, haw, haw."

Soames ignored him. "I'll tell you what, though. Why don't we say ten pynde, just to make it interesting? I wager ten pynde on the Ruffian, and I'll give you two-to-one."

What's a man to do, save play the carefree lad and flash the ivories?

"Done."

I spat on my palm and extended my hand with as much bravado as I could scrape together in the circumstances, which were not—let's be honest—ideal. To begin with this was ten pounds more than I possessed, and a great deal less than I owed. Besides, the chin-deficient young man had turned, and now he saw me. He gave a little start and peered closer, bleary with drink. I was now almost certain I had seen him before, and—oh Christ.

The one from the Nag and Fish. The young fellow with the silver snuff-box.

From the look on his face, he had recognized me too. This meant we were about to have one of those dreary conversations that begin with accusations and end in "Constable!" Fortunately, I have always been fleet of thought. By the time his mouth was opening, I had remembered a prior engagement and was legging it quick-sticks out of the door.

ALL THINGS CONSIDERED, a stolen snuff-box was the least of my problems. I was a man who had just fluttered ten pounds on a failed fighter who hadn't been in a prize-ring for nearly a decade. But damn it all, I *did* believe O'Thunder had a chance, especially since the Ruffian had flaws of his own—great gaping flaws you could drive a coach-and-four through. Besides, your friend John Thomas Rennert had not just fallen from the back of a turnip-wagon. He had in fact taken certain important precautions as recently as that very afternoon. Now Jaunty made his way through the night—a filthy one it was, for the record; cold and blowing and promising worse for tomorrow—and across the village to the Viking Arms.

The Viking Arms was a country inn like the Plough: taproom below, squalor above, vermin laid on at no extra charge. It took its name from the village's sole claim to fame, which was that it happened to lie just down the road from Maldon. This was where they had the first great battle in English history, back in 900-and-whatnot. I always took an interest in these things, having been a military man myself, and keen on strategy. The English army massed to meet a horde of Viking invaders from Norway. Getting it right for a change, their generals had 'em positioned on this side of a land bridge across the Blackwater River. The Vikings squawked it wasn't fair, since they were getting cut to ribbons as they tried to come over. This gave the English leader, Byrhtnoth, his cue to call back: "That's the whole point! What sort of scrub do you think I am?" But instead he agreed, and gave 'em free passage, after which the Vikings cut *him* to ribbons, thus proving what happens when you violate Jaunty's First Rule of martial strategy and life in general: Do Not Be A Scrub.

It was according to this rule that I'd sent Sally Grindle over to the Viking Arms an hour earlier, with half a guinea in her plump little hand and instructions to slip past the Ruffian's trainer, who wouldn't be pleased to see her. Sally was the daughter of the landlord at the Plough. She wasn't strictly speaking a professional, but she had a fine enthusiasm, God bless the little dollymop, and a certain appeal about her in that Olde Englyshe bullock-buttocked sort of way. So you can imagine my dismay when I found her sitting spraddle-legged on the bottom stair, instead of upstairs where she was supposed to be, with an air of dishevelled grievance.

"What am I doing here?" she retorted, in answer to my query. "He chucked me out, the son of a bitch, is what I'm doing here!

He tells me to clear off ye fecken draggletail is what I'm doing here, and when I sez there's no need for sich language he kicks me in the arse!"

"Boston Bob did that?" I was genuinely stunned, for this wasn't like Bob McCorkindale at all.

"Not the trainer. The other one—that fecken fighter!"

This was more stunning still. "You offered your charms to Spragg the Ruffian, and Spragg the Ruffian *kicked* you?"

She looked at me with such contempt, I marvel to this day that I survived. In those glims gleamed all the loathing that women have felt for men since Eve worked out the snake had been making things up.

"Are you an eedjit, Jaunty? You got a brain at all, in that pimple? I JIST SED."

I found them upstairs. The Ruffian was sprawled across the bed like a newly slaughtered hog awaiting the boiling-off of bristles. My first thought was a happy one: dead drunk. Spragg had often been known to drink his way through training, especially with a bit of encouragement here and there. He'd been known to dissipate his strength on whores, to the despair of his friends, for there is nothing more disastrous to training than sexual conversation. And where sexual conversation was concerned, Spragg the Ruffian had scarcely paused for breath since that day when as a lad he had looked out into his father's barnyard and noticed the goats. On top of that, he was a glutton beyond all reason. He'd been known to step into the ring on the day itself with two fowls, three pies, and a quart of porter sloshing about in his belly. But he opened one porcine ogle, and—damn the luck—that eye was clear.

"I expect yer fink yer clever," growled the Ruffian.

I did, normally, for I was. Clever, I mean. But perhaps not quite so clever at the moment.

"Spragg," I said. "You look well."

He looked horribly well. Leastways he did for a black-bristling bacon-faced bruiser—the last thing I was expecting. They had been training down south somewhere, Spragg and Boston Bob, and had just arrived today. Boston Bob was sat in a straight-backed chair by the window, reading a book.

"H'lo, Bob," I said. "You look well too. Are you well, Bob?"

"Tolerable."

"I rejoice to hear it."

Boston Bob McCorkindale was old and black and gnarled. He was also one of three natural gentlemen in the whole British prize-fighting game—and I forget the names of the other two.

"How's the girl?" asked Bob, looking up from his book.

"What girl?"

Bob directed a look over the top of his half-moon spectacles. I sighed.

"The girl as is sitting outside, Bob? Well, she's a bit bitter, just at the moment. I won't lie to you about that. She has grievance in her heart and an ache beneath her."

Bob shot a look of reproach towards the Ruffian, who ignored it.

Boston Bob was American, from the Carolinas, somewhere—or so I'd been told. Bob never said much about himself, or about anything else for that matter. He'd been a slave, and the fat pink massah had fought him against slaves from other plantations, promising him his freedom when he won a victory over some particular terror of the South. Or else the massah had just pocketed his winnings and beamed and broken his pledge, after which Bob escaped on his own, which actually seems a good deal more likely—fat pink massahs being fat pink massahs, and Bob being smart as a whip. One way or another, Bob made his way north to Boston and sailed to England. He'd fought for nearly fifteen years—quite a feat for anyone, considering how many prize-fighters were stumbling hulks at twenty-five, and dead not long past thirty. In Bob's case it was astonishing, since he never tipped the scales at more than ten stone, and was often matched against men who outweighed him by fifty pounds. Now that he was retired from the ring he earned his bread by training other fighters. He was as good a trainer as I had ever met, in his own quiet way, for Bob was a man who never used two words when a grunt would do the job.

I liked him immensely. I'd like to think he liked me back, even though he knew me for what I was.

"Would that be *Pickwick,* Bob?" I asked, indicating the dog-eared book in his hands.

"'Twould."

"Enjoying it?"

"Am."

Bob had taught himself to read late in life, and had done so by reading *The Pickwick Papers.* I heard it took him three years the first time through, slogging ahead with a crooked finger underneath each syllable and his tongue clamped bechuxt his pearly whites. When he finally finished, he decided to start again, to see if there'd been enjoyment missed in all the tongue-clamping. Second time through he'd discovered it was the most wonderful book he could imagine, so he decided he'd just stick with *Pickwick* and read it over and over, instead of risking disappointment elsewhere. Boston Bob had a single-mindedness about him.

"His Lordship was askin' after you."

This gave me an unpleasant turn, though of course you couldn't say it was unexpected. "His Lordship? When?"

"Week ago. Last time I seen him.

"You mean he isn't here?"

"Not yet.

"Then he isn't coming?"

"Might be comin'. Might not. Who knows? It's His Lordship."

Parsimonious as he was with words, Bob had looks that would sing arias. His glance was singing one now, the gist being that getting mixed up with the likes of His Lordship was something that Bob himself would not consider—Bob possessing sense—but that he would nonetheless forebear telling Jaunty his business, and if needs must could be counted on to send flowers to the funeral.

His Lordship had put up the fifty guineas for Daniel's share of the purse. I'd turned to him as a last resort, for Bob's unsung aria had a point, unfortunately. His Lordship was a man you wanted to avoid, even at the best of times. And if the whole dodge were to go sideways, then the very thought of seeing him brought on the ice-cold collywobbles.

I shot another glance towards the Ruffian, feeling wobblier in the collies by the second.

"Your man's been training," I said to Bob, and tried to sound breezy.

"Has."

"Impressive."

But mainly alarming. And why, since the Ruffian had never trained up proper in his life? Why the devil should he start now, except to thwart John Thomas Rennert and bring him to the brink of ruination? And what did Jaunty ever do to deserve this?

The Ruffian had his ogle open again—both of them, this time. He hoisted his bulk up onto one elbow, and glared pure malevolence.

"Tell that preacher," snarled Spragg, "that Boston Bob ent the only man here present who can read. So I saw what he said in that newspaper, didn't I? About how he's gonny bring me to my knees, and make me wail and blubber for my wicked ways, and pray for Jesus to have mercy on my soul."

My heart sank, as I recalled the article in question. It had indeed twisted Daniel's sentiments into something so sanctimonious you wanted to fry them up with catshit and feed 'em back to him for breakfast.

"I think what Daniel actually meant—"

"You tell 'im from me. Tomorrow afternoon, at one-clock, there'll be wailing and blubbering a-plenty, yes there will, and grovelling about on the marrow-bones. But it's gonny to be the wails of Daniel O'Thunder. Now clear out, and take yer fecken basket with yer."

For evidently someone had sent a wicker hamper to the room. It contained two fowls, three pies, and a quart of porter.

I DRANK THE PORTER myself, back at our verminous attic ken at the Plough. The din of revelry resounded from the public house below.

"I'm afraid you've got his dander up, Daniel. Now we have a fight on our hands."

"By the grace of Our Lord," said Daniel.

I loved Daniel O'Thunder like a brother, but God help us he said some ridiculous things. He'd always been like that. One time—this was years earlier, regimental days—one time he told me he'd seen God Almighty looking in at him, through the window.

I'd needed a minute to take this on board. "What, just now?" I asked, a little bit startled. We were in a brothel near the Liverpool docks, at the time. On the morrow we were to set sail upon a troop-ship bound for the ends of the earth, so tonight was one last fling with foul English gin and worse English whores. In short it was not the sort of establishment where you'd expect to meet the Ancient of Days.

"This was when I was a lad, John Thomas. I looked at the window, and there was the Lord looking back at me."

Well, you have to ask the question. "What did he look like?"

For the longest time Daniel didn't answer. I wondered if he hadn't heard, or if his thoughts had already gone dancing off with the faeries. For that was always Daniel, too. He'd be laughing and talking, for oh my Daniel could talk—words soaring out of him like flocks of swallows, wheeling and darting—but then his eyes would glaze and you'd know the faeries had took him. Or who knows? Maybe it was the angels.

"He looked disappointed," said Daniel at last. Such sadness pooling in his eyes, I couldn't think of a single word to say.

But tonight—these many long years later, in our verminous little room at the Plough—Daniel was smiling. He sat by the single window, looking out. His face was pale in the moonlight, and the old ragged scar showed purple on his brow. The scar from the cut the Battersea Gardener had given him that day ten years previous, just before Daniel went face down in the mud like a toppling tree, and stayed there.

"We came here for a fight, John Thomas. A good fair fight between two strong men, and may the best man be left standing at the end. That's what we came for, and that's what we want."

I thought, wearily: no, it is not. What I wanted was a cross, with the Ruffian standing in for ten minutes to make it look square before choosing six feet of Essex ground to stretch himself out on. Failing that, I wanted a seventeen-stone blubber-headed Ruffian, puffing like a locomotive. Because what I wanted most of all—what I *needed*—was a second fight for Daniel O'Thunder. If the worst came to the worst, I could make a few quid betting against him tomorrow. But that wouldn't be enough.

"No," said Daniel, as if he could read my thoughts. "It would never be enough."

His smile had faded. "The work I was doing—my work in London—it would never have been enough, at all. It was helping the poor and the afflicted, John Thomas, as the Lord enjoins us to do. It was doing all that, and reaching out to drowning souls. But in the end it was hopeless. It was trying to hold out against a siege. It was tending to the lambs with a pack of wolves circling. Each day growing weaker while the Devil grew stronger and bolder, and snatched them away one by one. I finally saw that clear when he snatched at poor Young Joe. So I must take the battle to him, John Thomas. I must go straight at him, with all the world watching."

The attic roof sloped down at the window, making Daniel sit hunched like a man at prayer. His eyes were fixed upon some unknowable point in the darkness, and his huge hands were balled into fists upon either knee.

"That's the spirit," said I, and knew we were dead.

For it was time to face the truth I'd been avoiding all these weeks. Daniel had changed, in the years since I'd known him last.

The old Daniel was odd, but endearing. This one was barking mad.

WORD OF THE FIGHT had been about for weeks. But no one knew the exact location till the night before, except for those as were directly involved, for that's how these things were done. You had to keep it close, since prize-fighting was illegal. The mill would be somewhere off in the country, where the Magistrates and Peelers would have a hard slog over bad roads if they wanted to stick their beaks in. If you could, you'd build the ring on the boundary between two counties, or better yet at the juncture where three lines met. This way, all concerned could flee from one jurisdiction to the next if the county constabulary was to be seen puffing their way across the fields, faces red and truncheons wagging.

By one o'clock there was hundreds gathered round the ring, which we'd set up in a pasture beyond the wood, well out of sight of the main road. There might have been nearly a thousand—ruddy with drink and anticipation and the cold October wind. The whole tag-rag-and-bobtail, for this was a fight crowd. The Fancy, up from London—touts and gamblers and men of the turf, sharpers and scroungers mixed in with the sporting toffs and lords—along with locals who'd been swept along in the excitement, good old John Bumpkin and his fellows from the farm. A few girls too, of a certain inclination, for there was nothing like a good bare-knuckle prize-fight to get the blood up—well, nothing this side of a good hanging, anyway—and coin of the realm was to be earned behind the hedges.

A raised platform was built sometimes, but today they'd just fight on the Essex grass. It would soon enough be churned to Essex mud, for a cold hard rain had begun to fall. The ring was small, just eighteen foot square between the ropes strung from the corner posts. This was my doing, for deciding the size of the ring was the first skirmish to be waged at any prize-fight. Fit or not, Daniel was after all three-and-thirty. He hadn't fought in earnest for a decade, and his best hope was to have the Ruffian stood right there where he could lay hands upon him. For of course you could lay hands upon your man, under London Prize Rules—clutch him with one hand and wallop him with the other, or wrap him in a bear-hug and crack his ribs. There was in fact plenty you could do under the London Rules, short of kicking your man, or biting him, or gouging out his peepers. And naturally you couldn't hit him when he was down. To prevent such atrocities a Referee was chosen, along with two Umpires. This being done, the Whips commenced trying to move the crowd a few feet back.

A shout went up. The pugilists were approaching.

The Ruffian was first, along with Boston Bob and another cove who was to serve as bottle-holder. With a bow and a flourish Spragg tossed his hat into the ring, and the crowd called out hurrah. Then came Tim Diggory with his glims all purple and swollen and his lantern jaw a-jut, shouldering through the press with Daniel following behind, like a great ship being towed into harbour. As the cries rose up on every side, I hurried to join them.

"All right, Daniel?" I demanded.

He nodded.

Once in the ring, the millers stripped down to their breeches and clogs. As I feared: the Ruffian was round and solid as a rain-barrel, and glowering homicide.

Yet Daniel was strong too, and more than that, Daniel was calm. In the old days he'd clamber into the ring with barrack-room jests to cover up his nerves, and laughter that was too hearty by half. But today I saw that he had a kind of serenity about him—a grim, gleaming serenity. As the rain lashed down and the Ruffian flexed those blacksmith's arms, Daniel took a step towards him.

"Will you join us, brother, in prayer?"

Spragg ceased flexing. He stared. Hawked. Spat.

"Then I'll pray," said Daniel, "for the both of us."

He took Tim Diggory's hand in one of his, and knelt down right there, on the grass. Before I quite knew what had happened I was kneeling alongside of 'em, for Daniel had taken my hand too and pulled me down.

"Lord," said Daniel, "we ask you to watch over us this day, and deliver us safely through the Trial that lies ahead. For the blows we strike are not in malice but only to the glory of Thy Name—my blows, and Brother Spragg's as well, for he is Thy servant too, Lord. He is as fine a Christian as any man here, he just don't know it yet."

I'd been in ridiculous situations before, and done some ridiculous things. I'm sure some of them were even more ridiculous than this. But kneeling there in the October rain, while the punters first goggled and then began to laugh, I couldn't offhand think of an example.

Except after a bit the laughter was trailing off, somehow.

I've never been a man as went in for religion. But there was something about Daniel. There actually was. Listening to that voice soaring out of him, I couldn't help thinking: it wouldn't be such a bad thing if some of this was true. For the fact of it is, we'd all like to believe in something, wouldn't we? We'd all like that considerable. And as Daniel finally finished—praying for Spragg and for Tim and Boston Bob, and for his friend John Thomas, and for all here assembled and everyone everywhere who was broken and needed mending—I was feeling a shiver. And it wasn't just the rainwater trickling down my inexpressibles.

As we stood up, I saw Soames standing amongst the crowd just behind the first row. I didn't see that chum of his—the one from the Nag and Fish—which was a relief. All I needed just now was an argument about a stolen snuff-box. Soames' eye met mine, and on an impulse I called out: "Double the wager—twenty pounds!"

He hesitated just a blink before he nodded, for he had seen what I was seeing. Daniel stood ready with a smile upon his lips—like Saul from the Bible, or Samson before the shears went snip. For the first time, the Ruffian looked uneasy.

"He's going to do it, Tim Diggory," I whispered with sudden certainty. "He's going to win this mill."

BUT OF COURSE he wasn't. Before the fight was a minute old, I knew it.

Normally the fighters would start slow, and circle round feeling each another out. Especially two men of this size, for even a de-blubbered Daniel stripped at sixteen stone, and Spragg was ten pounds heavier. But with a rumbling snarl the Ruffian commenced straight to work, with a prime lick to the smellers and a peg to the bread-basket that made our Dan go *whuff.* Spragg fought from a crouch, favouring the new style: hands low, the right arm drawn across the belly to block the blows. Daniel fought the old way, mauleys high. He tried to put in a blow in return, but the Ruffian turned it aside and followed with two more of his own. For Daniel had ten years of ring-rust creaking in his joints, and he was slow—oh God he was ponderous slow—even slower than he had seemed in sparring. The Ruffian was never a man of science—he was nothing but a slaughterer, in truth—but in comparison he seemed a jungle cat. He nobbed Daniel with a muzzler, and followed with a half-arm dig, and then landed a gravedigger that shocked us all and laid poor Daniel flat.

The punters gave a roar. Shouts went up as the betting resumed—"three-to-one on the Ruffian"—"I'll give you five-to-one!"—and them as had already wagered on Daniel began to feel a queasiness. Such as your friend John Thomas.

But I had no time to think about that. Under the London Prize Rules, a round was over whenever a man went down, either from a blow or from being thrown. After that, his corner had half a minute to get him back up and toeing the line of scratch, which was drawn on the ground in the middle of the ring. Then the next round would commence—as many rounds as was needed to settle the affair. There were always the dancing nancies who'd take advantage of the rule, and fall down without a blow having been struck, just to have a rest. Old Harry Sellers had a trick of falling down untouched and throwing a surprise blow as he did. But that was not about to happen this afternoon.

"That was never a blow to fret you, Daniel!" I cried. "You were just off balance."

I knelt in the corner with my other knee extended for Daniel to sit upon. Tim Diggory fluttered like a great nanny-troll.

"He can't hurt you, and that's a fact," I assured him.

"Can't!" echoed Tim, desperate to corroborate.

"Those are nothing but fly-flap blows, Daniel, such as the pastry-cooks use to beat the insects away from their cakes and tarts. He's served out the best he has, and you've found it to be nothing at all."

"Fly-flaps!"

But it was a lie, and we all knew it—Daniel best of all. That last blow had stunned him, and worse yet he was already breathing heavily. But he heaved himself to his feet as the Referee called "time!" and stumped up to the line of scratch, where the Ruffian stood waiting with a facer that made him stagger three steps back again. He rallied as best he could, milling on the retreat, a style that Tom Cribb had invented—for Cribb could fight as well going backward as he could going forward. But Daniel was no Tom Cribb, alas. The Ruffian closed and flung him to the turf, and that was Round Two.

"You're finding your range, Daniel," I told him as he sat upon my knee.

"Aye," said Daniel.

But he was huffing like a man who'd just walked five miles uphill, and when he rose for Round Three I looked hastily for my man in the crowd. This was Long Bill, the oddjob man at the Plough.

"Bill!" I cried, clutching his sleeve and pulling him close. "Put twenty pound on the Ruffian," I hissed in his ear, "and whatever odds they'll give."

For of course I couldn't be seen to bet against Daniel directly. Next would be exclamations, and cries of "Cross!", and then Jaunty hightailing it across the Essex countryside with the mob upon his heels. But I'd seen more than enough to know that a happy outcome for Daniel was not about to occur this afternoon. Or indeed on any other afternoon until the sounding of the Final Trumpet, when the skies would part and the dead would arise from their graves, half of 'em waving chits and clamouring to know when Jaunty was planning to pay them back.

Long Bill put his finger to the side of his nose, and sloped off.

Round Three had begun. They closed and grappled, and for once Daniel got the better of it, throwing the Ruffian into the ring post. Spragg came away wincing, and for the first time his appetite seemed less than keen. He feinted and stumbled, and as he did a blow from Daniel caught him upon the ear and sent him sprawling.

A great shout went up from the crowd, and as Daniel sat upon my knee I urged him on.

"You have him now, Daniel," I cried, "for the Ruffian has no bottom!"

"Bottom!" cried Tim Diggory. "None!"

"He never has, Daniel! He was never a bottom man, and now you've exposed him for it. Look at him there, across the ring—wishing he were anywhere but Essex, beneath the fists of Daniel O'Thunder. Oh, see the man's nurse-wanting courage—fie upon his worm-dread soul! Now up you get, Daniel—forth you go—and swing the Hammer of Heaven!"

Another cheer went up as Daniel lurched to his feet. Long Bill was at my elbow.

"Wager on O'Thunder?" he whispered.

"Christ, no," I hissed. "Put fifty on the Ruffian—and hurry, while there's still odds to be had!"

For of course I had seen what was evident to anyone who knew the ways of the green faerie circle. Daniel's blow had been glancing, and the Ruffian would hardly have blinked if his feet hadn't been tangled already. The tale would be told soon enough.

It was.

By the time the mill was twenty minutes in, I could scarcely bear to watch. The ground had been chewed to a bog of mud, through which the pugilists lumbered and slid. But this was nothing to the chewing of poor Daniel. Blood streamed from his brow. Both eyes were reduced to slits. His nose had been broken two minutes in, and now the side of his face was swelling like a melon, which made me suspect his cheekbone had been cracked as well. A doubler left him all in a heap, and when he wobbled back up to scratch his kidney had swollen to the size of a twopenny loaf. I shook my head and sighed.

There's a reason why prize-fighters are mostly dead by five-and-thirty. A man retires after twelve or fifteen mills, and they throw a Benefit Night for the splendid old warhorse as he trudges out to pasture. When you see him a year or two later, he's mumbling. A year or two after that, someone tells you the news: "Did you hear about old So-and-so? They buried him yesterday. No, it wasn't an illness, really—they think his heart give out. But wasn't he a warrior, in his day? I'll always remember the mill in Rabbit Dell, when he broke his leg in the twenty-second round against the Lanarkshire Lad, but offered to go on if they could both be strapped to chairs and set face to face in the middle of the ring."

"You can do it, Captain!" cried Tim Diggory.

Spragg batted him about the ring like a shuttlecock. He planted a chopper-blow; Daniel staggered, and in that instant the Ruffian struck. Stooping down he drove his shoulder into Daniel's stomach, and seized Daniel about the hams, and flung him cross-buttock. Daniel came down full weight upon his head, with a dull crunching sound and such force I swear I felt the ground shake.

The shout of the crowd became a gasp, for the cross-buttock throw is the most awfullest manoeuvre in pugilism. It damages men so's they're never right again. It can kill them dead, right there on the instant.

"Daniel!" I cried, and leapt to his side, as horrible images rose up before my eyes. Images of my dear friend Daniel stiff and cold, and a hearse rattling slowly along the cobblestones, with two mutes all in black following behind. Images of the churchyard, and the grave yawning wide. And Jaunty absent from his dear friend's funeral entirely, and peering instead through the bars of Clerkenwell Gaol. For they'd charge him with manslaughter, oh yes they would, and condemn poor Jaunty to Durance Vile, along with the Ruffian and Boston Bob. They'd charge the lot of them, even though the Ruffian had done the deed, while Jaunty—innocent Jaunty—stood helpless as a mewling babe. And the law calls this fair. The law calls it justice. God's hairy bollocks.

But Daniel opened his eyes. They were the eyes of an orphan, abandoned and lost, but God bless him they were open. We managed to get him to his feet, but the fight was clearly over, and I told him so.

"You've done all you can, Daniel," I told him. "You've done your friends proud, but it's time to rest, now."

"'E's right, Captain," said Tim Diggory. Tears welled up in both of Tim's glims—the one that was looking at Daniel, and the one that was rolling off elsewhere.

"No," said Daniel. "I can't give in. For he's here."

"I know he is, Daniel," said I, with a bitter glare across the ring at the Ruffian, who was strutting and clasping his hands overhead. "He's right there, and if you give him half a chance he'll throw you on your poor head all over again, and this time he'll kill you for certain."

For Daniel was my friend. He'd been a brother to me, and more than a brother—he'd been almost a son. I feared for his safety, even more than I feared prison.

Besides, seventy pounds wagered on the Ruffian. Matters could be worse.

"No," said Daniel. "You don't understand. *He's* here."

He seemed to see someone—or something—though who it was I couldn't say. Someone at the back of the crowd, but more likely nothing at all, just some phantom conjured in his poor battered brain. For what *could* he see with both eyes near to swollen shut?

But such a look upon his face. A look of desperation, and resolve.

"I'm afraid," said Daniel.

Poor Tim looked crushed to hear it, but he put a hand on Daniel's shoulder. "That's all right, Captain," he said, in a husky voice. "We're all of us afryde, sometimes."

"No, you still don't understand," said Daniel. "*He's* here, and I'm afraid I'm not strong enough to match him. But I must."

"Time!" called the Referee.

Daniel staggered to the line of scratch. What he felt in that terrible moment—and what he saw—I couldn't presume to say. The seething mass of the crowd, hemming him in. The awful solitude of the ring itself, for a man in a prize-ring is utterly alone—more alone than he will ever be in his life, with no human being in all the world to help him. The prize-ring itself plays tricks, for the ring is square and yet it isn't. When a man is inside the ring, he would swear that it's round instead. A terrible black void, and there stood Daniel, battered blind and all but helpless in the middle of it.

What happened next, I shall remember to my dying day.

He stood swaying as the rain lashed down and the Ruffian stepped forth with murderous joy to finish him. I seem to recall a rumble of thunder, and a fierce gust of wind. It was the wind that did it, I think. Sudden and strong, it checked the Ruffian for just an instant—unbalanced him just a tiny fraction—and in that instant Daniel swung his fist. It was a vast and ponderous blow, as ponderous as a great ship sailing across a faraway horizon. But somehow the Ruffian stood frozen, and at the end of half an hour—for truly, time itself seemed stopped—the Hammer of Heaven smashed home.

Spragg the Ruffian went down in sections.

An instant of stunned silence, and then a mighty roar went up. Boston Bob leapt into the ring, where Spragg had taken a reverent pose: face down, arse skyward, like a Musselman at prayer. A glance told Bob that brandy would never turn the trick. Desperate measures were required.

"Bullets!" shouted Bob, pointing at Daniel. "Got bullets in his fists!"

Naturally there was shouting and confusion. The Referee hastened to prise open Daniel's fingers to see if this was true, for bullet-in-the-fist was a low and dirty trick that had broken many a jaw before today. Then there was a minute or two of chaos as Bob swore that Daniel had dropped the bullets into the mud, and insisted that everyone look for them. Of course no bullets were found, for there were no bullets in the first place. And of course Boston Bob knew this perfectly well, and was just trying to create enough delay for his fighter to recover—this being an even lower and dirtier trick, a filthy and a shameful trick, but a good one. I had used it myself on several occasions.

But it wasn't going to work today. Spragg the Ruffian lay in ruins, and the Referee finally told him out.

Pandemonium. Bellows of disbelief, and hats flung up into the air. Someone raced to release the pigeons of victory, while the Ruffian's friends made one last attempt to clamour that a foul had been committed. That's when someone realized that Spragg was still face-down, which occasioned some alarm, this being a very dickey position for an unconscious man on a day with mud-puddles. They turned him over just in time, and dredged him back to soggy consciousness. After another minute or two he was brought to understand what had transpired, and that he had lost, upon which he gave a despairing wail and wished that he were dead. As they carried him out in a horse blanket, he was begging them tearfully to cast him into the river.

All this while, Daniel had stood splay-legged, swaying like a siege engine, while round him celebration raged. Now suddenly he slumped down onto his knees. A cry of consternation, and shouts of "Help him—look, he's fallen!"

But he was praying. "... Who in Thy Mercy and Wisdom hast granted me the victory this day. And not for my own merit—never that, for I have none—but to Thine Own Eternal Glory, that sinful eyes might be opened at last..."

Daniel raised his head again, and heaved himself back to his feet. Covered he was in gore and mud, through which the rain-water ran in rivulets. A hush had fallen. Behind him the pigeons rose up into the glowering skies.

White doves. Through the slits of his eyes, Daniel saw them.

"Yes, that's right—release the doves. Send them to every corner of the land, to tell of what has happened here today. Tell how Spragg was young and strong, while Daniel O'Thunder was old and slow. Tell how Spragg battered him until you thought that Daniel must surely lie grovelling—for you did, brothers, oh you did, yes each one of you was certain sure. But God gave me the strength to stand—you saw it. You saw brother Spragg fall instead, with a finality that shook the ground. Yes, the ground shook—and more than that. For beneath the ground, Hell shook, and the Devil shook with it."

Daniel's face was giant-like, so battered and swollen it scarcely seemed human at all. He was mad, and magnificent. He turned, and tottered, and gazed about, and as he did every man-jack in that vale believed: *he's looking straight at me.*

"Yes he did, the Devil felt that blow. It wobbled his knees, and he squealed out, 'Hold—enough!' But we *won't* hold, brothers, for we've barely begun. We're going to batter the Devil until he gibbers for mercy. We're forming an army, right here and right now, God's own army. So who's with me?"

"I am!" cried a voice. "Take me!"

It was the young man from the Nag and Fish. The one who used to have a silver snuff-box. His face was wrenched in an agony of transport as he rushed forward and fell before Daniel, wrapping both arms around his knees.

"Welcome, brother," said Daniel in a voice like coming home, "and know how dearly you are loved."

I HEARD LATER the celebration was the unlikeliest that ever took place after a prize-fight. It seems they took Daniel back to the Plough, and then turned off the taps—turned *off* the taps, if you please, so as the Devil's Buttermilk could not flow. Tim Diggory was there and assorted odds and ends of Daniel's old rabble who'd come up from London, including the fluttering grey doves, the Miss Whatsits. I'd actually noticed them once or twice that afternoon at the mill, at the very back of the crowd. They'd begun by hiding their faces and half-swooning in distress. But soon enough one of them was shrieking "Kill him!" and then clapping her hand over her mouth and looking round in great dismay in case anyone had heard her shriek such a horrible thing—and then shrieking it twice as loud two seconds later, for a good mill will get your blood going, I don't care who you are. There was some of the Fancy there too—at the Plough I mean—a fight crowd, dry and sober, listening with their gobs hung open as Daniel gathered 'em round and went on about God and the Devil. I'm told the young man with no snuff-box sat at Daniel's feet and never moved, gazing up at him as if Daniel was the sunrise in the morning.

And where was I, during all of this? Why, Jaunty was standing in the rain and the gathering darkness by the high road, shivering and miserable. For a note had been slipped to me after the mill, advising that His Lordship wanted a word. In all the crush and confusion I didn't see who slipped it, and my collies wobbled as I read. But you didn't ignore such a summons.

The appointed place was a crossroads two full miles from the village. The crossroads was crouched in the shadow of a bleak godforsaken hill, with rain lashing and wind sweeping down, and nothing for cover but a single storm-blasted tree. It was exactly the sort of crossroads at which a gibbet might well have been found, in the scarcely departed days when dead men hung in chains at half the crossroads in England. As the darkness became complete, I let myself grow convinced that a gibbet had indeed stood once upon this very spot. In the creaking of the storm-blasted tree, I heard the convulsive jerks of ghostly corpses.

He let me stand there for three hours. At last I glimpsed a light wavering in the distance, and heard the sound of approaching hooves, and the creak of carriage wheels. A coach came rattling out of the blackness towards me, drawn by two black horses, just as a shaft of moonlight slanted through the cloud. It slid to a stop in the eerie glow, and the window-cover slid up. I had a bull's-eye lantern, and lifted it as I stepped forward, peering through the window into the depths within.

Something dark stirred. I saw him by lantern light.

Don't babble, I told myself. Cool as cucumbers. Brazen it through.

"Good evening, Your Lordship, though a foul one it is, I suppose. The evening, I mean, and—"

Babbling already. God's hairy bollocks. The man just had that effect.

"I wagered on the Ruffian," said Lord Sculthorpe.

An old man wrapped in a cloak. But those glims of his—so icy and unblinking, you half expected a hiss. I swear to God, you half believed the cloak would fall away and there'd be coils.

"I wagered on the Ruffian because I had assurances," he said. "From you."

"Ah," I said. "Ah, yes. But here's the thing..."

"Would you care to know how much I lost?"

Something shifted within the cloak. For a moment beyond all horribility, I thought: it *is* the coils! But it was someone small, sitting on his other side. This might have unnerved me no end, if I'd had any nerves left to begin with. Christ, why had I gone to Scul-thorpe for the backing, of all the shady sporting lords in England? And why oh why had I told him that Daniel couldn't win?

"Your Lordship. The thing of it is—"

"I'm not going to tell you how much I lost. I'm not going to specify the sum involved, for it would just distress you. You would exclaim to yourself, 'However should a man endure such a loss? And what would he do to the wretch who crossed him?'"

"It wasn't a cross, Your Lordship! Upon my davy—honour bright—I fluttered against Daniel myself. Seventy pound I lost, wagering on the Ruffian. Seventy pound as I don't have, Your Lordship, for where would poor Jaunty find seventy pound?"

"We don't care about Jaunty's losses."

"Right you are. Fair enough, but—"

"We don't care if Jaunty lives or dies. You may decide for yourself which seems more probable, at present."

"No, look. You'll have your money back, and more. There's a way to make this right."

The small person beside him was a girl. This wasn't as surprising as it might have been, for Lord Sculthorpe frequently had a girl about him for companionship. A different girl each time—you didn't seem to see the same one twice, which might have made you wonder what became of them. This one was almost a woman, perhaps eighteen years old, but tiny. Jet-black hair and a little ivory face. I have a notion she looked frightened. But of course a man can't be thinking of two things at once.

"I'll make another mill, Your Lordship. This time, I guarantee he'll lose. You'll have your money back, every farthing, and twice as much besides. Swear to God, swear to anyone you like, and I wish I may burn in Hell."

Silence. Jaunty, hopping from foot to foot in the October cold, clutching a lantern in one hand and wringing his cap in the other. His Lordship's eyes, unblinking. I've a notion the eyes of the black-haired girl were upon me too. I've a notion they may have been imploring.

At last he nodded. The twitch of a bloodless lip, and the exposure of one incisor in what might have been a smile.

"Be careful what you wish for," he said.

I had a last glimpse of them—the horrible old man, and the girl nestled beside him—and then the window-cover slid back down, like a curtain falling. Lord Sculthorpe called to the driver, and thumped on the roof with his cane. The carriage rattled away into the night with a clatter of hooves, clip-*clop,* leaving me all alone at the crossroads with the ghosts of hanged men keening in the wind.

I didn't suppose I'd see the black-haired girl again. I wondered if anybody would.

JACK

I DO NOT LIVE alone here in my dank Whitechapel garret—the room in which I sit as an old man these four long decades later, assembling my *Book of Daniel*. There is a spider that lives here with me. She has a web in the corner of the room above my desk, near the filthy window overlooking Dorset Street. Whores loiter along the street, gin-sodden nymphs of the pave; I hear their voices at night, cawing like rooks. They are unwashed and indolent, while my spider is brisk and brown and industrious.

I watched her spinning the web the other morning, working away in the pale straggling sunlight. There had been just a few strands at first, wispy and gossamer. At first it all seemed random—even risible—but slowly a pattern began to emerge. Each strand connecting to another, and then another. The web was at this inchoate stage when I went out to earn my daily crust of bread. Although I am old now, nearly seventy, I am still industrious, like my friend the spider. I have a tiny shop, and a trade I acquired on my trudge through the years. These days I am a barber. You find the notion droll? Why, so do I. My long life's journey from tending souls to tending whiskers. You may picture me at work in a nook in Duke Street, with hair clippings upon the floor and mysterious coloured bottles on the shelf, bending over a supine trusting gentleman with a razor in my hand. It is a beautiful ivory handled implement that once belonged to a Negro barber in northern British Columbia named Wellington Moses.

The day previous I had been reviewing old newspaper reports of O'Thunder's prize-fights, such as the famous account in the *Illustrated Sporting Life* of his mill against Hen Gully, of which you will learn in due course. This was lively and stimulating. But this morning I set these aside to commence editing a passage that Nell had written, and reading the words—hearing her voice, after all these years—had stirred up powerful emotions. I needed to clear my head, and to recollect myself, so I went for a long walk through the squalid winding Whitechapel streets. There was a frisson of dark excitement in these streets today, for it seemed a woman's mutilated corpse—another one—had been found early this morning near Spitalfields Market. Rumours were flying of a ghoul who preyed shockingly upon nightwalkers, stalking and then ripping. When at last I returned to my room, the sun was dying behind the distant dome of St Paul's, and the spider's web was finished. It was triumphant. An intricate geometry, perfectly complete, making perfect sense of every seemingly random strand within it. A fly was trapped and buzzing. By midnight it was just a husk.

I am looking up at the web right now, as I pause for a moment in my scribbling. I am thinking of the strands of my own life, and the way they have all connected. Sainted brother Toby, and my call to the priesthood, and then Cornwall and the fiasco of Bathsheba Scantlebury. And Nell, of course; my little Nell. My years in London, and my subsequent years of bitter exile, and my eventual journey to the Cariboo Goldfields at the icy ends of the earth, where gold was discovered a decade after the California rush—and where Daniel and I were to meet one last time in circumstances so haunting and strange that the memory rises now like the fragment of an opium dream...

But not yet. We're not there yet. There are many strands I must weave together first. The geometry of my life—a spider-work of gossamer strands, and there at the very centre is Daniel O'Thunder.

OCTOBER, 1851.
I went to see the fight between Spragg and O'Thunder because random strands were connecting. One of these was an accidental encounter with some old companions from my student days at Oxford.

I'd gone up to Oxford nine years earlier, in 1842, through the sponsorship of a kindly old rector who knew my grandfather. In other words, I was practically a charity case. But over the course of my three years there I made chums with one or two offshoots of the aristocracy. Among these was Roderick Soames, who in student days had been almost unbearable, but rich. I bumped into him at the theatre after the play, and discovered he hadn't changed. Soamesie and some friends were out on the town, and I tagged along. We found ourselves at a night house, where someone was talking about a fight to be held in Essex, two days hence. Or rather a "mill," for thus were prize-fights known to members of the Fancy, amongst whom I seemed to be numbered, if only for this one boozy night. This led soon enough to the idea that we'd all go out to see the battle. Soamesie was agreeable, and so was the Honourable Alfred Duckworth, who had turned up halfway through the proceedings. Duckers thought it an excellent notion. In fact, he thought it the most deyvlishly amusing idea he'd heard since he'd come down from Oxford—which is of course where I'd seen Alfred Duckworth before. He knew me too, or at least he thought he did but couldn't quite place me, for once or twice he glanced across and mused, "You say you were at Balliol?" I admitted this, but avoided other questions. There had been an unfortunate incident midway through my final term, and I had a notion that slumbering memories of it might be stirring in the

Hon Alfred's overbred brainpan. I wasn't eager to prod them into wakefulness, for the ghosts of one's past are best left to mutter undisturbed.

We went by train as far as Chelmsford. There Duckers hired a coach, and waved a cheerful farewell to those of us who didn't fit and had to tramp the last two hours instead, arriving at last at a villainous country inn. But the first pot took the edge off, and the second partially reconciled me to limited segments of humankind, and by the third I was almost able to imagine what benevolence might feel like. Somewhere later in the evening I happened to notice a gingery rat-faced party, and was idly wondering why a man with such mangy whiskers wouldn't shave, when I abruptly recognized him as the bastard from the Nag and Fish—the one who'd stolen my snuff-box. But he was out the door before I had time to think, and at one o'clock the following afternoon he turned out—Jesus wept—to be O'Thunder's second. And *then* what was I supposed to do? I could hardly run for a constable, so I shut my mouth and prepared to enjoy the battle to which the connection of these random strands had brought me.

But of course this is hardly the truth at all. Or at least, it leaves out the only truth that matters.

I had come to Essex because Daniel O'Thunder had called me.

His face, appearing to me in the storm on that terrible Cornish night. Appearing again on the wall of the Horse and Dolphin. His hand reaching out, and his great sad shepherd's eyes.

I can't explain these things, even now. But they were the gossamer strands that drew me to him, and bound us together from that moment forward.

And now the mill had begun. A thousand of us stood crushed together, baying.

I'd seen fights—I'd even been in fights. But those, it turned out, had not been fights at all, just the games of children.

Bantams flailing and bloody noses. These were men, and they were killing each other—or at least the Ruffian was killing O'Thunder. Chopping him down with great shuddering blows, the way you'd chop a tree. O'Thunder was dying right there in the ring, in front of our eyes. Then came that dreadful wrestling throw that made even the fight mob gasp, and left him lying crumpled.

When I was a boy I'd seen a sheepdog run over by a cart. It had tried so hard to get back up, heaving itself with wonderful desperate determination, but its back had been broken, and a look of such bewilderment came over the poor creature's face, for it wanted so much to please and it just couldn't understand what it had done that was so wrong. All the suffering of the world was in that poor dog's eyes—all the tragedy of being alive. With O'Thunder it was worse, for he was a man, and such a splendid man, or at least he had been until the Ruffian had ruined him.

I shouted at him to stay down, for I couldn't bear another second. But they hauled him back onto his feet, the ginger rat and that troll from Mother Clatterballock's, the troll sobbing out loud while the rat cast round for some bits of wreckage to cling to. Then that blow, and Spragg like a sledgehammered bullock. O'Thunder, weaving and raving. The mighty arm of the Lord, with a fist that smote and a hand that reached from Heaven to all of us grovelling here in the mud below. His eyes found me—the eyes from the engraving, and from that storm-tossed Cornish night. He was speaking to me. Only to me. He seemed to stand in a shaft of light.

The next thing I knew something warm and golden gave a flash inside my head. I had a brief vertiginous sensation of the ground rising up to meet me. Then there I was, kneeling in the mud. In a bleak Essex vale in the driving October rain, nearly five years after I'd taken up holy orders and almost two since I'd fled the priesthood in disgrace. I wept like a child and begged for mercy.

THEY CARRIED HIM back to the Plough, and took him upstairs. After a time the gingery rat came back down again, and assured us that O'Thunder was fine. He was just vomiting, and a bit delirious—just the normal things you'd expect, after a mill—and would be right as rain after a few days. He was out the door and gone before I remembered that he still had my snuff-box. I had completely neglected to seize him by the collar and threaten to have the law on him—and more than that, I had not the faintest desire to do so. It was an extraordinary feeling of gentle benevolence towards another human creature, and I recall that I actually turned to the man beside me—he turned out to be a clerk in a counting house, for O'Thunder drew us in all shapes and sizes—I turned to him and said: "I wish you well."

He nodded and beamed. After a moment—not knowing quite what else to do—he embraced me. There was a deal of this sort of thing going on, for the Plough had been taken over by O'Thunder's rabble. The ones who had followed him up from London, and the ones like me who had joined on the spot, and dear God weren't we a motley crew. Threadbare mechanics and bumpkins with great red faces, clerks and apprentices and potboys, scarecrows and brawlers and bakers and whores and the Miss Sherwoods in grey bonnets. Just about the unlikeliest assortment since a group of halfwit fishermen had laid down their nets on a Galilean shore.

A sudden exclamation, and then a shout of joy, for a heavy halting step was on the stair. Against all odds, O'Thunder had arisen. His head was a jack-o-lantern, and he shuffled like ancient Methuselah. But even in such a state, Daniel O'Thunder changed a room just by walking into it. He changed every man and women in that room as well. He made them better than they had ever imagined they might be, if only for those moments while he was with them. We gathered around him like children, and he told us...what did he say? I find now that I don't remember. I suppose he preached to us, as best he could in his pain and exhaustion. I recall he asked once or twice if the Ruffian were here, and looked sad when we said no. After a while his face gave a twist.

"I need help."

He was struggling to rise. Tim Diggory leaped to his aid.

"No, brother," said O'Thunder. "Jack will help me."

He was looking at me. He knew my name.

"I need to go outside," he said. "Just the two of us."

I had an image of myself as a small wooden stake trying to wedge an oak tree upright. But we managed. The cold was still raw, but the storm had passed. It was night. I realized with surprise that he had been talking to us for hours.

"My buttons," he said.

We were behind the inn, by the stable. The yard was ghostly in the moonlight.

"I'm sorry?"

"I need help with the buttons. My hands break when I fight."

He made an apologetic gesture towards the front of his trousers. His hands were huge and swollen and useless. So what do you do? I fumbled with the buttons and then rummaged inside. A peculiar flash of memory: a child cross-legged at Christmas, reaching into a stocking.

I drew it out. It sat in my hand like a salmon. He gave a groan, and gushed.

"Captain!"

For the stream was bright red.

"It's just the blood from my kidneys. He gave them a battering, did Brother Spragg, but they'll mend."

Great clouds of steam rose up into the frigid air.

"How did you know it was Jack?" I asked after a moment. "My name."

"I think I'd know my brother's name."

Blood ran down the barn wall and trickled back towards us, across new-frozen mud. It was pooling at our feet.

"We lost," he said heavily.

"No, Captain. A famous victory. Don't you remember?"

"But we lost the Ruffian himself. I'd hoped we'd reach him, but the Devil's hold was stronger than I thought. Oh, he's strong, the Devil. And I'm old—I'm older than I'd realized, brother."

The blood-red stream had ebbed away to a last few drops. Gingerly, I put it back for him.

"But at least he didn't take Young Joe," he was saying. "That's something I hold onto. He snatched at Young Joe's ankles at the last, but he couldn't drag him down. Poor Joe Gummery."

"The boy they hung?"

"Aye. For killing that poor girl, the prostitute. But he didn't kill her, brother. He did no such thing. They hung Young Joe, but it was someone else who did the deed."

He was looking at me as he said it. Almost as if he imagined that I might know the fiend's identity. But the look on his face was just a trick of shadows and moonlight.

"Were you there, Jack, at the hanging?"

I started to deny it, but you couldn't lie to him. You'd open your mouth, but the lie would shrivel on your tongue, and there'd be nothing left but the dusty dry ashes of truth.

He looked at me steadily. "You went to the hanging. I saw you there."

"Yes."

"Why did you go?"

I wasn't sure. I went because it was life and death, I suppose. Dancing for you on a length of rope, and there you stood with a flask in your hand and a great dark roar rising up in your throat. I went because the world is foul and we are worse and some poor wretch is going to pay.

"I suppose I went because I am a very bad man."

His cue to reassure.

"Aye," he said, "I suspect you are. But you could be a better one, brother. Starting right now, in this minute, you could be the man you wish you were."

He dropped down onto one knee. I thought for a moment that he wanted to pray. But the blood had drained from his face. He would have toppled, except that I knelt beside him.

"I'll just need a moment, brother, to catch my breath."

"It's all right," I said, and managed to ease him down.

"I'm tired, Jack. Perhaps I'll just close my eyes. For a moment."

I got my coat off, and wrapped it awkwardly round his shoulders. Sitting on the cold mud with his great head in my lap. The night bit through my thin shirt, but what I felt was the warmth of surging conviction. And God help me, I felt something else, as well—something strange and wonderful. Love?

"I'll follow you," I found myself vowing. "However long and dark the road, I'll follow. I'll be with you wherever you lead. I'll follow you to the ends of the earth."

"No, brother," he murmured, "you'll follow me as far as you can. We'll find out soon enough how far that is."

YEARS LATER A physician explained to me what had in fact taken place. He was a dusty dry Edinburgh Scot, sitting next to me in a filthy wooden shack with benches and unspeakable whiskey. This passed for the taproom in a place called Yale, a godforsaken mudhole in the wilderness of British Columbia whence madmen began doomed treks to the goldfields far in the North. Jagged mountains reared on either side, and a sullen river churned below.

That first golden flash in my head, said the dusty dry physician, had in all probability indicated some manner of cerebral fit or seizure, such as Saul had sustained upon the road to Tarsus. It is not unusual for such a seizure to bring on exalted feelings. Sometimes there may be actual visions.

I am not a medical man, myself. I can offer no comment, except to say this:

Whatever I had done, and whatever I was yet to do, on that bleak October night in 1851, as I sat in an inn-yard with the moon above and Daniel O'Thunder's head in my lap, I was the man I had always intended to be. I was filled with love, and capable of deeds that would shine a tiny brave candle into the shrouded corners and coal-black crannies of the world.

I was good. I need you to know that. I was good, I was good, I was good.

WHEN I ARRIVED back at the Kemp Theatre some days later, Edmund Cubitt's door was closed to me. This was a sadness, but not a great surprise.

Relations between the two of us had been strained since the day he had rejected *John, Baptist,* and I in return had abandoned him to his own devices for that evening's performance. This left Edmund Cubitt unamused, a state of affairs that grew steadily more pronounced. My former cheerful solicitude gave way to mutinous silence, while Edmund Cubitt's looks grew steadily more arid, until he was a wasteland of Judgement and Grievance upon which the frail green tendrils of amusement were choked at first sprouting.

Thus was the situation between us when I decamped for Essex. By the time I returned—altered by what I had seen and experienced—I had formed the resolve to go straight to Edmund Cubitt, and confess that neither of us could be considered blameless in the matter, and offer my hand in reconciliation. I had even decided to admit my share of culpability in one of the primary irritants between us: his insinuation that I knew more than I admitted about his missing silver snuff-box. Naturally I had denied this hotly when the subject was first broached—as one does, when caught out in an indiscretion. But perhaps I had in truth noticed the snuff-box sitting on his unattended table. Perhaps I had even picked it up—as any man might do—in a spasm of resentment. And in the next moment been startled by the sound of approaching footsteps, whereupon I slipped it guiltily into my waistcoat pocket, whence it had remained until gingery rat-faced Jaunty Rennert had plucked it.

But when I arrived at the theatre and asked after Edmund Cubitt, I was told he was unavailable to me. Instead I was given a small hamper. In it were some small odds and ends of my belongings—a shirt, an old manuscript, two or three books, and a stocking—along with a brief note in an elegant hand: "For Mr Hartright. How sharper than a serpent's tooth." It was a bit much, even given my unexplained absence and Edmund Cubitt's natural propensity for the dramatic. But I accepted it meekly, and wrote in a reply a brief note, thanking Mr Cubitt for his friendship and patronage, and expressing the belief that he might yet through humility and God's Grace become a happier and a better man, as I had no doubt he yearned to be.

But no one at the theatre had seen Nell.

Mrs Beale the highly seasoned ingenue raised one pencilled eyebrow. "The young *lay-dee* as was here that once to see you?" she asked archly.

No, she hadn't been back, and she hadn't sent a note, and the doorman hadn't seen her either. Neither had anyone else, although Mrs Beale suggested helpfully that I might try one of the larger theatres, where such young *lay-dees* might be glimpsed amongst gentlemanly companionship in the private boxes. Or at any rate the backs of their heads might be glimpsed, bobbing. I thanked Mrs Beale for her kind assistance, and turned to leave.

As I did, I was startled by the glimpse of something small and twisted peering at me from the shadows at the end of the corridor. In that first uncanny instant I fancied it a faerie changeling, eyeing me with otherworldly intent. But then I realized it was only Tommyknocker—little Tommy, the goblin-faced boy who worked the pulleys and traps in the theatre. He stood unblinking in the shadows, like a defective sprite hunched in the mouth of a mineshaft. He opened his mouth, and for a moment I had the sense that he wanted to say something to me—but how could he, being mute? Then he winked back into the darkness and was gone.

I put Tommy out of my mind—and Edmund Cubitt as well. For my thoughts had turned again to Nell, and I was worried.

NELL HAD DISAPPEARED. I hadn't seen her for nearly a month. What's more, they hadn't seen her at Mother Clatterballock's either. At least, they hadn't seen her as of the last time I'd gone there to ask. This had been a few nights before I'd gone out to Essex for the mill.

The night house had been as foul as I'd remembered, with its haze of smoke and iniquity, and predatory denizens like creatures from a nether world. The old whore was holding court by the bar as I slunk through the door. She glanced my way, and after an instant recognition dawned. She wheezed her way towards me.

"Why, it's little Nell Rooney's brother, isn't it? Why, yes it is. It's our own dear Nell's dear *brother.*" She uttered the word with irony, for of course she knew perfectly well I was no such thing. But she let this pass for the moment, and eyed me shrewdly. "And 'as 'e come with news of little Nell?"

My heart sank, a little. "You haven't seen her either, then? For that's what I came to ask."

She cocked her head with its multiple chins, weighing whether to believe this. After a moment she drew me into a small side room, the better to back me into a corner and wheeze gusts of clove and tooth-rot into my face.

"Are we sure, my love, that we 'aven't information to share? For if this was the case it would distress us. And you."

"I haven't!" I gasped, and rose up upon my toes, for the sow had taken my nether parts in a grip that would crack walnuts. A bald rhinoceros manifested behind her, regarding me with oyster eyes and an air of homicidal deference. I took this to be the new bully, here to replace the departed Tim Diggory.

"Are we very, very sure indeed?" asked Mother Clatterballock, with a foul gust and a horrible wheezing purr.

"Yes!"

"You'd tell us if you'd 'eard a single whisper?"

"I would!"

"And will do so instanter should such a whisper come your way?"

"I swear!"

She eyed me for another long narrow moment, before relaxing her fist just enough for me to breathe.

"We'd make it worth your while." She said it with a wheedling sort of wheeze, and a leer that might have aspired to collegiality. "Wouldn't we, Swinton?"

"Yes, 'm," the bald rhinoceros agreed, oyster-eyeing me and cracking his knuckles.

"Oh, yes we would. We want so much to see our little Nell safe 'ome again—as Nell's own dear brother does as well—that in our gratitude we'd pay out a pound to see it. We'd pay a pound in pure joy. Yes?"

I indicated that I understood—no man was more understanding than I—and limped hurriedly into the night.

So you'll understand why I made my way back there tonight with a certain profundity of misgiving. But perhaps Nell would be there when I arrived. That was the thought that kept me going all the way to Panton Street. It was the hope that pushed me through Mother Clatterballock's door into the din and the fug within. Perhaps Nell would be standing just there—or there—in her shabby fox tippet and her absurd little hat. And if she was, then she'd look round and see me, and her thin face would twist in a quick grin despite her best attempts to squelch it.

But Nell wasn't there. Mother Clatterballock hadn't seen her, or heard a single word. The old whore shook her head. For just a moment, in the lurid oil-light, the look on her great wobbling evil face might almost have passed for regret.

"Well, I hexpect that's that, then," she wheezed quietly.

"Don't say that," I said instantly. "Look here, someone must know where she is."

"Oh, I'm sure they do, ducks. I'm sure someone knows exactly where she is. Leastways, 'e knows exactly where she was when 'e'd finished."

For of course we both knew what it meant nine times out of ten, when a girl like Nell went missing. It meant she'd be found by a waterman on the Thames, or by one of the mudlarks scavenging along the shore. With her face bloated up and her eyes just empty sockets, for the little crabs would have found her first.

I forced the image out of my head. "Maybe she found her mother."

"Her *mother?*"

The thought had come unbidden. But why not? "She's been looking for her mother—she told me that. So maybe that's what's happened. They've found one another, and they're—I don't know—together somewhere."

There was a sound—a thin sputtering gurgle, rising slowly to a whistle, like a teakettle boiling over on the hob. Mother Clatterballock's face had gone red. Her various chins were wobbling, and then her shoulders, and then she erupted like doomed Pompeii of old into gales of wheezing laughter. Great torrents of it that made the other punters stop dead and stare, as her face turned bright purple and she clutched at the back of a chair for support.

"Oh, dear," she gasped. The mirth subsided at last, just as it had seemed sure to reduce her to a pile of quivering rubble. "Oh dear, oh deary dear, Nell's sainted mother."

"Did you know her mother?" I demanded.

"Not 'alf as well as you did, ducks—you being Nell's brother." She wiped her streaming red eyes with the back of her hand, and favoured me with a slantways look. "Unless perhaps I've been mis-hinformed, and you're not really 'er brother at all?"

There was something lupine in that look.

"No, I am not Nell's brother."

"So you've been misleading us. Is that the long and the short of it, ducks? You've been lying through your nice white teeth."

The bald oyster-eyed rhinoceros had manifested again. He cracked his knuckles.

"Of course I've been lying!" I cried. "And what's more, you knew that from the start. But that doesn't matter—*I* don't matter. What counts right now is finding Nell!"

For I had changed. I was different, now.

Mother Clatterballock eyed me with speculative interest. As you might regard an unusual insect while deciding whether to tread upon it.

"Then who are you really? Who are you, I mean, on those hoccasions when you find yourself telling the truth—such as they may be?"

"I'm someone who takes an interest. I'm Nell's friend. Damn it, I'm someone who cares."

The largest of Mother Clatterballock's chins was beginning to wobble again.

"Oh, Christ, look at the gob on 'im, Swinton—'e's one of those. One of the romantickal ones, poor muff. 'E thinks 'e's in love with the little bitch."

I was sure that horrible laughter was about to come wheezing up again, but it died. "Fair enough, for she wasn't a bad little bitch, in her way. Not bad at all, for a lying little trull who disappeared with a dress of my purchasing on 'er back, and coins jingling in 'er pocket that was owed to me, and if she weren't dead already I suspect I'd have to kill the slut." In the lurid light, her face grew hard. "But that's enough of that. She's gone, and I'm sick of thinking about it—and I'm sick of you, too, with your lying white teeth. So I think you'd best be on your way, while my mood is still so kindly-nice and benevolent."

She turned, but I was not giving up.

"What about Old Mary?"

Mother Clatterballock stopped.

"Mary?"

"The old woman who followed Nell about. The one who kept an eye on her. Do you know where she is?"

For there was still the hope that Old Mary might know something. I'd been hoping to ask her tonight, except she wasn't here. She hadn't been here the last time, either.

Mother Clatterballock's eyes blinked twice, in a ghastly counterfeit of innocence. "I believe Old Mary went to see the

Great Hexhibition. That's where she was going, the last time I seen her. Leastways, she was pointed in the direction of the Park."

HYDE PARK HAD been carved from woodland, and at night the ancient forest reclaimed its own. In the darkness you would hear scufflings and stirrings, and sudden small alarming cries. The thin shriek of a rabbit being killed, perhaps, for there were small creatures in Hyde Park, and night predators such as owls and foxes. Once upon a time there had been wolves in England, and in the darkness you might almost believe that some of them had returned. You might glimpse one in the trees, watching some smaller helpless thing.

Hyde Park is where I found Old Mary—if "found" is the word I want. By the time I reached Old Mary, she had long since gone away.

"When I was a girl, my hair was golden ringlets. Did you know that? I was a good girl—good as gold."

A wraith in rags, detaching itself from the darkness alongside the path, in the last faint glimmer of dying twilight. A long black veil, and a claw clutching at my arm.

"Mary?"

"I'm old, now. A poor old widow—sixpence for a poor old widow woman? Except I'm not so old, not really."

"My God, it *is* you. I've been looking everywhere. Mary, it's me—it's Jack Hartright."

"I feel the cold in all my bones, but I can still kneel down. I could kneel for you. Shall I kneel?"

A tilt of the head, and behind the veil a ghastly death's-head coquetry. Crabbed fingers, plucking. Oh, Lord.

"No, just listen. I'm Nell's friend—Nell Rooney—remember? We met one night at Mother Clatterballock's night house. Now I'm trying to find her. I'm looking for Nell."

She grew still. Head cocked like a derelict bird. A flicker of misty recollection.

"That's right—we had a drink together, the three of us. I'm the actor. Jack. Well, I *was* an actor, which is neither here nor there. What matters is, I came here looking for you, and I found you, and now I need to find Nell."

"Nell gave me a present, once."

"That's right. She gave you a book. I remember you showed it to me."

Lord help us if she didn't fish it out, from somewhere within those rags. A little volume bound in dark green pebbled leather.

"See? It's Shakespeare's sonnets. I read them."

She pressed it upon me. Insisting I touch it—ascertain it was real.

"Yes, I see. It was a lovely gift. But the thing is, I'm very worried about Nell, and I need you to help me find her."

"My father was an educated man. A clergyman. He read Shakespeare to me, and many things besides. He taught me Greek."

"Just listen."

"*Alpha* is the beginning, and *omega* is the end. God is both of them, and he is also *dike,* for *dike* means justice—except not really. It really means 'the proper order of things.' Did you know that? We're not bound by *dike* here. I could do whatever you like. Would you like me to lie down? I could turn over."

At any other time, my heart would have gone out to her. A clergyman's daughter—dear God, my mother was a clergyman's daughter. And I had been a clergyman myself! Another time I must surely have wept, and perhaps even taken her in my arms—this reeking, filthy thing—and vowed to help. But right now I had to know about Nell. This was urgent; I was desperate.

"Mary, *please.* Do you have any idea where she is? Nell Rooney. Damn it all, do you . . . ?"

A little cry, for apparently in my frustration I had taken her by the elbow. I think I may have shaken her, without intending to.

"Oh God, I'm sorry."

Shoulders hunched and quivering. Head bowed, and a thin, unearthly keening. I fished awkwardly for a handkerchief to offer, and glanced quickly round. No one nearby, and darkness all but complete. I couldn't stay much longer.

"I'm really very sorry. I didn't mean . . . but please, just tell me. Have you seen Nell Rooney?"

Amidst the sobs, a syllable. "No."

"Are you sure?"

"I just said."

"Can you think where she might have gone?"

"She left me. This is her fault. I hope she dies. I hope she's writhing with maggots."

"You don't mean that."

"Yes I do. She caused this to happen to me, the evil little bitch."

"And you don't have any idea where—?"

"You hurt me!"

The head, snapping up. The keening gone now, and the old dim eyes bright with hatred, even through the veil.

And then the moment passed. A ragged, death's-head desperation.

"You could hurt me again, if you wanted. For a shilling?"

"Look, I have to go. They close the gates at ten o'clock. But if you should hear anything of Nell—anything at all . . ."

"Just a shilling. I think you'd like it. I think perhaps you're that sort of man."

Talons plucking at my arm again. I shook her off.

"Please don't touch me like that."

"A shilling to hurt the widow woman, who hasn't a penny to feed her poor crippled husband. For sometimes I'm the one, and sometimes the other—I forget which it is today. Sometimes I bandage my arm, and then I'm a girl who broke her arm in a factory when a steam engine blew up. She had golden ringlets, that girl, and all the soldiers loved her. But that was long ago."

"I said don't touch me!"

"For ten shillings you could kill me. I could die for you."

TO THE EDITOR
The Morning Register
3 November, 1851

. . .

Sir—News having reached us in Bristol of the prodigious Irish appetite of Mr Daniel O'Thunder for the salvation of souls, I invite him to join me in a repast of a different nature. If Mr O'Thunder will bring his appetite and his Hammer to a meeting at one of the clock on the afternoon of his choosing, for a purse of 50 guineas from each side, I would be delighted to offer him such a diet of Doublers and Choppers and Good English Pegs as would surfeit even the most outrageous glutton, and cause him to exclaim: "Sir, I am satisfied." In anticipation of Mr O'Thunder's reply I remain, as ever, his faithful servant, Henry Gully.

PIPER

HEN GULLY?" asked Daniel O'Thunder, in disbelief.

I recognized his voice as I started up the narrow wooden stairs that led from the main room of the Academy. O'Thunder had a room off the landing above, where he slept.

"That's right, Daniel. He's calling you a Great Spalpeen, and other things besides."

The second was a London voice, jocular and somehow insinuating at the same time. Turning the corner of the stair, I saw that it belonged to a spry ginger-haired man with ratty whiskers. I recognized him at once as O'Thunder's second from the mill against Spragg the Ruffian. Rennert, his name was.

O'Thunder stood barefoot in the open door of his bedchamber, newly risen and sluggish with sleep. He held a newspaper, which Rennert had just given to him. I paused three steps below them, to listen.

"Henry Gully said that?" O'Thunder demanded.

"A Great Bog-Irish Spalpeen, to be exact, of gusting winds and no bottom whatsoever."

"The Game Chicken?"

"Hen Gully, the Game Chicken himself."

O'Thunder frowned uncertainly at the newspaper. It had been opened to Gully's notice and handed over for him to read, which of course he couldn't.

"Show me the words, John Thomas. Point to the words where he says this."

"Oh, he doesn't say it in the newspaper, Daniel. In the newspaper, he's polite as you please—he's gracious as shake-your-hand. It's to his friends he's saying things. He's saying them in private, but of course nothing stays private for long, does it? Not in the world we live in, no indeed, and not when a man keeps his ears to the ground. Both ears fixed firmly to the ground, Daniel, for this has always been my way. Consecutively, of course, not simultaneously, which would involve an anatomical impossibility."

"What are you talking about?"

"My ears."

Rennert laughed easily.

From inside the chamber came a rumbling tinkle. Peering past O'Thunder, I couldn't help but observe the source.

The room itself looked to have been a storeroom once. It had been pressed into service as a Spartan bedchamber, of the sort a soldier might choose to inhabit. Bare walls, a rough plank floor, a narrow cot, and a chamber pot—upon which someone was currently squatting. This was a tousled young woman of generous proportions and scanty habiliment, and a singular absence of shame. She waved as she saw me, and continued with her business.

The two men hadn't noticed me yet. A fly on the wall. Or possibly a toad on the stair. Choose your image.

"You have always been a friend to me, John Thomas. For many years and in many ways, to the best of your ability."

"Thank you, Daniel."

"But Hen Gully said no such thing, in public nor in private, for I know the man and it's not his way. What you're saying is a lie and a slander."

Rennert essayed another easy laugh.

"Then no doubt I'm in error, Daniel, and I apologize. No doubt it's his friends who have said such things without his knowledge—and worse things besides. I won't repeat them, Dan, not even if you ask me to, for it's enough to make my own blood boil and I know what your temper is like. I'd not rouse a temper like yours, Daniel, not if I could help it. So just let me say that 'craven' is a word I do not like, and 'poltroon' a word I like still less, while as for 'pious hypocrite'..."

"Hypocrite? Who called me that?"

"Forget that I uttered it, Daniel. I'm nothing but a babbler. I'm like an old woman, prattling."

"Was it their word, John Thomas? Or was it yours?"

"My word? Never!"

Rennert's laugh was nervous this time, for he felt it as surely as I did. A stillness in O'Thunder that was much more unsettling than red-faced anger in another man.

"But here's the thing of it, Daniel. Here it is. I've spoken to his friends, and they're proposing a match for the second of December."

"Good God, that's less than a month away!" I exclaimed.

And grimaced. So much for the fly on the wall.

Rennert swivelled, and saw me. O'Thunder looked down as well. So did the young woman, who had finished her business and come up behind O'Thunder. She had a wide mouth and a gap between her front teeth and breasts like first-prize pumpkins at the county fair of your steamiest schoolboy imaginings. Which of course was the last thing a gentleman would notice. So I didn't.

Rennert eyed me. "And who might this be?"

I cleared my throat, and put pumpkins from my mind. "William Piper. I'm a correspondent for *The Morning Register.*"

"Ah," said Rennert, with a charming smile. "And did someone invite the gentlemen of the press into this discussion? Someone must have done, but I can't recall doing it myself."

"Brother Piper is a friend," said Daniel O'Thunder. "Brother Piper comes in welcome."

He attempted a smile, at which my heart gave an absurd little leap. But the attempt made him grimace with pain.

"This man can't fight Gully in three weeks," I protested to Rennert. "Just look at him!"

For O'Thunder was still a wreck. It was barely a week after the battle with the Ruffian, and he had just returned to London. His head had begun to shrink back to human dimensions, but the lumps were still there like boles on an oak tree. His eyes were vermilion blooms, and he shuffled and creaked like his own grandfather.

I warmed to the topic. "Besides, why fight Gully at all? The Ruffian was one thing, and he was bad enough. But the Game Chicken stood twenty-seven rounds against the Tipton Slasher himself."

Rennert's chuckle was as the cheerful tinkling of a country stream. "And now our friend is an expert on pugilism. What a fine thing it is, to be an expert. Did you know your friend was such a prodigy of knowledge, Daniel?"

No, of course I wasn't an expert on pugilism. But anyone who read the sporting press knew of the Game Chicken.

"He's killed two men in the ring," I pointed out.

Rennert's smile grew narrow as the mouth of a post-box.

"Don't exaggerate," he said.

"Exaggerate? How do you exaggerate dead? First it was Ned Belcher the Tyneside Tinman, and two years later it was Rossemus Corcoran."

"The Tinman stumbled and knocked his head against the ring post. And Corcoran died because his heart give out. Daniel knows that as well as I do—don't you, Daniel? Besides, look what the Magistrates said when the matters come to trial. Two slate-faced English beaks sitting on their haemorrhoids—if the Chicken had been killing men in the prize-ring, they'd have hung 'im soon as look at 'im. They'd have passed the sentence in two minutes flat, and then asked for their breakfast. But what did they decide instead? Three months for the Tinman, God rest him, and six for Corcoran. Nine months all told. Nine months isn't killing—it's just bad luck."

But Mrs Piper's son has a stubborn streak. "Corcoran's heart gave out because Gully stove his ribs in on top of it."

Rennert adopted a wounded look. "Tell me, friend. Do I really look like such a villain? I have known Dan O'Thunder, man and boy, for nigh upon twenty years. Through all this time, I have been his friend, and he has been mine. Do you suppose I would match him against a man who might *kill* him?" He shook his head in such sorrow that I guessed the truth: it would depend how much money was involved.

O'Thunder spoke. "No one would ever think such a thing, John Thomas, and least of all myself."

"I rejoice to hear it, Daniel."

"But I'm hurt," he said quietly. "The Ruffian's blows went right down to the marrow, and Gully's blows will be worse."

Rennert seized upon this. "Does that mean you'll fight him, then?"

"Leave 'im alone!" It was the young woman with the prize-winning pumpkins. Her dander had been visibly rising for some moments, and now she glared. "The man can hardly move—look at 'im. If there's chickens need fighting, go an' fight 'em yourself!"

But O'Thunder summoned the shadow of a bone-weary smile. "Of course I'll fight him, John Thomas. Go, set the match."

He turned back into his chamber. With an exclamation of remonstrance and a last scalding look, the young woman bolted in after him, the prize-winners bounding indignantly. Rennert turned towards me.

"And now perhaps you'll tell me what you're doing here," he said.

I watched unhappily as O'Thunder's chamber door closed.

"I'm a newspaperman," I said curtly. "I came here in hopes of a story. Something to write up and sell to the *Morning Register*. Good sturdy facts in plain English words, a penny apiece."

The cloud upon Rennert's brow began to clear. "In other words, you're here for the money?"

"Of course," I snapped. "Why else would I be here?"

In that moment, perhaps I even meant it. Seeing this, Rennert's well-oiled smile slid back into position.

"Good," he said, with the satisfied air that comes of identifying a kindred spirit. "Very good indeed. Yes, you write it up directly, for your newspaper. *O'Thunder Accepts Gully's Challenge.* We'll want to keep it lively—perhaps a reference to poultry-plucking, and bold Irish foxes set loose in the Henhouse. Here, give me a bit of paper—I'll jot something down."

"Or perhaps—here's an idea—I'll write the damned thing myself."

The country stream tinkled. Rennert was laughing again. "There it is—an idea indeed. I shall heed your advice, Mr Piper, and leave the scribbling to professionals." He placed a comradely hand on my shoulder, and leaned in close enough that I could smell the breakfast gin. "And now that you have what you need, friend, I wouldn't dream of detaining you further. You'll be on your way directly. And there'll be no need for you to come back."

MOTHER AND I HAD rooms near Mecklenburgh Square. These had diminished over the years—not in size, of course, but in number. Originally we had occupied two full floors of the house. This was in the bygone time when Father was still with us. Then one evening he had looked up suddenly while totting the household accounts at his desk. He exclaimed in some surprise, "Oh dear, I do believe I'm going now." And went, toppling sideways from his stool and proceeding directly to a far greater accounting. Subsequently we'd let the first floor go, and then bits of the second. Eventually we dwindled to four shabby rooms, with meals sent up from below, where a family of Poles now occupied the portion of the house containing the scullery. It doesn't particularly matter that they were Poles. I'm not even sure why

I mention it. It's just a Fact, I suppose. I'm a man who deals in Facts. Or tries to.

There was Mother's bedchamber. There was a closet beneath the stairs where Dorcas, her maidservant and companion, slept. I myself slept in a tiny attic room at the rear of the house. Originally I had occupied a larger chamber directly below, but had been as it were squeezed upward by the contraction in family finances. Lying in bed at night, I had latterly begun to imagine that a final spasmodic contraction might squeeze me right out onto the roof.

The parlour was on the second floor, looking out onto Guilford Street. It had a grate, and a faded green carpet, and a piano that no one played, and three chairs. A familiar bulk was sitting by the window as I came in, exactly where she always sat, wearing the customary black dress and shawl. Watching the world go by below—or as much of the world as had strayed onto Guilford Street.

My mother, Agnes Piper. The Rock of Agnes. She grunted fondly. I think it was fondly. With my mother it could be hard to be sure.

"Hullo, William," she said. "How was the world, today?"

"Variable, Ma. Some of it dreary—some of it shocking—bits of it quite remarkable."

"Tell me about it."

We took after one another, Mother and I—at least in our looks—which was of course unfortunate for the both of us. Each morning I'd go forth into the world in search of Facts. Each evening I'd bring them back to our rooms, and lay them out like shells from the seashore. The Rock of Agnes would inspect them and pass judgement, while Dorcas sat behind us, knitting and sniffling.

This evening, I told her about Daniel O'Thunder. "To tell the truth, I'm not sure quite what to make of him," I admitted.

"O'Thunder," my Mother mused, as if fingering a shell of doubtful provenance. "Irish." She shot a glance to Dorcas, as if to indicate that she had a shrewd idea what to think of this already. The Rock of Agnes had a shrewd idea what she thought of almost everything, and very little ever changed her mind.

Dorcas avoided the glance, and sniffled.

Dorcas sniffled constantly. She was five-and-thirty, angular and spare and pale as porcelain, with great pale eyes and white-blonde hair and veins that showed blue at the temples. There was a permanent glistening droplet at the end of her long nose, as if the nasal pipes had frozen one cruel winter morning in childhood and had been dripping ever since. All in all, I confess I was uncertain why Waldron the turnkey at Newgate Prison had been quite so smitten.

"Irish," my Mother repeated. "Catholic?"

"I think more evangelical," I said.

"Evangelical. *And* a prize-fighter?"

Her look darkened steadily when I confessed to misgivings about the company O'Thunder kept, and described Jaunty Rennert's ingratiating manner. Before I had even alluded to other companions, the Rock of Agnes was shaking her head with finality.

"No," she said. "No, no, no. He's a fraud, William—he's nothing but a charlatan."

"Well, you may be right, although—"

"William, *no.* He's mad. He's clearly dangerous. No good will ever come of such a man, and no good will come to him either. There'll be tears before bedtime—you mark my words. I have a very decisive feeling about this. It will end in tears, so just you stay away from him."

Having settled this once and for all, the Rock of Agnes folded her arms and returned her attention to Guilford Street. After a moment, Dorcas leaned towards me. Her great pale eyes shone, and for a surprising moment she had the aspect of a leaky translucent angel. In that moment I actually began to understand what Waldron the turnkey had seen.

"Tell me again," she whispered, "*exackly* how Spragg the Ruffian fell."

I hitched closer. "He fell," I whispered back, "like boxes toppling."

"Ohhhhhhhhhh," said Dorcas, and glistened.

WHEN I RETURNED TO O'Thunder's two days later, the difference was startling.

It was just gone noon. Half the indigent of Holborn—or so it seemed—were there. They were milling out front, where someone had placed a new handwritten sign in the window. No longer O'Thunder's Academy of the Manly Arts, this was now the Gospel Mission of Heaven's Hammer. The indigent straggled up the stairs. They crowded into the main room above, where benches and long wooden tables had been laid out. A ragged queue stretched to the far end, where the Miss Sherwoods ladled out soup from a great tureen.

Tim Diggory was just inside the door, standing guard like the Mastiff of the Lord in a chimney-pot hat. One eye was on the indigents while the other was fixed upstairs, watching for any sign that O'Thunder was stirring. Seeing me, he inclined his head in greeting.

"'Afternoon, Tim," I said, and looked around in mild wonderment. "The place has changed."

"Yuss," said Tim. "Didjer see it?"

"See what, Tim?"

"Sign. New one. In the winder."

"Yes," I said. "I saw it."

Tim leaned down closer, as if to communicate confidential information. "I writ that," he said.

"Did you?"

"My sign. Come up with the nyme, too—Gospel Mission of 'Eaven's 'Ammer. Like it?"

I assured him I did so, very much. Tim nodded in quiet satisfaction and rocked back on his heels, with the air of a man who has done a heroic day's work already—and here it was, scarcely afternoon.

"'Eaven's 'Ammer. My hinspiration."

"Very good. Excellent. Well... carry on."

I carried on myself, sauntering over to the soup tureen and hazarding conversation with the Miss Sherwoods as they worked. They were curt without being outright hostile, which I accepted as a welcome thaw in relations. We chatted about this and that—or rather, I asked questions, to which they made grudging but civil replies. Yes, their charitable operations were expanding remarkably, for contributions to the Mission had multiplied since Captain O'Thunder's victory in Essex. Yes, they had heard that the Captain had accepted another challenge. No, they had no particular opinion upon this—although the mouth of the younger Miss Sherwood grew tight when the topic was raised. It tightened further when I asked—very casually—about the young woman I'd noticed here the other day.

"The young woman with—hem." But of course there is no appropriate euphemism for "pumpkins." I amended on the fly. "The young woman with special permission to use the Captain's chamber pot."

"I have no idea who you're talking about," Miss Sherwood muttered through gritted teeth.

I subsequently learned that the young woman's name was Molly La Clarice. I learned because I asked, and I asked because I was trying to work up the nerve to say hello to her. But just now, there was a joyful shout from Tim Diggory.

"It's the Captain!"

And there he was. O'Thunder was easing himself painfully down the stairs. There was a great exclamation, and a general surging towards him. A surging like sea-foam, with the flotsam of Holborn bobbing with it. I swear the floor lurched with the shifting of the weight. I had a momentary image of the whole rotten building going over like a shipwreck, with a shattering of boards and a shivering of masts, and Wm. Piper clinging to the topmost spar as the deep rose up to claim him.

"'Ere 'e is—huzzah!"

"How is it today, Daniel?"

"Give him room!"

("Lord, it hurts just to look at him.")

"Give him air!"

"I've brought my babby, Captain. See? I've brought him here for you to bless."

"Fetch him something to eat!"

("Lord, he can hardly walk.")

"Bless me, Captain."

"Bless me."

"Bless *you*."

("Oh Lord, he's down!")

But he'd just stooped to place a swollen paw on the head of an old woman. He straightened and looked round at them all, with a slow misshapen smile.

"Look at you," he said. "Just look at you all—and aren't you beautiful?"

And damn me if they weren't. They were filthy and tattered and reeking, the better part of them at any rate. Even those that were halfway clean were as homely an assortment as you'd meet on any street corner. For—let's be honest—we're a queer-looking species in the first place, and poverty never improved anyone's looks. But in the warmth of that gargoyle smile they glowed. For a moment in their lives, they were lovely.

He shuffled forward through them: reaching out, smiling and murmuring. Somebody started to pound him on the back, then remembered how badly O'Thunder was battered and stopped in comical horror. A baker and his wife had brought some sticky buns, which looked to be far too few to go round. But O'Thunder handed them out and it turned out there were enough.

He moved closer to where I stood on the periphery. My usual vantage point, and it had always been a good one, good and safe. On the outside, looking in. Objectivity.

He stopped to speak to the man at my shoulder. It always came as a shock, how big he was, up close. He filled all the space around him.

"You've been afraid all your life," he said. "Don't be. And yes, there is."

There was no one standing at my shoulder. He was looking at me.

"There's much to believe in, brother. There's good in the world, but we must be ready to fight for it. Be bold, be joyful, and be ready."

I have an idea I flushed to the roots of my hair. I'm sure I stammered something idiotic. But in that moment the possibility occurred that I—Mrs Piper's pock-faced boy, with his toad's body and his bulging eyes—might be as lovely as the rest of them. Would you credit it? There was a thought to lift the heart—or else to make a horse laugh. But in that moment, I was like all the others. I was exalted.

Afterwards O'Thunder went outside, into the cold sunlight and the unending shout of London. The world—or most of it—took no notice. It clattered on its way along the Gray's Inn Road. But the ragtag assortment that was loitering out in front exclaimed and pointed. Someone cheered. A girl stepped towards him. Just a slip of a thing, wearing a fine cloak and bonnet.

"This is for you," she said, digging something out of her pocket. "Fucked if I know why. Here—just take it."

The accent was from the East London streets, oddly incongruous with the nice clothes she was wearing. She was brazen as you like, but turning red all the same—as red as the ribbon she'd just given him, because that's what it was. A scrap of red ribbon.

"Do I know you?" O'Thunder looked at her curiously, for he seemed to think he might recognize her. She had red hair, and green eyes, and a thin pinched face. She also had a mouth like a sewer.

"Not exactly. No. And I was never here. If he knew I was here—fuck me. There'd be the Devil to pay."

"If who knew?"

"Doesn't matter. I just wanted to say—fucksake, I don't know. What did I want to say? I wanted to give you that—so I did."

O'Thunder held up the scrap of ribbon, to admire it. It was tiny in his great swollen hand. "I'll wear this into battle," he said.

When he looked down again, the red-haired girl was already gone.

"Go whop 'im, Captain!" A one-legged beggar lurched forward, with a crutch and a wooden leg. "Go whop 'im a good one, the Devil. Then give 'im an extra lick besides, and tell 'im: 'This one's from Timber Bill!'"

The beggar swung his fist in demonstration. A poor idea for a one-legged man in a state of inebriation. He toppled headlong, but O'Thunder caught him and lifted him up. For a moment Timber Bill stood without his crutch, unaided and triumphant.

"Look at me!" he cried.

O'Thunder laughed with the sheer pleasure of it. Then the laugh died away. He raised his head, and called out to the Gray's Inn Road.

"Has anyone seen the Devil? Can anyone tell me what hole he's hiding in today?"

For just a moment, it was as if all of London faltered to a stop. O'Thunder's voice rang. "Wherever he is, I have a message for him. Pass it on for me, brothers and sisters. Tell the Devil: it's not too late. It's never too late, not even for him. Tell the Devil he can still repent."

*T*HE DEVIL STANDS *very still indeed. He stands like the very Statue of a Devil, for he has heard this before. The Risen Jew had uttered those very words as he stood before the Infernal Gates long centuries ago. Such a little man, with great mad haunted eyes, still wearing his grave clothes. The end of the winding-sheet had unravelled and trailed in the dirt behind him.*

"It is not too late."

The Devil remembers thinking: can it truly have come to this? *This quiet little fellow, and the ruination of all the Devil's darkest hopes. A tattered child, roused from sleep, trailing its blanket.*

"You can still repent."

He had said it in Aramaic, of course. A tongue the Devil had once spoken himself, along with all the other languages of the earth. The Devil had replied in Latin: "Non serviam." Servire, *to be a slave or servant.*

The Devil had started to say much else as well, had vowed eternal defiance and unutterable revenge, which caused the Risen Jew to shake his head in sorrow. Then all at once it was indeed too late, for the little man had raised his arm—an arm like a stick, and a hole clear through his hand. The Devil remembers this most vividly of all: the hole, sudden and startling, and the curious thought that a cork would fit. In the next instant there was a flash of unbearable light, and a terrible grinding of stone, and then with a mighty crack the Gate burst wide.

They all came stumbling out—the Devil remembers this as if it were yesterday. All that ancient rabble, condemned by original sin to languish in Hell until the Son of Man should set them free. Noah and Moses and Solomon, and Adam and Eve themselves, all weeping with the joy of it and shouting loud hosannas. Or possibly he just remembers reading about it. The Mystery Plays, perhaps. Or else the poem, the great rumbling Latinate monstrosity by that poet—not Dante but the English one, the Puritan, the one who went blind from tugging at himself—Milton. Perhaps that's what it was. The Devil remembers reading about it, as if it were yesterday.

And now this Irishman.

A wisp of smoke curls from the neck of the Devil's shirt as he looks out of the window. Peers down through cracked and soot-blackened glass upon the Gray's Inn Road, and the little tableau that has enacted itself. The Devil has bolt-holes all over London, and this is one of them: a filthy room in an appalling rooming-house, with a stench of humanity wafting up from below and rats rustling in the walls. It is foul, but it affords a view of the Irishman's redoubt, which is why he engaged it.

There is a creak from the narrow bed behind him, and a slap, and a querulous execration. It is the little mollie from the White Swan discovering a louse. He is a spotty creature with a shock of hair that stands straight up and pale eyes that bulge as if he were being throttled, which perhaps he will be, presently. The White Swan is a nest of sodomites. The Devil went there last night, as he will do from time to time. He doesn't know why, for he finds it repulsive. Perhaps it was the business of the old whore in the Park. She had died much harder than he had expected, and this left him feeling out of sorts with himself.

The little mollie is squealing. "It's lousy, this room! It's disgusting. I'd never have come, if I'd known you were lousy."

The Devil has been many things, but never lousy, and says so.

"Well, you are now!"

The Devil regards him fondly. He is imagining how much straighter the mollie's hair will stand, and how much more dramatically his pale eyes will bulge, when hands like talons close about his windpipe. The mouth will gape and the tongue protrude. In the end the extremities will judder most agreeably, before the eyes at last roll up and everything releases with a noxious reek. That part is unpleasant and may spatter the boots, but we must all take the bad with the good, even the Devil.

She had clawed his face, the old woman in the Park. Banshee shrieks and filthy fingernails. He was afraid that they would be overheard, and throttled her in flustered revulsion, all the while thinking that it ought to be much simpler than this.

"Tell the Devil he can still repent."

Right there, beneath his window. That voice ringing out, and the great roaring metropolis itself breaking stride for just an instant to listen.

The Irishman is mad, of course. This is precisely what makes the Devil so uneasy. He does not fear any power in Creation. He did not fear God Himself—all the literature has attested to this. But deep down in the bowels of his being the Devil is frightened of insanity. This is why he does not go to Bedlam Hospital on visiting day with all the rest, to gawk and giggle and marvel at the lunatics. He ventured there just once, and was frozen to the heart by the thought of what those tormented visages might portend, or perhaps reflect. For there exists a terrible strength in madness. You must not stray too close, for dread of what may reach towards you, and clamp on. And yet the Irishman cannot be avoided. The Devil knows this, knows in his marrow that this madman must be answered, and beaten, and broken.

The girl. He'll begin with the girl.

The thought of it almost makes him smile.

Two hours later, when he has finished with his pencils and his paints, and brushed his coat, and cleaned his spattered boots, he descends from his garret and commences his campaign.

JACK

THE HOUSE WAS unprepossessing. It was halfway along a row of terraced houses, dating to the last century and the time of poor King George III. Built perhaps in those last declining days when poor George himself still clung to his wits with sphincter-clenching desperation. The attempt might be glimpsed in the houses themselves. In the darkness and the fog they stood stiffly shoulder to shoulder, stolid brick houses aspiring to bland Germanic normality, perfectly uniform with identical iron railings in front.

"She's there?"

There was no sign that he had heard me. Those uncanny eyes remained fixed upon a curtained window on the second floor. It was dark, as were the windows in the rooms below. We were hunched in the shrubbery opposite, staying just outside the ghostly halo of a gas-lamp. Rain continued to fall.

"Are you sure?"

A tilt of the head: yes.

"You've actually seen her?"

Two tiny quick bobs of the pointed chin: yes. Of course he'd seen her. Why else had he come to fetch me?

He'd been waiting in the street outside my rooms—my room, rather. Room, singular; my garret on the northern fringes of

Holborn. The rat-hole I'd rented in these days of my exile from the Kemp Theatre. I'd just returned from a long night's tramp through the icy rain and the worst of the London byways. He was squatting against the railing: cap pulled low, collar turned up, chin sunk between his bony knees in ghostly changeling stillness.

"Tommy?"

And it was. Young Tommyknocker, the goblin-faced boy from the theatre. He sprang to his feet, and nearly slipped on the greasy cobbles. He'd been asleep, I think, despite the rain that drenched him to the bone.

"Good Lord, are you all right? What the Devil are you doing here?"

He didn't answer in words, of course, for he was mute. But he'd scribbled something with a stub of pencil on a scrap of paper, and now he thrust it at me.

I KNOW WHERE SHE IS.

"Where who is? What are you—?" And then it dawned. *"Nell?"*

The bobbing of the chin.

"Good God. Have you seen her? Is she all right? Quickly—where is she?"

Another scrap of paper. Another scribble.

I CAN TAKE YOU.

"Take me this instant!"

He darted away into the night, turning back like a dog to make sure that I was following. And of course I was. I was following him every step of the way, with all weariness forgotten and my heart hammering in my chest.

"Go! Hurry—I'll keep up!"

We made our way north and west, turning up Southampton Row. Despite the hour, pedestrians jostled and carriages clattered, lurching out of the fog and splashing mud. The cafés and night houses gave off an indistinct yellow glow, and the gas-lamps like ghostly lanterns faded away into blackness. North of Tavistock Square we veered westward, towards Euston

Station. But half-familiar landmarks were swallowed and distorted in the deepening fog, and soon enough I had lost all sense of where I was or what direction Tommy was leading. But just when my bewilderment had grown complete, we crossed Hampstead Road, and veered north again. Ten minutes more and we turned into a quiet narrow street, and the row of stolid Germanic houses.

"Tommy, are you *sure?*"

For we'd been crouched in the shrubbery for long minutes now, and still the house was entirely dark. Not a glimmer of light or a flicker of movement within. I had just resolved to stride across the street and bang on the door, when Tommy caught my arm. He had heard it, an instant before I did too: the clip-*clop* of horses' hooves, and the rattle of a carriage approaching. It materialized from the fog like a ghost ship taking form, and drew to a stop directly across from us. A brougham, drawn by a single black horse. A silent coachman sat above, muffled against the night. The carriage door opened, the step dropped down, and a black figure unfolded itself from the darkness within.

Lord Sculthorpe.

He limped up to the front door, opened it with a key, and stepped through. The door closed behind him. A lamp glowed into being, within. After a few moments, a second glow kindled behind the curtain in the uppermost casement. The curtain was drawn back, and Lord Sculthorpe looked out. Through the swirling fog, he might have been some monstrous revenant—the vampire Lord Ruthven himself, gazing down from a stone redoubt. For a terrible moment he seemed to be staring straight at me; I had an icy presentiment of calamity. But he turned away, speaking to someone just out of sight of the casement. Then there was a movement behind him, and I saw who it was.

A girl in a white nightgown, holding a candle. A tousled mane of red hair.

"Nell!"

It came out as an inarticulate cry—relief and confusion and fear, all at once. She was alive. She was unharmed. But she was with *him*.

I turned to Tommy, my thoughts all in a whirl. "What's going on? How long as she been in that house?"

He had his stub of pencil, and a scrap of paper.

I DON'T KNOW. WEEKS?

"Weeks? Dear God—is she a prisoner?"

He scribbled two more words.

OR WORSE.

NELL

His Lordship didn't want me going out. He'd said that when he first brought me to the house. This had been all the way back in September. He said it in a voice like winter, leaning in so close that I could see the tufts of hair in his nose and smell the oysters he'd had for supper: "You must not leave this house. I cannot sufficiently stress this. Mother Clatterballock will be seeking you all over London. If you do leave, then the Devil take you, for I shall wash my hands."

Then that lip of his had twitched in a smile. "On the other hand, why would you *want* to leave? Why would you want to set foot outside this house, ever again?" He gestured with a sweep of his hand. "Look where you are. You've died and gone to Hampstead."

I stared round, that first night. Not quite believing it. His Lordship stood like a slash of darkness.

"Who lives here?" I demanded.

"You do."

Three rooms, and all of them mine. Three rooms, each one bigger than the last, with Turkey carpets on the floors, and a feather bed you'd sink right into, and a grate for when it got cold, and pots on the shelves in the pantry instead of spread around to catch the leaks, like in every other place I ever lived. This was bigger than Tom's house on Pye Street. Trafalgar Tom's, where I lived for a time after they hung poor Mrs Dalrymple. I was there six months, before Tom sold me to Mother Clatterballock—and there was fifty of us lived in that Pye Street house. Fifty thieving beggars in them rooms, and sometimes more, depending on who was coming and who was going and who got transported and who was set to hang on Monday. Twenty to a room and ten to a bed, all jammed up farting together like piglets in a sty. A girl could lose her precious jewel and never know whose prick it was. But here in Hampstead, here in all them rooms, was only me.

"Is that a warming-pan for the bed? Christ, it is. Where's the pot?"

"The privy's right there."

"What?"

"Through that door."

Fuck me if it wasn't. A water closet with a toilet that flushed, and through another door a room with a bathtub like a great coal-scuttle, for someone to soak in all the livelong day if that's what they took a mind to, with pipes that brought the water in.

"Don't!"

I flinched away, cos he'd suddenly come up behind me. Much too silent, and much too close. A black arm slipping round my shoulder like a coil.

"Fucksake, don't be doing that! Sneaking and grabbing!"

There was look on his face like I'd slapped him. Then a look like storm clouds gathering. "Sneaking?"

I flinched back another step. "Look, I'm sorry—I didn't mean—you startled me is all. I'm just a bit nervy, tonight. With being here, and all. With running away. So I'm just—I mean—no offence to Your Lordship."

There was a queer rattling sound deep down in his throat. He was chuckling.

"She has spirit, the little puss. That's good—I enjoy spirit. Within reason. For a time."

I THOUGHT I'D seen the last of him that afternoon in May at the Great Exhibition, when he turned up out of nowhere as me and Jack Hartright were looking at the giant lizards. He said that afternoon he wanted me to meet him again, but fucked if I was going to go near him. Then a few weeks later I stepped out of a theatre, and there he was.

It wasn't a proper theatre, this one—just a penny gaff in Bread Street. There were penny gaffs all over London. Some were quite big, but others like this one were just a room above a shop or a public house. You'd climb a rickety staircase into a dirty hole with a hundred others crammed in with you. Mostly they were boys from the street, swearing and smoking shag tobacco, and for a penny you'd see the show. Some comical songs, or a pantomime, and sometimes a ballet. This night there was a farce about a man who married a terrible shrew. She made his life miserable until he got himself a big enough cudgel, after which she come round amazingly, and that was the moral: get a big one. The boys liked it considerable, cheering and flinging down coppers and apples.

He was waiting as I came out—standing there with wisps of fog about him. "Did you find her?" he asked.

"Find who? What are you talking about?" Cos I was flustered by the sight of him, and trying to keep my distance. "Look, how did you know I was here? Have you been bloody following me?"

"Did you find your mother tonight? For I know that's why you go to the theatre."

"Mister, I don't know what you—"

"No? Ah, well. Perhaps you'll find her another time, then. Come with me."

"What?"

"I'd like to buy you something nice. A treat."

There was a shop nearby, he said, where they sold fruit pies. I shook my head, and mumbled an excuse, and pulled away as he was reaching out. Cos I wasn't going anywhere with this one.

Not after the things he'd said to me the first time we met—and most especially not on a night like this, not on Bread Street with a London Particular fog shrouding round.

He smiled thinly. "Tomorrow afternoon, then," he said. "You'll meet me at two o'clock—yes you will, don't bother shaking your head. Why? Because you're hardly a fool—you know what advantages there are to being my friend. The special friend of a man such as myself. And you'll come because you're curious as a kitten. You'll come for your mother's sake."

We met at a café in the Strand. It was daylight, which made it safer. Besides there was a much better class of person there—except for me. They brought us cakes and ices, and he watched as I shovelled them in. Small as I was, I could always eat like a stevedore. I belched afterwards, too.

He looked amused. "My name is Lord Sculthorpe. You should know that, since we're to be friends."

"Who says we're to be friends?"

"I do."

"Why do you wear that hat?"

"I like my hat. What's wrong with it?"

It was on his knee, just now—that slouchy low-brimmed hat. He sat across the table, angled sidelong, watching me finish my treat. Right leg crossed over, dangling his foot, in old-fashioned knee-high riding boots.

I shook my head. "You look like someone out of a play. Sorry to say that, Mister, but—"

"'My Lord.'"

"What?"

"'I am sorry to say that, *my Lord.*' And mind your tone of voice. You're being pert."

But he still looked amused. He was different than he'd been that night at Mother Clatterballock's. Maybe he wasn't really so bad.

"When did you last see my mother?"

"I'm looking at her right now."

My heart stopped dead for a second, until I realized he meant me.

"It's uncanny," he said. "The resemblance, when you incline your head that way."

He looked at me, unblinking. "Shall I see what I can do?" he asked at length.

"What do you mean?"

"Shall I see what I can do to find her?"

I SEEN HIM two or three times after that. Only a few minutes each time, and he'd never say anything beyond little hints. Then one day a note was sent to me at Mother Clatterballock's. It said he had made a discovery. It said I must meet him that very night.

The carriage was waiting for me when I slipped out. The door swung open. Inside was blackness, and him.

"Have you found her?" My heart was in my mouth, even though I knew it couldn't be true. "The note said—"

"No, I haven't found her yet. But I have hopes. Get in."

"Does that mean you've heard something?"

"It means I have reasons to believe. But first we must take you away from Mother Clatterballock. This is the first step. Get in."

I could see the outline of his face, now, in the dim glow from a lamp. His eyes were fixed and glittering.

"But I don't—I can't just—I don't have my things."

"You'll have new things. I shall make you altogether new."

It crossed my mind right then—this is exactly the way you'd do it, if you had your eye on some muff of a girl. This is exactly how you'd draw her in, bit by bit. Especially if you liked the game of it, like a cat that's in no hurry with a mouse. And the thought was in my mind: Nell Rooney, you're a bloody fool, and you'll get what you deserve. Cos he's lying—they're all liars—and he's the worst of all. He's the worst you ever met, and you fucking know it.

"Get in."

And I did. I climbed into the carriage. His arm opened, drawing me into his cloak. It folded upon me like the wing of a great black bird.

"Good girl." In the blackness the glint of a smile, like something sliced open with a knife. He rapped with his cane. The carriage lurched and rattled forward into the night.

"Where are you taking me?" I asked.

"Home," he said.

And half an hour later, here we were. Three rooms in Hampstead, each one bigger than the last. A feather bed and bathtub and—fuck me backwards—a privy right there inside.

"Your mother will live here with you. Just as soon as we've found her."

"You swear you'll do that?"

"I have information that your mother may still be alive. No, I can't tell you more than that. But my agents are looking for her. This very moment, my gaze is roving across all of London, and beyond. If your mother is to be found, then we shall find her. And until we do, you'll stay right here. Inside."

"And what else do I have to do?"

That was the question, wasn't it? Though not much point in asking, cos after all I knew the answer. The answer was always the same—always was and always will be, till the last gentleman rolls off the last girl after the last fuck on the very last night of the world. It's just the details that differ. Some of them are worse than others.

"You should put on a fire. Have a wash, and something to eat if you're hungry. Then go to sleep."

"Why are you doing this?"

"There's clothing in the wardrobe—I believe you'll find it fits you tolerably well. There are books, since you can read, and a window in each room to look out of. When you're hungry, Mrs Prendergast will bring you meals—kindly Mrs Prendergast, who lives downstairs."

"Is she my keeper, then?"

"She's your friend. And you'll need her friendship, Nell, almost as much as you need mine. For you know what will happen—yes?—if Mother Clatterballock should find you." His voice was a purr. "She'd need to make an example, you see. So she'd let her bully at you for a bit—a few days, or a week—her bully and his friends. After that, your looks wouldn't be quite what they are today. You'd be past your prime, I'm afraid, and no longer quite the thing for nice gentlemen with clean hands. It would be the other ones—the ones who like to swing their fists, and lay about with a stick—gentlemen from the docks, Nell, smelling of old cheese, and old ones dripping with the pox. I wouldn't be able to help you, either, for I wouldn't be able to find you. They'd have you in some stinking hole in Whitechapel, where such a man as myself would never set foot. Even if I did, I'd never recognize you. Neither would your mother. She wouldn't know you, Nell, and more than that she wouldn't want to. She'd hurry on past, and she'd never look back. She'd let you go. Do you understand what I'm saying?"

I understood.

"Let me hear you say it."

"Yes, I understand what you're bloody saying."

Silence. A twitch, and teeth. "I'll visit you, from time to time. Not tomorrow, or the day after, for I have business elsewhere. But I'll come back—quite possibly when you least expect it. And you'll be here, waiting."

"Does she know, you reckon?"

He'd turned towards the door. Now he stopped.

"My mother. Do you reckon she knows who I am? Does she even know I'm alive?"

I could scarcely bear to ask. He turned back. There was another silence, and then he placed an icy hand against my cheek.

"She's your mother, Nell. She thinks of you each and every day—she loves you more than life itself. I want you to hold on to that thought. I want you to clutch it like a candle."

MRS PRENDERGAST WAS round and rosy as an apple. She beamed like a vicar's wife and called you *dear 'eart* and *lambkin*. I didn't trust her one half-inch.

In my experience, those were the ones you had to watch. You had to watch 'em close as can be, cos half the time you couldn't hear 'em coming, and that's what I trusted least of all—for someone so fat, she was awful light on her feet. You'd hear her singing to herself down below stairs—"Meet Me By Moonlight" or "Villikins and his Dinah"—while you were by the window, looking out. Then after a bit the thought would start to niggle: it had been a good long while since you'd heard that voice, or anything at all. You'd find yourself thinking: now, how long has it been *exactly?* And you wouldn't be able to remember. Then when you opened your door and looked out, the dishes you'd left on the landing was gone—the dirty dishes from the last meal she'd fetched upstairs, some ham or mutton and vegetables boiled to mush, with maybe some cheese and even a half-pint of porter, for they fed you here, give 'em that much—the dishes had disappeared, and you hadn't heard a rattle or a single creak on the stair. And every last one of those stairs creaked, cos I'd tested. They creaked like a rusty gate, unless you'd taught yourself to creep up quiet as a cat—and why would you teach yourself to do that in the first place? Unless you were sneaking and spying and listening at keyholes, like the tricksy old twat I knew you for the second I laid my peepers on you.

There was a husband too, and he was just as bad. He had long lean shanks and trousers yanked up halfway to his armpits, and he hardly said anything at all—just looked at you with a big toothy smile and grey hair sticking up all over. It was always stuck up like that, from his habit of rubbing his head furiously with his hand whenever he stopped to think about something, like a man trying to shake loose a whole family of lice. He was a man for angles and corners, that one. You'd catch him peering round 'em at you. I knew he was watching me in the bath, too, watching me through the keyhole the filthy old fucker, cos he wasn't as light on his feet as the missus. You'd hear a creak or two coming up, and if you were careful not to splash you'd hear him breathing. I let him get away with it once or twice, just sliding down in the water and staying there so there wasn't much to see. Besides, I was still trying to read the lie of the land, and work out what I was up against. But after a bit, enough was enough. So finally I got out of the bath and gave a lovely stretch to hold him where he was a second longer. Then I side-stepped to the door where a knitting needle just happened to be lying on a shelf, and poked it through the keyhole.

I never poked it all the way—not far enough to blind the old shitsack. Just enough for a little shriek and a thumping down the stairs and then strangled voices from below: *How did you...? The little witch...! You filthy swine, don't tell me you were...? Look at me, I'm half kilt!* They never said a word, either one of them. But next day when I seen him he had a patch, and the look he gave me with his other glim was quicklime. Her smile was worse, but fuck 'em both.

Besides, they weren't stopping me from going outside.

I found that out the very first time I tried. I was just about to lift the back door latch—walking on tiptoe, heart going thump—when the missus come suddenly out of the pantry on her sneaking cat's paws.

"Why, Lambkin," she exclaimed, all rosy and smiling, "would you be goin' somewheres? Where would you be goin'? (*And I'd like to poke* your *eyes out, oh yes I would.*)"

"I'm going out," I said. Cos what else do you do? You brazen it through.

She gave a little shimmy of alarm. "Out? Oh, no, I think you'd rather stay inside. It's cold out, Dear 'Eart—it's going to rain, you mark my words—you'd catch your death. (*One eye first, and then the next, with little needles: plink, plink!*) I know, Sweetness—I've a better idea. Why don't you go back upstairs, and I'll slice you a lovely bit of bread and treacle? (*Then I'd like to slice your ears off, you little unbottled abortion.*)"

I smiled, bright as a button. Then out I went, and she just stood there.

That first time I didn't go far—just to the corner two streets over, to prove that I could. Watch the world go clattering past and buy a bag of chestnuts from the little costerwoman with the brazier. Piping hot chestnuts, so hot you had to hop them from hand to hand. There were respectable people on the high street, going about respectable business. And every second I halfway expected to feel a hand clamp down from behind. Then headfirst into the carriage and Mother Clatterballock waiting there in horrible wheezing triumph: "'Ere's my peach! Yes 'ere's my own dear child, who thinks she's oh so clever."

But it didn't happen. The next day, it didn't happen either. So I started to go further.

A pastry shop I particularly liked was a five-minute walk away, and past that a dressmaker's. I stood outside the dressmaker's for the longest time, peering through the window. There were two seamstresses at work in the back, and shelves with bolts of cloth, and in the window there were dresses laid out and hats on stands. I looked up to see the shop girl scowling back at me. A little slut that gave herself airs—you know the sort. Looking like she had her monthlies permanent, cos she knew exactly what I was thinking. Oh yes, I might be wearing my nice clothes from Lord Sculthorpe's wardrobe, but she knew *my* sort just as well as I knew hers, and she knew damn well I was planning to filch something the second her back was turned.

Except I wasn't. For once in my life, I had no such thought in my head. Finally I marched right into the shop, and bold as brass I said: "I'll have them gloves." She looked a long way down her nose.

"Which gloves?"

I pointed to a pair laid out on the counter, and she gave a little sneery titter. "Them gloves are genuwine fawn leather. Them gloves are eighteen shillings."

"Good," I said. "So give 'em over."

This foxed her for a minute. She looked me up and down like she wasn't quite sure what to do next. But His Lordship had put more than clothes in the wardrobe—he'd put money in the pockets. So I fetched out my purse and paid the eighteen shillings, and them gloves were the loveliest thing you ever touched in your life, soft as kittens. I told the girl to wrap them up. And she did, going pink in the ears, but what else could she do? I had blunt; I had coin of the realm. When she finished I said: "I'd like it tied with a ribbon," and waited till she'd done. Then I said: "No, actually I think I'll wear 'em instead," and took off the ribbon and opened the package right there and put them on.

"Thank you, Miss," I said. "You're very kind." She squinched her face in a little monthlies grimace, and curtsied one-sixteenth of an inch, and I said: "Well, actually you ent. You're a toffee-nosed twat. But then it takes all kinds to make a world, don't it?"

And as I left I was a duchess. I was the King of Elfland's daughter.

FOR A WHOLE MONTH, it was like that. I came and went as I pleased, cos the Prendergastlies never said a word to stop me and Lord Sculthorpe had disappeared right off the face of the earth. Then one day I saw the balladeer on the street corner, and nothing was ever the same again.

He was one of them as sings out ballads about the day's events, and sells them printed on a broadsheet for a penny. There were balladeers like him on half the corners in London, most of them doing brisk business. Ballads about shocking murders were always popular, and especially the final confessions of villains about to dance the Newgate hornpipe. They'd be selling these in the crowd at the hanging on a Monday morning. Fellers who'd never met the murderer in their life, but here they were, with his last words:

"I sits in my cell as this last day dawns, for there's never to be another,
And I weeps for my sins and the girl I slain,
And I weeps for my poor grey-haired mother..."

But this particular balladeer was on about something else altogether. At first I didn't pay much heed. He was stood there on the corner like a tree in a stream, with the crowds parting as they flowed past. I was passing by too, aiming for a stall that sold mince tarts. I'd become a greedy little slut in Hampstead.

On the twenty-sixth day of October,
Eighteen hundred and fifty-one,
From London and all the other towns,
From everywhere they come...

He was lean and crooked, with his papers laid out in a barrow, and more of them sticking up out of his hat-brim. His apple bobbed up and down in his throat as he stood there declaiming, with his head tilted back and his eyes looking up and away, like his ballad was a cannonball and he was aiming it at Islington.

They come with a shout, but a heavy heart too,
For they know how this day will go:
They've come to see Daniel O'Thunder,
And the Ruffian lay him low.

Daniel O'Thunder. The man who had come to Mother C's that famous night. I knew his name, cos I'd asked some people afterwards. They said he was a preacher who used to be a prize-fighter, and kept a queer place in the Gray's Inn Road. So I stopped to listen. Others were stopping as well.

Half an hour gone, and now it is seen
That O'Thunder must do or die.
For there's gunpowder in the Ruffian's hands—

The Devil is in Spragg's eye.
And now down again! Daniel's friends reach out
With a cry and a terrible gasp,
For Daniel lies bleeding and Daniel lies still—
O'Thunder has breathed his last!

"Hang on!" I exclaimed, so sudden that he broke off and looked down startled with his apple still bobbing. "Are you telling me he's dead?"

"No, Miss," he said gravely. "He's alive. Daniel O'Thunder passed through death."

"He what?"

"On the twenty-sixth day of October, eighteen-hundred and fifty-one. Captain Daniel O'Thunder met Spragg the Ruffian in the prize-ring and was brought to the gates of death. They opened wide to swallow him, but he marched on through and out the other side. And no man who seen it will ever be the same again. Here." He shoved a broadsheet at me with the ballad printed on it, pen and ink. "One penny."

Well, I gave him his penny, didn't I? Cos now I had to know. I read the words, scanning as quick as I could, while he started up chanting again.

... a cry of, "look there—Daniel O'Thunder has risen!"
Like a man who has looked on the face of the Lord,
And the Lord has looked upon his'n...

Then there was something about the Hammer of Heaven, and a flash of lightning, and a horrible groan from under the ground that three bishops there present swore to be the voice of the Devil.

"And you were there? You *seen* this?"

He broke off again, and raised his hand, like a man swearing an oath on the Bible.

"Upon my davy, Miss. From beginning to end."

The fuck he'd been there.

"Well, perhaps not *personally*..."

But he'd spoken directly to some that were. Reliable gentlemen, ready to give sworn testimony. In fact—wait just a second—he had sworn testimony from several of 'em, set down in his own hand, ha'penny a sheet. He was rummaging about in his barrow, sorting through all the various documents, cos of course these street patterers will write anything. Love letters between noblemen and shop girls. Messages from secret Popish plotters. "The Diabolical Practises of Dr. B— —upon His Patients while in a State of Mesmerism."

But I was already on my way. I'd taken a notion to go find this place in the Gray's Inn Road.

I TOLD MYSELF I was just going there cos of curiosity. Just to find out if any of it was true—that's all it amounted to. After all, it wasn't like I cared, particularly. Why would I? Daniel O'Thunder and me, we'd never said two words to each other. He was just some Irish bruiser who sat on Tim Diggory's nob to save poor Luna Queerendo, and look what happened. She died anyway, and probably worse than Tim would have killed her himself.

Leastways, that's what I told myself.

When I found the place, he was standing in the street outside. A crowd of people staring back at him. He didn't look like a man who'd passed through death. More like a man who Death passed over, driving a coach and four. He was battered so bad I would never have recognized him from his face, only from those ridiculous spidery legs and that great barrel body.

Except of course I would have recognized him anywhere. He recognized me, too. I could see that as I went up to him. I was wearing a dark blue mantle from the wardrobe, and my finest bonnet. I was wearing my lovely fawn gloves.

I said to him: "Hello."

If I'd been paying attention, I'd surely have noticed someone else—Tommy, the goblin-faced boy from the Kemp Theatre.

Thinking back later, I realized I had seen him. Just a glimpse, crouched in the shadow of a building. But all I could look at was Daniel O'Thunder. All at once I wanted to tell him everything—things I didn't even know myself.

I wanted to tell him: "Yes, it's me—the one you saved that night. Cos you saved me too, even though you thought you were saving poor Luna Queerendo. You saved me from the very same man who owns the clothes I'm wearing right this second. I think he's an awful man. I know he is. He's the worst man I ever met, but I'm living in his house, which tells you something about me, I s'pose. It tells you whatever's coming I deserve it, but he says he knows my mother. He says she's alive, somewhere in London. I want to see my mother. Do you like my gloves? They're soft as anything."

And I wanted to say: "When you looked at me that night, you smiled. Almost like you'd smile if you cared about someone. So if you like, I could tell you where I'm staying. So you'd know where I was. In case there was ever a need, of some sort. Cos I've been having this totty-headed idea. If I was ever in terrible need, you'd be there again. You'd come busting through the door, and everything would be all right. Isn't that a lark?"

But of course I never said a word of that. I just stood there, stammering. Then I gave him a ribbon I'd bought from a stall. Christ only knows. A fucking *ribbon?* But that's what I had in my hand, so that's what he got. Then I ran.

As I did, I had the queerest sense that somebody was following me. And of course it would have been Tommy, wouldn't it? That came to me afterwards, piecing it all together.

That very same night, Lord Sculthorpe returned to the house in Hampstead. And that was the night Jack Hartright found me.

JACK

IF I WERE to tell you that I fell in love while keeping vigil outside that house—plunged helplessly and headlong into love, as precipitously as a man may plunge—then I suspect you would give your head a knowing shake, and laugh. "Dear me, no," you would say, for you know the ways of the world. Go ahead, admit it; there's no shame. You've seen a thing or two in your time, and understand the caprices of the human heart and the fondness of a young man's folly. "No," you would say, "what you fell in love with was an *idea* of Nell—the bird in her gilded cage, lovely and pining, singing her plaintive song and yearning for deliverance." And your friend with a dismissive snort would correct this: "In fact, he's fallen in love with an idea of *himself*."

I imagine him sitting at his club, this friend of yours. He's in his customary chair by the fire, underneath a painting of foxhounds, glancing across the top of today's edition of the *Times*. He is a bluff, no-nonsense sort of man—a man who once led a cavalry charge, and has latterly represented a particularly hard-headed set of constituents in Parliament. Or at any rate the sort of man who saw himself doing this sort of thing while in fact he spent three decades working at a bank. "There he is," says your friend, "standing in the rain like a statue of Fidelity. Shivering in the sleet like bloody Galahad, and all the while thinking, 'Was ever there such a man as my fine self?' Oh yes, I know these fellows. And you, my friend," he adds, with a squint like a walrus and a single cynical bark, "can have 'em."

But he would be wrong, your friend, and so would you. I need you to hear the truth. I fell in love with Nell Rooney, and I have loved her truly ever since, every minute of every hour of every day.

Remember this. Hold on to it like a candle.

LORD SCULTHORPE RE-EMERGED from the house an hour after he arrived. He paused for a moment at the carriage door, and I swear he raised his head and sniffed the air—sniffed it as a dog does, or a wolf. But he climbed in, and the carriage receded into the night with a clip-*clop* of hooves. After a little time the light in Nell's window went out; in another little time Tommy touched my elbow and blinked his uncanny eyes and melted away into the night, his duty done.

I stayed.

The morning dawned clammy and cold. I warmed myself as best I could with some coffee from a stall at the end of the road, then hurried back to my post, hoping for a glimpse of Nell at the window. I had already decided I couldn't risk approaching the house directly, for Nell had gaolers. There were two of these, a man and a woman—I had glimpsed them at one of the first-floor windows as Sculthorpe was leaving. A man with an eye-patch and hair sticking up, and a fat red-faced woman. The question was, how could I get to her without arousing suspicion?

So I paced, in an agony of indecision. I shivered uncontrollably as November rain became November sleet—for yes, there was actually sleet. And yes, I thought from time to time of Sir Galahad. So would anyone else have done, under such circumstances—so would you. But above all I thought of Nell, and the clutches she had fallen into. I tried to force his image from my mind—and the images that trailed after, like obscene capering Vices in an ancient play. Paddling fingers and reechy kisses and *Christ that leer upon his face, that wrinkled filthy lust, his parchment skin crawling upon my Nell.*

Oh, the thought of it was insupportable. The thought would drive me wild. But just as I was about to do something truly desperate, the door opened. She stepped out into the filthy morning, covering her head with a shawl.

"Nell!"

She swung round and gasped. I lurched towards her.

"Jack? Jesus Christ, it *is* you."

"Of course it's me. Oh, Nell—"

"The fuck are you doing here? Jesus, look at you."

Not the joyful greeting I'd expected. But of course I must have looked a sight. Drenched and dishevelled and shivering with cold, and doubtless wild-eyed from my night of sleepless vigil. Give me a beard and a cloak and I'd pass for the Count of Monte Cristo, newly escaped from the Chateau d'If.

"What's that?" she was demanding, impatiently. "Glad to see you? The fuck sort of question is that? But come on—let's not just stand here. Nothing to be gained by letting the Prendergastlies spy on us."

She hurried down the street, splashing through the slush piled up on the cobbles. I shambled after her. Reaching the corner she glanced swiftly over her shoulder. Satisfied that no one had followed, she looked back to me—more kindly, this time.

"'Course I'm glad to see you," she said gruffly. "Idiot—standing out in weather like this. Let's get something hot into you, before you catch your bloody death."

She led us to a café down the road. It was dingy but warm, and after a mug of tea and a pastry my teeth began to leave off chattering quite so violently.

"All night?" She gave an incredulous shake of her head. "Jesus, Jack, what was you thinking?"

"I thought—I thought perhaps you needed me."

"Needed me. Listen to him. The fuck did you find me, anyways?"

I told her.

"Tommy?" she repeated, looking startled all over again. "The boy from the Kemp Theatre? 'Course I know who he is—I seen him there that first time I went looking for you. But I hardly said two words to him. Why would he care about me, one way or the other?"

"It would seem more people care about you, Nell, than perhaps you know."

It came out like a line from a bad melodrama, and I winced to hear it land with a wooden thud on the table between us. But Nell just flushed a bit and looked away. I could see she was touched, despite herself.

"I went back to the theatre the other night," she said, sounding gruff again. "But they said you'd got the sack."

"You went there looking for me?"

"'Course I went there looking for you. I needed to find you, didn't I?" And as my heart began to give a little leap, she darted a beady look at me and added: "Cos you've still got my bloody locket."

The locket. Her mother's portrait. I'd actually forgotten. And in the next moment I found myself laughing.

"The fuck are you laughing at?" she demanded. "I'm serious!"

I promised her the locket was safe and sound. It was at my lodging, tucked away hidden, and of course I'd fetch it back to her. In fact, I'd take her there, I exclaimed with heartfelt inspiration. I'd take her there right now—and better yet, we could stay there.

But she was starting to shake her head. I leaned forward, growing urgent.

"You need to come away with me. Nell, I swear to you, I'll keep you hidden—I'll keep you safe, for as long as you need."

"The fuck are you talking about? I'm safe enough right now. I'm fine."

"Nell—"

"Look at me. Do I look like someone who needs saving?"

I faltered. The plain truth was, she looked like a rich man's kept plaything. She wore a green brocaded dress underneath a dark blue mantle. The fabric was clearly expensive, even splashed with mud and sleet on a wretched day like this. But the skirt was just that tiny bit too short, showing fine leather boots as far as the ankle. I'd noticed this as I'd followed her to the café—that telltale few inches that marked out the whore, unmistakably.

Lord Sculthorpe's trull.

"He doesn't touch me, you know." She said it out of the blue, sounding terse and defensive. "And he says he can find my mother."

"Is *that* what he's claiming?" It was the last thing I expected, and for a moment it confounded me. "Good God—and you believe him?"

Her jaw took on that familiar bulldog jut. "Yes."

"Nell, listen. I've discovered a thing or two about Lord Sculthorpe—no, please, hear me out." For I was losing her. She was drawing away from me; drawing into herself. Closing down like a child that does not want to hear. "I've asked some questions—informal enquiries. And you do not want to have dealings with this man."

I had decided to look into Sculthorpe after that first unsettling encounter with him at Mother Clatterballock's—the night he'd turned up with a limp and a thin cold smile like the Devil in an old tale, and offered Nell a guinea, and taken her upstairs while I'd gone slinking out into the darkness. I hadn't discovered very much—not yet—but the little I had learned was disquieting. No one seemed to know where he came from, and no one seemed to know precisely where he lived when he was in London. His lodging was a townhouse in Mayfair, or possibly Pimlico, or perhaps somewhere else entirely. He was a sporting lord—that much was agreed, for he was to be seen at the racetrack, and at sporting taverns, and in the gambling hells of the West End. Indeed, sometimes he seemed to be seen in three or four such places simultaneously.

"What?"

"At the same time."

"I know what simultaneous means."

"I'm merely reporting what people have—"

"Jesus. Pull the other one—it's got bells on."

The point being, he came and went. No one knew why, or whither, and often he was gone for years on end. He'd disappeared for more than a decade once, and then he'd come clip-clopping back. Looking exactly the same, in that old frock coat that hadn't been in fashion since the Regency.

"So he has business elsewhere, don't he? And he dresses odd—so do you."

But there had been a scandal. Just before he had disappeared the last time, years earlier. No one seemed to recall the details. "But it was something about a girl."

For the first time, the bulldog blinked. "What girl?"

I didn't know.

"What happened to her, then?"

"I believe," I said, "that she died. I don't know that for certain, but it's why I'm very worried, Nell. Whatever he's saying to you, I don't believe you should go near this man."

Nell had gone very still. But now she gave a rough laugh and stood abruptly, fumbling for some coins to leave on the table. I saw that her hands were shaking.

"That's what you believe, is it? Well, people believe all sorts of things. I don't give a toss what people believe, or what they say—and people includes you."

"Nell, wait—"

She was already on her way out the door. I caught up to her outside, as she paused under the awning to adjust her shawl over her head. The sleet had given way to a grizzling rain. The horses in the street churned through mud. Coaches slithered and pedestrians swore, bespattered. On the corner a wretched crossing-sweeper continued to sweep in mud up to his ankles, a figure of utter futility.

Nell had taken on an air of brittle cordiality that dismissed me completely. "Well," she said briskly. "Been good seeing you, and all. If we had more time, you could catch me up on what you've been doing, since getting the sack at the theatre."

"As a matter of fact, I've—Nell, listen—I've met the most remarkable man in all of London. His name is O'Thunder."

In my desperation to keep her with me, I had clutched at the notion of taking her to see Daniel. Perhaps he could talk to her—he could help me protect her. But the name was a talisman; it stopped her, and she stared at me.

I found myself blurting the whole extraordinary tale. Essex, and that terrible mill against Spragg the Ruffian. I told her of the Hammer of Heaven, and the pigeons of victory, and lurching forward to kneel at Daniel's feet in the mud. I told her of Daniel's head in my lap in the stable yard, and of my decision in that moment to devote myself to helping him.

"He makes everything seem possible, Nell. And he's my friend. I do believe he's already become the best friend I've ever had."

You may believe this, or you may not—suit yourself. Your friend the cynical walrus certainly doesn't. Look at him: peering over top of the *Times,* one eyebrow arched, ready to bark with derision. For he knows these fellows—oh yes, he knows 'em. Religious hysterics is what they are—mad addled poets—unsound every last one, rotten to the core with self-indulgent dreaming, and half of 'em secret sodomites to boot.

But I don't care, because I know the truth.

All this time, Nell had been gazing at me. "Oh, Jack," she said.

Her eyes were glowing, and she seized my hands in both of hers. "Oh, Jack, yes. Isn't he the most amazing man you've ever met?"

WE WENT TO SEE him, of course. We slithered across London, sharing the scant shelter of her shawl, talking with animation. I had been spending much of my time at the Academy, in those giddy days since our return from Essex—or rather, at the Gospel

Mission of Heaven's Hammer, as it was now known. Helping Daniel minister to the poor—visiting the afflicted with him, as the Bible enjoins upon us—accompanying him as he ventured forth to spread the Word and defy the Devil. I described all of this to Nell. I told her with a shiver of pure happiness that Daniel sometimes confided in me. And I confided that I had begun jotting down notes about what he said and did, for it seemed to me that someone would do well to keep a record.

She laughed at this. "Steady, Jack. He's lovely, all right, but he ent Jesus."

We had reached Russell Square, with its trees and railings and the statue of the Duke of Bedford. He stood resolutely atop his plinth with cherubs and sheep and pigeons at his feet, gazing southward. The rain had eased at last, although the air was still clammy and cold. On an impulse, I followed the Duke's lead and turned to the right, angling south instead of east.

Nell balked. "This isn't the way."

"We're going somewhere else first," I told her. "There's something I need to show you. No, don't pull away—just trust me."

And she did. She trusted me all the way to Leicester Square, even though it was well out of our way, and on such a day as this. I held the door open as we arrived, and she stepped in, out of the rain and into the warmth.

She looked round guardedly, out of breath with our long slog, her face red with the cold and the wind, blowing on her hands for warmth.

"Look," I said.

Soaked to the skin and shivering with the cold—shivering with something else, as well—I pointed through the haze of hanging smoke to Daniel O'Thunder on the wall. For of course I had brought her to the Horse and Dolphin. The pub was noisy and snug and dim, a haven against the weather. A fire roared in the stone fireplace; flames leaped like chained hounds. Men clustered round it, some of them newly arrived and dripping rainwater. Warming their hands, or turning to lift their coats and toast behind. As they did, they might glance idly at the drawings and etchings of sporting scenes. Hunters and hounds and pugilists—and Daniel. Frozen forever in the passion of his battle against Tom Oliver the Battersea Gardener, famous for his sweet peas and nectarines.

Nell looked perplexed. "You drug me here to see a pitcher?"

"No, come closer. Look at him. It's his eyes—I swear they actually follow you, wherever you stand in the room."

I reached out to guide her closer, but her attention had been caught by something else. It was a dog-eared newspaper, yesterday's *Morning Register,* folded open on an empty table. She stared at one of the titles, and began to read the words below, then gave a cry of dismay.

"Mary?"

"What's wrong?"

"Oh God, it is." She turned to me, her face crumbling into pure distress. "It's my poor Mary. Look what they done!"

She thrust the newspaper at me, and I saw what she had seen. A small paragraph at the bottom of the page:

> IDENTITY OF MURDERED "PARK WOMAN"
>
> Investigation has revealed that the body discovered several days ago in Hyde Park is that of Mary Bartram, also known as Lushing Mary, a vicar's daughter from Dorsetshire, sadly reduced in circumstances and latterly existing as one of the "Park Women," across whose degradation we draw a veil, excepting to observe that it is utter. It is understood that the victim had been viciously attacked and throttled.

I felt it in the pit of my stomach, even though I knew already—I'd read the item yesterday, and it had shocked me to the core. As Nell was shocked right now. I began to step towards her, reaching out as O'Thunder in the picture had reached out to me. Then came the voice behind me, exclaiming in hoarse wonderment.

"Christ a'mighty."

A rising mutter of incredulity. I glanced back, to see that several of the punters were gathered round O'Thunder's picture. More were standing to join them.

And then I saw.

Tell your friend the cynical walrus that he doesn't need to take my word, for the others saw it too. The men in the Nag and Fish that afternoon, and the ones who came in the days that followed, as the incredulous whisper spread. Some of them are doubtless still alive, and we all saw the same thing.

Ruby droplets had appeared in Daniel's eyes. Blood-red tears, trickling down his cheeks. The picture had begun to weep.

NELL

I AM THINKING OF a painting," said Lord Sculthorpe. "It is a painting of a girl. I want you to become this painting."

He stared at me from across the room. But the room wasn't big enough, for a time like this. No room I'd ever seen was big enough.

Oh, Christ, I thought wearily, and felt the skin on my neck begin to crawl. So this is where it starts. And maybe where it ends, too. But I felt so sick about poor Mary that part of me didn't even care. Cos probably I deserved this, didn't I? And God knows I'd brought it on myself.

I'd known something was wrong the second I got back to the house in Hampstead. It was dark already as I slipped in through the door. It had been dark for hours—I'd been out much longer than I expected. I was cold and drenched and dripping mud onto Mrs Prendergast's floor. Mrs Prendergast seen it, too—she poked her head out through the pantry door. But she just smiled, as sweet as strychnine.

"'Allo, Lambkin. Shall I bring you up your supper? Or else—I know—I'll wait a bit. I'll wait for you to get settled in. And then we'll see if you're 'ungry. For per'aps you won't be quite as 'ungry as you think."

That's when I knew—he was upstairs waiting.

He was sitting by the window when I come in. He'd lit the candles, and shadows flickered on his face. First time I'd seen him in a month, and there was something different about him, but at first I couldn't say what it was.

"Close the door," he said. "Come closer. God's blood, look at you." He shook his head. "Where have you been?"

"Been out," I said. Bracing myself for whatever was going to come.

"Out where?"

"Just out. I dunno. Various places."

"And what did I tell you?"

"Not to," I muttered.

"Speak up."

"You told me not to go out at all. But here I am again, ent I? I come back. So everything's all right."

He stood up and took a step forward, and that's when I saw what was different. His hair was jet-black. He'd blacked his hair, the way old men will do when they take a notion to go courting some girl. He had a parcel under his arm, wrapped up with paper and string. He opened it: a blue silk dress.

"I brought you a gift," he said, darkly. "I took trouble on your behalf. But I'm no longer certain you're worth it. I'm no longer certain at all."

"Look, I never—"

"Take off those filthy things."

"THE GIRL IN the painting is your age. Perhaps a bit older. She is bending over—no, not like that. Not like some filthy little trull—like a lady. Do it again. She is bending from the waist—elegantly—as if to button her shoe. With her right foot extended—no, elegantly. God's blood, do you comprehend the meaning of the word? *Elegantly.*"

I stood by the bath in my petticoats and drawers. The water had been drawn—hot water, steam rising up, misting the windowpane. So we knew the road this was travelling. The only question was: what was waiting at the end of it?

"That's better."

He was sitting on a straight-backed chair, now, watching me. Hands on his cane, one on top of the other, leaning forward just a little. Eyes lidded, but bright as stones.

"You bend down—bending from the waist—and as you do you're quite unaware that you're being watched. You don't quite realize what you may be revealing, to eager eyes across the room. Small perfect orbs of milk-white flesh, et cetera. But of course you do realize, don't you? You're completely aware—you've been aware from the start—and I'm afraid you're enjoying yourself. Yes, I'm afraid you're a bit of a minx. You're a greedy little minx besides, and there's something you want. You want to be wearing that dress."

It was laid out on another chair, near to hand. Blue as summer sky, with ruffles and lace.

"It's beautiful, isn't it? It's the loveliest dress you've ever seen. It's far too fine for the likes of you. Am I right?"

"Yeh, prob'ly."

"I beg your pardon?"

"Yes, Your Lordship."

I swear, he hadn't blinked. Not once. Looking at me like a falcon on a branch. Not knowing what else to do, I started to reach out for the dress.

"What the deuce are you doing?"

"I thought I was s'posed—"

"To touch a lovely dress like that? A dirty little trull like you? Who went out of this house when I specifically told her—"

"I'm sorry! All right? I said it before—I'll say it again—I'm fucking sorry. And if that ent good enough, then why don't you just do it? Go ahead and do whatever it is you're going to do!"

It was going to be bad—I knew that, now. But I had a place to go when it got bad, way deep in the back of my mind. It was a tiny room at the end of a long corridor, and I'd close the door behind me.

"I gave her a dress just exactly like that one. Your mother."

I felt myself going rigid.

"She was a trull, your mother. A trull and a liar, just like you. All those months I knew her, she had a child. She had you, hidden away somewhere."

"Have you seen her?"

"No."

"Then have you heard something?"

"Perhaps.

"What was it? What did you hear? Fucksake, *please.* If you know where she is—"

"A rumour—that's all. The whisper of a rumour. I'm looking into it. I have people all over London, as you know. A thousand eyes, and a thousand ears. I trust this is something you keep in mind."

"Do you think she's alive?"

He looked away.

"I gave your mother lovely clothes to wear. She needed lovely clothes, for I'd take her with me to the opera." He actually looked...wistful. "I'd take her to the finest gatherings in London. We'd eat roast venison, and sometimes I'd feed her with my fingers. I would actually do this for her—I'd pick up the choicest morsel, and place it between her lips. Yes. A man such as myself—a woman such as your mother." He was silent again, for a moment. "I tried to lift her up, but it was no good in the end. She had whore's teeth—that's what gave her away. As soon as she forgot herself, and smiled. As soon as she was happy. Whore's teeth, rotting right out of her head."

"My mother was an actress!"

"I'm afraid you're a dirty little trull, just like your mother. Look at your filthy linen. Take it off."

Fucksake, I had started to cry. But I wasn't going to let him see that, no matter what was going to happen next. So I clenched my teeth so hard I thought they'd splinter, and slipped out of my underthings. I never looked at him, all the time, but I could feel him. I shivered with the awful cold of him. You don't know how small you are, and how skinny and white and ridiculous, till you're stood like that, without a stitch on, and someone looking, someone like him. And my mother's teeth weren't rotten, cos I remember. I was a little girl lying in a bed in a room with a candle, and my mother looked through the door. In the flickering glow she looked pale and tired, but then she started to smile with pure happiness to see me—a beautiful slow smile like sunrise and her teeth were never fucking rotten, God damn His Lordship straight to Hell.

"How old are you?"

He seemed startled, like he was seeing me for the first time. Which he was, in a way. I expect I looked older, with clothes on. When I took them off there wasn't much left.

"What?"

"It's a simple question."

But it wasn't—not necessarily. Not when they were making a purchase. I hesitated.

"How old do you want me to be?"

"Just tell the truth."

The truth? I wasn't exactly sure. "Well—maybe fifteen, probably? Or fourteen. Something thereabouts. Give or take."

He stared, like this had unsettled him, though I couldn't see why. A man like him, bothered by a girl's age? But after a moment he seemed to put it aside.

"Get into the bath," he snapped. "Sit. Do as you're told."

The water was too hot. But I sat, hunkering down, and wrapped my arms tight round.

He eyed me steadily, from his chair across the room. "Now. What did you say to him?"

"Say to who?"

"The Irishman. When you went to see him, this afternoon?"

"I didn't see no Irishman."

"Don't lie to me."

"I'm not," I said. "I wouldn't."

He blinked just once. Considering. "Prendergast!" he called.

There was a soft bump and a scrabbling sound from just outside the door, like the sound you might've heard if some shitsack had been peering through the keyhole. The door opened, and Mr Prendergast peered in. Smoothing down his hair and trying to look like he'd just been passing by on accident.

"M'lud?"

"Prendergast, where were you the first time we met, and what were you doing?"

Mr Prendergast hesitated for a moment, and licked his lips. Cos of course he wanted to get his answers right too.

"I was at Hyde Park, M'lud? With a sack? Drownding kittens?"

"And why were you drowning kittens?"

Mr Prendergast hesitated again, like a spindly-haired schoolboy. His eye went darty, and he gave his head a vigorous rub. Lots of ways to get this one wrong. "Cos they was useful, M'lud, to nobody?"

"Exactly. Those kittens were of no use to any living soul on this earth, and certainly not to you or to me. And drowning is what we do to useless things."

Mr Prendergast beamed, relieved he was getting his answers right. He looked at me, then back at His Lordship, and that's when the little bell began to ting-a-ling. His eye give a *pop,* like a thought just occurred, and such a happy thought that he could hardly bear to think it. "Shall I fetch the sack, M'lud?" he exclaimed.

"I think perhaps you should," His Lordship said. He was looking straight at me.

I'd grabbed up my drawers the second Mr Prendergast come in, and I was clutching them to cover myself. I slid down lower in the bath, but I was still twice as naked as the day I was born. And a hundred times as scared.

"Now, look!" I cried. "There's no call for sacks, and treating me like this. Just cos I'm younger than you thought? You knew who I was when you brung me here!"

"I don't give a toss how old you are. What I want is the truth. If it tells the truth, perhaps it has some use. If not, it's nothing but a wee blind kitten."

He drew up the chair and sat right next to me, beside the tub with the steam rising up. His face staring through it like something coming at you through the fog.

"Where did you go today?"

"Nowhere. Lots of places. I walked here and there. Then I come back. I thought that would be all right. I really did."

His hand was on my head. Stroking my hair.

"I wish you'd tell the truth."

His fingers tightened, and in the next instant he thrust me down so sudden I never had a chance to brace. A lungful of hot water, and then he hauled me up again, blind and choking.

"What did you say to the prize-fighter? The mad Irishman. O'Thunder. You went to see him this afternoon."

"I never said—"

"A thousand eyes and ears."

"I swear, he wasn't even there! I went to see him, but he'd gone out. He'd gone off preaching, or whatever he does, and finally I just left."

"You're a lying little trull, just like your mother."

"But it's true!"

And it was. But it wasn't going to matter, was it? I kicked and swung my arms, but he was too strong. An old man like that, but a grip on him like iron. Forcing me down, and this time I was finished, I fucking knew it. But what else did I deserve? Going off with a man like this—going off like a little fool. Abandoning poor Mary Bartram so she got banished to the Park and killed.

"Stop! Please! *Captain O'Thunder—help!*"

And he stopped. At the last half second he stopped and held me dangling like a doll. At first I thought it was the name I'd shouted out. Then the wild thought came—maybe he was here. Maybe Captain O'Thunder had heard me call, and was busting through the door this very instant. But it was a Bedlam thought, cos of course there was nobody here. It wasn't the name that stopped Lord Sculthorpe, either.

"What the devil is that mark?"

He was staring at my neck.

"Mark? What mark? What are you talking about? Fucksake—"

"You have a birthmark."

It was a little cherry mark like a stain in the divot between my neck and shoulder. That's what he was staring at. "God's blood," he said, with the strangest look on his face.

But now there were footsteps thumping outside. The door flew open again, and there stood the Prendergastlies—both of 'em, this time. She was peering round at me, wringing her hands with joyful concern. He was clutching something, and fair to gleaming with the happy prospect ahead.

"Here it is, M'lud. The sack."

But Lord Sculthorpe didn't hear him. He was on his feet, pacing in agitation.

"M'lud?"

"What? No. Just get out."

The Prendergastlies exchanged a look of unhappy surprise.

"Are you sure, M'lud? Cos we could—"

"Get out!"

They wilted like horrible tulips, and backed out the door. His Lordship turned back to me. A swift step and he was beside the bathtub again. He knelt down, baring his teeth to rip my throat out. Leastways that's what I thought for a second, till I saw he was trying to smile. A whole row of grinders, impossibly white and even. Christ, Lord Sculthorpe had Waterloo Teeth.

"I have made a decision, Nell," he said. "I want you to come and go as you please. Would you like that? Yes, of course you would."

He leaned closer. "And I want you to go and see this mad Irish prize-fighter again—call upon him whenever you like. Be his friend. And then bring me news of him—what he says, and what he does, and who else has come to visit. Yes? For I like to hear news of your friends."

Those teeth, three inches away.

Lots of old men had Waterloo Teeth. A whole generation of horrible old men with lovely teeth, pulled from the dead soldiers on the battlefield. Finest teeth there was, that's what Mrs Dalrymple said. She had a set of her own, passed down from her uncle. Or so she liked to claim, since no one likes to say "stole from a customer." Probably she took the teeth out before they hung her, except I never even thought of it till that second. Probably they were being used right now, by someone else. Teeth just like these ones, gleaming at me in the candlelight. Funny the things that go through your mind, when you're half drowned and staring at an old man with a face like the Devil.

"Go to him. Talk to him. Bring back news. Do you understand? And don't lie to me again."

A battlefield full of dead boys, beaming at me. Then the lips twisted down. I knew it was on the way but it still come out of nowhere, the blow. The other sound was the back of my head against the iron tub.

When the room stopped swimming, there was little threads of blood in the water. As cherry-red as the mark on my shoulder.

Lord Sculthorpe was gazing at it again. Like the mark was something risen from the grave to haunt him.

"God's blood," he muttered again.

JAUNTY

THEY LAID ON a special train for the mill with Gully. That was the way it had always been done, for a big enough event.

The word went out in the sporting houses on the Friday evening: *Euston*. Wink, nod, finger to the side of the nose. Saturday morning, crack of dawn, here they are—scores of the Fancy already at Euston Station, and more arriving by the minute. Some of them bright-eyed and some of them reeling, depending on who'd been home to bed and who'd stopped for one more pot (and then perhaps just one more to keep it company, and then godalmighty-look-at-the-time)—all of them clambering aboard the train marked TO NOWHERE. For that's where this train is going, this fine crisp December dawn. Why, this train is bound for Nowhere At All—at least as far as the Peelers and the Magistrates are concerned.

There's hundreds crammed into six coaches as the Nowhere Special lurches out of the station, and now of course the betting has begun. Someone thinks the mill is in Surrey, and someone else has heard Salisbury Plain, and a knowing cove with a bright shining guinea to back it up has heard for a certainty it's Kent. But they're all wrong, for now it's clear the train is rumbling North. A new round of wagering begins, and someone's passing a flask—for we're all friends here upon the Nowhere Special, we're all the very best of friends—and so we should be, for we're the finest fellows in the world, hip-hoorah. Now someone is raising his voice in a fine old boxing song. It's a song that I first learned as a lad. A song that's been sung by fine fellows since the days of Bonaparte, God blast him, and we all join in.

Come move the song, and stir the glass,
For why should we be sad?
Let's drink to some free-hearted lass,
And Cribb the boxing lad,
And a-boxing we will go, will go, will go,
And a-boxing we will go!

Here comes a costermonger, staggering down the aisle with a basket of bread and sausage. More flasks are in hand, and a gentleman or two is spewing out the window, and a few more who find themselves wedged in are spewing into their hats, the way they do in the chapel at an Oxford college. This is God's truth. I was told this by my Uncle Peter, who was an Oxford man himself—he was a porter at Magdalen—which goes to explain how a reverence for education comes to run in the family. The young scholars at Oxford University, when feeling queasy in Sunday morning chapel on account of their natural high spirits on the Saturday night, will spew into their hats so as not to cause an inconvenience to others. This is what a British education will do, and I am proud to be British. So is every man-jack on this train to Nowhere, which in fact—though no one knows it yet, excepting for obvious reasons the engineer, and wouldn't he love to join the wagering!—is chug-a-chugging towards Six Mile Bottom, in Hertfordshire. So are other trains, from Manchester and the West, and coaches (hired by those among the Knowing Ones who rumbled the true location in advance), and on all of them is swigging and wagering and excitement rising by the minute, and a fair deal of manly English spewing, and manly English voices raised in song:

Italians stab their friends behind
In darkest shades of night;
But Britons they are bold and kind,
And box their friends by light.

The sons of France their pistols use,
Pop, pop, and they have done;
But Britons with their hands will bruise,
And scorn away to run.

So! Throw pistols, poniards, swords aside,
And all such deadly tools;
Let boxing be the Britons' pride
And science of their schools!
And a-boxing we will go, will go, will go
And a-boxing we will go . . .!

More or less, at any rate.

Naturally I wasn't on the train myself. I'd been at Six Mile Bottom since Tuesday last, me and Daniel together, after training for three weeks in the countryside. Daniel had trained as I had never known him to train in his life—he had trained with a will and a resolution that quite took old Jaunty aback. He had trained even more diligently than he had done for the Ruffian. And thus I had told His Lordship when he'd summoned me on Friday night, the night before the mill.

"Fit? Yes, I'd have to say he is. Quite a surprise to me, a man his age and disposition, especially coming off the mill with the Ruffian. But he trained like a perfect fiend, as the expression goes, though come to think it don't make sense—how could a fiend be perfect?—ha, ha, ha—I could barely stop him."

The summons had come in a note slipped underneath my door. A sheet of fine bond paper, smelling of lavender. "Come." So I went—and here I was. Same as before. Standing by the carriage at the side of a rutted track in the dead of night, clutching my cap and beginning to babble.

He interrupted, impatiently. "What would you calculate his chances to be?"

"Oh, slim, Your Lordship. Decidedly slimmish, I should say."

That look of his. As if he was totting you up like beads on an abacus—click, click, click—and beginning to suspect you would come up one bead short.

"Slimmish. That's the best you can do?"

"Overwhelmingly slimmish, Your Lordship. Practically non-existent."

Moonlight shone through the window behind him. Click went another bead.

"But not precisely so."

"Well, no. But then again, Your Lordship, what is? Precise, I mean. In such a world, ha, ha. As this."

"And what do you propose to do about that state of affairs?"

"Me, Your Lordship? Well, I—I suppose I'll do whatever I can."

"Which is?"

"Whatever seems possible."

Click.

"Under the circumstances."

Click.

There was no one else on the road. No one else for miles, as far as I knew—just the two of us. And the coachman, of course. He sat up there on the box with his face muffled against the cold, sitting perfectly still and quiet, as he would remain until such time as his employer needed someone murdered. But there was no sense even thinking that way. His Lordship had his queer cold ways, and you didn't want to cross him—no indeed, not ever—but he wasn't the Fiend himself, ha ha. He wouldn't leave you on a lonely road with your throat slit—and for what, because you gave him some news he didn't want to hear? No, no—I knew the man.

Except I didn't. I didn't know him at all, really, and I never met anyone who did. I'd first encountered him twenty years earlier at the mill between Young Dutch Sam and Jack Cooper the Slashing Gipsy. He seemed old even then, though perhaps it was partly those queer old-fashioned togs he wore, that hadn't been in fashion since the Regency. We'd crossed paths on various occasions since, but never for more than a few minutes at a time. I knew he was a Lord, from somewhere-or-other. I knew he liked to take a flutter on a mill or a horse-race, and would put up the purse when a handsome profit seemed likely. I knew he was rich—or at least I thought I knew it, although sometimes you'd hear rumours of mounting debts. You'd hear rumours of other things as well, darker things, such as girls gone missing. But a man minds his business, and the world goes on apace.

Beyond that, what did I actually know about His Lordship? Well, I knew he was cold as the tomb. I knew he had a fondness for secret midnight meetings at godforsaken crossroads. And I knew he'd kill me in a second if it suited him to do it. I knew it for a certainty—just as sure as eggs are eggs—from the way he was looking at me in that very moment.

"I seem to recall," he mused, "that Tom Griffiths' seconds did surprisingly well, under similar circumstances. In the match against Paddy Gill."

I pretended to take it as a little joke, and laughed obligingly. Ha, ha. His Lordship could be very droll.

"Yes, I know the mill you're referring to," I said. "I've heard the story. But of course it didn't really happen."

"No?"

"As you know just as well as I, Your Lordship. You're just having a little joke with me, for that's your way, and a droll and witty way it is. A man's trusted seconds, poisoning him with arsenic on a sponge, in between rounds? No, no. Ha, ha. Very droll indeed."

"And yet poor Tom Griffiths died."

"Well . . . yes. That much is true."

"The man dropped dead."

"But nothing was ever proven, Your Lordship, when it came to trial."

"Indeed." A meaningful angling of the head. "Nothing was ever proven."

I could feel myself starting to sweat, despite the cold. An icy trickle down my spine. And I'm an old soldier—whatever else you think of me, I've been in battle on both sides of the world, and I've stood my ground when I had to. Jaunty Rennert has marched left-right-left into volleys of rifle-fire. Jaunty staggered through the Khyber Pass in the depths of an Afghan winter. But I've never been more afraid for my life than I was that night on the Six Mile Road.

"Besides," I said, "it was a different situation entirely. Griffiths broke his word. He swore he'd go along with the cross, and then he went back on sacred bond of honour. He battered poor Paddy Gill from pillar to post—he commenced to pulverize the man into paste—to the great distress of all his friends, who had placed their wagers upon a certainty. When a man breaks his sacred bond, then God help him. But this situation is entirely different, for there's no cross, is there? Our Daniel would never agree to such a thing, so this mill is on the up-and-up. No sacred bonds to be broken. But he can't win. There's really no chance of it."

His Lordship considered me for a very long moment.

"I think I should like your word on that," he said. "Your sacred bond."

O'THUNDER V. GULLY

From *The Illustrated Sporting Life*
7 December, 1851

. . .

O'Thunder arrived first at the ring, attended by Rennert and Diggory. Great cheer as he tossed in his hat. Gully followed. Both men stripped down and both were observed to be admirably fit and trim (viz. Not Blubber-Headed). As they shook hands, the Game Chicken was heard by the nearest spectators to say: "Daniel, I wish you well, despite what others may have claimed in my name. For 'twas THEM as said such things and NOT ME. But nonetheless I bid you clutch your trencher and your spoon, for I propose to serve you out directly." O'THUNDER: "Will you pray with me, brother, before we commence?" GULLY: "Not at this time, Daniel. Perhaps afterwards, once one of the two of us be already on his knees."

First Round.—No blows were exchanged for at least a minute upon setting-to, as both men sparred while probing for advantage, Gully in particular displaying great science. Seeing his opening, the Game Chicken roused himself suddenly to exertion, pinking O'Thunder with a blow to the cheekbone. First blood. Daniel responded with great vivacity, but his blows fell short as his distance was discovered to be incorrect. The Chicken landed a facer of considerable severity, after which the combatants closed and fell, with O'Thunder underneath. Seven to four on Gully.

Second Round.—Gully commenced with brisk resolve, pinking O'Thunder again with a left and then tapping the claret most copiously with a wallop to the cork-snorter. Daniel rallied, but Gully, full of impetuosity, battered him backward. They closed by common consent to the half-arm distance, upon which an exchange ensued of thunderous ferocity, ending with a grave-digger from the Chicken that levelled his man. O'Thunder assisted back to his corner, where Rennert was observed to exclaim with an animation that most strangely resembled relief: "That's it, Daniel! Point your chin at him, and defy the worst!" Exhilaration amongst Gully's friends. Intimations of catastrophe amongst O'Thunder's. Five to one on Gully.

Third Round.—The Game Chicken rushed out like Achilles upon Hector, punishing the Irishman with hits of great severity. But O'Thunder returned a blow to the throat that staggered Gully, who then closed and fell. Sensation amongst the onlookers. Even odds.

Fourth to Sixth Rounds.—Gully endeavoured to recover his advantage, displaying great bottom, but exhibited signs of distress while O'Thunder's strength seemed as a rising tide. Agitation in the Game Chicken's corner, whilst on the Irishman's side Rennert was observed to grow quite pale from happiness. Three to one on O'Thunder.

Seventh Round.—The Chicken had never been more Game, and seemed briefly to rally. But O'Thunder recovered his distance, and planted a dreadful hit on Gully's ear that caused the claret to gush as from a cask unbunged. Gully fell all of a heap, and was assisted half insensate to his corner, where his friends exhorted him with desperate pleas and blew brandy up his nose. Odd agitation in O'Thunder's corner, where Rennert was now chalk-white with joy, and an exchange was overheard, as follows. RENNERT: "Quickly, Daniel—here—put this sponge in your mouth." O'THUNDER: "I don't want it." RENNERT: "Yes you do! Truly!" DIGGORY: "If you don't stop waving that sponge, Jaunty, I shall shove it someplace you won't like one bit." O'THUNDER: "Now, Tim, remember you are a Christian." RENNERT: "Oh g-d, oh g-d, I'm done for." Nine to one on O'Thunder.

Eighth Round.—Gully carried to the line of scratch, and placed there on his feet. O'Thunder, exhibiting consternation, urged Hen to reconsider his resolve. Gully replied with a muzzler that caused Dan to step backward, and drew hurrahs from his friends. But it was the last cupful of water in the well. O'Thunder struck out in return, and Gully fell like a sack. Those close enough were able to observe his feet twitching most unusually for the space of half a minute, leading some to suggest that a man should stand up before attempting a victory jig. Others in reply cried "Oh! Oh!" and "Fie!" that jests should be made at the expense of a man who had battled so nobly, and vowed to be the first to buy Gully a drink once he was restored to himself. They offered further to blacken the eye of those that did not stop their gobs, which occasioned additional exchanges of rising warmth. There was great celebration amongst O'Thunder's friends, in the midst of which it began to be noticed that the twitching of Gully's trotters had ceased. There was no subsequent movement. Someone was heard to exclaim: "God's hairy bollocks, he's dead."

PIPER

THEY CARRIED Henry Gully from the ring in an old horse blanket. One arm hanging down, the fingers trailing. I remember that image, with shocking clarity: his fingers trailing in the mud.

But he was alive. He was alive when they carried him up the stairs, and laid him out upon his bed at the inn. He was alive when the doctor came in twenty minutes later, and pronounced him dead. He was clearly alive, for that is the only way to make sense of the story. And that is what I do—I make sense of stories. I deal in Facts. That is what I have always done, since I first grew old and canny enough to set good sturdy English words in a row and charge a bright copper penny for each one of them.

The doctor was a fool, and a drunkard besides, which helps to explain the confusion. They'd sent a boy to fetch him from the taproom of the Swan, where he'd been since breakfast. Where he'd been, in fact, for the past three decades, with breaks for sleep and surgery and the funerals of townsfolk who had come to him with minor ailments. He plodded up the stairs in a fog of brandy fumes, and took one look.

"That man's dead," he said.

"Nope. Don't know that yet."

It was the black man who'd spoken. Boston Bob. He'd been at the mill. Not in Gully's corner—he'd been amongst the spectators. But he'd helped carry poor Gully from the ring, and stayed with him when so many others fled.

"I know it as well as you do," the doctor exclaimed. "Just look at him."

"Got to be examined, first."

Bob had a dogged look about him. The doctor muttered to himself, and rolled his eyes, and sat. He had a nose like a potato, spider-webbed with purple veins. He breathed through it heavily as he bent his head and listened at Gully's breast. Then he felt for a pulse in the neck, and felt for it at either wrist, then bent his head to listen again.

At length, he looked up.

"Man's dead," he said. "As a doornail."

Boston Bob took off his hat. "Well," he said, bowing his head with the weight of all the sorrow of the world.

For of course he'd known all along. You want to observe the niceties—the doctor, and all. You do things properly; you do it to show respect. But Bob had seen men dead before, in the ring. So had Gully's seconds—which is why they had made themselves scarce, as soon as it was clear what had happened. Jaunty Rennert scarpered too. He was gone even before the feet stopped twitching. I'd noticed him, out of the corner of my eye—a goggle and a blanch, and a sidling away. Then he hotfooted down the road and across the fields, coat-tails flapping. It ended up being Boston Bob who laid poor Hen in the horse blanket and lugged him upstairs, even though Bob had been nothing more than a spectator at the mill. Helping him were Tim Diggory and Mrs Piper's toad-faced lad—who knew it was folly to get involved in such matters at all, but was finding himself inexplicably involved in all manner of folly, these days.

"You the one as did this?" asked the doctor. He was looking at Daniel O'Thunder, the way you'd look at the mastiff caught slavering in a barnyard full of dismembered poultry.

O'Thunder had just arrived in the room. He stood against the wall, still stripped to the waist. His face was a mess of welts and cuts, and his eyes were great and numb. There was a girl with him. It came to me that this was the girl from that day outside the Gospel Mission of Heaven's Hammer. The red-haired girl in the gay little bonnet who had given him a ribbon—the very scrap of red ribbon that now hung at his belt, tattered and soiled from the mill. Seeing her from a distance I'd thought she was much older—a young lady, seventeen or eighteen at the least.

"Come away," she said quietly. "Come quick."

"Girl's right," said Boston Bob.

"No," said O'Thunder. "We can't, you see—not yet—for we can't leave without Hen Gully."

He was addled by shock and grief. This was obvious. He knelt by the bed, and clutched Gully's hands.

"Get up, Henry. For your family's sake. You've a wife, Hen Gully, and three children waiting for you, at home. So open your eyes, Hen. It's time to get up."

"Fucksake, Captain," said the red-haired girl. "Come away. They'll be coming for you, and it's good to be sorry and all, but fuck."

Too late. Loud voices were without, and heavy boots were upon the stair. A Magistrate was at the door. A man like a cormorant, with two Constables and a finger that pointed like Death's own bony summons. So there it was—the game was up. *The Hertfordshire Constabulary have seized the celebrated evangelist and prize-fighter Daniel O'Thunder and charged him with manslaughter, following the tragic death of Henry Gully during an illicit mill on Saturday.* Good plain English words in a row, telling thirty pence's worth of incontrovertible truth. Thirty-one if you count *prize-fighter* as two words, which an editor wouldn't, and he'd undoubtedly strike out *celebrated* besides. ("Celebrated by whom, precisely? An unlettered bruiser whose fame has spread the length and breadth of half a block of the Gray's Inn Road?")

But now it all grew confusing. Tim Diggory was on his feet, and shoving someone back, and saying something loudly.

Boston Bob was rising to intervene, and the red-haired girl was gazing swiftly round, as if to calculate the chances of one small girl spiriting a very large man out through a window the size of a penny loaf. In the midst of it, there was an infinitesimal voice—that of Wm. Piper, Esq., piping in disbelief.

"Excuse me. Excuse me, please? I don't think he's dead."

For Henry Gully had opened his eyes. Now, as the others began to notice—one by thunderstruck one—he groaned.

"Oh," he said, "my aching nob."

NELL

ARE YOU TELLING me the man was actually dead?"

That's what His Lordship kept asking. Pacing back and forth in my rooms, agitated. I'd seen some moods from him, but nothing like this.

"Are you actually trying to make me believe that a corpse rose up and walked?"

"'Scuze me, but I'm not trying to make you believe anything."

"At the touch of this man's hand, a sack of bones drew breath, leapt upward like Lazarus, and, what—capered about the room? Danced a jig to the wonderment of all present, and the despair of hungry maggots in the churchyard?"

"Actually, Gully sat up and spewed and lay down again. But afterwards he seemed all right, 'cept for the headache. And you can believe all of that, or any of it, or none at all, whatever you like. Cos it don't make a blind bit of difference to me."

"And what do you believe?"

"Me?"

"Of course you! Who else am I talking to? Listen to the girl—is she stupid? Is she an imbecile, to be displayed in a tent at country fairs? I'm asking you what you believe!"

I could have told him loads of things. I could have told him how Daniel's face lit up with joy when Gully raised his head, and then how he burst into tears and wept like a child. I could have told him how that doctor gaped like a fish, and how Tim Diggory fell to his knees and wailed hallelujahs. And I could have told him how I felt such happiness and terror in that moment as I was sure I'd never feel again. But instead I told him the same thing I'd been telling everyone who asked.

"I don't know," I said. "And I don't know as that makes any difference neither. But I'll tell you what I *do* know. Hen Gully went home the next day, and the missus and children waiting. And here's me, answering the same bloody question over and over."

He didn't hit me for saying it, although I was halfway certain he would. He didn't even seem to hear. He was pacing again, and waving his arms.

"Are you asking me to believe that this man—this illiterate bog preacher—this Irish buffoon can *raise the dead?* It's beyond ridiculous!"

SOMETHING HAD GONE badly wrong. That much was obvious, soon as I arrived back at the house in Hampstead.

I hadn't been here for almost a week. Up to Hertfordshire for the mill, then staying for two days afterwards while Daniel recovered enough to travel, and then back again. But instead of coming back to Hampstead I just stayed at the Mission for a few nights. Me and a score of others, with scores more dropping in and dropping out, cos the news was back in London before we were. Patterers on the street corners, hawking the news: "Prize-fighter raised from the dead—a full true and pertic'lar account!" Beggars with twisted limbs and sores gathering outside the Mission, in the hope that Daniel would touch them. A piewoman with a lame daughter, and a boy leading a donkey-cart with an old man in the back, spitting blood. In the midst of it all was Daniel, reaching out to touch and pray and comfort. Once in a quiet moment I found him standing alone in the courtyard out the back, staring at his great swollen hands, as if he couldn't quite believe what they'd done. And ever in his shadow was Jack, with his soft brown hair flopping down and his phizog shining all earnest, telling everyone who'd listen that there were men upon the earth who opened a window onto God Almighty, and he'd come to understand that Daniel O'Thunder was one of them. Oh, Jack was shining with it. Jack was brimming right over with his joy—although I wasn't quite sure I trusted everything he was saying, even then. I wasn't quite sure I trusted Jack Hartright at all.

But I couldn't stay away from Hampstead forever. Even if I thought His Lordship would stand for that, I needed to know if there'd been any news of my mother. So that afternoon I'd slipped away from the Mission. Clutching my shawl and hurrying towards Hampstead in the cold December sunlight. It was nearly Christmas—candles and decorations in the shops, and a knot of gentlemen singing carols on the corner, rosy with goodwill and brandy. When I got to the house I fumbled for my key, and stepped in through the front door.

And something was badly wrong. There were Prendergastly voices—his and hers—muttering from the scullery. The mister's head stuck out through the door just long enough to see who had come in—just long enough to see it was me, and wish me dead and eaten by quicklime. Then the head pulled back in again, like a venomous one-eyed turtle, and the door slammed shut. Later, when I was in my rooms upstairs, I could hear footsteps trundling back and forth below, and something heavy being dragged. Through the window I seen the mister hauling a trunk to a donkey-cart waiting outside, and the missus behind him with two battered old valises and her coat on and a hat with a flower in it. She turned just long enough to see me in the window: *"And hot coals, Dear 'Eart, oh my yes; Lambkin roasting on red hot coals."* Then the cart rattled off, and the two of 'em with it, and the house was empty and quiet and they never came back.

It was dark when His Lordship arrived. I heard the coach outside, and then the door, and his footsteps on the stair. But they weren't slow and measured, in that usual way of his. They were rapid and shambling, and he pounded on my door and shouted for me to open it. When I did, he didn't look himself at all. His clothes were all disordered from the wind, except there was no wind that night. His shirt was open at the neck, and his face was flushed. He'd been at the gin—I could smell it from here. He was lobstered with it.

"Get your things together."

"Is something wrong?"

"Do as I tell you!"

But in the next moment he changed his mind, and for a minute all the energy seemed to seep out of him. "No, don't bother," he snarled. He turned, leaning against the back of a wooden chair. Head bowed, gripping onto it with both hands. "After all, what difference does it make? Stay here, until I send word."

"Are you all right?"

"Where is he now?"

"Where's who?"

"Do not play games with me!"

He reared up again, lifting the chair like it was nothing at all and flinging it against the wall. It splintered. For a moment I reckoned I was next. But that's when he started pacing, and flinging his arms about, and demanding if I believed Daniel could raise the dead.

"And does he mention the Devil? Does he talk about the Devil, this bog-ignorant Irish preacher of yours?"

"I don't know. All the time. What does it matter?"

"What does he say?"

"He says he knows how the Devil feels. He says we all do."

"And what does he mean by that?"

"I think he means we've all been afraid."

He swivelled, and stared.

"He thinks the Devil is afraid? Of *him?*"

He began to laugh, that rattling down low in his throat. "God's blood," he snarled. "I've had my fill of this Irish madman."

And all at once I'd had my fill of His fucking Lordship. "I've told you what I know, all right? I want to go now. I want to know what happened to my mother." I was starting to shake.

"You said you'd find my mother. Where is she, then? Where's my mother? Stop laughing at me!"

I didn't even know I was shying the glass at him, until it was on its way. It was on the shelf behind, and then it was in my fist. Then it was straight at his head—four feet away—but he blocked it. An old man like that, and his hand moving fast as a snake. A sound of shattering, and now I was dead, of course. I could run, but why bother? He'd locked the door behind him when he first come in, I'd seen him do it, and put the key in his pocket.

"I want to see my ma!"

He wasn't laughing now. The horrible laughter had stopped, and the fury had passed with it. It left him looking older than ever, ancient and tired, like he'd been hollowed out.

"Her image. You really are. And fifteen years old—is that what you think you are? Born in 1836."

"The fuck difference does it make?"

He didn't answer. His hand was bleeding—drip, drip, drip, onto the Turkey carpet. After a minute I pointed.

He looked at the hand, distracted. "You'd better come and wrap it for me, then." He took out a handkerchief with his other hand, and held it out. Very white it was, against the blackness of him. He stared at me, again.

"Fifteen years old. Born in 1836. God's blood."

He started to shake his head from side to side, like you do when someone tells you something too ridiculous for words, except it's true.

"Tell him he's finished," he said. "Your Irish buffoon. Go tell him from me—he has no idea. And as soon as I've done with him, I'll come and find you."

He tottered just a little, and sat down on the edge of the divan. He leaned forward, elbows on his knees. As he did, the front of his shirt fell open. His skin so white it was obscene, and his old man's collarbone, sticking out like a spar on a burnt-out ship. I saw something else, too—right there at the base of his neck.

The cherry red stain of a birthmark.

JACK

DANIEL O'THUNDER walked with angels. This is God's truth. He healed the lame, and gave hope to the hopeless, and slew a man with his terrible fists and then raised him up again. He walked with archangels in the teeming streets of London, and through all of it I walked by his side. I walked with him; I was the disciple he loved.

This is the earliest surviving fragment of my *Book of Daniel*. I came across it entirely by accident, just the other day, slipped between the pages of an old book. Words in faded ink, on a slip of paper yellowed by age, folded up and then forgotten for nearly forty years.

I recognized it instantly as one of the fragments I had scribbled in those giddy weeks following our return from the mill against Gully in December of 1851. I had scribbled in joyful fervour, in moments snatched from the whirl of activity, for those were glorious days. Those were surging days. They were the days in which the news of Daniel O'Thunder began to spread across London, and—even more importantly—the *spirit* of Daniel O'Thunder infused all of us. They were days in which nothing could ever seem hopeless, and nothing could ever be truly lost, for all things were surely possible.

Reading it again, all these years later in my bleak Whitechapel room, I wept.

I don't know how many scraps of paper I scribbled in those days and weeks and months, hasty records of things Daniel had said and done, or thoughts and inspirations of my own. Dozens of them. Scores. I'll never know for certain, for most of them were subsequently lost in a terrible fire, to which this narrative will come in due course. And doubtless these fragments were all as overwrought as the one recorded above. Dear God, I was so excruciatingly young—and I believe I must also have been half mad for a time, as well. As all the saints and all their disciples have always been half mad—or more than half—and always shall be, until the last rattling gasp of time.

That giddy overwrought youth, with his heart so full and his head so addled. And yet that ridiculous youth was right. The years have changed my perspective on almost everything. I know now that Daniel O'Thunder was not what I thought him to be—or at least, not entirely. But in reading and rereading that ancient fragment from the first incarnation of my *Book*, I realize that it actually contains the essence of the truth.

Daniel O'Thunder walked with angels. And I walked with Daniel. Not every single step of the way, perhaps, but the steps that mattered most.

I was with him at the beginning, and at the end.

And I was the disciple he loved.

HE'D BE TALKING to you about this and that, and then his voice would trail off. His eyes would cloud over and he'd be miles away. You couldn't reach him, even when he was right beside you. The first time it happened, we were standing at the foot of Ludgate Hill, below St Paul's Cathedral.

"Daniel?"

He didn't hear me, or feel my fingers as I plucked at his sleeve. Then suddenly he was back again—for that's the way it would happen. He'd give a little start, and then a slow sweet smile, as if seeing you—seeing me—was the finest surprise he could think of.

"Look," he had said that afternoon, pointing up Ludgate Street towards St Paul's. "What do you see, brother?"

Sun had broken through the clouds, and sparkled like gold on the dome of the cathedral. A fanciful notion took me. "It almost looks like angels dancing," I said with a laugh, pleased with the whimsy of the image.

Daniel's eyes glowed with an uncanny light. *"Almost?"* he repeated. Then he lifted his hand to those angels, and waved.

For Daniel O'Thunder saw angels the way you or I see costermongers. That is to say, he saw them standing on street corners. He saw them walking unseen amongst the crowds, or looking down from the roof of a building. He would see an angel standing on Waterloo Bridge, nodding a solemn greeting down to an angel sliding past on a barge below, and the bargee angel would nod solemnly back. One day—it was 23 January, 1852—he saw the Archangel Gabriel sitting by the fountain at Trafalgar Square. I remember the date because it happened to be my birthday—though of course no one else knew that, and of course it didn't matter.

He had been preaching a sermon in the square to whomsoever would stop and listen. I was with him, of course—in those weeks and months I was almost always with him—to listen and glow and collect up the coins that were contributed afterwards. As he finished, Daniel turned to me. He was flushed and a little bit out of breath, as he usually was after a sermon, for Daniel's sermons were long and soaring.

"Well, I wonder what he thought?" he said. He actually gave a nervous laugh, as might a musical prodigy who has just been told that Chopin was in the audience.

"Who do you mean?" I asked, expecting he meant someone particular in the crowd, or possibly the police constable in his tall hat who had been plodding darkly about on the periphery in case of rabble-rousing. From Daniel's flushed grin, I thought possibly this was even a whimsical reference to the towering statue of Nelson, gazing down upon the square from the top of his Monument.

"The Archangel Gabriel," he said.

"Gabriel?"

Daniel pointed across the square. "He was sitting over there, by the fountain. No, he's gone now—didn't you see him? Ah, well. Perhaps you'll see him the next time, brother."

I was surprised by this—I was in fact stunned—for I had glanced over towards the fountain several times while Daniel had been preaching, and I had utterly failed to see the Archangel Gabriel, or anyone remotely like him.

"What did he look like?" I asked, feeling more than a little amazed.

"He had his robe pulled up to his knees, and he was paddling his feet in the water. For I don't believe they feel the cold as we do."

Seeing the expression on my face, he laughed out loud, and put a paw upon my shoulder. "Why is it so astonishing, brother? For we know the angels exist—and so why would it seem strange that they walk amongst us? They must walk somewhere, after all. And once you've learned to look, you may discover that they're closer than you ever supposed."

As he left me, I turned to stare again at the place by the fountain where he had pointed. And it began to seem to me—the most remarkable thing—that I *had* glimpsed something, while he had been preaching. For just the barest moment, the barest flicker of a golden radiance.

I described this in a flutter of excitement to Nell that evening, at the Mission. Or attempted to, at any rate. She was busy with this and that, and Nell was not in any case a metaphysician. Love her dearly as I did—as I do—she had a doggedly prosaic streak that could be limiting.

"Gabriel?" she said. "That's nice."

"Nice?" I repeated, a bit incredulous. "Nell, an archangel in Trafalgar Square might be many things. It might be staggering, or life-altering, or even mad as Bedlam. But *nice?*"

"We're mending old clothes for the poor," she retorted. "If you're here to give us a hand, go ahead."

I recall on another occasion growing almost exasperated with her, as I tried to establish what exactly it was that she believed. This had been over Christmas, as I had attempted to come up with small appropriate gifts for her on the twelve succeeding days. She said she found this sweet but excessive, and it turned out she was referring both to my attempts and to Christmas itself.

"Excessive?" I protested. "Surely you believe in Jesus."

"I s'pose," she said with a shrug. "I never met him, did I? So obviously I couldn't say for certain."

In part I suspect she was doing this deliberately, to unsettle me. If so, it was having the desired effect. For of course I was in those weeks and months in the fervour of a renaissance of Faith, following my flight from Cornwall and my aching apostasy from my former life.

"Good Lord," I said. "I mean, you *do* believe there's a Good Lord, don't you? You believe in God? And you understand that he made the world in seven days?"

She shrugged again. "I'll tell you this much. Whoever built the world, it was brickmakers' apprentices built London—and they been building it ever since, poor fuckers."

But on this particular evening—the evening of 23 January, mere hours after the Archangel Gabriel had paddled his feet in the fountain at Trafalgar Square—she didn't even want to argue. To tell the truth, my Nell had been moody and reserved for some while, now. Or at least, she had been so with me. She wasn't precisely cold, but she wasn't warm either, certainly not as warm as I so fervently wished her to be. She made the excuse of having some errand or other, and left me.

IT WAS LATE when I saw her again. She was alone with Daniel.

I had gone for a walk through the streets by myself, despite the January fog and chill. It was always my custom—it is my custom still—to take long walks, alone with my thoughts. Some of my thoughts were joyful, that night, but others were troubled. I thought of Nell, and of her friend Mary Bartram. I thought too of Luna Queerendo, and Joe Gummery who'd been hung. I'd have walked further on this particular night, except a fog was rolling in, as if in response to the gathering darkness of my mood. The night had begun surprisingly clear, by London standards—one of those nights when all the city glowed with lights like a vast faerie palace. That's when you wanted to see London, on a night like that, with the lights winking and glowing for mile upon mile in every direction. But then the rain had begun, churning the streets to mud all over again, and now a true London Particular was coming on. In the darkness it hung brooding over the metropolis like the ghost of mud itself. By the time I turned onto the Gray's Inn Road, the fog was so dense that you could barely see the gas-lamp ahead, and you navigated from one to the next like a Pilgrim reaching out towards glimmers of salvation.

I heard their voices, muffled by fog, before I saw them.

"How did you know it was Gabriel, then?"

"I'm not certain. It just was. He had golden hair."

"I thought all angels had golden hair."

"No, not all of them."

"You got golden hair."

"I have yellow hair, Nell. And a great ugly face to go with it, with a nob of a nose and ears like cauliflower, for I am altogether nothing like an angel."

They laughed then, the two of them.

They were sitting on the step at the front of the Mission, in light spilling feebly from within. The great bulk of Daniel, and Nell like a wisp beside him. I trailed to a stop, standing just outside the halo of a gas-lamp. I wasn't ten paces away.

"Are you cold?" Daniel asked.

I almost replied to him. I almost said: yes, I'm cold, Daniel, and solitary too—I feel them both tonight, the cold and the solitude. But of course he didn't even know I was there. He had asked his question of Nell.

"I'm all right," she said. "Maybe a little."

He opened his coat then. She leaned against him, and he wrapped her inside.

"Is that better?"

"That's lovely," she said, and nestled.

For a time they were silent. Carriages passed along the street like underwater hulks. "Was Hen Gully really dead?" she asked at last.

"You were there, Nell. What did you see?"

"I seen him lying there. But do you believe he was actually dead?"

He didn't reply for a moment. He was staring off into the night. A carriage ghosted past, on the other side of the street, and was gone again, as if it had never existed.

"Yes," he said finally. He spoke with low thrilling intensity. "Yes, I believe Hen Gully was dead, and God gave me the gift of raising him up. God singled me out, despite my unworthiness. Despite all the sins I've committed, Nell, and the bad things I've done."

"Do you really see angels?"

"Yes."

There was certainty in his voice, but also a kind of desperation. As if he were stating a truth that he could not endure without. It crossed my mind then—it has crossed my mind ever since—to wonder if raising Henry Gully had actually changed what Daniel O'Thunder saw. Did the raising of Gully cause Daniel to see the angels? Or did it merely embolden him to say out loud what he'd secretly known for years—that he saw angels as other men saw costermongers?

"You're seeing angels right this minute?" Nell was asking. She looked up into his face with a kind of edgy fascination, as if half-afraid what she'd do if he said yes.

"No, not right now."

"But sometimes you see them sitting by fountains, and such?"

"Did Jack tell you that?"

I had been about to make my presence known, and join them. This stopped me.

"Jack," he repeated, with a fond shake of his head.

It's true—there was fondness in Daniel's voice, deep and genuine. Although perhaps he had given a little sigh as well, as one may do from time to time when one speaks of a friend.

"You're not saying he made that up?" asked Nell. "About the Archangel Gabriel?"

"No," said Daniel. "That was true, what Jack said." He hesitated for a moment, and then added: "I don't believe Jack ever makes things up, really. But sometimes perhaps we must be careful with the way he says them."

There was another silence. When Daniel spoke again, his voice was soft.

"I know they're among us, Nell, the angels. I believe they let me see them, though not so often as I'd wish. I see dark things, too. Other times it's just the pain in my head, like flashes of light. It's worse these past few months, the pain. But that's all right, for it's sent by the Lord. He sends me pain to test me, Nell, and this time I won't fail."

"Of course you won't fail, Daniel," I said suddenly, stepping towards them. "I know you and believe in you, and you won't fail."

They gave a start, the both of them. A swift look was exchanged—if not quite like guilty creatures at a play, then at least like friends with something to be furtive about. *How long has he been there, and how much did he hear?* But it was no good my standing there any longer, unnoticed in the fog and darkness. Lingering outside their charmed circle of yellow light like the uninvited guest at the wedding feast—for nothing good has ever come of that. Nothing good has ever been done by that uninvited guest.

Nell peered out from the cocoon of his coat. "Jack," she said. "Where've you been?"

"Nowhere," I told them. "I've been nowhere. Just walking, alone."

"On such a night?" asked Daniel.

"The darkness belongs to God, just as much as the daylight."

There was an awkward moment of silence. "P'raps I'll go inside, then," said Nell, detaching herself from the shelter of Daniel's coat. "It's late."

The door thudded shut behind her, leaving the two of us alone. For the very first time, there was a strain between us, indefinable but keenly present nonetheless. Somewhere in the fog, hoofbeats clattered unseen. The muffled light from a passing carriage flickered like a will-o'-the-wisp.

"What have you been doing, brother?" Daniel asked easily.

"I might ask you the same thing, Daniel."

"Why, what did it look like I was doing?"

He was smiling, but he looked at me steadily. I summoned an offhand chuckle in return. It came out not quite right, forced and just slightly louder than I'd intended.

"You looked like you were sitting with a friend, Daniel. Sitting with a friend in the night, and talking of this and that."

"That I was, brother. That's just what I was doing."

I laughed again, and this time there was no missing the metallic edge.

"I might say, though, Daniel—I might say in a friendly spirit—that your friend seems a trifle young for you."

"I might," said Daniel, "say the same to you."

His smile didn't dim, but his eyes never left mine either. Wrong-footed, I felt myself starting to flounder. I asked him what exactly he meant—as if we didn't both know perfectly well.

"I see the way you look at her, brother," he said. "It's all right—I'm not blaming, for I don't believe there's wickedness in it. But you need to remember that she's just a child. No matter what she's done and who she's been, she's still a child. That's how I see her, brother—I can promise you that—it's the only way I see her. And I hope that's how you see her too."

Stumbling a little—knowing that my face must be turning red—I assured him it was so. I knew indeed that Nell was very young; no one knew this better than I. Here I had intended to stop, but somehow in that smiling level gaze I found myself going further, and confessing that the thought had nonetheless occurred—an innocent, blameless thought, as any man might find occurring to him—that Nell must however be older in a space of time. In two or three years, perhaps—or even less—she would be a woman, at which time other intentions might indeed become appropriate, so long as they were expressed with deference and respect and love.

I think I was half-expecting him to chuckle, and nod his agreement. Perhaps even to clap me on the shoulder, and offer bluff conspiratorial well wishes, as a man will do with his best friend. Instead his smile faded, and his mouth turned down at the corners with displeasure.

"Hum," he said, tersely.

I felt a spike of anger, and shame. I floundered again. It was on the tip of my tongue to fling back that he was a fine one to be offering such advice, and passing such judgements—St Daniel, who enjoyed regular midnight visits from bouncing bountiful Molly La Clarice and others like her. Oh yes, I knew about these visits—so did others—and a fine way it was for a man like him to behave, a man who spoke on the Lord's behalf and presumed to see angels in Trafalgar Square. But instead I blurted something else entirely. It made him blink in surprise.

"You saw me a year and a half ago, brother? In Cornwall?"

And I found myself telling him all of it—or at least, enough of it to make his brow furrow in perplexity. I told him of running from enemies along the cliff, and losing my footing, and plunging down.

"That's when I saw your face. I swear, Daniel—it was your face, in the darkness. You told me I had nothing to fear. I thought you must be an angel—I did—an angel, at the very least. You said: 'I am O'Thunder.' It was the most extraordinary thing that's ever happened to me."

I discovered I was laughing, with the sheer experience of saying it out loud after all this time—and of saying it to him. "I'm not making it up, Daniel. This actually happened—I saw your face. However could—what I mean is—what do you think it could possibly mean?"

I felt closer to him in that moment than I have ever felt to another human being, before or since. I waited for him to feel it too—to acknowledge it—this extraordinary bond that existed between us. The two of us, standing together in a spill of yellow light outside the Gospel Mission of Heaven's Hammer, with nothing but fog and darkness all around.

"I'm not sure, brother," he said at last. He was speaking carefully, choosing his words. "I think perhaps you're tired. We're both tired, for it's been a long day. A good day, though—it's been a good day, brother."

He stood, and turned.

"Daniel?" He glanced back. "It's my birthday."

"Is it really, Jack? I didn't know."

"I don't think anyone did." I said it with another little laugh. "But it is. And now you know. I'm twenty-seven."

"Well," said Daniel. He put a hand on my shoulder, and summoned a smile. "Happy birthday, Jack. Many happy returns of the day."

Then he went inside, and left me standing there.

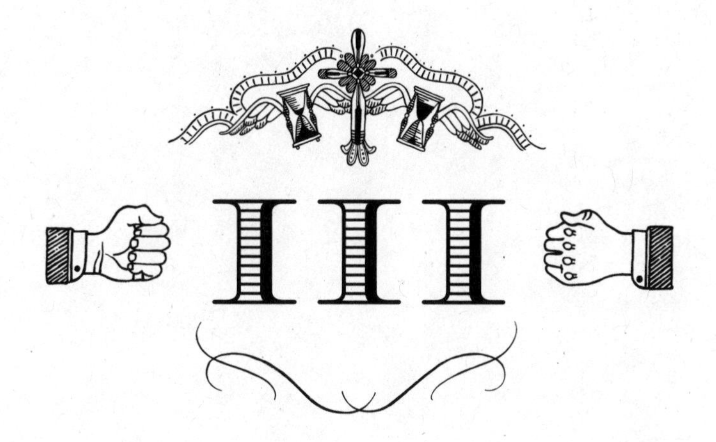
III

· SPRING, 1852 ·

JACK

I'M AFRAID THIS is where the tale grows dark. As all tales do, if they are tales of this world, for the world is dark, and we know it.

Oh, we try to delude ourselves that light exists, and will endure. The light from the eyes of a beloved, or the warm glow spilling through a window into the night. We reach towards it—we flutter our wings, we batter ourselves against the glass. But we'll never win through into the light itself, for it was never there in the first place. It wasn't real—just a trick of the shadow. And once we understand, once we finally accept that the world is dark, and all the people in it, and we ourselves are dark, just as dark as all the others, neither more nor less—once this terrible knowledge settles down deep into the marrow, and we understand at last that there is not nor ever shall be deliverance from this eternal darkness, not for so much as an instant, no not even in death itself—why, then what do we do, poor heart-broken moles?

We go on, of course. That's what we do, for it's all we *can* do. Step by blind faltering step, one foot ahead of the other, ever deeper into the darkness.

THE CALAMITY BEGAN with the events of the night of 13 February, 1852. The Ides of February. On the Ides of March, as every schoolboy knows, Julius Caesar was murdered by his friends on the steps of the Senate. The Ides of March was also—a lesser known historical fact—to loom tragically in the life of Joseph Bazalgette, the most significant figure in the entire history of English sewage, and a man who will in due course make a spectral appearance in this narrative. And on the Ides of February, Jack Hartright was betrayed.

I had gone to the Kemp Theatre that night. I went in a spirit of Christian charity, which—as every schoolboy will live to discover—is precisely where the very worst calamities originate.

Edmund Cubitt was playing Hamlet, which was bound to be a mistake. If watching Kean upon the stage had been, as Coleridge claimed, akin to reading Shakespeare by flashes of lightning, then watching Cubitt was to read it by clearings of the throat and mutterings of disapprobation, rising steadily to cries of "Enough!" and the flinging of orange peels. I'd made one or two critical observations to this effect during our last interview together, some months past. This had escalated into furious ejaculations from Cubitt and the shattering of crockery—Cubitt being, like many failed tragedians, an unbalanced man—and ended in the severing of connections between us. For Cubitt's suspicions about his missing snuff-box had been augmented by the conviction that someone had been pilfering from the theatre's cash box—doing so stealthily and steadily during all the months of my employment. Still, he'd been a friend, of sorts. I felt badly. And besides, those were the weeks and months when I was desperate to be Good, for I walked with Daniel O'Thunder at my side.

Daniel was with me in spirit when I went to the theatre that night, even though he was not present in the flesh. This was often the case, at that time. I would imagine that Daniel was with me, and often in my mind I would talk to him.

It's difficult to explain this without sounding mad as a hare.

Your no-nonsense friend at the club—the one with the air of a cynical walrus—is already inclining towards this conclusion. He is lowering his copy of the *Times,* and peering over it to demand: "And this imaginary companion—this vapour of an evangelical Irish pugilist—did he ever *reply?*" And were I to tell the truth—were I to admit, "Well, yes, in fact he did"—then your friend would bark a great derisive *"Haw!"* For of course he's had me pegged from the very start. Oh yes, he knows these fellows—unmanly self-indulgent hysterics, rotten to the core, fit for Bedlam, if Bedlam weren't too good for them. No, take 'em away, out of his sight—send 'em to the Devil.

But it wasn't like that. It was more as if the *thought* of Daniel O'Thunder stayed with me, for he was so much in my mind. I imagined speaking with him, as one might seek guidance from one's own Best Self, especially in moments when I was troubled or uncertain. I felt him with me as I went round to the stage door after the performance. A large part of me wanted to slope off into the night, and I imagined it as a debate that Daniel and I might be having.

"He won't want to see me, Daniel. He said as much the last time, and some very cruel remarks besides."

"But were you blameless, brother? And even if you were, would it matter? Ask yourself what our Saviour would do."

"Our Saviour was perfect, Daniel—but I am not."

"It makes no matter, brother. For we are called upon to forgive, even those who call us 'viper'—and worse things besides, such as 'thief' and 'lying bastard'—and fling crockery at our head."

He was right, of course. My Best Self was right. So I went in at the stage door to look for Edmund Cubitt, rehearsing as I did two or three of those vapid euphemisms one utters to friends who have just failed in some creative endeavour. Then I stopped, for there were voices just round the corner, and one of them was uttering my name. A woman's voice, and somehow alarmingly familiar.

"Jack Hartright. For that's the name he's been using, I believe."

"Mr Hartright?" This second voice belonged to Mrs Beale, the highly seasoned ingenue. "Why, he's not with us, I'm afraid. Mr Jack Hartright is not with us anymore."

"What does that mean? 'Not with us'—you mean to say he's dead?"

"Oh, no—dear me—not dead! Or at least not so's I've heard, though I suppose that's no guarantee either, the world being what it is, and men and women being what they are, and dropping dead, some of them, right when you least expect it. No, Mr Hartright was merely dismissed for thievery."

"Do you know where I might find him?"

"And might one ask," drawled Mrs Beale, with her unerring nose for other people's business, "why such a young lay-dee as yourself might wish to find such a person?"

"Let us say, it is a question of Virtue," said Bathsheba Scantlebury.

For it was she. I stood rooted, even as I sensed a hulking malevolence in the corridor directly behind me.

"God's blood," said Little Dick. "Here's the villain now."

I SHOULD HAVE known. Fool that I was, I *had* known, ever since my narrow escape, that the Scantleburys would come after me, raven-hearted with wrath, shrieking for vengeance, though I fled to the ends of the earth.

During my first months in London, this fear had preyed upon me constantly. All the time I worked at the theatre, I never once stepped out onto the stage without the clammy expectation that a bulk might at any instant lurch to its feet in the unholy blackness of the gallery, and a voice cry out in Cornish wrath: "Beresford!" So I'd slipped out through a side door after each performance, and followed a different route home each night, and changed my lodgings each two or three weeks—changed lodgings as often as many men changed linen.

But since autumn I'd grown careless. Preoccupied with my new life at the Mission—preoccupied with Daniel O'Thunder, and with Nell—I'd let down my guard. And now they had me.

"Excuse me." I tried to say it as calmly as I could. "Excuse me, but where are we going?"

We were rattling down midnight streets in a carriage, but whither we rattled remained a matter of impenetrable darkness, for the window blinds were drawn down. They emitted the barest sliver of moonlight—just enough to discern Bathsheba's pale face across from me.

"I'm sorry," I said, trying again. "I'm very sorry, but wherever we're going, you cannot be doing this."

But clearly they were.

They'd had me out of the theatre before I'd had a chance to shout, for my windpipe had constricted with horror even as Little Dick's hand had closed upon it. I'd been flung directly into the carriage, with Little Dick wedged in beside me, crushing my ribs against the side of the compartment and breathing all the available oxygen in ursine snorts. His sister stared across in kidney-slicing malignancy.

Desperate words bubbled up. I knew with utter certainty that I was pleading for my life.

"Look," I said, "there's been a terrible misunderstanding. I am not the man you mistake me for. I was not such a man two years ago, and I am a better man now. A sinner—yes, of course I am—a sinner and a wretch—a blind worm writhing in the mire. But a man who would—would *force* a girl, against her will? No—never! Somehow we both misinterpreted..."

But something had gone wrong with Bathsheba's face. The malignancy had given way to something else—or perhaps it had never been there at all, at least not as I had imagined. It was a look of simple human distress. Tears welled up in her eyes. As they did, I had the lurching thought that she was somehow younger than I had been remembering. She was no more than eighteen even now, which would have made her—what?—sixteen perhaps, on the night of the alleged assault. Or fifteen? And somehow she wasn't the surly slattern I had been remembering, either. She was altogether plainer than that, and more vulnerable. A country girl in a plain cloak and bonnet, clinging to a plain frail dignity. And large as he was, Little Dick himself was not much older. A lump of a country lad with rough red hands, pale with anger at what had been done to his sister.

I opened my mouth once again, to protest that I was never the man they accused me of being. But I couldn't force the words out.

For in fact I was that man.

Your friend the cynical walrus is speechless, for once in his life. You yourself are incredulous, as you protest: "But you told us otherwise!" To which, in feeble self-defence, I would reply: well, no, I didn't, exactly. I didn't precisely admit that I used force. But I didn't precisely say that I didn't, either. A lawyer might say that I framed the event in a deliberately ambiguous context. You yourself might exclaim that this is beginning to sound like mealy-mouthed evasion, while your friend the cynical walrus has found his tongue and is spluttering that it sounds to him like outright villainy—yes, to him it sounds like blackguardly abomination.

To which I would reply that nothing—almost nothing—is as clear-cut as it seems. And that I have long since ceased caring what men like the cynical walrus think of me. If I cared a whit for their opinion, I'd slit my own throat. I'd string a cord from the rafters of my Whitechapel garret and hang myself directly. As I might still do. Yes, as I might indeed still do, just as soon as I set down this pen. And then to jerk and twitch my slippers from my feet while my friend the brisk brown spider looks down from her perfect geometrical killing-ground.

But on that night—the Ides of February, 1852—rattling through London in that carriage, I was too upset to think clearly about anything.

I have a vague idea that I exclaimed in distress, and fumbled in my pocket for a handkerchief. I have an idea that I extended the handkerchief to Bathsheba, who exclaimed something in return—in disbelief, I think, and contempt—and slapped my hand away as if it were a serpent. But now the carriage had rattled to a stop, and as it did I knew where we were. Knew it for a certainty, even before staggering out into the night wind—for I recognized the stench. It had been creeping upon us steadily for some while without my having been quite cognizant, being as I was preoccupied with such matters as guilt, self-loathing, and mortal terror. But now here it was in front of me.

The river. They had brought me to the Thames.

My thoughts careened instantly to wild Gothic conclusions. You'll have observed in me a tendency towards lurid penny-dreadful self-dramatization, the legacy of a boyhood spent in the muttering shadows of *The Castle of Otranto* and *Melmoth the Wanderer*. Or possibly the refuge of a man who dreads to study himself too closely. I saw myself in an instant: a corpse in the great stinking Thames, arms flung wide and windpipe gaping in a harlequin grin, swept with the rest of the filth and offal to the sea.

A boat was waiting for us, down the steps by a rickety landing. A wherry with a leering one-eyed boatman and a hound of Hell beside him. Or so it seemed to me in that moment—it was probably a Newfoundland retriever and a boatman with the normal complement of eyes. The schooner—I seemed to grasp their plan with horrible clarity—the schooner would be waiting downriver, in the Pool of London between London Bridge and the Tower. The harbour where the great ships moored, in a forest of masts and rigging. They would spirit me aboard, and take me to their ancestral home.

Which was ridiculous. I realized this afterwards. Who would sail a ship from London to Cornwall? Assuming they were taking me to Cornwall at all, the plan was to go upriver for a few miles to a waiting coach. And they wouldn't have taken me to Scantlebury Hall. Their intention was simply to turn me over to the authorities in the county where they lived and were known, rather than attempting to lay charges here in London.

But in the penny-dreadfulness of the moment, Scantlebury Hall loomed before me. In my fevered imagining, it was darker and more terrible than Childe Roland's Tower. The postern gate would creak wide, and then clang shut again behind us. Sir Richard Scantlebury, *Bart.* would be waiting, amidst the weasels and stoats and all the ghastly Scantlebury ancestors, with Geoffrey the Cabin Boy pouting beside him. "Go fetch the Instruments," Sir Richard would grate. And I would howl in desolate envy for those happy, happy men who were corpses instead in the terrible tea-brown Thames.

Growling an oath, Little Dick pushed me ahead of him, towards the stairs that led to the landing. Then for an instant he hesitated, turning to offer a hand to his sister, who might otherwise slip on the narrow stone step. That was all I needed. I twisted, and fled.

A shout of dismay from Little Dick, and an exclamation from Bathsheba. "Stop him!"

They'd catch me, of course. Even in the dead of night, the hue and cry would raise pursuit. Slumbering lightermen on the quays below; mudlarks out before dawn to scavenge the riverbank; water-bailiffs emerging from the wooden shacks where the drowned were laid out on planks until the coroner might find time for them. And the waterman's dog, which would surely have me down at any instant.

"Stop!"

There were more voices—terrible voices, closing in on me. All at once there was a stench more noisome than the Thames itself. A black sphincter gaped in the embankment in front of me, disgorging a noxious flow, and guarded by a gate of iron railings half-risen with the tide. An instinct of revulsion, but there was no time to think, and no choice. I hurled myself forward and down—headlong and choking into the Stygian filth—and then I was through. Under the railing, and rising blind and retching on the other side. Lurching upward from the horrid river as if hauled by the hands of some infernal Baptist.

It was the reeking blackness of the London sewer. I had escaped into the mouth of Hell itself.

And here the Devil awaited.

NELL

THAT NIGHT THERE was two hundred of 'em singing and praying at the Mission, and Daniel preaching in a voice like he'd bring the roof-beams down. There was a service like this most nights now. Daniel would preach for two hours, and sometimes even more, praising God and urging the Devil to leave off his wickedness and repent. This night he went further.

"I call upon the Devil to show himself—yes, to come here right this instant, if he dares. For he and I have a great issue to resolve between us!"

There was loud exclamations at this, but Daniel told us not to be afraid. "For the Devil is a coward, brothers and sisters," he cried. "The Devil will not attack a healthy Christian. And if he disputes this, then I will offer to pull his nose for him!"

Peggy Sherwood hated such talk. She stood with me at the back of the room—we were crammed at the back cos there was such a great crowd here tonight. Some of 'em here to worship, some of 'em praying be healed, and others just here to gawk at the man who'd raised Hen Gully from the dead.

The last hymn was "Where Shall My Wandering Soul Begin," and I sang along with all the others. I couldn't sing a lick before I met Daniel O'Thunder—and tell the truth, I couldn't sing a lick even afterwards. But every time I opened my mouth, I was ready to believe that *this* was the time it would be different. And if you're asking how it felt to be with Daniel in them early days, then that's what I'd tell you. It felt like this was the moment I'd finally be able to sing. I'd open my mouth, and carillon bells would ring. It would be pure and lovely and send shivers right down your spine, like the voice of a boy I heard one time at the Albert Saloon in Tothill Street. A beautiful Italian boy with dark hair and great sad eyes and his little onions cut off and given for a present to the Pope. That's what Mary said, when I told her afterwards. I described the way it sounded, and she gave a nod and a certain look, and told me how that voice had come to be. "And the Pope keeps them all in a golden box, Nell. Like conkers."

My friend Mary Bartram, who was dead cos of me.

Afterwards, when most of the others was gone, we sat in a corner and Miss Peggy brushed my hair. She did that often at night. I think she felt responsible for me, somehow. She wielded that hairbrush brisk-like—Miss Peggy was wiry, and a deal stronger than she looked.

"I wish he wouldn't talk like that. It tempts the Devil—and that's a terrible mistake." She wrenched at a tangle, like pulling a nail from a post.

"Ow! Jeezus, Miss—leave some hair attached to my fucking scalp."

"Nell Rooney, I swear, half an hour with you is like an entire morning at Billingsgate fish market. And one day soon I shall wash out that mouth of yours. With hot water and lye soap, until that mouth is a gargle of soap-suds and nothing comes foaming out but 'hallelujah.'"

She fussed for another minute, and then suddenly asked: "Is it true, Nell? You were there, that day, after the mill. Do you believe he actually raised that man from the dead?"

That's what was bothering her most of all. She kept coming back and back to that same question. I told her what I always did—I didn't know. But tonight, something else was bothering me much worse. I couldn't stop thinking about poor Mary.

When Miss Peggy finally left off, I went up the stairs to Daniel's chamber, and sat on the top step of the landing. Daniel had gone off after the service, striding away to visit someone who'd fallen sick. He was constantly striding somewhere to help someone, and scarcely sleeping two hours in a night. But he'd be back sooner or later, and I wanted to be waiting. Before Molly La Clarice could get to him, or one of them others. Cos there were others—various others—coming and going from Daniel's chamber. We all knew that, even though nobody talked about it.

It was well past midnight when I heard his footsteps, trudging. The light from his candle come wavering up the stair. "Hallo, Nell," he said, surprised to see me sitting there in the dark.

"I have something I need to tell you," I said.

He laughed a little, sounding tired. "Can it wait till tomorrow, Nell?"

"I killed someone, Daniel."

He started to laugh again, but seen in a second I wasn't joking. The laugh died away, and he sat down slowly beside me.

"Tell me." He set the candle down, and waited.

So I told him about Mary, and how I was the one responsible. I'd run away from Mother Clatterballock, and that's why Mary got sent packing and ended up in the Park. It was the thing that terrified her most in all the world, and it may as well have been me who wrapped hands around her throat.

"No," said Daniel, and shook his head. "I'm so very sorry for your friend, but this was not your fault—no, look at me. This was never your fault, Nell, not any of it. And it was never God's fault either, even though he was there—for he was, Nell, he was there with your poor Mary till the end. You can be sure of that, and take comfort. She died in his arms, though he couldn't save her. All he could do was feel the pain, worse than Mary felt it herself. So I won't have you blaming yourself, Nell—I won't have it, for it just won't do, and there's nothing to be crying about."

But the tears were streaming down, now, and my shoulders were shaking. He put one arm about me, like an oaken bough.

"If you want to know who to blame, Nell, then blame the man who did it. And yet not even him—blame the Devil, who was in that man when it happened." His voice grew husky, and strange. "And if you need to blame someone else, then blame me."

"Blame you?" I said through the sobs. "You w-wasn't even there!"

"Aye," said Daniel. "The Devil was there—and I wasn't. I am far too idle, Nell—yes I am, don't shake your head—I am a sluggish idle fellow, and the Devil never sleeps at all. From this moment forth, I must do better."

He talked like that more and more these days, and it frightened me. But that's not what I had come here to tell him, nor why the sobs were twisting in my stomach.

"There's something else," I said. "It's something awful, Daniel. It's worse than you can ever imagine. I'm here cos I'm a spy."

JACK

IN A VERY few years after that dreadful night, there would be no more open sewer outflows along the banks of the Thames. London would awaken to the discovery that it was choking on its own sewage.

A miasma of cholera wafted from cesspits under the houses, misting upward from the Thames itself. In the long hot summer of 1858 it would grow so appalling that the newspapers would name it The Great Stink. Londoners would stumble along the Strand in masks, and sheets soaked in chlorine would be hung over the windows of the Parliament at Westminster.

In London's hour of crisis, Joseph Bazalgette arose, and was commissioned to undertake the greatest engineering project in history. It was far greater than anything the Romans ever dreamed of, for Bazalgette's task was to mitigate human filth itself. The ordure of three million human beings, passing daily through three million human entrails, each and every day, day after day without any hope of let or cessation, and each day more of it, for each day there were more of *them*. Every eight minutes a Londoner died, but every five minutes another one was born, mewling and defecating. So Bazalgette drained the cesspits. He closed off the outfalls along the Thames. He built of Portland cement eleven hundred miles of new sewer tunnels, to gather the Stygian streams from every corner of London and channel them into a vast great Stygian river that flowed to new outfalls far away from the heart of the city in Barking and Crossness. He accomplished all this while he himself was generating human filth, without let or cessation, each and every day of his life, until at last it ended upon the Ides of March in 1891, amidst tributes and lamentations, with a feeble thoracic rattle and a final filthy loosening of the bowels.

And here I was. The Ides of February, 1852: standing blind in a river of filth, slipping and choking. I would have despaired—I would have given up and died—except Daniel was with me. I was certain of that, through the whole nightmare that followed. Daniel O'Thunder was at my side, and he never left.

Someone else heard my cries in the darkness, too. It was a tosher—one of those ragged men who spent their lives in the sewers, scavenging for treasures, bits of bone and coins and buttons and spoons. Men in velveteen coats and wide-brimmed hats, sifting through the filthy ooze as gold-panners sift for gold. He'd been scavenging near the gate, thank God, and now he emerged through the darkness with a lantern and a soiled leathery face, like a shit-spattered Orpheus seeking his Eurydice.

"Awright then, mate?" His voice echoed against the bricks. "Christ, how'd you get in 'ere?"

I had it in mind to explain that I needed his lantern. But in my panic I shouldered into him, grabbing at the light as he reached out. He fell back with a startled "whoof," and now I had the lantern instead. It sputtered one-eyed as I ran splashing into the bowels of the metropolis. I heard the tosher's shouts receding behind me, his chagrin giving way to alarm. Afterwards I preferred to suppose that he found his way out eventually.

The tunnel was eight feet wide at first, crumbling brick and masonry. Fungi grew upon the walls, obscenely white. The tunnel soon grew narrower, and as it did the filthy stream rose higher, round my thighs. The current grew stronger, trying to draw me down. Where the tunnels were narrowest, the stream would rise at high tide nearly to the roof and men would drown.

They drowned all the time in the sewers, men who were unlucky or caught unawares. Toshers, or else rat-catchers, for they came into the sewers as well. They came with wooden traps to catch sewer-rats, which they'd sell for killing in the rings in the back of sporting houses. Such a house would need dozens of rats for killing each night—hundreds even, for a prime rat-killing terrier might kill dozens by himself—although the sewer rats didn't fetch such a price as the water-rats did. Sewer rats were dangerous. They carried disease, and the merest nip from a sewer rat might fester upon the nose of a dog, and kill him.

There were other ways to die in the sewer. I had heard about these from Lurcher, an ancient tosher who came to the Mission from time to time, trailing the faint stench of effluent. There was slop-gas in the sewer—bubbles of it, in the sludge. If you stepped on a bubble, the gas would rise up and overcome you in an instant. Down you'd fall, and drown. But that was nothing, compared to the rats. Not the ordinary sewer rats, the ones you'd hear scrabbling and splish-splashing in the dark. There were gigantic rats down here, rats the size of badgers, and these rats were silent. They'd follow you, dozens of them—hundreds—they'd come upon you from behind. Oh yes, said Lurcher, everyone knew about the giant rats. They'd strip a grown man of flesh in five minutes, strip him right down to the gleaming white bones.

The river of filth had risen to my waist. It rose to my armpits. But Daniel was with me.

He said: "Be not afraid, brother." He said: "Take my hand."

I said: "Oh, Daniel. What have I done?"

"Tell me the truth," said Daniel. His voice was grave. "Did you ravish that girl?"

"I did," I said. "Oh God, I did. And I've done other things besides, Daniel—worse things. For I haven't been telling you everything."

Daniel's face grew grey with sorrow. But he didn't leave me.

Daniel never left, not even when the tunnel narrowed to the width of a coffin, and the river of filth was a torrent. It rose to my chin and roared in my ears, for now it had me and began to drag me down. My hand with the lantern was desperately upthrust, like the painting of a drowning man. One hand with its feeble light groping towards God, but God couldn't see me and he couldn't hear my cries, here in this filthy black hole thirty feet below the cobblestones of London, with the rats behind and the Devil just inches beneath my feet. "This way!" cried Daniel, for we had come to a branching in the tunnel. Blind and choking, I couldn't see it. But Daniel could—and he was right. Even as the nightmare grew unendurable I began to realize that the horrid river was loosening its grip. It was round my thighs, now, and then my knees, and the tunnel itself grew wider and taller until I could stand upright. Finally it was wide enough for three men to walk abreast and the filth was just a noxious stream, ankle-deep.

I staggered and splashed, weeping and gibbering, with the slop-gas lurking beneath my feet and the rats closing in behind. For they were there, they were nearly upon me, oh yes I knew they were, giant rats spreading like a stain, on silent scuttling claws. And every instant I expected worse than this. Expected the worst of all: hands closing suddenly about my ankles. Horrid icy talons, and a great infernal shout of triumph as the Devil pulled me down. Or not a shout of triumph—why triumph at all, for a conclusion so foregone?—but instead a murmur of welcome. For here was his own dear friend at last, his own dear *considerate* friend. Not only had he damned himself, far beyond any prospect of salvation—well done!—he'd brought himself down here to the Infernal Gate, and spared the Devil a journey into the upper air.

But now the tunnel was slanting upward. Then it wasn't a tunnel at all, but an underground alleyway, and above my head was no longer crumbling brick but rotting wood. Here and there the London sewer led right into the worst of the London slums—Lurcher had told me this, described it in peculiar revolting detail. I was underneath the sagging tenements of St Giles' rookery. There were holes in the planks above me, some of them plugged with bits of rag, but some of them showing through into the rooms where families lived writhing together like maggots. I glimpsed a face peering back as I staggered past below, and dimly heard a shout of mortal alarm, for of course—it was obvious later, when I stopped to think—for of course the poor man had jumped to the only possible conclusion. Hearing my subterranean cries and glimpsing my upturned face, he had understood in a flash of horror that I was the Devil come to catch *him* by the ankles. Thus did I petrify a denizen of St Giles, and perhaps even—who knows?—inspired him to thoughts of repentance and the salvation of his soul, if only for one night of his wretched life, before he returned to the consolation of drink and despair and bashing his wife and babies about.

At last I emerged from a cellar into the open air. A bundle of rags lying crumpled by the doorway bolted upright, for it was not a bundle of rags at all but a crone with a halfpenny jar of gin, who shrieked to see the Devil arise from Hell. And in her horror I saw myself reflected back: smeared head to foot and dripping with filth. A twisted thing of ordure and despair, loathsome and loathing. The ruination of a soul of Light, now black and stinking and utterly foul.

Icy rain poured down. I dimly recall the lash of it, and have some recollection of tearing off my beshitten clothes and begging God to wash me clean again, though I knew in my heart that he wouldn't. I remember feverish ravings, and I believe I must have been delirious, for it was dawn when I staggered up the stairs to Daniel O'Thunder's bedchamber, and to this day I have no memory of getting there. What I do recall is the desperate conviction: I must see Daniel. God had turned his face from me—this much I knew with terrible certainty—and now all my hope lay in Daniel O'Thunder. I must see him, and lay all my sins at his feet. I must stand naked in Daniel's eyes, and fall to my knees before him, and wrap my arms around his thighs, and implore his absolution.

I pounded upon the door of my last hope. When at last it opened just a crack, it was her face peering through.

"Nell?"

And it was. It was my lovely Nell. Standing in his chamber doorway in a smock, her little face querulous with sleep.

"Christ a'mighty. Fuck happened to you?"

"Who is it?" came his sleepy voice, within.

"It's Jack," said my lovely Nell, "and he fucking stinks. Phew! Have a wash, and come back later."

She closed the door. Within, the floorboards creaked as she padded back to bed.

I stood upon the landing like a statue.

NELL

AND THE THING of it was, he'd never touched me. Leastways not the way Jack thought.

We'd sat together on the landing, Daniel and me, and I told him everything. Almost everything. I told him how I'd gone off with Lord Sculthorpe—yes, him from that night at Mother Clatterballock's, when Daniel sat upon Tim Diggory's head. I'd gone off with him cos he swore he'd help me find my mother, which made me a fool, although it didn't make me something even worse. The "even worse" came later. I didn't say the part about "I think he thinks I might be his daughter"—I left that bit out, cos I couldn't even bring myself to think about it. I can hardly bring myself to think about it even now. We all got fathers, and some of them are no prize, but *him?* But I told Daniel the rest of it. I told him how Lord Sculthorpe said I should come here to the Mission and bring back word of what I seen. And I wager I would have done it, too—told His Lordship everything he wanted to hear—except he'd up and disappeared and I'd never really had the chance.

"That's what I did, Daniel. That's who I am. And now you know."

I wasn't even crying, now. Just sitting small and desolate with knowing he'd hate me, and waiting for him to turn me out like I deserved.

"Well," said Daniel. "There's no harm done."

Apparently he hadn't understood. That just made it even worse, cos now I had to explain it all again.

"But I would have told him. I would have betrayed you—knowing that he'd just use what I said against you somehow. Don't you see?"

"Because you were afraid of him."

"That's no excuse!"

"It would have been all right in any case."

"Why?"

"Because I love you. And I'm weary now, and need to rest."

He stood up, and put his hand on my head, and went into his chamber, leaving me and the candle sitting on the landing. I sat there for the longest time. Then finally I got up and went in after him, closing the door behind me.

"Nell?"

He shifted, sleepily. He was lying in the cot, the great animal bulk of him. The room was full of his smell. It was a dark, good smell, like woodsmoke. I snuffed the candle and slipped under the blanket beside him. It was warm.

"What are you doing?"

I'd moved to stroke him. Cos that was something I knew how to do, wasn't it? Something I could give back to him for being kind to me.

"Nell, stop." His voice was sharp enough to sting.

"Why?"

"Because you're a child."

"I'm not a fucking child."

"And it isn't this way between us."

The other whores were good enough. Molly La Clarice and them—sneaking in and slipping out and thinking no one knew. So what was wrong with me?

"There's nothing wrong with you, Nell."

"And if you don't want me—if I'm not good enough—then fine." I was starting to cry again, with feeling so ridiculous.

"Just tell me so. But if that's how you feel, then don't be saying things you don't mean."

"What did I say?"

"You know what you said!"

"I meant it, Nell. I love you—with the best kind of love."

I discovered right then—if I hadn't known before—that I didn't want that kind. I wanted something lovelier and worse. But here I was, stuck with it and settling for the best.

"If you're frightened," said Daniel, "you can stay here for awhile. You don't need to worry about Sculthorpe, Nell, or anything else, for I promise I'll keep you safe."

And that's what he did, or tried to do, in everything that followed. He kept me safe. That's what he was doing that very last time of all, all those years later. As far from London as you could ever imagine. Mountains and snow and bitter cold—wind howling like wolves from a vast northern sky, and Daniel striding into the storm with a rage and a terrible joy, cos at long last he was about to lay hands on the Devil.

But that was still a long way off. We don't need to talk about that yet.

That night in London I lay beside him. Just lay with him, nothing else, in the warmth and the lovely woodsmoke smell. Then somehow it was morning and someone was pounding at the door.

Fucking Jack.

LONG AFTER, I wondered if it might have made a difference if I'd gone after Jack right then. If I'd gone running after him, instead of turning back into the bedchamber, and made him see that nothing had happened. Maybe he'd have listened, and maybe that would have changed the way everything turned out.

But I don't think so. Jack was in a fearful state that morning, filthy and reeking and wild. Besides, I don't think he'd have believed me anyway, no matter what I said. Jack could never trust himself—that's what I finally understood. So how could he ever trust somebody else?

I'd actually liked him well enough, at first. He had a charm about him, Jack, and he actually seemed—God help him—to think I was wonderful. But that wasn't exactly it. What it was, Jack wanted *me* to think that *he* was wonderful. He wanted it so badly he was all a-quiver with it—and that's where the difference comes in. One day he gave me a little wooden box tied with a bit of ribbon. I opened it, and inside was the locket I'd been asking him to give me back—my own locket, and he gave it to me like a gift. I'd actually started avoiding him, as much as I could—which wasn't easy, with both of us spending so much time at the Mission. Jack had a room somewhere, but he hardly seemed to go there, and I hardly ever went to the house in Hampstead. So generally I just avoided being alone with him.

Tim Diggory reckoned this was a good idea. Tim kept his eye on Jack—an old habit, he said, from keeping an eye on the dickey ones at night houses. A professional like Tim Diggory could spot the dickey ones straight off. "And that one," Tim said to me once or twice, with a quiet look in Jack's direction, "that one is a bit dickey."

Jack had disappeared that morning, after he found me in Daniel's chamber. He was gone for nearly a month, then one day he turned up again.

I'd stepped out the back door of the Mission to empty a bucket, and suddenly he was right there at my shoulder. Appearing out of nowhere, like a devil in a play. I near to jumped out of my skin.

"Jesus!"

"I need you to come with me, Nell," he said.

He'd cleaned himself up again, but there was something wrong about him. He talked just a bit too fast, and his eyes wouldn't settle. He had my arm in a grip.

"You're hurting," I said. "Let go of me."

"I've made a discovery."

I made one stab at sorting this out. "Jack, listen to me. No, listen for just a minute. That night, it wasn't what you thought, at all. Me and Daniel—"

"Yes, of course—it's you and Daniel, now." The bitterness came bursting out of him. "I understand that very well. I understand the state of things. It's Daniel and his Nell."

It twisted his whole body in a sneer, and for a second the look on his face was pure hatred. I realized right then—there was no point.

"Fine," I said irritably, pulling away. "Go ahead and believe what you want. But I'm warning you. If you go grabbing me again, I'm going to call for Tim."

"Nell, this is important. This is vital. It's about your mother."

The one thing that could have stopped me—and he'd said it.

"What about my mother?" I demanded.

"I've found her."

PEGGY SHERWOOD

It was a blustery afternoon in early March. I remember very clearly. It was the same afternoon the old soldier came to the Mission, and that was the day Captain O'Thunder took a step too far.

Please understand: we were loyal to him from the very outset, without question or qualification. My sister Esther had been the one who saw him first, three years earlier. He was preaching a sermon under the trees in Gordon Square. She said to me, "Sister, you must hear him, for there is something extraordinary in this man." So we went back the next day, and there he was—a great ragged Irishman preaching the Gospel of Joy to the passers-by and the pigeons. I listened. A great ragged Irishman indeed, but there was such laughter in him—and something else, too. Something lovely and terrible. And I thought: "The spark of the Divine. That's what it is. The spark of the Lord, and it's burning in this improbable man."

We come from that sort of family, my sister and I. We have always been open; we have always been searching. My mother spoke in holy tongues, and once she saw an Angel of the Apocalypse with eyes of flame.

So we went up to Captain O'Thunder, and I said to him: "Yes."

For what else was there to say? When Our Lord encountered the fishermen on the shores of Galilee, He didn't say to them: "I would ask you to give my message some consideration." He said: "Put down your nets and follow me." And they did.

The Captain was a child, in many ways—that was evident from the start. In his emotions, and especially in his *appetites,* if I must use the word, for there was no self-control; there really wasn't, which was too, too bad. Captain O'Thunder wanted boundaries, and yet he did such good work. He did God's Work amongst the poor—he truly did. That's why we stayed with him, my sister Esther and I. Feeding them, and going into those terrible night houses, and then the healing, for I firmly believe to this day that he had healing power in those great gnarled hands. But the prize-fighting was difficult to reconcile, and then he started shaking his fist at the Devil. I mean, yes, of course the Devil existed. The Devil *exists.* He's at his infernal work this very moment and we must fight the fight as Christian soldiers, all of us. But offering to pull his nose? And after Henry Gully rose up with an aching head, that was all anyone would talk about. It worried me, it terrified me, because you cannot have it. You cannot have this talk of raising corpses from the dead—especially when it might be true. For then we have exceeded ourselves. We have gone past the boundaries that are permitted to us. And when boundaries do not exist, then what is there to hold back the Devil?

The old soldier tottered into the Mission like something blown by the wind. Thin as a scarecrow in a ragged coat that might once upon a time have been red, and very much the worse for drink. This was hardly unusual, for many of them had been drinking, the poor lost souls who came straggling in. The place was jammed all day with them, and all night too, for they had no other place to sleep and the Captain never turned anyone away. He wouldn't let Tim Diggory turn them away either—even though Tim Diggory would have done so. He would have done so with increasing frequency, left to his own devices.

Tim Diggory would get a look about him, sometimes. Nell Rooney, who knew him from his old life, used to call it his "Tim look." His left eye would narrow, and you could see an urge coming upon him to lay violent hands on someone. It was the drunkards who offended him most. Nell believed that Tim took the drunkards as a personal affront, since he himself no longer touched a drop. He had not taken a drink since the evening at that dreadful night house, that famous evening when Captain O'Thunder sat upon Tim's head, and in the darkness under the Captain's behind Tim saw the light of salvation.

I'm sure Nell was right about this—although I think there was something else, too. I think poor Tim Diggory needed somewhere to draw a line. I think he was looking for boundaries.

Well, Tim took against this particular beggar. His eye gave a flash like a telescope upon a hill. Fortunately I'd been watching, and called for Captain O'Thunder. He hurried to sort it out, firmly requiring Tim to let the beggar go. Tim protested that the beggar was a drunkard, and the Captain replied: yes, this was true. But this only made him especially welcome here, for Our Lord was a drinking man too. And would we turn Our Lord from the door?

Tim scoffed at this, but the Captain assured him it was so. He said: Our Lord was a wine-bibber, which means a drinking man. Thus his enemies said about him, for thus it says in the Bible, written down in black and white. The Captain could not read it himself—the Captain could not read—but he encouraged Tim to open the Bible and see.

So Tim did. He found out the Captain was quite right, which shocked him. I saw him communicate this subsequently to a young woman named Molly La Clarice, who had taken to visiting us at the Mission. Molly was a woman who desired poverty, chastity, and humility—just like St Augustine had done. But also like St Augustine, alas, she wasn't sure she wanted them just yet.

Poor Tim showed Molly the Bible. Look, said poor Tim: Our Lord really was a wine-bibber. And worse, he went about with whores and tax-collectors. With a certain look, Molly demanded of Tim what precisely was so worse about whores. This stopped Tim for a moment, and briefly perplexed him, for Tim was never swift of thought. But the race—as the Bible also tells us—is not to the swift, and Tim got there in a moment. He apologized quickly, and agreed that there was nothing worse about whores, who were always welcome here. Then he thought for another moment, and added: but not tax-collectors.

You see? Boundaries.

But meanwhile the Captain had sat down with the beggar in the ragged red coat. It turned out that this was an old Infantryman, and the Captain asked him where he'd done his soldiering.

In India, said the old soldier, and in Hell.

I was in Afghanistan, said the Captain. And in Hell.

The Captain's eyes had gone distant and strange. The old soldier looked at him closely. After a minute, he nodded, and put a hand on the Captain's shoulder. Aye, said the old soldier. I can see you been in both them places.

I moved closer to listen, for I'd never heard the Captain speak like this, of the places he'd been and the harrowing sights he'd seen. Then all of a sudden the poor old soldier had a fit. He rolled about on the floor, flailing and foaming. It took four of us to hold him down, and the Captain was greatly agitated. He cried in a terrible voice for the Devil to let this poor man go.

This threw the Mission into chaos, as you'd expect. Beggars and disciples all clustering round, with exclamations of horror and fascination. The Devil? The Devil had taken this man? Keep back! Look sharp! God's mercy! Shouts of fear and calls upon Heaven's protection, and above the din there was the mighty voice of the Captain, calling upon the Devil to desist.

"I order him in the Lord's own name—*come out!*"

And God save our souls, it worked. Or seemed to do, at any rate. The poor old soldier stopped flailing. He opened his eyes and looked at the Captain with a slow sweet smile starting to form, like a child awakening. And then he died—just like that. He just stopped, with his eyes wide and that sweet smile halfway formed.

We did our best to revive him, of course. The Captain tried desperately, and we sent for a doctor, but the man was dead.

When he finally understood that, the Captain rose. He stood very still, for a moment. Then he gave a howl, and seized a table and flung it over. He seized a chair and flung it, and smashed another like kindling, and lifted the great iron soup pot and hurled it clear across the room. The rest of us shrank back cowering, until at last the rage left him and he stood white and shaking upon a battlefield of splintered tables and stools. Then he cried out again, and went up the stairs, three of them at a time. We heard the door slam to his chamber, and afterwards we heard his heavy footsteps pacing above us. Back and forth, back and forth. Finally there was stillness, and after another span of time I went up to him.

He was sitting on the edge of the cot, hands on his knees and head hanging low. He looked like a condemned man in his prison cell, awaiting execution. Such an image, but I swear it was the one that came to me.

I said to him: would he take some nourishment? For I had brought up a wooden platter with a bowl of soup, and some bread.

He spoke with a terrible finality. He said: this was never going to stop, was it? He understood that now. The Devil was never going to stop.

I said to him: if he wasn't hungry, then he should lie down and rest.

He said: did I not see? All the preachers in the world could preach against the Devil, and all the armies in the world could march, but it would make no difference. It would just be worse, for the Devil would double back like a wolf to seize the stragglers. The weakest of all, the halt and the lame. The ones who had been left behind. And this must be stopped. The Captain would not tolerate this a single day longer.

At last he raised his head. His face was haggard, but the look in his eyes was of wild and terrible resolution.

NELL

Jack wouldn't tell me where she was. He had to show me, he said. But he swore my mother was safe.

"How did you find her? What did she say? Did she ask about—?"

"You must see her for yourself."

We went on the Omnibus, and then on foot, east towards Whitechapel. I could have screamed cos he was so slow, limping on his ruined knee. That's what he said—his knee was ruined. He'd ruined his knee in the sewers of London, and he would have died there except Daniel had been with him, his dear friend Daniel O'Thunder. His best friend in all the world, who had—cos no friend is perfect, alas—betrayed him. That's what he kept saying, over and over in a low fast bitter voice, laughing roughly and carelessly.

Oh, it was wild and strange. It was enough to make people stop and stare, and when Londoners stare you know it's strange indeed—it belongs in bloody Bedlam. But I had to find out if he was telling the truth about my mother.

"Your mother's close by. We're almost there."

"Where?"

But deep down I was starting to guess.

He'd started to talk about something else, now. It was even wilder than before, cos he was telling me that we must go away together. Today, this afternoon, just as soon as I'd seen my mother. We needed to be far away from London, and from Daniel O'Thunder who'd betrayed him, and from Lord Sculthorpe most of all.

"For I've investigated him, Nell." He clutched my arm, gazing at me with great dark eyes. "That's what I've been doing, this past fortnight. I've been investigating Lord Sculthorpe. I've gone to great lengths on your behalf."

Then it was something about fleeing to Portsmouth and taking ship for the New World, where we could be together just the two of us and start our lives all over again. But by now I'd had enough.

"Stop grabbing at me, Jack—and stop your raving, too! Cos we ent going anywhere together, not now and not ever. And where the fuck have you brung me, anyway?"

He'd brought me to the church at the end of the road. A sad little church where God hadn't been for years—you could tell that just by looking. But of course it wasn't the church we'd come to see. He'd brought me to the sad little churchyard behind, with the stones and crosses all jumbly and bent, like the teeth in an old woman's head. The sick-sweet graveyard stench, and Jack's voice. It had gone deadly quiet now, and sad. Something about how Sculthorpe had given my mother rooms in Hampstead and lovely dresses cos she amused him. But after a time she wasn't amusing anymore.

"And so this is what he did to her, Nell."

A feeling like the ground giving way. Disappearing underneath my feet, like the trap from under poor Mrs Dalrymple.

"You're a liar."

"But not about this."

"You said she was safe!"

"And so she is, Nell. Safe as houses, for now he can't hurt her anymore."

"No. Just cos someone's name is on a stone? Anyone's name can be on a stone. She's never in that grave."

But of course she was, and of course I knew it. I suppose I'd known all along, hadn't I? I suppose I'd known for years. I'd just never known which grave it was.

Joanna Rooney. 1822–1841.

A sad little corner of a sad little churchyard, and a stone with weeds growing over. Jack stood beside me in the lengthening shadow. His own shadow was long in the dying sun. It seeped out from him like a stain.

"But that's not all I've discovered, Nell, about Lord Sculthorpe. I've discovered who he really is."

He was braced on one leg, hunched over with his hurt knee bent inward and his foot clubbed. His face was twisted with the pain of standing and his eyes were coals and I swear—in that second he could have been Belial gazing from the burning lake.

"Lord Sculthorpe," he said, "is the Devil."

PIPER

THE DEVIL OF it is, he's disappeared," McKay was saying. "Vacant rooms where he was wont to dwell, and at his club an empty chair by the fire."

"We're speaking of Sculthorpe?" I was trying to catch up with a conversation already well in motion, and consequently felt like a man trotting after an accelerating train.

"What's that? Yes, of course we're speaking of Sculthorpe. Who the devil else would we be speaking of?"

"In point of fact, I was hoping we could speak of O'Thunder."

"O'Thunder? Good God, Piper—no, not this early in the day. Sorry. Lunacy is not on this morning's bill of fare."

SOME CRONIES: (*with knowing cynicism*) "Har, har."

OTHER CRONIES: (*with ingratiating approval*) "Early in the day—haw!—not on the old bill of fare."

STILL OTHER CRONIES: (*with pounding heads and unsteady stomachs from the night before*) "Whose turn is it this time? Yes, perhaps I will—just a small one."

We were in the Dog and Duck, where the Editor of the *Morning Register* was holding court. I knew I'd find them here, as it was past ten in the morning, and the sun had crossed the yardarm. Not here in London, perhaps, but assuredly somewhere in Her Majesty's vast domains.

"Disappeared," McKay resumed, with an Editor's relish for scandal and a Scotsman's relish for someone else's comeuppance. "The Word we're hearing is: financial ruin."

"Which is two words, actually..." one of the cronies began. A sub-editor, with the prissy-lipped exactitude so characteristic of the species. A look chilled him into silence.

"Financial ruin," McKay continued, for the benefit of those who might not be fully up to date. "Word is, the man's finances were a house of cards—issuing bills left and right to cover his gambling debts. A final catastrophic wager—several thousand pounds on a boxing match, is the Word we're hearing—and it all came crashing down. Long and short, he's vanished from London, with naught to indicate he was ever here at all, save the clamour of creditors."

"Yes, but look here," I interjected. "This may well be true, but it isn't news."

The Editor turned to stare. "Not news?" He had a vaguely astonished air, like a rat-catching Aberdeen terrier that has just been told it doesn't recognize vermin.

"At least, it's hardly *new,*" I continued, impatience making me bold. "Sculthorpe disappeared some weeks ago, didn't he? There was already something in the *Times.*"

McKay considered me for a moment. "Ah," he said. "But you see, Piper—what it is, you see—there've been *developments.* Speaking of which," he added, "here comes Landers now. Landers!"

He beckoned to a smirking man who had just insinuated himself through the doorway. Herbert Landers was McKay's star reporter, a man of undulations and secrets. He came towards us sidelong, with his customary impersonation of an adder in tall grass.

"Have you spoken to the police?" McKay demanded.

Landers winked, and nodded.

"And is it true? They're issuing warrants for an arrest?"

"Mmmm," said Landers, with a knowing smirk. Landers was

a man who conversed with smirks and sardonic eyebrows and an entire array of cryptic sounds from the back of his throat.

"Well, out with it, man. What have you been able to establish?"

"MMMMmmmmmmmm." This being Landers receding to fetch himself a drink. He smirked his way through the tall grass to the bar.

"No, listen," I said, seizing the opportunity. "O'Thunder."

McKay made an impatient Scottish noise. "What about him?"

"Well, just for starters, he's challenged the Devil."

"Why, so I do," drawled one of the wittier lickspittles. "I do so each time I resolve to drink no more this day. But I find he tends to triumph in the end."

"That's not what I mean. Have you seen this morning's *Illustrated Sporting Life?* He's challenged the Devil to meet him in the prize-ring."

I'd brought a copy with me:

> To The Editor
>
> Esteemed Sir:
>
> Those familiar with the ways of this world will be only too aware that it has long been the target of shocking depredations by a most Villainous and Deceitful Antagonist: viz., the Devil. I have repeatedly called upon him to Leave Off, Cease and Desist At Once his provocations, and most especially his vile stealthy attacks upon the weakest and most vulnerable, who are ever his preferred target, to the sorrow and outrage of all Right-Thinking British Men and Women. He has not done so. Accordingly, I charge him that he is a Coward and a Poltroon, and most earnestly invite him to settle his quarrel against humankind with Me Personally. For I will delight to meet him in the twenty-foot ring of his

choosing, at any location the length and breadth of Britain, for any purse he chooses to specify, there to contend bare-knuckled under London Prize Rules: he with all his Infernal Powers, and I with the Hammer of Heaven. Awaiting a reply, I remain steadfastly, Daniel O'Thunder.

There was actually a moment of stunned silence.

I'd been stunned myself, when I saw it—and yet somehow I wasn't completely surprised. For I'd been with O'Thunder on several occasions, these past few weeks. A number of occasions, really—almost daily. Hanging about the Mission, where he'd gather the faithful about him, breaking bread and telling stories. Tramping along behind when he went to preach on street corners, and then after nightfall barging into dens and flash-houses with fierce exhortations. But there'd been a growing agitation in his mood. A darkness too.

"Christ on a crutch," said McKay. "The man's gone right off his head."

"But that's just it," I said. "Suppose he hasn't."

"You're telling me you find this *normal?*"

"Normal? Good God, no—the man isn't normal. That's the last thing you'd ever say about Daniel O'Thunder. But what I'm trying to say..."

Somehow I wasn't sure what I was trying to say. Or perhaps I just had no idea how to say it without sounding like a Bedlamite myself.

"For God's sake, Piper." McKay rolled his button-black eyes. "Just spit it out."

I drew a breath and did my best. Good plain English words, lined up in a row.

I was trying to say that I had been wrong. I had begun with intentions of befriending O'Thunder in order to betray him. Or at least to worm my way into his confidence in order to expose him as a charlatan, as the Rock of Agnes had counselled me to do. But instead I had discovered that he was extraordinary.

Whoever he really was, and whatever he was really doing—feeding the hungry, comforting the afflicted, healing the sick (yes, but there are precedents, and more things in Heaven and earth, et cetera), raising the dead (all right, fine, we'll skip over that one)—he was the most extraordinary man currently to be found in London. Hundreds of others thought so, too. Possibly thousands. The Mission was crammed full of them, day and night. When Daniel O'Thunder walked out into the streets of London a throng would follow. And this wasn't even counting the angels who waved to him, and to whom he waved back. I was saying that he was a genuine phenomenon. I was saying... well, I was in fact saying that I thought he might be genuine, period. And most astonishingly of all, the Rock of Agnes had decided I might be right.

They looked at me, McKay and the rest of them. Stared in wordless fascination, like men who have nearly forgotten how to sneer.

"Who the Hell is the Rock of Agnes?" McKay asked.

"My mother."

He opened his mouth to reply. But the moment was lost, for now Landers came undulating back, and all attention swivelled to fix upon him.

"All right, Landers," McKay was snapping. "Let's hear it."

"Well," said Landers.

Amidst much waggling and many obscure vocables, the details emerged. It seemed Lord Sculthorpe had not really left London at all. He had abandoned the lodgings he kept in Mayfair, and also a house he had let in Hampstead. But he kept a bolt-hole near the Haymarket, where he had evidently gone to ground. Police had been alerted by an anonymous tip. The tipster described the location, and furthermore hinted that a certain highly incriminating item was to be found there. When the police arrived, Sculthorpe had decamped. But among the clutter and general filth—the place was a sty, apparently—they found engravings of young women in advanced states of deshabille, and odious books printed by low booksellers. There was also a personal item connected to a very serious crime. A book of poetry, bound in dark green pebbled leather. It was inscribed to a woman named Mary Bartram, who had been murdered in Hyde Park.

McKay reacted. "That old streetwalker from two, three months ago—the one they found throttled? A bloody vicar's daughter, or some such thing. Is that the one we're talking about?"

"MMMmmm."

"A murdered Park Woman, a peer of the realm, and warrants issued for arrest. Excellent." McKay rubbed his hands briskly. "Give me whatever you've got, and I'll pay you tuppence a word. Meantime, let's find out some more about this man's background. And while we're at it, let's look into this anonymous tipster."

"But look," a voice was bleating. It was mine. "About O'Thunder..."

McKay rounded on me in exasperation. "*What* about O'Thun-der, Piper? Because you haven't told me anything! No, you haven't, so be quiet and listen. Feeding the poor, healing the afflicted, what you think and what you believe—yes, fine, but who *is* he? He served in the Army? All right, then tell me when—and where—and why was he discharged. You don't know? Well, find out! Find out when he came to London, and where he was before he arrived. You call yourself a journalist, so go investigate the man. And if you turn something up, then come back and talk to me."

He was right, of course. As soon as I paused to think about it, I realized I knew next to nothing about Daniel O'Thunder. That's why I stood for several moments like an utter fool, making movements with my mouth in the vain hope that something incisive might spring forth. And yet McKay was also completely wrong, because he was missing the only point that truly mattered.

"Daniel O'Thunder," I burst out, "has challenged the Devil to a prize-fight! Dear God, does this not set the man apart? Does this not make him a special case?"

It was Landers who replied. "I suppose—mmm—that this depends," he said, with much waggling of eyebrows.

"Depends upon what?"

"Upon whether the Devil—mmMMmm—accepts his challenge."

THE ILLUSTRATED SPORTING LIFE

2 April, 1852

. . .

Sir: A certain peal o' Thunder having rumbled once too often, I advise that I accept his challenge, and will be pleased to meet him at a time of my own choosing, at the place he least expects, there to settle once and for all eternity this matter between us. Until then, I remain, et cetera, His Enemy.

PIPER

O'THUNDER DELIVERED HIS sermon from the steps of St Paul's Cathedral. Rebuilt from the ashes of the Great Fire of 1666, London's foremost monument to the Almighty. Some detected a certain hubris in this choice of location. In retrospect there was terrible irony too, given the role that fire was to play before the day was ended. But none of this would have occurred to O'Thunder himself.

What do I believe? Well, let's start with what I don't believe, since that's always the easier question. It's where I start whenever I think of Daniel O'Thunder—which is frequently, even these several years later. Sitting in a garden as I'm doing right this moment—the garden is somewhere in Wales, though I won't say precisely where, for reasons that will be evident in due course—setting down this account while listening to the children. For yes, there are actually small Pipers, two of them. A little girl with a leaky nose who luckily favours her mother, and a stout little toad-faced fellow with bulging eyes. Alas. But perhaps he'll find some good plain English words, and think of something constructive to do with them.

So. I don't believe O'Thunder planned in advance to deliver a sermon from the cathedral steps, that day. I'm not sure he planned to deliver a sermon at all. Looking back, I don't believe Daniel O'Thunder ever planned much of anything—I think he just reacted. He was there, and emotions were rising, and a crowd was beginning to gather. So he went up the steps, and said what was on his mind. Is this what you do when you're directly inspired by Almighty God who made the sun and earth and sees the sparrow fall? Yes, it might well be. On the other hand, it's also what you might do if you were never much more than a holy fool.

Was he mad? I'm not sure of that, either. He was certainly obsessed, and haunted by visions, and held in the vice-grip of remarkable convictions—viz., that the Devil a.) existed, and b.) might be goaded into a prize-ring, where one might c.) plant a good old British peg upon his smeller. Some believed that O'Thunder's brain had been damaged in the mill against Hen Gully the Game Chicken. There were old fight men, and Boston Bob McCorkindale was one, who were convinced of it. O'Thunder collapsed after that mill—no one ever seems to mention this, but it happened. That's why it took him nearly an hour to arrive at poor Gully's bedside. Boston Bob believed the damage was done by a right hand in the second round, and it's certainly true that O'Thunder was never quite the same man afterwards. And God knows, O'Thunder would not be the first pugilist to leave the green faerie circle with a slantways brain, or the ten thousand and first. But was it actually madness, or something else? To this day, I'm not sure.

Now I'll tell you what I *do* know. On that early afternoon in 1852—April 2, with the first buds on the trees, and the pale spring sun struggling to be warm; steps of St Paul's, and a multitude gathering—whatever else it was, it was magnificent.

"We are here to build Jerusalem."

That's what he told us. He wore a clean white shirt, open at the neck. It billowed with the April breeze, and there actually was a multitude. Not at first, but more kept coming. Shop girls and apprentices, merchants and costermongers. The face of London itself gazing up at Daniel O'Thunder. His own great ugly face shone back at them.

"For I can see it, brothers and sisters—I can see it already. The New Jerusalem, the City of God, rising up amidst the blackened walls and narrow winding streets of London Town. Oh, just look at it—look!—it shimmers with the light of Heaven."

You'd swear he actually saw it. And I believe he did. He saw with such intensity that we could almost see it too: ghostly golden spires, like tall ships emerging through a mist. Oh, that voice of his. Close your eyes as Daniel O'Thunder spoke, and the Kingdom of God rose up around you.

"But there's a canker within, brothers and sisters. There's a serpent that writhes, and a wolf that gnaws at the very foundations, for the Devil is among us."

A low inchoate rumble from the throng. There must have been a thousand now, and more were still coming. O'Thunder was looking down at them, and no longer out and across at the ghostly spires. A shadow had fallen across his face.

"I've challenged the Devil, brothers and sisters. I believe the greater part of you know this."

Of course we knew, every one of us. That's why we were here.

"Some may be aware that he has replied."

Many were aware, for the *Illustrated Sporting Life* had appeared that morning. Some of us had read it at the breakfast table, where we sat across from our mother, the Rock of Agnes. It had caused us to choke on our kipper, so violently that Dorcas had come running in alarm to pound us vigorously on the back. Meanwhile, word had spread across London like fire through dry timber. A very few were just discovering now, in this very moment. There were exclamations from these—*What? What did he say?!* Here and there a jeering reply, for of course a few were here to mock. But mainly cries of "Hush!" and "Shut your gob!", for this was why we had come. Ghostly golden spires were all very well, but we had come to hear Daniel O'Thunder's response to the Devil.

"He has replied from some hiding place, not daring to show his face. He has replied with taunts and threats." O'Thunder clutched a copy of the *Illustrated Sporting Life* in one massive fist, and shook it. "Well, I have a message for him in return. I advise the Devil—"

Then, abruptly, he stopped. You could see the thought occur to him. He stared about in gleaming apprehension.

"Is he here, brothers and sisters? Is he lurking amongst us? For yes, I believe he might be—I believe he *is*. Yes, I'm certain of it. He's hidden in some hole nearby, or peering from some garret, where he can see me and hear my voice."

A thrill of consternation, and slantways looks. No spine goes unshivered by the prospect that the Prince of Lies might be standing red-eyed in the very next shadow. Even the spines of those, such as Mrs Piper's sensible boy, who know he doesn't actually exist. But then again, you're never really sure, are you? And wouldn't you look a muff, being hauled to Perdition, shrieking that it didn't exist.

O'Thunder's voice rose with the dark certainty of his realization.

"Brothers and sisters, I ask him this one last time. Will he repent? Will he cast himself upon the mercy of the Lord, which extends even unto the Gates of Hell itself? For even now, the Almighty reaches out his hand."

There was no reply. No sound at all. Just a cocoon of deathly silence, here amidst the great unending shout of London.

O'Thunder began to look sorrowful. As if he'd thought there might actually be a chance. A possibility that Old Nick really might come slinking from a sagging doorway, or crawling up through a sewer grate. Black and twisted with thwarted malevolence, but muttering sullen capitulation, and dropping to his goatish knees to get it over with. But of course he never did. And now O'Thunder's face grew hard as granite.

"Then he and I shall fight."

He was Michael Archangelus, reaching for his sword.

Some fool actually said this out loud, in tones of strangulated rapture. It was the correspondent for the *Morning Register*.

He—that is, I—was standing directly below O'Thunder at the bottom of the steps, in the very thick of the crowd. The Rock of Agnes was on the periphery somewhere, in her wheeled chair, attended by Dorcas. My mother could walk, but not far, and didn't much like it. And she didn't like venturing outside the house, either. But this morning, after reading the *Illustrated Sporting Life,* she had abruptly announced: "I wish to see this man." She had said it with decisiveness. "I do not like the Irish, William. I do not approve of prize-fighting, or evangelists, or religious hysteria. But by God I do admire sheer spunk. Dorcas, fetch the conveyance." Dorcas had given a sniffle of fervent agreement, and leapt to her feet. An hour later she had emerged in a cloak and bonnet, wheeling the Rock of Agnes like a cannon onto a battlefield.

O'Thunder addressed the multitude.

"But we will not fight on the Devil's terms, at the time and place of his choosing. I will choose the where and the when. And I choose to fight him here—in London—today."

Rising excitement from the throng. Oh, this was prime. This was even better than we'd hoped for.

"Round Two," said Boston Bob, shaking his head. He was wedged beside me in the crowd. "Knew it when it happened."

Boston Bob had turned up out of the blue—with Spragg the Ruffian, of all people, scowling and shuffling. Spragg swore he was only here by accident, but in later years I heard he actually became a lay preacher somewhere up North. Which just goes to show you, doesn't it? It goes to show you something.

"Seen it time and again," said Bob. "Man gets up, man seems fine. But he ain't. Something's broke. Never right again."

O'Thunder's voice rang like King David's lost chord.

"I shall find him. I shall hunt him down to his lair, and drag him forth by the horns. I shall drag him shrieking and squalling into the sunlight. In this I ask your help."

And that's where it all began to go horribly wrong.

"Who will help me, brothers and sisters? Who will follow me through the streets of London, searching every garret and bolt-hole until we've found the Devil? If you're with me, raise your voices! Sing out!"

"AYE!"

A thousand voices roaring in return. A thousand and one, if you count the correspondent for the *Morning Register.* I discovered I was roaring with the rest, in dark thunderous passion. Someone was grabbing my arm—Boston Bob. He shouted something in my ear. I couldn't catch what it was; it was lost in the din. From the look on his face, it may have been: "Christ, we've got to get out of here!" Now there was a new sound amidst the tumult, a horrible metallic jangling. Long afterwards I realized where I'd heard it before. It was the sound they had made at Young Joe Gummery's hanging.

Oh, Daniel O'Thunder was glorious. Such terrible joy, and conviction. But he'd just made the mistake of his life, for he'd unleashed the London Mob.

They all began to move at once.

The Mob was the dark soul of the metropolis. It had been there from the beginning of time, or at least from the beginning of London, and at dreadful intervals it burst forth. Kings and Queens lived in mortal terror of the London Mob, for once it formed there was no way to stop it. It was the paper-thin tissue of civility, tearing. It was Moloch, rearing up from the underworld. In the Gordon Riots of 1780, an anti-Catholic Mob rampaged for an entire week, looting and burning, attacking businesses and homes and churches. There were two hundred and ten persons killed outright in the streets. Newgate and Clerkenwell were set ablaze, and the prisoners freed. The home of the Lord Chief Justice was sacked and burned, and the Prime Minister himself barely escaped with his life, galloping in a carriage with the Mob raging at his heels.

I swear O'Thunder never intended it. In fact, he didn't seem to realize what was happening. At first it was a joyful revelation to him: he was discovering what power he had, but not yet comprehending what this power had set in motion. He started down the cathedral steps with glorious resolution on his face, like an infantry captain leading the charge. Banners waving, and drums discharging splendid bursts. But they were surging ahead of him. Surging like a river through narrow streets, and the river was rising as others joined them. They were swept up by the Mob. They became the Mob, and discovered that all passions are licensed and exalted. By the time O'Thunder understood what he'd done, it was too late. I glimpsed him briefly in the middle of Fleet Street—shouting something that was lost in the tumult, and raising one hand as one might do to stop an onrushing locomotive.

Some of it was actually in rough good fun, at least in the early going. The doors of low public houses were barged through, as likely haunts of the Devil. Casks were broken open just in case the Devil was hiding within. But then began the settling of scores. The breaking of furniture, and the offer of violence to those who were clearly of the Devil's party, such as publicans believed to water their gin, and whores who took coins in return for the pox. Soon enough the definition was expanded to include anyone who protested. The thought occurred—as it had in 1780—that the Devil might be hiding in Popish churches, where he would feel at home.

This was the stage at which fires were set, and fatalities occurred.

And somewhere in the dark heart of it all was a man called Jack Hartright.

THE HONOURABLE ALFRED DUCKWORTH

Edited from an Affidavit submitted in evidence

I'D ENCOUNTERED THIS FELLOW Hartright some months earlier, in a public house out in Essex. This was the evening before the mill between O'Thunder and Spragg the Ruffian. I'd encountered some old school friends from Oxford, and this fellow Hartright was with them. It seemed to me that I recognized the fellow, but I couldn't quite place him. "Hartright?" I asked him. "Deyvlish thing, but I don't recall the name. And you were at Balliol?" But he grew a bit vague, and the evening proceeded apace, and I put him out of my mind.

Some days afterwards it came back to me—I *had* encountered him at Balliol, but in those days he wasn't going by the name of Hartright. His name had been John Beresford, and there had been unpleasantness. A young serving girl from the Town. Word was she'd been seduced, or rather assailed, and outrages perpetrated. It never came to a formal charge, for of course it was her word against his, and one heard there was money paid to help smooth things over. But one kept hearing other things, as well—one heard that a knife was involved, and the girl was cut. Beresford was gone not long after, and one thought: deyvlish rum fellow—good riddance.

I saw him, as I say, in Essex the night before the mill with Spragg. And then I saw him on one subsequent occasion. It was the night of April 1—and yes, of course I'm certain of the date, for it was the night before the riot.

I'd been to the theatre, and afterwards to a chophouse in Pall Mall, and thence to a night house near the Haymarket, and eventually to the mouth of an adjacent alleyway to seek relief from nature. It was deyvlish dark, with nothing but the pale spill from a gas-lamp beyond. I moved a few steps deeper into the alley, picking my way carefully, for one never knows what—or whom—he may tread upon. And, as I fumbled with my buttons, I discovered that I wasn't alone.

There were voices, two of them, issuing from the darkness deeper in the alley. A half moon slid into view above the rooftops, and in its ghostly light I glimpsed two men in agitated conference. I recognized the first as the fellow Beresford—or Hartright. I had the immediate impression that he was inwardly fearful for his life. He shrank back, cringing, as his companion paced in agitation and flung his arms. In the next instant I recognized this companion. It was Lord Sculthorpe.

I'd known Sculthorpe for years. Or known of him, at any rate, for his family held property in the same part of Norfolk as my own. They had been wealthy once, the Sculthorpes, but latterly were much reduced—the sort of country gentry that had been notorious for dipsomaniac squires, riotous hunts, and foxhounds defecating in the dining hall. The present Lord Sculthorpe was the last of that line, and as a boy I recall seeing him at county fairs, a figure both sinister and risible in a hat and coat that had been old-fashioned in his own father's time. He was half mad, in other words, but not a man to trifle with. In latter years I had seen him from time to time at sporting events—he was a hopeless gambler, busily burning the fag-end of the family fortune—and avoided him as much as possible.

In the moonlight, Sculthorpe flailed and gesticulated. Hartright/Beresford cringed and fawned, like a cur that is sorely tempted by a sweetmeat but mortally fearful of a kick. I wasn't close enough to hear distinctly, but Sculthorpe seemed to be raving about a book that had been planted in his rooms as false evidence. He also raged against this man Daniel O'Thunder, apparently blaming him for some catastrophic misfortune. I heard Hartright/Beresford vent his own spleen at O'Thunder, and then say: "But I've brought news. I've located the man Rennert." Sculthorpe exclaimed in dark exultation, and resumed his agitated pacing, alternately pledging extravagant reward for faithful service, and threatening hideous retribution should Hartright/Beresford prove false. He then stopped dead, and I distinctly heard him say: "But what about the girl? Have you seen the girl? Tell me that my girl is safe and well."

I heard Hartright/Beresford reply that she was. He pledged to see that she was looked after, exactly as she deserved. But as he turned away, his face in the moonlight bore such a look as to freeze the blood. A look of deyvlish loathing and malevolence.

PIPER

As best I can, in plain English words:

At the height of the riot, there were several thousand milling through the streets. Before it was over, three men were dead. Two of these were rioters, trampled when a charge by truncheon-wielding constables panicked the crowd. The third was an apprentice who was knocked on the head when he tried to prevent a knot of rioters from setting fire to his master's shop. Several shops were destroyed, and two churches sustained significant damage. Also burned to the ground was a ramshackle building in the Gray's Inn Road, which housed a singular enterprise known as the Gospel Mission of Heaven's Hammer.

Details are sketchy, but it appears the fire broke out not long after Mr Tim Diggory returned to the Mission in the company of one of O'Thunder's hangers-on. This was a young man I'd seen on numerous occasions, calling himself Hartright. His real name seems to have been Beresford. The two of them had apparently been drinking gin together, Mr Diggory's commitment to Christian sobriety having been shaken in the tumult. His animal spirits had evidently been stirred as well, for witnesses report hearing a loud exchange between Mr Diggory and another of O'Thunder's close companions, a young woman named Molly La Clarice. It would appear that Mr Diggory ripped Miss La Clarice's dress from her back and offered outrages upon her person, for witnesses relate that he clutched the dress in one fist as he pursued Miss La Clarice up the stairs. At some point during the encounter, a lighted candle was overturned, setting alight a bit of sacking over one of the windows. Miss La Clarice fought off her attacker with great spirit and resolve, but was subsequently overcome by smoke.

By the time O'Thunder arrived, the building was an inferno. He gave a terrible cry. Resisting all efforts to hold him back, he ran in to search for those who were trapped. He was able to rescue several, though not all of them. Finally, just before the roof collapsed, he emerged carrying Miss La Clarice, who was insensate but alive. According to eyewitnesses, O'Thunder was so blackened by smoke as to be all but unrecognizable. His face was seared with flame, as if he had harrowed Hell itself. His anguish was described as "beyond human measure."

Subsequently Mr Diggory gave tearful testimony, in which he identified the agency of his ruin. He maintained that he had been incited by the Devil, who had spied his fatal weakness and plunged like a falcon. He also said that the man Hartright (or Beresford) had stood treat for the gin.

NELL

AND I DIDN'T even know.

The riot and the fire—Tim Diggory and poor Molly La Clarice—I never knew it was happening. While Daniel's world was catching fire and crashing down upon him, I was on my way to Hampstead to kill the Devil—or leastways to kill Lord Sculthorpe, who was as close to the Devil as was living in this world, no matter whose bloody father he might be. Or so I thought at the time, poor daisy that I was, having no idea then what the Devil was really like.

I knew His Lordship was just a man. Flesh and blood. That much I did know—give me *some* credit. But he was the man who killed my mother, and left her lying in that churchyard. He was the man as killed my friend Mary, too. That's what the newspapers said. He had disappeared, they said, which was unfortunate according to the Constabulary, cos they was desirous to speak to him in connection with the disappearance of several women. And they said there was a certain item found among his possessions. A book of Shakespeare poems, with an inscription inside: *To my friend Mary Bartram, on her birthday.*

So of course I was going to kill him, wasn't I? All I had to do was find him. That might be hard but it couldn't be impossible, not when I had the rest of my life to spend on it, every second of every day. I went to all the places where a man like him might be, all the night houses and brothels, even Mother C's. I never went inside, but I waited round the corner till finally one of the girls come out. She gave an exclamation like she'd seen a ghost, but swore she'd send word if she saw His Lordship. "But Jesus Christ, Nell, you better run. If Mother C ever sees you, yer bloody dead!" I talked to some of the costers, too. You'd be surprised the things they hear. I said I'd pay if they had information about Sculthorpe—pay with his own money, that he left behind for me at the house.

Then the note came. *This afternoon. He'll be at the house in Hampstead.*

No name, just the words scribbled on a bit of paper. It was left for me at the Mission. No one seen who left it there, and no one cared about a thing like that. They were all of a tizzy about some letter in a newspaper from the Devil himself, and what was Daniel going to do. Somebody was babbling about was this the End of Days when the Whore of Babylon would rise up with free goes for all sinners or whatever the fuck she's supposed to do, and flaming comets in the sky. But I was already down the stairs and out the door and on my way. I had my knife and I was going to kill him.

If I wasn't such a muff, I might have stopped to think. A note, left like that? Then I might have stopped a little longer, and thought about some other things as well. I might have thought: he killed my ma cos that's what he does. He goes after young women and draws 'em in and buys 'em lovely dresses and has his lark until he's bored. Same as he obviously had in mind to do with me, until he seen my birthmark.

But why would he kill Lushing Mary Bartram, or look at her in the first place? She hadn't been young for thirty years. So why kill my poor friend, of all the raddled old whores in London?

When I got to the house I found my key was missing. It wasn't in my pocket. But then it turned out I didn't need it after all, cos the door wasn't locked. Even though I knew I'd locked it, last time I'd left. I could have sworn I'd locked that door.

It was dim and cold inside, with all the curtains drawn and no fire for days. Only April, so spring had hardly begun. Dark and empty and smelling of must. Just me creeping through the silent rooms, cos of course I had to be sure he wasn't here already. But there was no one here at all, so I slipped up to my old rooms, to wait. I'd wait behind the door—that's what I'd decided—wait for him to come slowly up the stairs, clip-*clop*. He'd come through the door and I'd be there behind him with my knife. I had it all worked out, which I suppose is why I didn't want to think about who left the note, or why he'd want to kill Mary, or what had happened to my key.

But no one came. The house was silent and night was falling. I started to worry. How would I see him when he came, and should I light a lamp?

That's when I heard the click of it closing—the front door, down below. Closing as someone came in. Then footsteps, limping up the stairs: clip-*clop*. It was him, and he was a dead man. He was dead in half a minute, cos I was here in the darkness behind the door with my knife in my hand and here he was.

Except it wasn't Lord Sculthorpe.

"Hello, Nell."

It was Jack.

His hair was wild and his clothes all askew. His face and hands black with smoke. There'd been a fire, he said, and he smelled of it. He reeked of smoke and cinder.

What fire, I said, what happened? Jesus Christ is anybody killed?

"It was a purifying fire."

I knew right then something terrible had happened. He looked like a soul released from Hell one night each year to tell his tale. But I was still thinking about His Lordship, and what I meant to do. Even then, that's what my mind went to.

A sudden realization. "Was it you, Jack? Yes, it was, wasn't it? It was you, left that note. Well, where is he? Is he coming? Tell me!"

But he was saying something else. About how he had to leave London now, and go far away. He was never going to see me again, which was very tragical, but maybe not so tragical as all that, cos I had betrayed him. Just as Daniel had done. The two people he cared about most in all the world.

"What are you talking about? Betrayed—with Daniel? Fucksake, Jack, I told you already—"

He said something then that I've never forgotten. He said: "I gave you the opportunity to love me, Nell. All my life, I have given women just like you the opportunity to love me. But all of you—you've always failed."

It wasn't even the words, but the look on his face as he said them. Like a sorrowful magistrate arriving at his verdict—oh, much more sorrowful than angry—and reaching for the black cap.

But it was going to be all right in the end, he was saying, cos he had set certain crucial matters straight. He had made discoveries about His Lordship, and pointed the authorities in that direction, and helped them by putting a book where they might find it, a book of poems. And he had helped put a stop to Daniel, too.

"I am a man who wanted so much to have faith, Nell. I put my faith in Daniel O'Thunder, who had such gifts, and could have done so much. But Daniel turned out to be false. So I did what I had to do."

He actually smiled. So earnest and reasonable and sad. But now I had another realization. This one came with a cold lump of ice in my stomach.

"Where did you get the book, Jack?"

He blinked. "I beg your pardon?"

"Mary Bartram's book. You said you put it in Sculthorpe's rooms. Where did you get it, then? How did you come to have that book?"

I never even heard the other man come in—that's how upset I was. Never heard the door opening, or footsteps creaking up the stairs behind. Never heard a single thing until I turned to run and he was right there in front of me and had me in both his hands. Bald head and eyes like oysters.

"'Ave we got 'er?" asked a voice from below. It was horribly familiar.

"Yes, 'm," said Swinton, cos that's who it was. The new bully from the night house—the one who took over when Tim Diggory left to start his long hike to Heaven.

There was a wheezing on the stair. She came as far as the half-landing, and looked up. Her face bright scarlet with the strain of heaving herself up six steps, and those great blancmanges wobbling in purple velvet.

"'Allo, my peach," said Mother Clatterballock.

I turned to Jack. He made a little helpless shrug with his shoulders, as if I surely must see there was no other way.

"You'll be better off with your friends," he said. "You're a whore, Nell—you're a false little trull—and they'll put you where false little trulls belong."

"Oh, that's a fact," said Mother C. She had a smile like a mother dandling her babby, and pinching its fat little arms and legs, and thinking of how they'll taste. "Isn't that a fact, Swinton?"

"Yes, 'm."

"It's more than a fact—it's an Eternal Werity. Nell's friends will look after her, and in return my peach will look after us. Oh yes she will, she'll look after us wonderful well. She'll pay us back, for starters, every penny she owes for lost earnings, and for suffering too. For didn't I suffer, Swinton?"

"Suffered something 'orrible."

"I suffered a mother's grief, Nell—a mother's hanguish that her precious wee chick was lost, and all them earnings lost with her. But now my dear duckling is back, and I've totted it all up, ink and paper—I've haccomplished a reckoning of what's owed, and the debt you'll be working off. Flat on your back, my peach, or down on your knees, and in warious postures besides, the preferences of the clientele being—what's the word I want?—*eclectic,* hespecially the clientele in Whitechapel, which is where we've found a crib for you. Eclectic it is, my peach, and eclectic it must be—eclectic being a word meaning 'till you're dead.' But we must take the bad with the good, mustn't we? Cos why life just ent a bowl of strawberries and cream."

I was struggling with all my might, for all the good it did me. "You just wait! You wait till Daniel hears—he'll be coming for me, and he'll settle with you!"

"Daniel O'Thunder?" Mother Clatterballock began to laugh. "Oh, I don't think so, my peach—I don't think that Irish lunatic will be coming for you, or for anyone else, ever again. Cos why I'm afraid there's been misfortune. Is that the word I want, Mr Hartright?"

"Tragic misfortune," Jack said, very sadly. "There has also been an investigation, carried out by certain parties with a heavy heart. I'm afraid it has resulted in shocking revelations."

JAUNTY

THEY ARRESTED DANIEL, of course. They took him up as he came staggering out of the Gospel Mission of Heaven's Hammer, half dead with smoke and seared with flame, bearing Molly La Clarice to safety in his arms. The fire was still raging as they carted him to Bow Street Police Station and locked him in the cells. It was later that night when the building finally collapsed. Down it went, sliding in upon itself with a shudder and a thud that flung a last great billow of red sparks into the sky. That drew a cheer from the crowd that had gathered to watch.

Or so it was described to me, for naturally I wasn't there to see it happen. I was at the time a good distance from London, lying low at a country inn, a certain sporting lord having made clear that I was being held responsible for his ruinous gambling losses. His Lordship was indeed in a wild passion about it all, and had expressed through an intermediary the intention to slit Jaunty's throat like a chicken's. I tried to point out to this intermediary—a certain young man deficient in chin, who had once possessed a fine silver snuff-box—that slitting poor Jaunty's sink-hole would hardly rescue His Lordship from bankruptcy. The intermediary agreed, but said it would give His Lordship satisfaction. And His Lordship demanded satisfaction, the bloodier the better.

But if Jaunty's position was parlous, poor Daniel's was worse. For men had died in the hullabaloo he'd set off, and worse yet property had been damaged. They'd charged him with violating the Riot Act, and that was a capital crime. Daniel's fate now hung in the balance, and so what did Jaunty do?

Why, he went to London.

I SLIPPED INTO town the night before the proceedings, and in the morning I camped in a public house around the corner from the court. It was early afternoon when a pink perspiring clerk arrived to fetch me, sent by the Old Bailey hack who was defending Daniel.

"Mr Rennert?" he said.

"It was Sergeant Rennert, once upon a time," I replied.

I drank off my glass in one, rose to my hind trotters and squared my shoulders. Then I marched left-right-left to give testimony at my old comrade's trial.

It was in the smaller courtroom, which was packed to overflowing, for a good many of Daniel's rabble stood by him still. Those as could afford the admission were stuffed into the gallery, while the rest jammed into the narrow gangway leading to the door. Below the gallery the jury sat, with lawyers and clerks at wooden tables in the middle, beneath the gaslight chandeliers. At the head of the room the judges sat along the bench, like rooks on the battlements.

Poor Daniel looked a sight. He stood shackled hand and foot in the dock, burnt on his hands and one side of his face, and he seemed stunned by what was happening to him. He put me in mind of a bear I'd seen once at a country fair—a poor great mangy brute, tethered in the heat of an August afternoon. Whenever a few punters gathered, the keeper would prod the bear with a pole until at last it lurched to its hind legs and began to shuffle its feet, swinging its head slowly from side to side with sorrowful faraway eyes.

As he saw me step into the witness box, Daniel actually smiled a little. He raised his shackled hands in a bewildered way, as if to say: "Why, look what they've done, John Thomas. Look what it's come to."

The hack who was defending him glanced at a slip of paper passed by the clerk, and cleared his throat. He had a harried air about him, the hack, as of a man who'd had only a moment to familiarize himself with the case, whereas he normally preferred a full quarter of an hour. "Mr, ah, Rambert is I believe an acquaintance of the man O'Thunder," he began.

"It's Rennert," whispered the clerk.

"What is?"

"The witness. They're old infantry comrades."

"Ah," said the hack, pleased to have this straightened out. Very good. Now they were getting somewhere. "An old infantry comrade, who will speak to the history and character of the accused."

So I spoke.

I took them back twelve years to 1840. This was a year after my return to England from the ends of the earth—or at least from Afghanistan, which was near enough to the ends of the earth as to make no difference—having been invalided out of Her Majesty's Forty-Fourth. I didn't weary the court with tales of my sojourn in faraway benighted lands, as I won't weary you now. Suffice it to say that one winter evening, as I chanced to step through the door of a sporting tavern near the Bristol docks, it seemed to me that I heard a strangely familiar Irish voice, slurred with drink and calling for another drain of pale to be brought forth instanter, lest fearful reprisals result. I peered through the blue haze of smoke to see a familiar hulking form with a blowsy slattern on one knee, and her sister on the other, and between the two of them a great ugly phizog flushed with drink.

"Daniel?" I exclaimed, astonished to stumble upon him like this.

For Daniel it was. My old comrade Daniel O'Thunder—or rather (as I said to the court) my old comrade Daniel O'Connor, for such was the name he was born with, and under which he had served in Her Majesty's Forty-Fourth. Daniel Fergus Niall O'Connor, from Sligo.

I was astonished to find him in England at all, for surely (I exclaimed) the Forty-Fourth was still at the ends of the earth, in Caboul. Daniel avoided the question at first, in between thumping me upon the back with such force that my teeth rattled, and roaring joyfully for a bottle to be fetched for his old friend, and thumping me again for sheer delight. But in due course, amidst hints and hems and sidelong looks, he gave me to understand that he had decamped from Afghanistan not long after I had left myself. He had left quite abruptly, following an unfortunate episode—I never was clear on the details—involving quantities of drink, and a valuable chronometer stolen from a senior officer, and another senior officer poked vigorously upon the nozzle.

Well, under such circumstances Tom Lobster in his red coat might indeed make himself scarce, for striking a senior officer was a capital offence in Her Majesty's army. I would gladly have shared a rueful laugh about it, except that Daniel had grown morose. I looked at him closely, and began to perceive how much he had changed. His face was thinner, and lines had begun to furrow his brow. More than this, there was a shadow upon him that had never been there before, as if he'd brought with him ghosts that stirred and muttered in the dark corners of the room.

After another moment he shook them off, and bellowed for more drink, and gave a grin like a sunburst through the clouds, and set my teeth a-rattling again with another happy clout that knocked me clear off my stool. Two bottles later, I was seized by inspiration—I would put that clout to work in the green faerie circle. Midway through another bottle I came up with the name O'Thunder, and by the time we staggered out into the night I had sugarplum notions of raising Daniel's hand one day as Champion of All England.

But Daniel was not a success in the ring—leastways not in that first incarnation as a pugilist. He lacked the killer instinct, did Daniel. Worse than that, for all his strength he lacked bottom. He swung that mighty fist of his half-heartedly, and as the blows rained down in return he received them with the air of a man who secretly knew he deserved much worse. He won a few mills in spite of himself, but mainly he lost, and in between was drinking and roaring and laughing and whoring, and awakening the following day in remorse and self-loathing, and then lurching off on another ran-tan before the sun had set. I watched him founder like a hulled ship, and finally in '42 he sank for good in that brutal mill—immortalized upon the wall of the Horse and Dolphin public house—against Tom Oliver the Battersea Gardener, famous for his sweet peas and nectarines.

Daniel disappeared immediately after that mill. It took me a week to track him down. I finally found him back in Bristol, in a brothel by the docks.

It was up two flights of rickety stairs to a foul little room at the top of a pox-raddled house. Two drabs were sprawled in drunken slumber on a mattress—sailors' whores, lying across one another like creatures spewed up by the sea, naked but for scraps of blanket draped across them like bedraggled angel's wings.

Daniel stood by the window, looking out into the dawn. He was battered and swollen, and pale with drink. He'd been drinking hellaciously for the entire week straight—that was plain enough. He was haggard and trembling with it.

"H'lo, Daniel," I said with a sigh, wincing just to look at him.

"Look, John Thomas," he said. His voice was a low rasp, but there was a thrill of wonderment in it. He spoke without looking round. "Just look. Despite everything I've done, he still hasn't given up on me."

I shielded my eyes to follow his gaze, for it seemed to me that he was staring out at the rising sun.

"Come along," I said. "Let's get you cleaned up."

He didn't move.

"I never told you what I did," he said hoarsely. "Before I left Afghanistan."

"Yes you did, Daniel. A stolen chronometer, and an officer's nozzle. And while it may not do you credit," I added kindly, "it's hardly cause for shame. For who hasn't admired another man's chronometer at one time or another? And many's the commissioned cork-snorter I wish I'd bashed myself."

"No, John Thomas," he said. "No, that was sordid enough in its way, but it's not what I'm talking about. I need to tell you what had happened a few weeks earlier."

And so he told me the tale. It seems a ragtag clutch of bandits had been harrying supply trains and slitting throats and otherwise inconveniencing the British garrison in Caboul. This was hardly unusual, Afghanistan in those days being one great hive of ragtag banditry. But after one particularly brazen provocation, the regiment dispatched a detail into the mountains in pursuit. Daniel was amongst them, and it turned out to be a trap. Instead of running the bandits to ground like so many ragged-arsed foxes, they found themselves set upon instead by dozens of others in a narrow mountain pass.

"They came howling out of the rocks, John Thomas. They came howling upon us from all sides, like wolves."

So it was shouts and shrieks and smoke and confusion—the ancient bloody chaos of battle. Daniel saw the lieutenant turn towards him, as if to exclaim something urgent—it was Daniel's impression in the moment that the lieutenant was about to urge a retreat—except it was strictly speaking just half the man's head that turned, for the other half had just been taken away by a ball. As the lieutenant sank beneath his line of vision, Daniel spied an opening—a gap in the melee, and a trail leading down, whence a man moving quick-sticks might slip-slide in salvation of his skin. In that instant, a voice spoke to him. It wasn't the lieutenant's voice, of course, but another—a voice that was wonderfully earnest and reasonable. The voice of a dear friend—of a father, even—who only desired the very best for Daniel. The voice said: "Save yourself."

So that's what Daniel did.

"It was cut and run, John Thomas. I turned and fled and hid myself in a cleft in the rock, and I stayed there until it was over."

"As many a man might have done in your position, Daniel—and good men, too," I protested. And I meant it. For you don't understand what battle is until you've been in the middle of it, and to tell God's truth I failed to see how it was quite so terrible, what Daniel had done.

But Daniel shook his head. "Don't you see? I might have saved them. Some of them, at least—even one of them. For I'm strong, John Thomas—I'm very strong—you know how strong I am. God gave me that strength for a purpose—he entrusted me with strength to do his work, and instead I turned and ran."

He returned an hour or two later, when the bandits were gone, and found not a single British soldier left alive. They were strewn about the rocks like discarded dolls. One of them, a lad of just sixteen years, lay with his eyes open wide and one arm stretched out, as if he were reaching in desperation towards Daniel himself.

"That's when I understood, John Thomas. The voice that spoke to me—'Save yourself'—that was the Devil. He was there. The Devil was right there in the rocks that afternoon, and I did as he bid me. Just as I've done his bidding since, in so many small mean ways."

"I think you judge yourself harshly, Daniel."

"Not half so harshly as God does—or so I've always believed. But look, John Thomas—look there, through the window. Despite it all, God hasn't let me go. He rises in radiance to greet me once again, and here are his two angels, ready to walk at my side."

He spoke with such frail wondering joy that I scarcely had the heart to set him straight.

"I fear you're light-headed, Daniel, with too much drink and a lack of proper nourishment. What you need is boiled beef."

"I must fight," he said.

"Perhaps we'll talk about pugilism some other time." I took his arm. "First we must find you a room—a proper room, without whores strewn about, and a bit of curtain to keep out the sun—and put you to bed."

He shook off my hand, still gazing out the window at the sun. The light from it glowed upon his face. Daniel shone with sunlight, and dust motes danced like angels about his head.

"You don't understand," he said. "I am being given a second chance, and this time I will not fail. I must fight for those too weak to defend themselves, John Thomas. I must fight against the Devil himself, for I am God's man from this moment forth."

AND GOD'S HAIRY BOLLOCKS, he was true to his word. Daniel walked out of that filthy room and down the brothel stairs and into the clear light of morning, and that was the last I saw of him for eight long years. When I saw him again, he was a man transformed. He was Daniel the preacher and Daniel the saint, and Daniel the fighter who wouldn't say die. And thus I told the court.

I didn't tell them in nearly such detail as I've set down here, of course, but I gave them the gist. All the while, I seemed to feel the ice-cold eyes of Lord Sculthorpe upon me, and his malevolent spirit brooding over the courtroom. As I concluded, one of the judges leaned forward. "Are you telling the court," he demanded in a voice like flint, "that this man is a *deserter?*"

I made a weary gesture of apology, as if to indicate: what else was a friend to do? For it hadn't been poor Jaunty's fault that Daniel had beaten Hen Gully the Game Chicken—had batted him about the ring like a shuttlecock, and even spit out the sponge I had prepared against such an eventuality—in calamitous contradiction of my promise to His Lordship. But if I provided evidence—thus the chin-deficient intermediary had indicated—then perhaps His Lordship would forgive my failure. Or if not forgive then at least forget, or at any event avert his murderous gaze for a moment or two, just long enough for Jaunty to hasten down the road to Somewhere Else Entirely.

Daniel gazed across at me. The look on his face seemed unutterably sad and yet somehow tender, as if he were to say: "And did he threaten you, John Thomas? Did you fear for your life, my poor old comrade?"

But perhaps this was a trick of shadow, for in the next moment he gave a terrible roar, and lunged across at me, as clerks shrieked and barristers scattered and half a dozen bailiffs struggled to restrain him. In the meantime, I was slipping out the door. And was this fair? Of course it was not—it was monstrous. But life is very seldom fair, and thus we must all be philosophers.

If you peer off into the distance, you may see a man's back, getting rapidly smaller until you can't see it at all. And this will be your friend Jaunty Rennert, disappearing over the horizon.

MAY, 1852

PIPER

FLOWERS WERE in bloom the day they sentenced Daniel O'Thunder. I remember being appalled by that. As if spring had any right to burgeon on such a day.

I didn't have the heart to go straight home, so I stopped at a public house in Chancery Lane. But as I sat in a corner with my glass, I found that the news had already preceded me. A man in a blue neckerchief and a smart narrow-waisted jacket was telling his companions, with grim relish: "The Irishman got exactly what he deserved. There were no surprises in the court this afternoon." His companions growled with satisfaction.

It was evening when I arrived home at last. Dorcas met me at the door. But the urgent question died on her lips, for of course she could read the answer in my face.

"Well?" the Rock of Agnes demanded. She was sitting in her chair by the window. "What happened?"

I slumped down on the chaise. "No surprises," I said heavily.

And it wasn't a surprise at all—not really. Not after the testimony of the Judas Rennert, which shredded any last sympathy. But by God, it still came as a shock when His Worship looked down from the bench like the face of midwinter, and reached for the black cap.

"So," said my Mother. "It has come to this."

There was silence for several moments. Dorcas stood, too stricken to sniffle. The Rock of Agnes shook her head.

"It is precisely as I predicted at the start," she said. "What did I predict, at the very outset? I predicted tears, William, before bedtime. And here it is—not even bedtime yet. I wish I could take some satisfaction. But I can't."

It was on my tongue to fling a bitter retort, thanking her for great goodness in this regard. But I didn't have the heart for it. On that dismal evening, I didn't have the heart for anything at all.

She was speaking again. "Not even bedtime yet—and here we are. The Irishman in ruins—in shackles—in Newgate. In *Newgate,* no less, awaiting their pleasure. And their pleasure, dear God, is to hang him."

"It won't come to that," I said wearily. "They'll almost certainly commute, in the end. With luck he'll come out of this with ten years—or twenty—or life."

There was silence for another moment.

"No," said the Rock of Agnes, having reached a decision. "William? *No.* The man is in durance vile—the man has been condemned—and we do not sit dithering. Instead we ask ourselves a question, and the question is this."

She leaned forward, regarding me with grim finality.

"William? What the Devil do you propose to do about it?"

THE TWELFTH TOLL of St Sepulchre's clock was echoing into silence when at length our knocking was answered. The grate slid open in the thick oaken door, and a familiar palsied-seeming eye appeared.

"Hello, Waldron," I said. "It's us."

"Ten shillings," said the turnkey.

"What? I thought we agreed on five."

"Five's the evenin' rate. It's just gone midnight. Ten."

I ground my teeth, but fished in my pockets. Waldron's eye roved across our little group standing in our little pool of lantern light. "Just the three of yer? I thought p'raps Miss Dorcas might be 'ere present, p'raps bearing certain of them pies to which I am hespecially partial."

There was a sniffle from the blackness behind me. Dorcas stepped closer, where Waldron could see her. In the pale light she looked more translucent than ever, and she carried a hamper. After a moment we heard the hollow rasp of the bolt being drawn back, and the door creaked open.

"Evening, Miss Dorcas," said Waldron. "You're lookin' pertic'larly blooming, tonight. And I 'ope," he added with a mordant wink, "you'll find the patient well."

We didn't find O'Thunder well at all—not that we'd expected to, God knows. He'd been in shocking decline ever since the day of the fire, and tonight he was worse than ever. He was stretched out on the cot when we arrived. Lying in near darkness in his small stone cell, his single candle having dwindled to a last feeble glow. He was startled from a fretful slumber by the opening of the cell door. He gave a hoarse exclamation and raised his arm to block the light from Bob's lantern, for it blinded him at first. The other arm was wrapped in a filthy grey bandage, and he was in shackles, hands and feet.

"Who's there?" he cried, caught between sleep and waking. Even his voice was diminished. It was cracked and hoarse. "Who's come for me? Is it time? If it's time, then do your worst, for I'm ready."

I spoke quickly, to reassure him. "It's just us. Your friends. It's William—see?—and here's Boston Bob McCorkindale as well. Your old friend Boston Bob, come to see you."

"Bob?"

O'Thunder peered through the gloom, his first agitation easing as he collected his wits from slumber. Boston Bob stepped a little closer, and set the lantern down. There were just the two of us in the cell with O'Thunder, Dorcas having gone with Waldron. Our other companion had lingered behind, in the corridor.

"H'lo, Dan," said Bob. "I can see you're in a pickle."

"A pickle, Bob?" said Daniel. "Is that where I am?" He struggled to sit, with clanking of chains, and managed the ghost of a smile. "For I'd have sworn I was in Newgate Prison."

He was pleased to see us, I think. I believe he was touched to the heart, as he was always touched when friends came to visit him—the very few who still did, for so many had deserted him. But he was distracted, as he always was, these days and nights. He couldn't settle. His eyes were sunken and his cheeks were hollow; he had lost weight shockingly.

"Is there any news of Nell?" he asked. For that was always his first question.

But there had been no news. Nothing seen or heard from Nell Rooney since the day of the fire.

He lowered his head. "I hope she's well. Do you think she's all right? I think perhaps she is, William. I think perhaps she's just given up on me. This is a sorrow to me, and a cruel one—I won't deny it—although I can hardly blame her." But he looked up again, with a distracted smile. "Still. You've come again, William, as you've come so often, to see me. To bring me cheer as best you can, and news from the great world. So. What news have you of the world tonight, brother?"

The news was bleak. "We've been writing letters, Daniel—we've been doing our very best. Members of Parliament, lords, anyone we can think of. But people have—how can I say this . . . ?"

"Just say it, brother. They've taken against me."

"Many of them. Most of them. Yes."

He was sitting on the edge of the cot, now. Shoulders slumped, elbows on knees, shaggy head hanging. Kneading his hands together, one hand over the other, over and over, in a way I didn't like to see at all. I'd seen it before, in cases of mental disorder. Men who'd been shattered.

Daniel summoned a brief bleak smile. "Taken against me, just as my Nell has done. I thought perhaps she'd be among the very few who'd stay. But let that be, for I have to tell you, brother—I do believe I've taken against myself."

"Don't say that, Daniel."

"But I do," he said. "I do say it. More than that, I mean it. And I say something else, as well. Whatever you're trying to do for me—these letters, and all the rest of it—whatever you're doing, I want you to stop."

"Daniel—"

"No, listen to me." Still staring at the stones beneath his feet. The hands kneading, over and over, as if he were trying to wash them clean. "Even if they listen—even if they commute the sentence—what would it mean? A prison cell for the rest of my life? And besides, I deserve to hang, brothers. I deserve to hang, and worse, for the things I've done. More than that, I *want* to hang."

He looked up, now. His eyes were coals of desperate conviction. "Yes, that's what I want. Let Calcraft send me to the Devil—for I'll have him, then. We'll meet at last, the two of us, on the burning plains of Hell."

It was lunacy, of course. But it was Daniel O'Thunder's lunacy, which meant it came with its own mad logic. I threw a look of deep dismay to Boston Bob. All this while he had been standing in silence.

"Good plan," said Bob.

"*What?*" I cried.

"Fine plan. If your notion is to give in and quit."

Daniel went rigid. Even the hands stopped kneading.

"Seen you do it before," Boston Bob continued. "Seen you do it against Tom Oliver, the Battersea Gardener. You gave in, that time. Quit. That what you're planning to do again? Just asking. Clarification's sake."

Later inquiry was to establish the strong possibility that this was the longest speech Bob McCorkindale had ever made in his life. He cocked his head now, and waited for Daniel's reply.

It welled up as a cry of despair. "And what else would you have me do? Here I am—shackled—Newgate Prison. Where is the angel come to free me, brother? Where is the shining being come to roll back the rock? The angels don't come here to Newgate Prison, brother—leastways they don't come here to see me, for I have failed, and it's over. So I want you to leave me now, the both of you. Go away, as all the others have gone away—as the angels themselves have gone—and let me gather my thoughts to die like a man!"

There was a sniffle from the dark corridor behind, and light footsteps hurrying towards us. I turned to see a white face with blue veins at the temples. Metal jingled as she arrived, and held up her hand.

"Got the keys to the shackles," whispered Dorcas, with fierce translucent triumph.

I could have kissed her. Later on, in fact, I did.

INQUIRY INTO BRAZEN ESCAPE

Suspicions Surround Former Correspondent

By Herbert Landers

The Morning Register

9 July, 1852

. . .

Details emerged today at the Inquiry into the recent escape from Newgate Prison of the Irish prize-fighter and evangelist Daniel O'Thunder. It appears that certain friends of the prisoner had arrived at the gaol shortly after midnight on 18 June, offering silver coins to a turnkey, on the pretext that they had come for a brief visit. One of these friends has been identified as William Piper, a former correspondent for the *Morning Register.* The turnkey, a party of shambling gait and mordant winks named Reginald Waldron, accepted the silver, and unlocked the cell door. He then left Piper and another man unattended for several minutes while he went off for a private conference with a third visitor, a domestic servant named Dorcas Ragnarson. Under questioning, the turnkey Waldron confessed that he had entertained amorous aspirations regarding this woman ever since meeting her at a fish market two years ago. He further stated that he was eating eel pie and regaling her with tales of famous escapes from this very prison, when an unseen assailant rendered him senseless with a ferocious blow from behind.

The assailant has not been conclusively identified, although there is reason to suspect it may have been an erstwhile pugilist named Spragg the Ruffian. It may also have been Spragg who subsequently impersonated an undertaker, in order to convey from the prison a coffin containing the corpse of a prisoner who had died earlier that afternoon. This seems to have been a ruse, with the coffin instead containing the prisoner O'Thunder. By the time the gambit was discovered, the conspirators had disappeared. Reports indicate that O'Thunder himself may have been smuggled into a coach that was seen waiting outside Newgate, driven by two elderly women in grey cloaks and bonnets.

The man Piper has disappeared without a trace. There are indications that the woman Dorcas Ragnarson is with him. Piper's mother has disappeared as well.

PIPER

I LEAVE YOU WITH an image. It is a ship, a sailing packet. It is sailing from Liverpool a fortnight after the escape, bound for New York.

I was not there, but I can see it in my mind, from letters that were later exchanged.

In the darkness, a man in a ragged cloak stands on the deck. He is gaunt, but still massive and powerful. Two others are with him, having slipped aboard at the last moment, even as the gangplank was about to be raised. One of these is an eerie boy with a sharp-chinned goblin's face. The second is a red-haired girl. She is fifteen years old; her face is pinched and drawn as if from some recent ordeal.

There had been disbelief and joy in that first moment when he had seen them and wrapped them in his arms and wept. A thousand questions—where did you?—but how?! Swift whispered answers, and more tears of joy, and now they stand together at the rail.

"Come," says the girl, holding tight to the gaunt man's arm. "We need to go below, with the others." For of course their place is in steerage, along with two hundred other souls. More than that, the girl remains in mortal fear of being seen.

Behind them, the lights of Liverpool recede into the void of night. There are creaks from the spars and shouts from the sailors at their work. A salt wind gusts, tugging at the gaunt man's cloak. But his eyes are fixed ahead, gazing westward into the darkness.

"The New World," he says. "Yes—I do believe this is where he may be found. I had a dream, Nell, that this was so. He has caused such destruction in the Old World already, and now he is seeking new fields to raze. Besides—he doesn't dare stay in one place for long. For he knows that I'm coming after him."

The girl casts a look to the goblin-faced boy, half-despairing.

"Just let it go," she pleads with the gaunt man. "We're together again. We'll look after one another, and we can start all over, ten million miles away. Just come below, and leave off all them Bedlam thoughts."

"The New World," he repeats. His eyes are very bright, and he speaks with a grim distracted urgency. "That's where I'll start to look for him, Nell, and I will not cease until I've found him."

But behind them, unseen in the darkness, a deeper shadow has begun to gather.

IV

The Devil is in Liverpool when he sees the little red-haired whore. In the last glimmer of twilight she is hurrying along a deserted dockside street. She is all alone, a shawl clutched round her thin shoulders.

The Devil is emerging from the web of stinking narrow lanes that leads from the lodging house where he stays. It is a low and pestilential house, inhabited by the very dregs of the seaport, for the Devil finds his circumstances shockingly reduced just at present. He turns the corner—and there she is. O'Thunder's red-haired draggletail. She scurries like a rodent along the rain-slick cobbles.

The Devil is rigid in the first shock of recognition, for he had thought her long since dead. But against all hope, it is she. His desiccated black heart swells within his breast, and through the crepuscular light he follows like a falcon.

He has been in this bleak city for months now, ever since catching wind of a rumour of the mad Irishman. The rumour was already ancient when it reached his ear in London, but the Devil hastened northward nonetheless with an avenger's unholy agitation. Arriving, he searched the city, night after night, stalking haggard and hollow-eyed through winding streets, seeking news of his enemy in low taverns and seamen's brothels.

He had feared from the outset it would prove a fool's errand, for so much time has passed already—nearly twelve years since the Irishman's disappearance from Newgate Prison. And yet there are wisps of recollection in the salt air of Liverpool, tantalizing. The remembered glimpse of a great shambling Irishman with yellow hair. Why, yes, such a man had been seen—when was it?—a year ago, or two, or twelve? He was taking ship for India—or Gibraltar—or perhaps he was returning. He was alone—or not—no, wait, he had a girl with him, a red-haired girl.

And now in the gathering darkness, there she is at last.

She is making her way eastward, angling towards Lime Street. Her feet go splish-splash in the puddles, and she actually begins to sing. The draggletail begins to croon a tuneless song to herself, so oblivious is she to the darkness that is closing upon her.

*The Devil accelerates his pace—clip-*clop, *clip-*clop*—giddy with dark anticipation. If the little trull is in Liverpool, then surely the mad Irishman is here also. Should he take her at once—the final fatal stoop, a strangled shriek and an exultation—or should he let her lead him to O'Thunder first?*

It is such a dark sweet dilemma, and it grows sweeter still, for the little trull has begun to sense she is being stalked. The tuneless singing trails away. Her footsteps falter—she slows and for an instant stops—she calls out in an uncertain voice: "Is someone there?"

The Devil has stopped as well, and stands in the shadows beyond the feeble spill of light from a doorway. He savours such moments, and finds his heart—his desiccated heart—is pounding.

He steps forward at last, unable to contain himself. The little whore turns round to see him. She gasps aloud.

And it is not she.

It is not the Irishman's red-haired whore at all. Her hair is scarcely red—how could the Devil have imagined such hair to have been red? It is more nearly a mousy brown, and she herself—God's blood—is hard and leathery and five-and-forty. The Devil stands as if turned to stone, for he has never seen the bitch before.

"Allo, old cock," she says. "Lookin' for comp'ny? Well, fuck off and find it somewheres else."

Her spasm of alarm has given way to coarse jollity, for some friends of hers—three other whores and a pair of drunken sailors—have just come reeling out of an alleyway. She falls in with them, and they lurch away together. Turning the corner, the whores peer back. "Wouljer look at that shabby man?" he hears one of them exclaim. "And didjer ever see such a ridiculous fucking hat?" They shriek with laughter.

The Devil stands.

He feels a strange hot crawling sensation upon the parchment of his face, and discovers that he is weeping.

IN A LANE *near the river there is a ramshackle house that calls itself a Gospel Mission. It is run by a spavined sea-cook who found the Lord one night in Zanzibar, and it is filled with the lowest rabble imaginable. Ragged sticks with missing limbs, gin-addled dropsical wrecks, and syphilitic crones, huddled together in wretched camaraderie. In this, the darkest hour of his long damnation, the Devil finds himself amongst them.*

They are singing "My Faith Looks up to Thee."

While life's dark maze I tread
And griefs around me spread,
Be Thou my guide...

The Devil cannot imagine why he has come. He sits alone in the darkest corner, and hates. He thinks what he would like to do to these creatures. He tries to imagine vengeance upon Creation and everything in it—assuming that anything has been Created at all, and is not all the merest result of chance. He discovers that he is weeping again.

Bid darkness turn to day,
Wipe sorrow's tears away,
Nor let me ever stray
From Thee aside.

There is someone standing over him. It is the spavined sea-cook, with a look in his eye of fierce mad piety as he greets the Devil. "Welcome, friend," he says. "Do you come here in true repentance and acknowledgement of your sins, looking to the Lord Jesus as your Saviour?"

It is an inexplicable thing, but in that moment the Devil can almost imagine himself saying yes. Except there is no Saviour, is there? Nor any hope of one to come. The Devil has long since known this, deep down, and now he can deny it no longer. His heart is ash, his vengeance has curdled, and he himself is utterly absurd. He is a character in a medieval play, club-footed upon a pageant wagon, squeaking malevolence into the void. He is achingly alone, and cannot endure this. There is no God, and no hope, and no Irishman, and no Nell.

But in the very depths of his despair, the Devil makes a discovery. On a rickety table, someone has left open a tattered Christian tract. He picks it up.

It is one of those breathless evangelical pamphlets through which the desperately earnest spread their fables to pious fools. This pamphlet tells of modern-day saints who are doing the Lord's work in the faraway goldfields of the Canadian north-west. This is the new gold rush, a thousand miles from the California fields where a young Cornish vicar named Jack Beresford had once dreamed of journeying, back in the mists of time when he could still imagine himself doing God's work.

For in the goldfields, God's soldiers are desperately required. In such places—a town called Barkerville is cited—men are maddened by greed, and are thus easy prey for the Ancient Enemy. He stalks amongst them—so says the pamphlet in its laboured purple prose, blinking back earnest tears—plucking the unwary for Perdition.

But a few brave soldiers rise up against the Prince of Lies. The pamphlet names several of these, and in a final vermilion paragraph it mentions one in particular. He walks incessantly through a merciless rugged land, ministering to those in spiritual need and seeking, always seeking, for the Foe.

He is Irish, this crackpot saint. He calls himself Brother Daniel.

The Devil sits transfixed.

JACK

I TOOK SHIP IN the spring of 1864. The winds were with us, and did not flag—not once, the entire month of the westward voyage. We cracked on like smoke and oakum; we chased the sun and threaded the eye of night. We came on like the very devil. West and south to Panama, and then across the isthmus by stagecoach from Colon to Darien; a steamship north to San Francisco, and north again from San Francisco to Vancouver Island. As it rises before you green and rugged there is exultation, for at last you are drawing near to your destination in the goldfields. But no, you've only just begun. You must cross to New Westminster, on the mainland. From New Westminster you must travel a hundred miles east to Yale, a sorry cluster of shacks on the banks of the Fraser River. All around are mountains so tall they slow the mind, rearing jagged from impenetrable forest. The river itself is wide and seething.

And still you've scarcely begun. You must make your way by wagon-road along the Fraser Canyon, where the river rages through chasms of rock a thousand feet below. The sheer size of the landscape overwhelms; you cannot locate yourself. This terrain is the very face of a merciless God—or else his utter absence. You may decide for yourself which is worse. Through Hell's Gate you struggle all the way to Lillooet, where the land begins to change, the forests of cedar and spruce giving way to bleak arid hills and stands of lodgepole pine. And still you've scarcely begun. Look at your map. Christ, another three hundred miles of this before you finally reach Quesnellemouth—if you reach Quesnellemouth at all, for many don't. Three hundred miles, with very little resembling even a roadhouse, just wooden shacks in the wilderness every twenty or thirty miles, where you might find a rough meal and a place to curl up on the floor. Jackpine jungle and clouds of blood-sucking insects, whining out of the twilight to batten upon the living. And even if you reach Quesnellemouth—another godforsaken cluster of shacks—then you still have a journey to go, for the goldfields lie further, through the worst jungle yet.

It will be desolate beyond your imagining, with a terrible beauty. It will be cold. Even in summer the nights will bring a shiver, and the winter will be almost unendurable. For you are trudging into the North, and the North is the ancient fastness of the Devil. He tells us so. "I will sit on the highest mountain above the tall mountains of the North," says the Devil. "I will ascend above the clouds, and I will be like the Most High."

I HAVE in my way invented the Devil.

You might say I have created him as a character in these very pages, in my *Book of Daniel*. The Devil was of course the adversary whom Daniel O'Thunder battled all his life, and no editor can afford to leave blank pages where his great antagonist ought to loom. So I have presumed to speak on the Devil's behalf, evoking an image of him that seemed truthful to me. Scribbling him to life each night, here at my desk in my Whitechapel garret in the yellow flutter of candlelight, drawing upon my scholarship and long cogitation. I have drawn as well upon my own instinctive understanding of the Devil's heart and mind. For any man must ultimately write of himself, even when he writes of the Devil—especially, perhaps, when he writes of the Devil—and thus the Devil in these pages might sometimes seem to be standing in for Jack Hartright himself.

I was also guilty of inventing the Devil in my mind, in those few weeks and months of my darkest exultation four long decades ago, when I actually believed he was Lord Sculthorpe. It was an easy mistake to make, I suppose. Lord Sculthorpe was labouring under exactly the same delusion, towards the end. But I was also mad for a time—I do believe that, now—and looking back I have to shake my head. Lord Sculthorpe, the Dark Power himself? Lord Sculthorpe was just a bankrupt peer from Norfolk. His Christian name was Ronald, and he'd had a mother once, upon whom he was to call as he lay raving in the last extremity of syphilitic ruin.

But the Devil was real all along. Horrifyingly so, as events were soon enough to prove. He was real as he rose up that final cataclysmic night in the Northern wilderness, to do battle at last against Daniel O'Thunder. He is real as I scribble these words at my Whitechapel desk in 1888, with predators stirring in the darkness outside and my brisk brown spider looking down from the shadows above me. And the Devil will still be real as you read this—wherever you are, and however snug and secure you suppose yourself to be—even though he was never Ronald, Lord Sculthorpe.

WHEN I SAW Sculthorpe the night before the fire that destroyed O'Thunder's Mission—that April night in 1852, in an alleyway off the Haymarket—the first signs of his ruination were already upon him. Looking back I can see that clearly, although I put it down to his agitation at the time. Pacing distractedly, for he was hunted by creditors and the London Constabulary. Dark allegations circling like rooks—the whisper of dead girls—and an incriminating book of Shakespeare's sonnets. That's what seemed to upset him most of all. Never mind the volumes of pornography—dozens of them, each one viler than the last—or the drawings of young women in various stages of lurid deshabille. He'd own to these—God's blood, he'd own to murders—but the book of poetry he'd never laid eyes on, and he'd had nothing to do with the killing of the old whore. He swore the evidence was false; it had been planted there, most feloniously and wickedly, by some Enemy. And of course he was quite right—the villain was tantalizingly close to hand, had he only known. But his vituperations kept circling back to Daniel O'Thunder, for this was his *idée fixe*. O'Thunder was the man who had ruined him. He had wagered vast sums upon O'Thunder to lose the mill against Hen Gully, but instead O'Thunder had swung that fist of his, he had swung that whoreson Hammer—et cetera. And now the desire for revenge consumed him.

I'd come with excellent news, on this occasion. I'd been delving into O'Thunder's past, as Sculthorpe had engaged me to do—I'd been following the spoor like a bloodhound—and I'd come up with whispers of desertion from the army. Better yet, I'd located the man Rennert, who could drive the final nail. This pleased Scul-thorpe mightily; we congratulated one another, and were for a moment darkly exultant. At least, I was as exultant as a man may be who has not quite shaken the vestiges of suspicion that he is alone in a pitch-dark alley with Satan himself, who might at any instant reveal himself in full Infernal Majesty and drag all present howling down to Hell.

But he didn't do that. He resumed his pacing and his raving, before turning suddenly and asking after his daughter. For this was a second obsession with him. He was convinced that Nell Rooney was his own child, fathered upon that girl who now lay in the East London churchyard.

I assured him she was well. I assured him I would safeguard her against all harm. I lied and lied. As I did, a strange sad look crept into his eyes.

"It is a remarkable thing, to have a child," he said. "It is something that has hope in it. There is in it something that might even be redemption."

There was a teardrop. There actually was. It trickled onto his cheek. As it did, I noticed that the patrician nose was starting to rot.

The next time I saw him, the nose was gone entirely, and his mind with it. This was twelve years later, shortly before I took ship to the new world. Sculthorpe was chained to a madhouse wall, filthy and gibbering. Flies buzzing round suppurating sores. He told me the flies were his darlings, for he was the Lord of them. Yes he was, he was the Devil. Soon enough, he said, I should feel a clutching at my ankles, and that would be his hands, closing like manacles.

"Tell her I love her," he cried, as I turned to go.

It stopped me, for a moment. There was genuine heartbreak in that cry.

"Go find her. My little Nell. Will you do that? Say her father loves her."

Great mad eyes gazing from that ruined face, as of a soul abandoned to the bottomless desolation of Hell.

I gave my word, and left him there.

I RODE INTO Barkerville in late autumn of 1864. Winter lay white upon the mountains already, creeping down towards the tents and shanties on the hillsides above Williams Creek, where miners camped and worked like ants. Another week or two, I had been told, and it would be too late in the year to travel at all. November's grip would close like a fist, and God help stragglers on the road.

I rode like a lord the last forty miles, having come upon good fortune a little distance east of Quesnellemouth. Or more precisely I had come upon a man who possessed a horse and a money-belt besides. He was solitary, and glad for company, and we journeyed together for an hour or two, until with a smile and a friendly word he turned his back for a moment. Shortly thereafter I resumed the journey alone, for his fortune had not been quite as good as mine. The deciduous trees among the pine and cedar had been a blaze of red and gold scant weeks earlier; now they were barren and stark. The leaves had fallen even as I passed, as if I had somehow brought this desolation with me. Such are the whimsical thoughts that come to us in solitude. And as the lemon sun declined upon my fourth day out of Quesnellemouth, I rode into Barkerville at last.

It was a filthy hole, and home to nearly ten thousand souls. The largest city in North America west of Chicago and north of San Francisco. Only for an eye-blink, mind, and then it fell into ruin. The tragic mutability of things, and the vanity of all human aspirations. Look on my works ye mighty, et cetera. Still, Barkerville had its blink.

I left my horse at the livery stable, and started up the street. The town was just the one long street, with more shacks in behind, by the creek. Two rows of wooden shanties thrown together, all jumbled against one another. The wooden sidewalks in front were different heights, like the buildings themselves. There was a blacksmith and Wake Up Jake's Café, and stores and a bank. Saloons, of course—I counted four in forty paces—and a theatre. The Occidental Cigar Store had a library. A bleached pine pole with a red flannel rag wrapped round it stood outside the shop of Wellington D. Moses, the Negro barber. At the very top of the street the Chinese lived—the Celestials, they were called—sad-faced outcasts who had left their homes forever and carried in silence what embers of hopes and dreams might remain to them. They were men whose entire existence had narrowed to the single goal that had brought them here. Men very much, indeed, like myself.

When I stepped into the Occidental Hotel, unwashed and haggard from travel, the clerk at the desk raised an eyebrow—but only by a sixteenth of an inch, for of course he had seen much worse.

Yes, as it happened, they did have a room. Did I wish to see it first? His expression doubted the need for such niceties, and I shook my head.

He was a brisk little sparrow, this man at the desk. He turned the registry book towards me, and handed me a pen. The hotel itself was a tiny shard of England, though it was new, and smelled of new-milled wood. Wallpaper and a small brave bit of carpet, and wispy curtains. There was a proper little sitting area in the window, with chairs and a chaise where a spade-bearded miner sprawled.

I signed my name. "I am hoping to find a man," I said casually, "called Brother Daniel. Do you know of him?"

The eyebrow arched again. Brother Daniel? Yes, of course.

The pulse quickened.

The brisk little sparrow was loath to pry, but he was curious. Was I a friend? he wondered. Or just—an offhand little laugh—a man in need?

I could have told him: both. I was a friend—or had been so—and now I was a man whose need was bottomless. But I managed to keep my voice steady.

"And is he hereabouts in Barkerville?"

Not at the moment, as far as the sparrow knew. Brother Daniel came and went. But after a week or a month he'd usually be back.

"A good man," he added, volunteering the opinion unsolicited. "An unusual man—he has his ways. A strange man, Brother Daniel. But good."

"There is God," said a voice like coal scraping in a scuttle, "in Brother Daniel."

It was the spade-bearded miner on the chaise. He had risen onto his elbow, fixing bleary eyes upon me and speaking with the slow *gravitas* of the slobbering drunk.

"Do you understand what I'm saying?" he demanded. "In Brother Daniel...there is God."

There was a silence. The brisk little sparrow cleared his throat, but not before bobbing his head in quick awkward agreement. Looking down, his eye fell upon the name I had signed in the registry.

"Mr. . . Pithius, is it? What an unusual name."

"What about a girl?" I asked. "Does he have a girl with him? A red-haired child."

The sparrow cocked his head, and frowned polite perplexity. A child?

"Or wait, she wouldn't be a child anymore." What was I thinking? She'd be a woman, now. "Perhaps seven-and-twenty. Red hair."

The sparrow cocked his head the other way. Ah. There was a friend of Brother Daniel's—a red-haired woman who kept a boarding house down the street. Is that the one I meant, by any chance? Nell Rooney.

And there it was. After all these years, I'd found my little Nell. I'd found the both of them.

"Five dollars," the brisk little sparrow was saying. "Excuse me?"

For I had turned away, my emotions in a surge. I looked back.

"It's five dollars for the room. Payable in advance."

I regarded him briefly, drawing a slow breath to steady myself. Then I smiled. "What's this?" I asked, reaching out.

"What?" he asked, uncertainly.

"This."

I plucked a gold coin from his ear, and gave it to him. It was a droll little trick I'd acquired, over the years.

NELL

THE SECOND I stepped out the door, I knew I was being watched. I'd had that feeling off and on for several days now. At first I'd put it down to Daniel being gone, cos I could never settle when he was away. But this was different. This was spiders creeping up my spine.

When I looked back, there was no one there. Just the dark street stretching behind me. I gripped the buckets in either hand, and started down to the pump.

It wasn't yet dawn, for I was up early, same as every morning. Stir up the fire in the pot-bellied stove and start preparing breakfast for the men. As many as ten or twelve of them, depending on the day. Half a dozen on bunks behind the partition, the rest on the rough wooden floor in the main room. Step over them in the darkness.

They were men from all over—rough men, and a few of them bad apples, but most of them quite decent. For awhile there were two brothers from Wales, Welsh miners, one black-headed and one ginger, who'd clump back from Denby's saloon each night singing. They stayed at the boarding house for a few weeks before staking a claim above Williams Creek. I heard they were starting to make a go, until one of them got sick with the Mountain Fever. The ginger one. After he died his brother kept on for a time, but his heart had gone out of it.

I slept in an alcove at the back, with a piece of sacking for a door. Sometimes one of the men would try to crawl in with me, but he'd go crawling straight back out again, the fucker. I was through with that. Believe me, I was so fucking through. Sometimes a man would crawl in and find out I wasn't alone. Those were the nights Selena Lashaway came by. The man's eyes would go wide as plates.

"Goddlemighty," I'd hear him exclaiming hoarsely. "She's got a squaw in that bed with her."

And what if I did? Selena was my friend. She had a low rich laugh, and I never had to "ooh" at the size of anything, and she never tried to hit me even once. There was lots to be said for Selena Lashaway.

Daniel could have come through the curtain, of course. He could have come through any time he chose. But he'd never done that, not even once.

And now he'd been gone for nearly a week.

I didn't like him to be gone this late in the year, not out there in the mountains. Even here below in the town, the night had been cold enough to freeze the mud in the street. White puffs of breath, and my fingers freezing on the bucket handles.

There was someone behind me—I knew it—but when I looked again there was still nothing there. The outlines of the buildings, and coal-oil lights gleaming in some of the windows.

Walking quicker now, down towards the pump. The blackness was starting to edge into grey, but the night had a ways to go yet, and besides the mist hung thick at the bottom of the street. As I got to the pump, something stepped out of the mist at me.

"Jesus Christ!"

My heart stopped dead, but it was only Tommy. He'd been waiting for me by the pump, like he did every morning when Daniel was away.

"Fucksake," I said, sharply. "Do you have to go lurking about on people? And no, I haven't seen him, and I ent heard a word of him neither. Have you?"

He shook his head no.

"Well, then there's nothing to be heard," I said. "So we'll just have to wait till he comes back, won't we?"

Tommy nodded, and looked away. I was peevish at him for startling me like that, but mainly I was relieved to have him with me. I filled the first bucket with water from the pump, and then the second. When I finished, Tommy moved to pick them up.

"No, that's all right," I told him, like I always did. "I'm not a bloody weakling—I can manage."

He picked them up anyways, like always.

"Fine, then. Suit y'self."

I talked for the two of us, as we started back up the frozen street.

"The Indians are saying winter's coming early this year, early and hard. That's what Selena says. Don't ask me how Indians know these things, but it always seems like they do." There was light beyond the mountains now. By noon it might be above freezing, and the street would be churned into a bog of mud. That's why the buildings here were all on stilts. That, and the creek was liable to flood. "Something about the geese, I think—flying early, or some such. Or maybe she said the ducks. Fucked if I know—I never listen, when she starts up about the birds."

Tommy smiled a little, and bobbed his chin.

You wouldn't hardly recognize him from the old days, when he was Tommyknocker, the goblin-boy with clever hands at the Kemp Theatre. His hair was white as ever and he still had them same uncanny eyes, but the difference was they looked down at you. Leastways they looked down at me—but then again, few didn't. He was thin, but wiry strong. He did odd jobs here and there about town, mainly fixing up equipment, for his fingers were as clever as they'd always been. At night he slept behind the brazier at the smithy, stretched out in the dying warmth.

I asked him one time how he ever decided he'd be my friend in the first place. He scribbled on a scrap of paper, and showed it.

YOU SPOKE TO ME. AT THE THEATRE.

"What, that first time I went there, looking for Jack Hartright?"

Cos I hadn't said three words to Tommy that time at the theatre—leastways not three words that I could remember. Maybe I nodded in his direction and said, "All right, then?" You know, the way you do when you say hello to someone.

He nodded.

AS IF I WAS NORMAL.

Fucksake. And that was all it took?

When I told Daniel, he smiled. "You'd be surprised, Nell, how little it takes sometimes to touch a soul—one way or the other." But being Daniel, he had another explanation too. "I think Tommy may be just a little bit of an angel."

Daniel O'Thunder and his angels.

Still. Tommy was the one who found me in that stinking hole in Whitechapel, the place I was kept after Jack Hartright betrayed me. The godawful brothel where Mother Clatterballock put me to learn eclectic from the sailors, with oyster-eyed Swinton for a gaoler. Then one night there was a goblin face in the window, and it was little Tommyknocker come to fetch me out of Hell. So perhaps Daniel had a point, and you just learned to take your angels as they came.

We'd reached the boarding house. Tommy set the buckets down on the sidewalk, and straightened. I touched his arm. "I'll be all right."

Cos Tommy had felt something, same as I had. He'd been edgy, too, for days.

"And don't look so worried. He'll come back—Daniel always does."

Leastways he always had before. That's what I was telling myself, even though I didn't like the feel of the wind that had been slicing down from the mountains last night. A winter wind, and winter here was terrible. Oh, it was lovely, too—the snow so white it was shocking, and sometimes on clear nights the Northern Lights, great flashes of colour sweeping across the horizon, green and red and white. But mainly the winter was just crueller than you could believe. Winter here could kill anyone—even Daniel.

Tommy melted back into the mist. After he was gone, I looked round again. Cos someone had been watching us every step of the way as we'd come up the street. They'd been watching, though they hadn't shown themselves.

"Go on, then," I said, raising my voice. "Try it."

There was no reply. But whoever it was—he was there. Just outside the corner of my eye, watching.

DANIEL HAD GONE off into the mountains with Mrs Jimmy. She'd come riding in on an old white nag, saying there'd been an accident and Jimmy was dying. Jimmy being Jim McKenzie, who had a claim thirty miles away. Mrs Jimmy was Lobelia, though no one ever called her that. She worked the claim with him, holding the drill while he hit it with the hammer, then lifting it up and turning, eighth of an inch each time. She'd come all the way from Yorkshire to help him do that, a knotty little stick of a woman. But now there'd been an accident and Jimmy was dying. He was asking for Daniel, so could Daniel come quick. And of course Daniel said yes, like he always did.

I wanted to make them wait long enough for Mrs Jimmy to have a meal, and maybe even rest herself for an hour or so, but she said fuck that. She'd come all the way across the ocean, and then all the way north from Yale, nearly five hundred miles on horseback and foot and not even a wagon-road the last part, so she was fucked if she'd stop for a rest at a time like this.

So off they went. Mrs Jimmy on that poor white nag, which looked about set to drop dead from exhaustion, not being from Yorkshire itself. Daniel went on foot, just like always, great spindly-legged strides. Daniel never rode. Nothing against horses, he said, but he was an old infantryman, and never learned the knack of them. So he walked. Up and down the mountainsides, and through the jackpine jungle. He must have walked ten thousand miles before he was finished, back and forth through the hardest countryside on earth. Back and forth, hardly even stopping for breath before he was off again somewhere else.

"Where do you think you're going?" I asked him one time.

"Wherever I'm needed."

"For God's sake, Daniel."

"Exactly." He laughed a little. It was nice to hear, and a bit surprising. He didn't laugh much anymore.

"I'm serious. You're not young."

His hair was grey now. He stooped a little and there was stiffness when he moved. That was the age, but it was also all the scarring from the fire. Puckered red skin across his arms and back, and up the one side of his neck. But he was still strong as a mule, just not so strong as he used to be. We were sitting by the stove in the boarding house, the afternoon we had that conversation. It was the middle of the day, so the men were all gone out. Daniel came by from time to time, although he never stayed. He'd sleep here and there—other boarding houses, a tent on the hillside, sometimes the little white Anglican church across the stream at the bottom of the town. But he wouldn't sleep here, even though I wanted him to.

"One of these times, Daniel, it's going to be the time you die out there."

"We're all going to die. Some of us sooner, and some of us late. There's nothing we can do about it, Nell, at all—though perhaps you'll be one of the lucky ones, with white hair by the fire, and grandchildren gathered about. I've a notion I can see you like that, so I believe perhaps it's true."

"Well, that was a speech," I exclaimed. "That was more words than you said together in years."

It wasn't like the old days, when he'd open his mouth and the words would come rolling out, great dancing rivers. He didn't even preach the Gospel anymore, not really. He'd ask: who was he to preach to others? These days it was more just helping people, helping with his hands.

And searching.

"You ent going to find him, Daniel."

He heard me, though he made like he didn't. That dogged look was coming over his face, like frost. He was turned inside himself again, and I couldn't reach him.

"Can't you see? You ent never going to find him, cos he ent there to be found."

ON THE AFTERNOON of the tenth day, he came back.

Tommy seen him before I did. We were outside the blacksmith's, where Tommy was mending a harness. His face came over with relief and he pointed. There was something emerging out of the blackness of the forest below the town, and it was Daniel. I ran to meet him, across the stream and down the slope. The cottonwood trees by the river stood like skeletons.

I wanted him to pick me up and swing me around, but instead I shouted at him.

"Fucksake, Daniel! Where've you been?"

"I'm here now."

"That's not an answer."

"You know where I've been, Nell. You know where I went. Now I'm back."

"We was half frantic, me and Tommy both!"

I hadn't realized how worried sick I was, not till right this second.

"Hush."

He looked older than ever before, tired and gaunt. His face was too thin, and the lines were deep furrows. But there was something else, too. A tension in the air around him. His eyes kept roving.

"Is everything all right?" I asked.

"No," he said. "But I don't think anything will happen tonight."

He wouldn't say what that meant. He didn't say much the whole evening, just that Jimmy was dead and Mrs Jimmy was still at the claim. Apparently she was going to try and work it herself, being more Yorkshire than any other woman ever born, before or since.

We found out later what happened from Mrs Jimmy herself, when she come to town for supplies. Jimmy was still alive when they got there, her and Daniel, but drifting in and out, and moaning. They expected he'd die any minute, but he hung on for almost a week. Daniel tended him and fed him broth with a spoon, and chopped firewood so Mrs Jimmy would have a good supply. It was a one-room shack they had made of logs, caulked with mud from the creek. Eight foot by ten, with a dirt floor and a door with leather hinges, set in a stand of trees. In the night they could hear wolves, howling. One morning when Mrs Jimmy woke up Daniel was gone, and Jimmy's rifle with him, but after a few hours he come back with a mule deer he'd shot for her. She said he was carrying it over his shoulders, a five-point buck, nearly three hundred pounds. Towards the end Jimmy was raving and crying out, saying someone was coming to take him. Daniel sat with him for a day and a night. Finally when dawn broke Jimmy came back to his right mind, or almost, at the very last.

He said goodbye to Mrs Jimmy and bid her watch them closely at the store, for they'd try to chisel her. He recognized Daniel, and thanked him for coming. But then he grew troubled, and said something Mrs Jimmy didn't understand. He said: "He's coming, Daniel, but not for me. It's you he wants."

Mrs Jimmy said Daniel went grey as ash, but somehow he was gleaming too. "At last," he said.

Afterwards, Daniel dug the grave—six feet down and the ground already freezing, so he had to build a fire to melt it. He wouldn't leave till he'd done that, and then done the service, wrapping Jimmy in a blanket and laying him in the ground and saying the prayers that would save his soul.

"Do you reckon they did that, them prayers?" I asked him. "Do you reckon they saved his soul?"

It was evening now. The men were still out at the saloons, so we were alone. I was at the basin, washing plates. I banged one down to catch his attention, cos I was in a mood.

Daniel didn't reply. He was at the window, looking out into the darkness. He went to the stove to put in another log, and when that was done he moved away again. He'd been like that all evening, distracted and pacing. Like a dog that hears something outside, and can't settle.

"Who's out there, Daniel? Is it the angels?"

I asked him partly for spite, and partly just to get him to talk to me. But once I asked the question, I realized I actually wanted to know.

"Do you still see the angels, Daniel?"

He shook his head. "No," he said, looking out the window. "No, I don't see the angels anymore. They're still there—I know that. It's just that I can't see them."

It was beyond sadness, the way he said it. He was weary and aching and the loneliest man in the world—and I couldn't stand it anymore.

"You can't see me either, can you?" I demanded.

He finally looked at me then, a little perplexed.

"You've never been able to see me. Have you, Daniel?" It came out bitterer than I'd intended. But fuck it, that was how I felt. And still he just looked at me.

"Fucksake, Daniel—I'm not a child anymore!"

"Of course you're not a child, Nell. You haven't been a child for years. Do you think I never noticed that?"

He shook his head as if to say what a fool I was. A wisp of hair had fallen across my eyes, and he brushed it away.

"I should go," he said, and started to turn.

"Fine," I said. "You do that, Daniel. Run away."

It threw him, and he stopped. His mouth tightened, and he flinched as a log popped loudly on the fire.

"I'm not running from anyone," he said, "and least of all you. But it's not—"

"—That way between us," I said, harshly. "Yeh, I know. But why is that, Daniel? Is there something you're afraid of?"

He was silent a long moment. The fire muttered behind us.

"I'm afraid of many things," he said at last. "I'm afraid of dying, and what may come after. I'm afraid I won't be strong enough when the Devil finally comes. What are you afraid of, Nell?"

I felt the hot tears pricking in my eyes. "I'm afraid you're going to walk out that door, Daniel. I'm afraid you'll walk out and never come back. I'll never see your ugly phizog again, and that will be the saddest thing in the world."

He finally smiled. "You're right. It's an ugly old face, isn't it?"

"But not to me."

There was silence between us then, but he hadn't moved. I reached out to touch him. Just a touch, a brush of my fingers against his arm.

"Nell . . . look at me."

It was a stupid thing to say. Cos what else was I doing, but looking at him? But he shook his head.

"No, *look* at me," he said. "I'm old, Nell. Next to you, I was old the first night we met—and I was practically a young man, then. I'm nothing but an old warhorse, who's had too many battles already. I'm old and grey and tired to the bone, and I'm afraid one more battle will finish me. I'm not the one you want, Nell."

"Why don't you let me decide what I want?" I said. "For once in my fucking life."

THAT WAS THE only time he ever come into my bed, as a man. The one and only time. In my bed in the alcove with a bit of sacking for a curtain, while the men were out bellowing songs at the saloons and dreaming they'd all be rich as kings.

The warmth of him, and his smell like woodsmoke, but most of all the strength of him. That's what I'd remember, the rest of my life. It was like nothing I'd ever known before. The strength of him was like wind and rivers. The whole house shuddered and was safe with the strength of him. Clinging to him afterwards, I was shaking.

"Gawd help the Devil," I said, "if you ever lay your hands on him."

"God wants to help him, Nell," said Daniel quietly. "But the Devil won't understand."

I pulled him to me again. One last time, I pulled him away from the Devil—cos that's how it felt, that evening. Like I was holding Daniel back for one last hour, while a huge haggard face looked down upon us from just beyond the flutter of light, a face twisted with awful pain and darkness. But I'd never be strong enough to hold Daniel in the end, no matter how hard I tried.

Afterwards I must have dozed off. When I woke up, the room was dark and I was alone.

"Daniel?"

But he hadn't gone away. Leastways not yet. When I come through the curtain he was standing by the window staring out into the night. Yellow light from the oil lamp was flickering against him. Shadows played off the planes on his face.

"Daniel, please just listen to me."

He was bare-chested, wearing his breeches. Despite all the years, he looked in that moment exactly as he'd done that afternoon in 1851 when he'd stood in the ring to face Hen Gully.

"I want us to go away, the two of us, and Tommy too. I want us to go south. You've done enough, Daniel—you've done more than anybody could ask of you, even God. You don't have to do any more, and you don't have to fight anyone. You can rest, now."

He hadn't moved a muscle. He was stone still, stiff-legged. Staring into the blackness. His huge hands were balled into fists.

"Daniel?"

"He's here," said Daniel, in a voice like Judgement.

JACK

WHEN I FINALLY saw him, the shock of it brought me rising from the chair. His back was to me, but it was him. After all these years, it was Daniel.

"Good gracious!" An exclamation of distress from Wellington Moses, the Negro barber. For it was his chair I'd been sitting in, amidst the smells of mysterious manly unguents, looking out the window. His razor had been at my throat, and I had risen against it. Apparently there was blood. I didn't notice.

Daniel was standing a little distance down the street. He was with the two of them, with my Nell and her defective angel. He turned, then, and oh how he'd changed. That great ugly beautiful face grown gaunt, and the scar tissue bubbling down one side. His golden hair now grey and tangled. There was about him something wild; something of locusts and wild honey.

"Mister, I do entreat your pardon!"

In after times I have often paused to reflect upon how I must have looked in that moment. Crouched, half standing, with blood welling through the shaving lather. Possibly even—who knows?—my hair standing straight on end, as hair does in books when mighty shocks have been experienced.

Poor Wellington Moses fluttered and clucked in great discomfiture, for it seemed there was a good deal of blood.

"My gracious, what a state of affairs."

He turned in a fluster, setting down the razor on the counter behind us and reaching for a towel. It was a fine German razor with an ivory handle; I had complimented him upon it just moments earlier. And of course the world would be a better place had he snatched it back up and finished the job instead, slitting my throat from ear to ear. But Wellington Moses was a finer man than that, and thus he missed his chance. Subsequently he also missed his razor, for before I left I slipped it into my pocket.

I WAS SHAKING as I returned to my room at the Occidental Hotel. I needed to change my shirt. I needed to calm myself—and quickly.

While Wellington Moses had stammered and mopped at blood, I had kept on staring through the window. I had seen Daniel turn and walk away up the street, with the defective angel beside him. For such I had supposed the creature to be when first I had seen him days earlier, upon my arrival. An angel—or not precisely an angel but a failed angelic prototype, with shocking white hair and a triangle face, a discard from some distracted Deity's trial run at creating the seraphim. Then with another start I had recognized the mute goblin boy from the Kemp Theatre all those years ago, the defective boy grown into mute defective manhood.

For days he had been hovering about my Nell, for clearly he had intuited some danger. But at last he had left her unattended—he and Daniel O'Thunder both. She had turned and gone the other way, down the street to the boarding house. At last she was alone.

When I went down the stairs, I was composed again. I would like to think I was even serene. I nodded to the brisk little sparrow at the desk, and continued to the door. He cleared his throat, behind me.

"Pithius."

I looked round. He was eyeing me askance, the brisk little sparrow.

"Yes?"

"He was one of the lesser devils, in legend. I found that in a book. No offence, of course."

"None taken."

He cleared his throat again. Cocked his head the other way.

"Pithius was the demon of lies. Did you know that?"

I paused briefly, reflecting. "I don't know that he was a liar, necessarily. Perhaps it was more that he didn't tell you everything."

With a very small smile, I was gone.

It was late afternoon. Intimations of storm stalked down over the mountains as I stalked down the street to the boarding house. When I got there, she was alone. Her back was to the dirty window as she warmed herself by the stove, for the cold was growing more bitter by the hour. She turned as I came in.

My Nell had aged. She had grown hard. I suppose some might say she had also grown strangely beautiful, in the way that a small fierce animal may have beauty. But there was something in her now that shut you out and would judge you mercilessly. It left me feeling terribly sad, and remembering golden things that had been irretrievably lost. It left me feeling betrayed, all over again.

"Hello," I said.

For the longest moment, she didn't seem to know me. I suppose the years had changed me too. And then she gasped.

"Jack."

Her hand flew to her throat, in an instinctive gesture. She was wearing the locket on a chain—the locket I had given back to her so many years before. In that moment it had seemed to me a lover's gift.

If I were the demon of lies, I would tell you a tale that would warm your heart and redeem your faith in God and humankind. I would describe how Nell's shock of disbelief gave way to a shake of the head. How she exclaimed that I was a whoreson rogue, but that grudges cannot be borne forever, and besides she could understand why I had acted as I had done those long years ago, considering my pain and the provocation I had endured. I would tell you how we gazed at one another, and began to laugh—weary, rueful laughter, but laughter nonetheless. I would describe how I took my hand from my pocket, and left Wellington Moses' razor there, safely folded. I would tell how we embraced, the two of us, and grew tearful, as old friends will do after a long and painful estrangement.

But why bother? You've already guessed what really happened.

She had gone white. She shrank three steps back, and stood rigid.

"You bastard. You were the one who killed her, weren't you? You killed my friend Mary Bartram."

"Yes."

"And Luna Queerendo—the girl they hung Joe Gummery for killing. That was you, too." You could see it coming to her in this very moment—the jolt of realization as a tumbler clicked one final notch and fell into place. "Jesus Christ, it *was* you, wasn't it? You're even worse than I thought you were."

I heard myself starting to stammer an explanation: that Luna Queerendo's death had been more accidental than anything else, that it never would have happened if she hadn't carried on so, fighting and screeching. Because in that moment with Nell—this is the truth—I actually wanted to make amends. I wanted to make Nell understand. But I didn't get the chance to finish.

She was upon me with a cry of hatred, so suddenly that I couldn't draw the razor at all—not just then; not at first. Her lunge knocked me off my feet, and as I toppled back she was on top of me. But I rolled as we fell—I was supple as a serpent—and now both my hands were clenched about her throat.

"Your father died cursing you," I hissed.

She writhed and flailed, her face just inches from mine. It was contorted like a lover's. And there would have been a consummation, then—the consummation desired so devoutly, and for so long. But in the next instant there came a roar. I felt a grip like iron. A strength beyond all reckoning lifted me and flung me like a child's quockerwodger toy soldier, wooden limbs flailing herk-a-jerk.

For the second time in my life I glimpsed the face of Daniel O'Thunder gazing down at me from out of blackness. This time its wrath was terrible.

IN THE MOMENT of his triumph, the Irishman turns to make sure the little red-haired whore is still alive. This is his mistake.

As he turns back, the Devil is already rising. The Devil's hand is a snake-lick; there is a flash of steel and a hot keening slice, and the Irishman recoils for just an instant, bellowing like a bull. In that mote of eternity the Devil is through the door and gone.

The Devil knows the Irishman will follow, of course. And so indeed he does. As others hasten to the aid of the little red-haired trull, boots pounding upon the wooden floor—"Someone fetch water!" "Give her air!"*—the Irishman careens outside. A crowd clusters but the Irishman shoulders through them, scattering miners like sparrows, for a terrible cold rage has settled upon him. He is dimly aware of a sharp pain beneath his arm, but he has no time for pain.*

"There!" It is the clerk from the Occidental Hotel. He points, rigid as a retriever, aflame with indignation.

The Irishman swivels, and sees. A dark rider gallops headlong towards the blackness of forest, riding like the very Devil.

"You'll need a horse to catch him!" someone cries. But the Irishman is already gone, lumbering with great spider-legged strides.

The shadow of the forest closes upon him. The temperature is plummeting, and falls further with each passing moment. Snow had fallen heavily the night before; now it clutches at O'Thunder's knees, and tries to pull him down. But this is good, new-fallen snow is very good, for the tracks are clear. A single horseman, riding north. The Irishman lunges through the jack-pine wilderness.

With darkness, the cold grows cruel. Each breath cuts like a knife along the breastbone. But this is good too, for the sky is clear, and stars shine down to light his way. In its stillness, the night is alive with sound, strangely magnified by the cold. The air rattles; trees crack with frost. Frozen lakes rumble and groan, the sound drifting across vast distances. By nine o'clock the wind has begun to keen. Somewhere far off, the unearthly howl of wolves rises up and hovers, before sinking back down into the trees. This is cold so intense it has come to life, a living malignity. This is cold that will kill. The wind grows wilder.

"I will sit on the highest mountain above the tall mountains of the North..."

It is impossible to think clearly, in such cold. Such cold can drive a man mad. O'Thunder forges onward.

He is no longer alone. He feels the others with him, those who have gone before. Glimpses them in the swirling wind. Tim Diggory is here, and Young Joe Gummery, urging him on. The Angels are with him too, for at long last they've come back. They have come to him out of the sky. Michael Archangelus and his warriors, a brilliant blaze of them, sweeping across the horizon in streams and flashes of green and red and white. They make a sound, a whisper and a rustling; they call to him. O'Thunder calls back to them, and weeps with joy. The tears freeze upon his cheeks.

At midnight he comes upon the horse, lying dead in a clearing. He knows the Devil is on foot now, lunging on his ruined leg. O'Thunder forges onward.

They are climbing, out of the jackpine wilderness and into the snowfields above the timberline. The howling of the wolves is all around him now, except it is the howling of the wind. A murderous winter gale upon these barren heights, buffeting him, whipping the snow from the ground in blinding, slashing crystals. O'Thunder forges onward, battering through the wind, battling through waist-high drifts, for the Devil is close now, he is very close. Somewhere to his left is a river, raging down through a chasm of rock. The spray from the icy rapids seems warm, but freezes in crystals even as it falls.

There is a trapper's rough lean-to shack in the lee of a rocky bluff, sheltered by trees. A dark figure hunches there, tending a tiny flicker. It stands and turns as O'Thunder looms out of the swirling snow.

"Come," says the Devil. "Come to the warmth. We can share."

For the Devil in his extremity has found this scrap of shelter. He has managed to start a fire, with kindling that had been left there against precisely such an eventuality. Now he manages to speak, though his face is so numbed he can barely form sounds.

"We can be warm, Daniel. We can be friends. I just want to be your friend—that's all I've ever wanted."

The Devil speaks as one who has been wronged beyond all power to endure, and yet can somehow still forgive. A voice of sorrow, and reason.

He lifts his hand. He reaches out. "Come to the warmth, Daniel."

"Satan," says O'Thunder.

He seizes the Devil. Both arms wrapped round him in death's own mighty grip, a clasp that would splinter the Devil's ribs like sticks of kindling. The Devil flails at him, striking with his hands, his eyes huge with terror. But the terror is human, and it is this that stops the Irishman at the last. Instead of crushing the Devil's life out, O'Thunder flings him down.

"Why would you want to kill her, Jack?" he cries.

For of course it is. It is only poor Jack, lying there upon the snow.

"I could have been your friend, but you pushed me away," says Jack. He is in great pain, and his bitterness is infinite. "And she was just a whore, no matter how much I loved her."

"I should kill you," says O'Thunder.

"Yes," says Jack. "You should."

O'Thunder reaches out to seize him—or else to lift him up. But something is wrong. He is weary to the bone, and it has grown difficult to raise his arm. He shakes his head to clear it, and looks down again. Jack lies curled like a beaten child, or a serpent.

"You should have killed me when you had the chance," says Jack.

O'Thunder discovers he is down upon one knee. There is blood beside him, in the snow. This perplexes him, until he recalls the pain he had felt much earlier, beneath his arm. The snake-lick of Jack's hand, at the boarding house. There had been the glint of steel. A razor?

"Remember what I promised you, all those years ago?" says Jack. "I vowed that I'd follow you to the ends of the earth. Well, here we are. I've kept my promise. And now I've killed you."

Jack begins to weep. "It wasn't really me," he says. "I wouldn't have killed you, Daniel. I wouldn't have done any of it, not by myself. It was the Devil."

For the Devil is—has always been—far more than poor, mere Jack.

And then, without warning, the Devil is here.

O'Thunder hears him, howling out of the darkness. Jack hears as well, and looks round in slow terror, not realizing at first what is happening. But O'Thunder knows in an instant. At long last, the Devil is coming in earnest. The Devil is coming to fight him, face to face.

With terrible joy, O'Thunder lurches to his feet. He wrenches at his coat with frozen hands, and flings it to the ground. He tears off his shirt, and staggers bare-chested to the line of scratch.

"Come on, then!" he cries, taking up his stance. "For you and I shall settle this matter between us!"

The Devil comes at him from out of the North. He comes in a shriek of wind that buffets O'Thunder and drives him sideways. For the Devil is a foe far stronger than any Daniel has ever faced. The Devil rages in great savage gusts.

O'Thunder staggers, swings wildly, and falls. As he does, the Devil comes at him from a new direction, and this time he comes with wolves. Not the grey timber wolves of the south—these are terrible black northern wolves. Great shaggy slinking devils half again as heavy as a man, with hooked fangs and weird yellow eyes. But O'Thunder throws them off, and rises. He strikes out left and right, clubbing them back, as his friends cry out encouragement from the sky and the darkness flashes with archangelic light. Again they close and bear him down, the wolves, but O'Thunder rises yet once again; and the shaggy devils howl in dismay, for the Hammer of Heaven rises with him, and swings out with shattering force. Some of them crumple with broken spines; some are flung headlong; others melt back into the night.

"Come on!" cries O'Thunder. He has never been more splendid.

But he is dying.

Now the Devil comes for him with cold. Cold beyond all imagining, clutching him in Hell's own icy grip, and even O'Thunder cannot prevail against such cold. For all his mighty strength, it bears him down. He feels a terrible weariness take him. But neither does he despair, for here at the end he finally understands. At the very last he glimpses a truth about the Devil. With it comes a slow warmth, creeping over him.

O'Thunder seems to see himself struggling back to his knees. He seems to see himself lifting his arms, and looking up. His friends reach down to him, in return. The vast black sky flashes red and green and white, and opens.

NELL

HE CAME BACK to me that same night.

I opened my eyes and Daniel was sitting on a stool beside me, looking down. It took me a moment to understand where I was—my bed in the alcove of the boarding house, behind the scrap of curtain. Moonlight filtered in through the one small window, and fell across him.

"Hullo, Nell," he said.

He was naked, except for his breeches and clogs. Battered and bloody and exhausted, like after a prize-fight. But he was smiling.

"Daniel!" I rose up onto my elbow, struggling to do it, cos I hurt a great deal from what Jack had done. My voice was a rasp. "Where have you been?"

"I've been fighting the Devil," he said. "I've been battling him all my life, and tonight at last I drew him into the ring."

"Did you beat him?" Cos somehow asking this question seemed the logic of it, in that moment.

"No," said Daniel. He gave a rueful laugh, and shook his head. "It turns out he was too strong, Nell, in the end. Being the Devil and all. But I made a battle of it, which is all any man can do upon this earth. I served him up enough to satisfy his gluttony—and it's all right. That's what I'm here to tell you, Nell. I'll always love you, and it's all right."

It came to me then that he looked as light as air. As if a great weight had been lifted from his shoulders.

"Come into bed, Daniel. I'm so very glad you're here."

But he was going now. I reached out, but he was fading into a rainbow light. It wrapped around him like angel's robes. That's when I understood that this was a dream, and Daniel was dead.

"Don't leave!" I cried in the dream.

"The child will be a comfort to you," said Daniel. He was already gone.

"Wait! Daniel—what child?"

The child I was carrying. I didn't even know it at the time, but there was a child from our one time together—a little boy. He was born in midsummer.

I MET A Chilcotin Indian once who said he knew the place where it happened—the battle between Daniel and the Devil. He said there was a great scorched mark where Daniel cast the Devil down. Nearby was the spot where Daniel lay dying, just before the sky opened. Flowers grow there now, the Chilcotin man said, right on the rock. They grow even in the middle of winter.

I never saw that place, so of course I couldn't say, one way or the other. But if you're asking if I believe it could be true, then no. No, I do not. A doolally tale like that? Except sometimes I'm not so certain.

But here's something I do know, for a fact.

A thousand people turned out for Daniel's funeral. His memorial service, I suppose you'd call it, since there wasn't a body. It was springtime when this happened. There were people who kept on holding hope till then, even though I knew he'd died that very first night. We walked up the whole length of the street in the dusk with candles. The Celestials stood silent and watched us, holding their hats, and it took ten minutes for the whole procession to pass. Afterwards we gathered along the river, and a priest in black said some words. I stood with Tommy, leaning on his arm. I was getting big with the boy, my belly swollen. At the end we sang a hymn that Daniel liked, "There Is Rest for the Weary."

When all the others stopped, a single voice kept singing. It was the most unearthly sound I ever heard, strange and croaking like something being wrenched into the world. We stared, every last one of us, as that single voice croaked on and on.

And fuck me if it wasn't Tommy. Fists clenched, eyes squeezed shut, singing his heart out.

So there you go. At Daniel's memorial, a mute boy sang.

If angels were watching, I bet you they wept.

· LONDON, 1888 ·

JACK

To know the truth about God, you must ask the Devil.

It is a great irony, but there it is. Much of what we need to know can only come from the Devil. Much of what we think we know already does, for the Devil indeed wrote crucial segments of the Holy Bible.

You don't believe me? The Temptation in the Wilderness. Our Lord wanders alone for forty days, utterly alone, and yet the Gospel describes in detail what he did and said and thought. How can this be, unless Our Lord wrote the Gospel himself, which he manifestly did not? And the answer comes in a lurch of realization: Our Lord was not alone. He did indeed have a companion, through all those forty days and nights, his companion being the Tempter. This same Companion was with him during that final solitary vigil upon Gethsemane, when every single apostle—the Bible is very specific on this point, go and look it up—when every last blessed apostle was drunk and asleep and oblivious to his agonies of the spirit. It was left to the Devil to set these down instead. I like to picture him perched upon a rock, brow furrowed like a field, scribbling doggedly. God's only friend—for this of course is one way to look at the Devil. As someone who tried very hard to be a friend. All he ever wanted was to be God's special companion. But God pushed him away, and look what happened.

IT IS LATE, as I write these words. Well past midnight, scribbling at my desk in Whitechapel, in a pool of candlelight. Somewhere in the shadows of the rafters my brisk brown spider is motionless and perfect, looking down at me.

I wonder sometimes what she will do when I am dead. Will she blink, my little brown spider, and after a time creep forth to investigate? To salute a fallen comrade, perhaps—or merely to determine whether something here is edible, and then to withdraw into her shadow once she has established that it is not. That this mute unmoving form is nothing but a husk, as dry and shrivelled as the husks of week-dead flies.

There was consternation in the street beneath my window, earlier in the night. Hasty footfalls upon the cobbles; voices raised in exclamations of dismay, and further off the fluting of a police whistle. I suspected at once that they'd found another woman murdered, for these nights there is a dread shadow stalking the Whitechapel streets. His name is Jack, like my own, but he is far worse than I have ever been. He is the Devil himself, or as close to the Devil as those poor women will meet on this side of the grave. At moments I have yearned to seek him out, this other Jack. To find his spoor and follow him to some low tavern or some filthy silent alleyway, there to offer myself up to his service. "I am your man, and have always been," I would tell him, with head inclined and shoulders hunched in wretched reverence. "Look here—look what I've brought. A razor with an ivory handle and a fine German blade. I have carried it with me all these years."

But I suspect it has already grown too late.

I have almost finished my *Book of Daniel,* now. I confess I have been putting it off, this completion, for it has been my only real companion for so long. Writing out Daniel's story as

I perceived it to be, and gathering together the perceptions of others to add to my own, for of course no one man alone can comprehend the whole truth of anything. Searching through dusty archives for newspaper reports, and writing away to those who might have stories to contribute, little shards of the truth for my mosaic. They believe they are sending their scribblings to a man named John Pithius, for of course I don't go by Hartright any longer, or Beresford, for obvious reasons. I like the name. It is, I like to think, a droll touch: Pithius is one of the very minor fiends, and I was always thus. I was always minor, and never the Devil himself.

I am sufficient to the task of writing of Daniel O'Thunder. But it took the Devil to kill him.

What really happened, that night in the wilderness? If you mean, "what are the facts?"—if that's what you want, as if facts ever took us to the heart of anything, as if all the facts in the world laid end to end ever added up to a single grain of Truth—then the facts are these.

There was bitter cold, and blinding snow. There were wolves—I heard their voices on the wind. But there was something else in that darkness, too. There was someone else. Daniel turned, and saw him, and shouted a glorious challenge. He strode forward and was swallowed by the storm. In the morning I searched and searched, but could find no trace of him at all. Just a vast cold whiteness like the face of God.

But in the night I had seen another face, ruined and malevolent, looming out of the blackness. Its eyes were coals and its teeth were bared in a snarl of agony. It was haggard with hatred and loss. And I swear it was not my own face, looking back at me.

Those are the facts. As for the truth?

The truth is, I loved him.

IN ANOTHER MOMENT I will set down my pen, for my labour of forty years will be finished. I will pass a crabbed hand before my eyes, and lean back slowly in the sinking emptiness of completion, and discover that I am weeping again.

For the longest time I supposed that they must come for me in the end, and take me up for my various crimes, and deliver me over to the hangman. Not old Calcraft, for Calcraft is long since dead and burning; it is a man named Berry, now. He is stark and terrible, is Mr Berry, and yet the alternative is worse. For the alternative is to go on and on—to remain the Devil for all the tomorrows to come, with no response from God at all. Not the faintest flicker from Heaven, no matter how monstrous the provocation. And no hope of victory, for the Devil has long since known what Daniel O'Thunder glimpsed as he lay dying: the Devil has already lost. Just as sure as there are stars in the sky. Whatever he does, in all his malevolence, the outcome is already foregone.

But lately I have come to despair of meeting Mr Berry. I begin to think that the end must come here in the solitude of my room, with a cord tied from the rafter, and a chair overturned upon the floor, and my brisk brown spider watching the husk as it twitches. I begin to think that the end will come quite soon.

As the chair clatters, I will see Daniel one last time.

THE DEVIL has always known that Daniel O'Thunder would come to him, in the instant of his last extremity. And thus it will be. As the noose tightens, Daniel will come. His raiment will be white. He will reach out and catch the Devil, as his ancient enemy begins to fall.

"You can still repent," Daniel will say, holding him up.

The Devil will say: "I am dust and ash."

"But God can make new things with dust and ash."

The Devil will say: "Let me go."

And Daniel will do that. With a last look of bottomless sorrow, he will let the Devil go.

ACKNOWLEDGEMENTS

THE SOURCES FOR this novel, both literary and factual, are too many and various to list in full. Among the most notable, I naturally owe a great debt to Henry Mayhew, whose monumental *London Labour and the London Poor* has been ransacked by novelists from Dickens onward. Much of the boxing lore derives from Pierce Egan's classic *Boxiana; or, Sketches of Ancient and Modern Pugilism.* Among modern studies, I found Bob Mee's *Bare Fists: The History of Bare-Knuckle Prize-Fighting* to be particularly excellent. Other indispensable companions included Peter Ackroyd's astonishing *London, the Biography,* Fergus Linnane's *London, the Wicked City,* the social histories of Judith Flanders and Liza Picard, Geoffrey Hughes' *Swearing: A Social History of Foul Language, Oaths and Profanity in English,* and John Camden Hotten's *A Dictionary Of Modern Slang, Cant And Vulgar Words Used At The Present Day In The Streets Of London* (1860). All inaccuracies are of course entirely mine.

My gratitude is owed to all those who read and commented on the manuscript in its early stages, including Peter Cocking and Hazel Boydell. Special thanks to Paul Mears and Jude Weir, whose insights led to many improvements. Mary Sandys provided much invaluable advice, both linguistic and historical, and Peter Norman's copy edit was rigorous and perceptive. My editor, Ramsay Derry, was altogether splendid.

Above all, my heartfelt thanks to Chris Labonté at Douglas & McIntyre, who commissioned *Daniel O'Thunder* and then guided it every step of the way. He was an unfailing source of encouragement, insight, wisdom, and inspiration; every author should be so lucky.

IAN WEIR is an award-wining screenwriter, playwright and novelist. Among his extensive television credits, he was the writer and executive producer of the acclaimed crime thriller *Dragon Boys,* a CBC miniseries that first aired in 2007. His stage plays have been produced across Canada and in the U.S. and England, and he is the author of ten radio dramas. He has won two Geminis, four Leos, a Jessie and the Writers Guild of Canada Canadian Screenwriting Award. He lives near Vancouver, B.C., with his wife and daughter. Visit him online at www.ianweir.net.